THE
MISSOLONGHI
MANUSCRIPT

THE MISSOLONGHI MANUSCRIPT

FREDERIC PROKOSCH

Farrar, Straus & Giroux NEW YORK

CONTENTS

FOREWORD

FOREWORD

I

One April evening, four years ago, at a cocktail party in Via Sistina, I found myself on a sofa beside the Marchesa del Rosso, a lady in her sixties, who was dressed in a suit of black garbardine. She was an American, née Miss Whitaker, and lived in the Piazza Navona. She had iron-gray hair, drawn resolutely back from her forehead; a fine Minervan nose, a Massachusetts chin, and the piercing implacable eyes of a condor. She casually mentioned the "memoirs" which Byron had written in Missolonghi. I expressed, with some amazement, my total ignorance of any such memoirs, and added tactfully that my dissertation at the University of Kansas had dealt with Byron.

The Marchesa lifted her brows and gazed intently through the window. She sipped at her highball, then lowered her voice and informed me curtly that these memoirs, as luck would have it, were in her own possession, and were safely tucked away in a trunk in her attic.

"Most intriguing," I said. "You choose, I gather, not to release them."

She placed a finger against her chin. "For several reasons," she said thoughtfully. "They appear, from my casual perusal, to be controversial in content. They are far from reticent on sexual matters and sometimes border on the slanderous. Furthermore, while I firmly believe them to be absolutely genuine, I neither can nor wish to adduce any positive proof in the matter. And

3

finally (though this is a point I hardly expect you to agree with) I feel an old-fashioned pleasure in possessing an unknown manuscript which, if it ever were published, would lend itself to a vulgar publicity."

I looked slyly at the Marchesa, and was about to murmur something when she glanced at her wrist-watch (a rather large one, with a platinum band) and remarked with agitation that she was already late for a dinner engagement.

That was the only time, alas, that I saw the Marchesa. I wrote her three letters, but they all remained unanswered. Two years ago I was told by a friend of mine (a young poet who lived in Assisi) that she had died, during the winter, of cervical cancer. I promptly wrote to her secretary, a Miss Meldrum from Philadelphia, and after a month's correspondence was allowed to visit the palazzo where Miss Meldrum still resided, in order to inspect these curious "notebooks."

For five days I sat by a window which looked down on the Bernini fountain, making my copy of the "copy" (see below) by Colonel Eppingham. This copy of my own I then transferred to a typewriter: so that the version here presented is really a copy of a copy of a copy. Since the manuscript itself was to be eventually transferred to the library of Trinity College, Cambridge (see below), I am risking a defiance of any pertinent laws of copyright.

The authenticity of the original manuscript will be impossible to establish until it emerges (if it ever does) from its present obscurity. We can only hope that whoever has absconded with it will eventually send it to Cambridge; or at least, *faute de mieux,* submit it to an auction room. For all we know, it may be rotting in a rain-soaked jungle in the Andes. The sinister possibility exists that the manuscript was destroyed intentionally. (Some earlier "intimate" journals were burned in the home of the publisher John Murray as a sop to the sensibilities of Lady Byron, Hobhouse, *et al.*) When and if the notebooks appear, we can

4

leave it to the experts to determine, by an analysis of the ink, paper, glue, calligraphy, etc., whether they are indeed in Lord Byron's own handwriting.

There are admittedly quirks of phrase and oddities of vocabulary which are un-Byronic. And the syntax seems in general unusually disciplined for Byron. (Byron's spelling and punctuation were at times highly arbitrary, e.g., *Mephistofilus* for Mephistopheles, *Michel Agnolo* for Michelangelo. He used dashes instead of semicolons, as well as numerous abbreviations: L.H. for Leigh Hunt, C. for Caroline, A. for Augusta.) I myself in my transcription was forced occasionally to guess at a word, and the spelling may at times have been inadvertently modernized. Certain details seem not quite plausible. Could Byron, for instance, have known Archilochus? But most startling of all is the change of outlook (to put it mildly), which brought a visual precision quite at odds with his earlier manner. And it seems likely that his memory may occasionally have deceived him, or that he deliberately invented or distorted certain episodes.

This is not quite the place for a literary analysis, but I cannot resist a comment or two on the style. *Le style, c'est l'homme.* True enough. But the truth lies deeper. The style is not the man, of course; it merely reflects the man. But it reflects not only the present spiritual texture of the man but the multiple pangs of the past which combined to create this texture. The style of *The Tempest* is very different from that of the *Sonnets*. But something of the *Sonnets* still echoes miraculously in *The Tempest*. The style of Beethoven's last sonata is very different from the first, but the first already contains the magical seeds of the last. Rembrandt's paintings of his youth are very different from those of his later years, but the latter can be seen as an intensification of the former. Maybe I over-emphasize the notion of "magic" in an artist's development, but what I mean is that the tight and almost "modern" phraseology of some of these passages is not so much in conflict with the poet's earlier style as in a subtle and secret and self-developing harmony.

5

The thing, of course, may be a forgery. But if it is argued to be a forgery, we are confronted by an even greater enigma than before.

What could have been the forger's motives? Financial gain? Obviously not. Notoriety? Most improbable. The zest of deception? Possible, but unlikely. It may conceivably have been written by the Colonel himself, in a fit of almost lunatic ingenuity, and driven by an obsessive transposal of identity. Or it may even have been done by the gray-haired Marchesa, who then invented the mythical Colonel and the half-blind Baron (see below).

And so we are left with the final enigma. Not only of Byron's own character, not only of a metamorphosis which was psychic and sexual as well as philosophical, not only of an artist's animadversions on the meaning of art; but of the iridescent nature of a poet's own past when resuscitated and reinterpreted in the clear sad glow of an autumn solitude. That, to me, is the final paradox of this puzzling and disquieting document.

I append a letter from the Marchesa which was fixed to the papers by means of a safety pin. I have been unable to identify the intended recipient, Stefanella. (When I asked Miss Meldrum about this person, she merely replied with an irritable snort.) I also append a letter to the Marchesa from the mysterious Colonel Eppingham, which was attached to the manuscript by means of a ribbon.

And now I leave the reader to his own speculations.

T. H. APPLEBEE,
Bryn Mawr College,
November 7, 1966   Bryn Mawr, Pennsylvania.

Letter from the Marchesa del Rosso.
(In black ink on lavender stationery.)

10, Piazza Navona,
15 September 1963.

Dear Stefanella,

Here is the manuscript I told you about. (I hope that poor Lois behaves decently about it.) Do be careful with it, dear. You know that I trust you implicitly.

I remember strolling one evening with Colonel Eppingham in the garden of the Villa Borghese. A cool misty sun gilded the bronze-coloured ilexes. I remember peeping into the distance at the temple of Aesculapius.

We talked about Keats and Shelley. (I loathe Shelley but worship Keats, you know.) Somehow (not unnaturally, I guess) the conversation turned to Byron. The Colonel is a haggard, slightly ratty-looking eccentric, with masses of kinky hair, a vulturous nose and dirty tweeds. He described a manuscript which he had bought in Missolonghi from some penniless Baron, and when I expressed my curiosity he consented to let me have a peek at it. We made a rendezvous for the following Tuesday at Miss Babington's Tea-room.

There he was, sitting in the corner by the fireplace when I arrived. I ordered some toasted scones with lemon marmalade, as usual. He had a brownish parcel lying on the table by his plate, but before mentioning Byron he embarked on a diatribe against "modern poetry"—Auden and the rest of them, you know. (Is Auden still considered a "modern"?)

I finished my cup of tea and he unwrapped the parcel wistfully.

It was written in a kind of upward-wandering scrawl on pale grey paper.

"But surely," I exclaimed, "this isn't Byron's own hand-writing!"

"Heavens, Marchesa, of course it isn't," said the Colonel condescendingly. "This is merely a copy. I wouldn't dream of parting with the original."

I took the thing home and read it through in three days. (I skipped here and there; some of the descriptions didn't interest me.) Still, I felt distinctly privileged about it all, dear Stefanella. There were parts that shocked me horribly but other passages still haunt me. Do read it, but promise to return it without fail to poor Lois.

Oh yes: the reason I still have the manuscript in the house is the following. I was about to return it to the Colonel by a special messenger to the Via Cassia, when a letter suddenly arrived. I have tied it to the manuscript by means of a ribbon. I never heard from the Colonel again. I wonder what he was up to in the Andes.

Take care of yourself, child, and do watch your diet. (I hear that the food in Damascus is utterly vile.) *Bon voyage* and write to me immediately on your arrival, *carina*.

Your loving *amica,*

Jessie.

III

Letter from Colonel Eppingham.
(In pencil on a dirty page torn from a ledger.)

23 Via Cassia,
10 October 1959.

My dear Marchesa,

Owing to unforeseen circumstances (please forgive me if I don't enlarge on them), I am leaving for Naples very early tomorrow morning. From Naples I am sailing on the SS. *Isabella* to Peru. I shall write you again, I trust, from some outpost in the Andes.

A word about those Byron memoirs. You will never visit Missolonghi, I suppose. A squalid town, utterly charmless—just a group of huts in the middle of a swamp. I went there as a pilgrim. (Byron has always been a God to me!) His house in Missolonghi was turned into a fortress after his death and subsequently destroyed, presumably by fire. Nothing is left of it but a tumbledown fence which surrounds a rain-streaked monument, on which there is a carving of the poet's head.

Missolonghi is not an appetising spot to spend the holidays. There is nothing which can even euphemistically be called a "hotel". I lived for two months in a small grey house with an iron balcony, engrossed in my essay on "Supernatural Symbols in *Mazeppa*". In the course of my saunterings I met a decomposing personage, the Baron von Haugwitz, who lived on the outskirts of the town (in sin, I suspect) with a young Greek ragamuffin.

I treated the Baron to a glass of *ouzo* and we spoke of Byron. I was startled by his familiarity with the "darker" side of Byron's life. Then he revealed to me that he had found, some six months previously, a Byron manuscript. He was prowling (I don't know

9

why) through the former dwelling (now a butcher's shop) of a certain Dr Vaya, who had been officially attached to the Suliote corps in Byron's time. Here he found (so he said) in a big wicker box, amongst some garments, sheets, blankets, medical treatises and surgical instruments, three old note-books, yellow with age and on the verge of disintegration.

We happen to know that Dr Vaya was present on the day Byron died. It is quite possible that he filched these note-books from the room of the deceased. In any case, when the Baron showed me these documents two days later, it was obvious to me at once that they were in Byron's handwriting.

I spent a fortnight trying to coax the Baron to part with his *trouvaille*. (He was a pitiful old figure, nearly blind and riddled with syphilis.) We finally agreed on a price of sixty-five pounds—not much, you may think, but a decent sum under the circumstances. I immediately made a copy (the one I gave you at Miss Babington's) and wrapped the original manuscript in a piece of blue muslin. This treasure I shall keep with me as long as I live. On my death it will be consigned to the library of Trinity College, Cambridge.

So I leave my own copy under your aegis, my dear Marchesa, and I hope that you will find it thought-provoking as well as *piquant*.

My best wishes, and thank you for the tea.

Your humble friend,

C. V. Eppingham.

THE
FIRST
NOTE-BOOK

It is raining as usual. The drops are lashing the dirty window-pane. I asked Tita this morning to fetch me some paper in town, and he brought me these little monstrosities— three small note-books bound in a sickening mauve. He also prepared some fresh ink for my writing-set. I shall begin a new diary.

The bells are tolling midnight. The rain muffles their clangour, and they sound like the wail of some lonely muezzin.

The flame takes a leap. I look up in surprise. Was that a face peering through the window? Bearded and bulbous, like a gorilla's? Are those footsteps shuffling through the hall, followed by a clanking of chains? Who knows? This house is haunted, but not by the usual kind of ghost. It belongs to one of the Ephores of this abominable town, a hairy old patriarch named Apostoli Capsali. My room is an oblong chamber looking out on the lagoon. I have covered the walls with Turkish sabres, French pistols, rifles and swords, guns and blunderbusses, a Hydriote helmet, a Bulgarian trumpet. The smell of a sweating masculinity pervades the place. I have enjoyed playing soldier. I have enjoyed chatting with my captains about nothing but sieges, surprise attacks and am-buscades.

My page Loukas is lying in the corner, fast asleep on a pile of cushions. I can hear my valet Fletcher snoring noisily in the neighbouring room. Through the half-open door I see my blackamoor crouching in the corridor. He is growling to himself as he peels an orange. He eats all night, and sleeps in the day-time.

The rain has stopped at last. An arrowy shudder runs through the house. An earthquake? No, no, nothing as violent as that. Merely the stirring, I imagine, of one of these Missolonghi phantoms.

Nothing of interest happened to-day. I feel worn, disenchanted. I shall snuff out the flame and try to sleep. (I am suffering from sleeplessness.)

26 January

There is a breeze that blows from the hills. A whiff of freshness, thank the Lord. Loukas brought me some flowers (rather like hyacinths, but nearly black. Where on earth did he find them? I forgot, inexplicably, to ask him). He is growing a delicate honey-hued moustache.

Colonel Stanhope came for a chat and we spoke about Scotland: the cloudy Highlands, the flashing rivers, the white-pebbled estuaries. Finally he left. I am sitting alone by my open window, looking down on the marsh-lands, sniffing the sour smell of midnight. I have noticed something unusual. Little by little (especially at night) the visions of the past are beginning to obliterate the present. As I sit by my window and look at the stars, my mind keeps roving back to blacker nights and brighter stars.

I have kept innumerable diaries and journals in my life. The first was at Harrow when I was sick with a fever, the last in September in Cephalonia. But it is time that I spoke from a deeper "recess" of my being than this series of shallow pedestrian scribblings. I shall jot down the daily events (they are usually wearisome and pointless): then an asterisk (I have always loved asterisks, and a star, in Persia, symbolises destiny): and after this chaste symbolical asterisk I shall rove into the past, I shall prowl through the night in my search for deeper "recesses".

*

Very well. Let us begin at the beginning.

But, of course, there was no beginning. There were only mountains and thunder-storms, fishes and dragon-flies. There was a troll squatting by the mill-pond and a gnome crouching in a willow-tree.

When I was nine my mother and I spent the summer in the valley of the Dee. We lodged with a farmer, a Mr Robertson, not far from Ballaterich, and the peak of Loch-na-garr loomed majestically in the distance. Sometimes we strolled to the shores of the foam-furrowed sea, but more often we walked to the estuary for our swim. One day I rode on my pony to the ancient bridge we called Brig o' Balgonie. It spanned a deep pool which was surrounded by woods and I peered into the water, where a fish was hovering motionless. Old Mrs Robertson, the farmer's wife, had sung me a song:

> Brig o' Balgonie,
>   black's your wa',
> Wi' a wife's ae son,
>   on a mare's ae foal,
> Down ye shall fa',
>   Down ye shall fa',
>   Down, down ye shall fa'!

I tethered my pony and walked into the woods. There was still dew on the gooseberries. A spider hung from his dewy web. Birds sang to the sunlight which filtered through the leaves. And quite suddenly I fell in love with all that I saw around me, and stranger still, I felt that I was loved in return. At this moment, quite inadvertently, I invented my secret God.

15

I walked to the edge of the stream and knelt in the moss. Tiny tadpoles and minnows were darting about. On the surface some water-spiders were skating about ecstatically. Were they born just to be happy? Was I, too, born to be happy? I walked on and saw a dark furry thing in the grass: a vixen, eyeless and udderless, hollowed out by the seething maggots.

Was she, too, born to be happy? But why not for ever? What went wrong? What was this hideous thing that had happened to her? What was this wormy, horrible stillness?

I felt sad all of a sudden and sat down under a yew-tree. I wrote my name carefully in the dust with my forefinger. Then I studied it thoughtfully. BYRON. What a very curious name. It rhymed with iron, but there was certainly nothing iron-like about it. It had a strangely evasive and ephemeral look to it. This Byron—was it I? Why in the world should my name be Byron? And come to think of it, why should I be sitting under a tree by the Brig o' Balgonie? I drew a large circle around this curious patronymic and then I caught a grasshopper and placed him in the middle of it. But, far from solving the riddle of my identity, it merely deepened it: the grasshopper gazed at me with his pea-green eyes and then jumped into the bushes, leaving my name slightly blurred. The letters had been ruffled into something which resembled EVRUN.

I lay on my back and looked up at the sky. Infinitely vast, infinitely old. This too, like death and identity, was incomprehensible. But I was seized with a violent longing to fly through the sky and lie basking on one of those bubbling white clouds. I envied the birds that sang in the trees. I always envied them; and I still envy them. In one of my childhood dreams I stood in a glittering salon, and to the general amazement, I started to fly—not in a flapping, feathery fashion but in a cool graceful glide, cleverly weaving my way past the crystal chandeliers. "Look at that boy, he is flying!" cried the ladies, clicking their fans.

I strolled by the edge of the stream, gathering pebbles as I went. I found an egg-shaped pebble and dropped it in my pocket. I untethered my pony and rode back through the dappled woods, plucking leaves from the overhanging boughs and singing "Brig o' Balgonie".

My mother was sitting by a rose-bush under a large yellow parasol. She was eating a plum and the juice of the plum ran down her chin.

She regarded me gravely, and then a film of suspicion clouded her eyes.

"Sit down, lad. Where have you been?"

"Down by the Brig o' Balgonie, Mother."

"Heavens, child, you are perfectly filthy. Your breeches are covered with leaves. Why must you always behave so recklessly? Why can't you be like other boys? Look at your hands! Reeking with filth, toads, slime, abominations!"

"I am sorry, Mother," I said.

"You did nothing improper, I trust?"

"Not," I said, "that I am aware of."

"Listen, lad," she said solemnly, wiping the juice from her chin, "there is something I must warn you against. You must never abuse yourself."

I sat motionless, with downcast eyes. "I shall try not to do so, Mother."

"Do you understand?" said my mother.

I shifted my feet and folded my hands.

A large brooch covered with opals stirred fretfully on my mother's bosom. She said, more in sorrow than reproach, "You are like your father. The same chin, the same eyes, and much, I fear, of the same naughtiness. Dear boy, your little rose-bud was given to you by God. It is sacred. It is more precious than rubies or amethysts. You must never toy with it or fondle it, or a curse will fall upon you! Nightmares and chimaeras, twitches and torments, and finally a raving idiocy . . ."

That evening I strolled from the farm-house down the

17

path to the willow-grove. Loch-na-garr rose in the distance like the head of a witch. The air grew hushed and dim. A single star peeped joyfully down at me. Now a large icy moon rose from the summit of Loch-na-garr, but its face was like the mad white face of an unknown ancestor.

27 January

A red-cheeked English sailor came and knocked at my door this morning. He said that the *Anne,* under the command of Captain Parry and loaded with supplies from the London Committee, was waiting at Ithaca for my further instructions.

I said to the sailor: Let the *Anne,* as soon as she can elude the Turkish vessels, head for the coast by Dragomestre. From there we can bring the supplies by boat.

*

I remember the cold that came down in November. One morning I awoke and saw my window covered with frost, a pattern of diamonds which crumbled as I touched it. I crept into the garden and stood there enchanted. The sun was still misty and the grass was furred with white. The breath from my mouth shone like a puff of gleaming smoke. The stalks of the Michaelmas daisies were crowned with tiny crystals and the fallen oak-leaves were crusted with spangles. The pebbles in the path shone like the scales of a fish; the acorns were carved out of a cold white agate. Then the sun grew suddenly bright: the frost died away and the magic dissolved, like the foam on the far-off sea.

One day I sat by the hearth on a red plush-sofa, reading slowly, by the light of the flames, the story of Sinbad the Sailor. I looked through the window and saw that the sun had crept through the clouds. I put on my mittens and raced down the corridor; I flung open the door and ran out through the snowy rose-garden.

I entered the woods and followed the path to the lake. The snow was already patterned with delicate embroideries: pine-needles and owl's feathers and the footprints of rabbits, and small yellow tunnels where a deer had paused to piss. A feather of snow fell down from a twig. I caught it in my hand, filled with joy, as though it were magical. But it was nothing, it had vanished away; it was neither a feather nor a snow-flake; it was merely a small dark stain in my mitten.

I came to the mill-pond where the skaters were swirling about. Their scarves danced in the wind, their tasselled caps were as red as raspberries. Tommy Duncan was doing some magnificent figures of eight in front of the girls and in the wood-hut Mrs Fothergill was pouring punch from a copper pitcher. The sun was setting: the tracks of the skaters shone like brightly-burning wires. Willy McDiarmid picked up his fiddle and started to play and old Jane Fothergill cocked her head and started a jig. Soon it was night and Mrs Fothergill lit her lantern.

Now a sleigh was tinkling in the distance and came to a halt at the cross-roads. The skaters leapt into the sleigh, which slid away with a rippling of sleigh-bells, leaving behind only the fresh brown balls dropped by the mare, which steamed as they sank in the rutted snow. Jane Fothergill took her lantern and Willy McDiarmid picked up his fiddle and with a merry "Time to be home, lad!" they headed for the woods, and all I saw was the swinging lantern tossing its glow on the snowy boughs.

Then it was dark. The sleigh had gone, the sound of the sleigh-bells died away, Jane Fothergill's lantern vanished in the depth of the forest. The moon rose over the hill and shone on the empty pond, where a tangle of fine silver hairs shone on the ice.

I shivered with cold and headed for home again. But the

woods were dark and forbidding, filled with a stillness which was like a threat. A snow-covered bush looked like a dwarf with coal-black eyes; a snow-hooded rock looked like a beast waiting to pounce on me. At last I caught sight of the fire-light shining through the window-panes and I ran into the kitchen where May Gray was crouching by the oven.

May Gray! What a terrible woman she was! She sat by my bed in the evening, reading aloud from the Book of Ecclesiastes. Then she belched with disdain and read the Twenty-third Psalm. (I disliked the New Testament but tolerated the Old; best of all I liked the hair-raising tale of Cain and Abel.) When she finished reading the Psalm, May Gray reached into her bosom, plucked out a small lime-drop and popped it into my mouth.

She was drunk. She had been "bousing at the nappy" in the ale-house. She peered at me blearily and growled, "Well, what little tricks to-day, my lad?"

She drew back the blanket and regarded my hairless body. The strands of her hair tickled my belly when she leant over me; I caught the autumnal stench that oozed from her powerful body.

Once she lifted her skirt to give me "a blink" of her "fer-lie". I was amazed by the masses of curly red hair and the wound-like aperture, half concealed by the billows of flesh. She was, I think, on the point of providing an even fuller view of her anatomy when we heard footsteps in the hall, and she pulled down her skirt and hurriedly picked up the Bible and started to read, with a bull-like resonance, the Ninety-third Psalm, which begins "The Lord reigneth, he is clothed with majesty".

She had her own spicy vocabulary, that terrible May Gray. (I cannot hope to reproduce her furrowing, orotund accent.) My buttocks she called my "hurdies" and my penis a "tousie tyke". "Show me thy wee waulie crummock and they twae wee nits," she muttered. "Tis a right meikle bogle for sic a wee laddie!" She tickled my poor little membrum, tossing it this way and that, and finally she stuck out her tongue and daintily licked at my tiny testicles. "Ah, ah," she cackled triumphantly, patting me briskly on the belly, "some fine day we'll see a drappie come louping fra' thy birkie!"

And suddenly a glaze of icy indifference passed over her eyes. She drew back her hair and tied it in a bun on the back of her head. Her hideously leering visage was transformed into the face of a martinet, and she glared at me with a cold, cruel hate in her eyes. She picked up her Bible, straightened the folds in her dress, and went staggering out of the bedroom.

28 January

Missolonghi is a quagmire. But I insisted on my daily ride, and together with Pietro and the Colonel I hired a boy (named, appropriately, Christophoros) to ferry us across the lagoon in his boat. We found a deserted olive-grove where the ground was hard enough for a gallop.

*

Newstead Abbey! I was never so happy, or so good and gentle, as I was at Newstead. There was nothing left of the chapel itself but an ivied skeleton. A wasps' nest hung in the corner like a great wicked melon, and the spiders wove their fine octagonal tracery between the windows. The reception-hall was empty and smelled of earthworms, and at night the wind whistled as it dived through the recesses. The refectory of the monks was still littered with rotten hay: food for the cattle who had once been stabled in the Priory parlour.

The lake lay still as a looking-glass, reflecting the Gothic skeleton, and on the western edge of the lake rose the Folly Castle with its moss-furred turrets. I rode on my pony with my wolf-dog following behind me and came to the glade, where a straw-stuffed target stood by an elm-tree. I shot my feathered arrows and when I finally hit the bull's-eye I leaned down and patted my dog. "Well done, good old Woolly!"

A butterfly lit on my wrist. It was blue as the sky. I looked at the silky wings and thought: How fine it is to be blue! Then I looked at the sky and wondered: Why is it so blue? Is it blue because blue is the colour of emptiness and infinity? Or is it blue because blue is the colour of freedom and happiness? The green all around me was a fresh and restful colour, and the red of the briars was a vivid though troubling colour, and the yellow of the buttercups was a gay exuberant colour, but it struck me that blue was the colour of magic, and that the answer to the mysteries of the world lay in the colour blue.

Mary Chaworth came riding from Annesley Hall one autumn day. It was a Sunday. There were pheasants and a gooseberry fool for dinner. After dinner we sat in the parlour and looked into the dazzle of my kaleidoscope. I took Mary by the hand and led her down to the edge of the lake. "Come, Mary, let me show you the Folly." And we wandered down to the Folly. We passed the old kennel and stepped through the thicket of ferns and waded through a wilderness of dry, rattling leaves. We came to the Folly and climbed the lichenous stairs that wound to the top of the broken tower.

It was dusk. A night-bird went swooping over the lake. "Tell me, Mary, do you ever expect to get married?"

Mary regarded me with dignity. "Yes, certainly I shall get married."

"To whom?"

"To a lord with a four-horse carriage," said Mary calmly.

"You'll have children, will you, Mary?"

"Yes, certainly I'll have children!"

I looked thoughtfully at Mary: she was a solemn little girl with dimples in her chin and enormous black eye-lashes. She wore a raffia-coloured dress with a round lace collar and a large moiré sash, the colour of fleur-de-lys. I thought for an instant of the worm-like nastiness of human procreation: the sickening odours, the prowling organs, the hanks of hair, the oozing fluids. But in the presence of Mary such nauseous visions were dissipated and what was bestial had been transformed, by adoration, into something lovely.

"Look! A shooting star! Quick, make a wish!" cried Mary Chaworth.

I made my wish. But the moment I made it I forgot what it was. Did I wish for immortality? Eternal happiness? The colour of blue? Did I wish that my ugly foot should suddenly be straight, like Mary's feet? Did I wish for the power to fly into the over-arching night? Or did I wish for the wonderful lamp which Aladdin rubbed with his fingers? Did I wish for the gleaming rubies which lurked in the depth of Sesame?

I don't remember. I remember a star that shot through the dusk and I remember saying to Mary, "May I kiss you, please, Mary?"

But at that moment, as I held her cold little hand in my own, a bat swooped out of the castle and dived into the gloom; and Mary screamed, "Goblins! This place is full of goblins!"

Then the moon rose over the lake and another moon swam on the water, just as bright as the moon itself, but faintly aquiver, like mercury. I picked up a stone and threw it at the reflection, and a bright spray of arrows burst over the water.

We walked through the thicket and Mary whispered: "I am frightened, darling." And then she suddenly cried: "Something has stung me! Something has bitten me!"

She moaned softly and held out her thumb, on which a drop of blood was gleaming. "Only a thorn," I said consolingly. "Just a thorn on a rose-bush." I took her little hand and sucked the blood from the tip of her thumb and caught the scent of her flesh, pink and virginal, like that of a rosebud.

I see that the Turkish squadron has returned to the gulf. From my window I can see the sails floating on the water like a swarm of butterflies.

*

I still remember the wintry December dusk, fragrant with mud and rotting leaves. The mist crept out of the woods and hung motionless over the lake, and the ruins stood like a ghost in the wandering half-light.

Ruthven and I stole through the wet leafless woods with our guns. (Lord Ruthven was a ruddy young scoundrel of twenty-three, with apple-green eyes and a boxer's body. He had leased Newstead Abbey for five years with my mother's consent: I was no longer the lordly heir but merely a shy, resentful visitor.) The mist slowly settled and a cold half-moon shone through the branches. Lord Ruthven cocked his gun. (We were looking for roosting pheasants.) A shot rang out in the gloom and a feathery corpse fell through the branches.

At that same moment a blunt, shaggy beast went scampering past us.

"What was that?" I cried softly.

"A wolf, I'd say. Or maybe a werewolf!"

"A werewolf?" I whispered.

"Scared, Byron?" cackled Ruthven.

"No," I murmured. "Merely incredulous."

Ruthven laughed. "You'll have to get used to uglier things than a werewolf . . ."

The night was black as a cistern when we finally returned to the Abbey, and a fire was roaring in the enormous stone hearth. A plate of cutlets and a bottle of claret stood on the table in front of the fire. Ruthven rang for his valet (named

O'Higgins, if I remember rightly) and he came and dragged a wooden tub into the room. Buckets of steaming hot water were poured into the tub and Lord Ruthven threw off his garments and started to lather his mighty limbs.

"Come, wash yourself, Byron. You're spattered with mud," he said nonchalantly.

He filled his glass with wine and lay down naked in front of the fire. I bathed myself gingerly, with my back turned modestly to the leering Lord. Then I squatted by the fire with a towel round my waist, fondling the ears of the sheep-dog Nero, who lay curled in front of the andirons.

"There's a ghost here in the Abbey," grunted Ruthven, draining his glass. "Did you know you were letting a ghost along with the Abbey, my good Byron?"

"A headless monk," I admitted grudgingly. "He wanders about on top of the refectory."

Ruthven laughed. "There's not much use for a headless monk, is there, Byron? Now a nun might be different. What do you say to it, Byron?"

"There never were nuns in Newstead Abbey," I said carefully.

"The more's the pity," said my host with a yawn. "Fill my glass, will you, Byron?" He scratched his hairy armpit and held out his glass.

The wind swept over the lake and a twig of ivy scratched the pane. Nero lifted his head, cocked his ears and growled gently. I could hear the valet's footsteps shuffling down the empty hall, and the clatter of closing shutters and the bolting of a door.

Ruthven reached over and plucked a slice of rosy meat from the platter.

"You're a virgin, aren't you, Byron? You're a pretty lad but you're still a virgin. Your brain is precocious but your body is as pure as a baby's. You haven't yet learnt the pleasure of mounting a woman, poor little fellow. Once in

Nottingham I slept with six young harlots in a single night. Do you believe me? I can do it ten times in a row. D'you believe me, Byron?"

"I don't doubt it," I said dejectedly.

"I am a bull of a man," said Ruthven, "and there's none that can beat me. Look, Byron. See that cock of mine? Would you like to see me straddling a woman?"

"It would be instructive, I'm sure," I ventured.

Ruthven laughed and patted his belly, and gazed with a gloating smugness at his rising phallus. "It's a pity you aren't a lass, Byron. I'd have use for a pretty lass." He peered at me ominously. "Come, take off your towel. Take it off and we'll see what a fine little lass you can be!"

"I would rather not, if you'll excuse me."

"It is time," declared Ruthven, "that you learnt a thing or two," and his voice took on a furry, carnivorous quality. He got up with a snort and stood barbarically in front of me and held out his phallus in the crook of his forefinger. "There's no woman in the house, my lad, so you'll have to serve me instead!" He shook with secret amusement and tossed his wine-glass into the flames, where it burst with a delicate, bell-like resonance. "Come, get down on your knees, Byron. Suck it, you sly little bastard, suck it!"

I regarded with horror the prong of flesh that quivered in front of me. I said hoarsely, "I cannot do it, Ruthven! I cannot and will not!"

He glared at me scornfully and started to roar with laughter. "Pure as a baby!" he sneered. "And just as stupid and just as ignorant! There's much you'll be learning in life, my pretty lad, but you'll never forget this evening in Newstead, I promise you!"

He spat into the fire and picked up his dressing-gown and then he flung open the door and strutted down the hall.

I left Newstead on the following morning without saying farewell. And many years later when I saw the mist floating through the ruins, I suddenly remembered the bulbous flesh held in the crook of a big white forefinger. Am I exaggerating, am I dwelling unduly on these carnal vignettes? Why do they loom so insistently over that fog-filled horizon? And why did these sexual visions, which in childhood seemed merely amazing, take on in adolescence such a hideous humiliation? There were things I never forgave and there were things I never forgot. The line between love and loathing is as fine as a knife, and just as deadly.

30 January

One of my young Suliote captains is standing by the lamp under my window. He is wearing his *fustanella;* his buckles and buttons gleam like quicksilver. He lowers his breeches and squats in the mud. He has decided to snub the latrine, which is a hut adjoining the chicken-coop, with a four-leafed clover carved on the door.

It has been raining all day long but now the air is marvellously clear. I can see the peaks of the Morea in the moonlit distance and far away, across the gulf, the hunch-backed summits of Cephalonia.

*

I still remember the high dark building on top of the hill, with its sharp slated gables and bleak uncurtained windows. I still remember the thumb-worn Ovid left on the stairway and the rain-soaked cricket-bat in the hall. I still remember the line of boys wandering slowly across the lawn: red-cheeked boys in high black hats, sharp-tailed coats and tight-fitting breeches. I still remember their faces—Harness and Tatersall, Clare and Dorset, the pock-marked Claridge and the wild-eyed Wingfield. I was miserable at Harrow, but it was a

27

misery tinged with pride. I remember Harrow with a thrill of nausea as well as a pang of secret triumph.

Once again my mind goes prowling through the dismal rubbish of sexual discovery. We think of childhood as pure and innocent. It is anything but pure, anything but innocent. Wayward glimpses which in maturity are dismissed with a shrug of tolerance bloom in childhood into a livid, almost legendary nightmare. I was a boy, I would suppose, much like the other boys round me: a bit more "sensitive" (as my mother put it) and more "intractable" (as my tutor put it), and in general perhaps more sensual and rebellious and moody. It isn't easy for us to remember the "simple realities" of childhood. What one remembers is the monstrous, the grotesque, the elegiac.

I remember an autumn evening as I sauntered back from the library. Two boys were lurking in a nook under the stairs at the end of the hall. They jumped out as I wandered past— freckled Smithers and pimpled Boulton, and Boulton seized me by the right arm and Smithers by the left.

"Hush," said Smithers. "Keep your mouth shut. We have something to show you, Byron."

They dragged me past the stairs and opened a door of a dusty store-room, where a mottled green light seeped through an elongated window. In a corner lay a heap of red autumn apples, which mingled their scent with the smell of ancient saddles.

Boulton turned the key in the lock and slipped it ominously into his pocket.

"So," he growled, "you're an atheist, are you?"

I blushed and lowered my eyes.

"That's what you told us yesterday, isn't it? A bloody little atheist, are you, Byron?"

"I am an agnostic," I murmured primly.

"It's all the same," said Smithers, leering. "Atheist, agnostic, bloody pagan. It all boils down to being a pig. You don't believe in the Lord Almighty—is that what you told us, Byron?"

"I neither believe nor disbelieve. I await the evidence," I said with a tremor.

"You are," said Smithers calmly, "an arrogant little swine."

"As well as a foul blasphemer," added Boulton, "of the basest variety."

Smithers picked up a whip which lay on the floor among the harnesses. "It is time," he said darkly, "that you learnt a lesson in humility."

"Quite," said Boulton. "Sit down, Byron." He pointed to the heap of bright red apples. "We must have a theological discussion. We must settle this thing of God."

I crouched in the dust. Smithers lifted his whip. Boulton towered in front of me with outspread legs and arms akimbo.

"Unbutton your breeches, Byron!"

"I would rather not, if you will excuse me."

"Unbutton your breeches, Byron, or I'll whip you unmercifully!"

I meekly undid my buttons and stared at the floor dejectedly.

"That little thing you have hanging there. Do you know what it is, Byron?"

"I believe I do," I ventured.

"Well, what is it?"

"A male appendage."

Smithers burst into a falsetto scream. *"Male appendage!* He's a quaint one, ain't he? We call it a sugar-stick. There, now, Byron, take hold of your sugar-stick!"

"For what purpose, may I enquire?"

Now it was Boulton who shook with laughter. He mimicked my words with venom. *"For what purpose, may I enquire?* We'll show you for what purpose! Kindly grasp your appendage, Byron, and we'll teach you all about God in Heaven."

I had already observed the bulge under his tight-fitting trousers; now he opened the slit in his breeches and drew out his genitalia and proceeded, with an air of casual expertise, to masturbate.

"Come, Byron. Show us your style. Show us that you have a bit of spunk in you."

And so, with Boulton looming in front of me and Smithers poised with his whip to the left of me, I proceeded (with an air, I suspect, of never having done it before, and stimulated, possibly, by the sight of the whip) to imitate the suave and sophisticated gestures of the pimpled Boulton; until finally, scarcely visible in the gathering twilight, two tiny droplets welled forth and fell like tears on the dusty floor.

"Bravo, Byron!" said Boulton mockingly. "Your foot may be crippled but that fine little prick of yours is amazingly agile."

And Smithers said virtuously, "Now you see the evidence, I trust. Those little drops, my dear fellow, are the visible proof of the ways of God." He lifted his whip. "Repeat my words, please, Byron. I have witnessed the proof of the Lord Almighty."

I echoed miserably, "I have witnessed the p-p-p . . ."

"Go on, damn you!" snarled Smithers.

"I have witnessed the proof of the Lord Almighty," I whimpered feebly.

"A convert!" hissed Boulton, rolling his eyes with an air of piety.

"One more soul," said Smithers triumphantly, "saved from the toils of the infidel!"

Boulton drew out the key and softly opened the door of the store-room, and we stole on muffled steps down the hall that led to the library.

After this occurrence, I was obsessed for several months by the thought of the store-room; the upraised whip, the rotting saddles, the ruddy apples, the buzzing wasps. I remember

sitting alone in the copse with my Virgil, struggling bravely
to scan the dactylic hexameters:

> *In freta dum fluvii current, dum montibus umbrae*
> *Lustrabunt convexa, polus dum sidera pascet,*
> *Semper honos numenque tuum laudesque manebunt . . .*

And mingling with the thought of Dido wringing her
hands on the shores of Carthage came the vision of young
Boulton plucking urbanely at his swollen flesh: the dactyls
and spondees gradually dissolved into a stealthier metric,
until finally a small white drop fell on the centre of the page,
blending its own secret sorrow with the invisible tears of
Dido.

31 January

Rain again, all day long. Nothing but rain, filth, mosquitoes. I find myself struggling with a growing exasperation.
First of all, with the Greeks: a cozening, pilfering populace. I
came to Greece to fight for her freedom, but are the Greeks
still capable of freedom?

And the climate. Everything mildewed. Lice and fleas and
perpetual headaches.

And my Suliotes: a drunken and avaricious bevy of
ruffians.

And even my friends—Pietro has purchased (at my expense) some bolts of cloth. He might have had the decency to
tell me about it. Colonel Stanhope is sinking more deeply
into his pamphleteering mania. And queer old Mavrocordato, who has no feeling or taste for leadership, is revealing
himself as a kind of Byzantine *lunaire*.

I came to Greece out of a longing for self-renewal and self-
forgetfulness. I was intent on achieving some final all-obliter-

31

ating act of valour. I wanted to hurl my body into battle and bloodshed—but even here I was deceiving myself. It was not, *au fond*, out of heroism, or a dedicatory urge, or a selfless idealism. It was from a need to shed the serpent-skin of my selfish, brutal past.

*

Harness and Tatersall, Clare and Dorset, the pock-marked Claridge and the wild-eyed Wingfield: I can still remember their faces, and the dearest of all was Clare. There was a translucency about Clare. He was utterly guileless. His heart and his mind were as clear as a trout-stream. When he sat beside me in the chapel or the rain-soaked pavilion I longed to fondle those curls, I longed to kiss those luminous cheeks. But I never quite dared. Once he was a slave-girl in a play by Plautus—the *Captivi,* I believe—and he looked so exquisitely vulnerable that the tears rolled down my cheeks.

One April morning we were strolling across the green with our cricket-bats. We walked through the churchyard and sat down beside a grave. The clouds sauntered lazily beyond the over-hanging boughs, the grasshoppers were hopping in the deep clover.

"Tell me, Clare," I said sadly. "Don't you wonder occasionally?"

Clare looked at me with gravity. "What about, my good Byron?"

"Why we are born, for example?"

"We are born by sheer accident."

"No doubt," I said wisely. "But consider, please, Clare. You and I were only one out of a thousand spermatozoa. It was purely by chance, admittedly, that we happened to win the race. But the puzzle remains. How did I happen to be Byron? And how did you happen to turn into Clare? Along with the thought of the infinite stars, which I find quite unimaginable, and the thought of the eternal centuries, which I find incomprehensible, I must say that the problem of identity continues to baffle me. Here I am, sitting by a tombstone, talking to another boy named Clare; thinking my own mysterious thoughts and having my own secret feelings. I find it, I tell you, Clare, profoundly bewildering."

"You keep looking for mysteries, Byron. We must look at life as it is."

"How can we know what it really is?" I cried. "Look at those clouds! What are they, Clare? Look at these graves. What has happened to the people who lie under these gravestones?"

"Death," said Clare, "is an awful thing and I do not like to think about it."

"But if death is awful, Clare, then life too must be awful since no life exists without death, and no death exists without life."

"You think too deeply, Byron. You should be a poet and not a philosopher."

"I find poetry," I said, "detestable. It hides the reality of things, and substitutes a hollow gesticulating phantasm."

I wandered down the lane towards the blackberry-copse. A family of gipsies had pitched their camp in the shade. A mule was grazing peacefully and the gipsies lay sleeping beside him; all except for a withered hag who was sharpening a knife on a piece of pumice-stone.

"Good-morning," I said politely.

"Morning to you!" cried the hook-nosed harridan. "Come, my boy. Do you have a penny? I'll tell you your fortune for a penny!"

I pulled a coin from my pocket and dropped it in her palm. I caught the smell of onions rising from her bright orange petticoat.

"There," she muttered, "sit down, my pussy-cat, and show

33

me your hand. Beautiful fingers, like a prince's, and nails as white as pearls! Crippled, are you? Never mind, there's uglier things than a twisted foot." She peered at me through the thick oily strands of her hair. "Water," she moaned, "is your native element. You will live and die near the water." She drew a wrinkled finger over the fat of my thumb. "Much is the love that lies a-waiting for you. Much and mottled, and some of it miserable. And always to the end the love in your heart will wear two masks." Two stumpy black teeth shone in a vulturous grin; the breath from her mouth stank like that of a scavenger. "Beware of your thirty-sixth year. Beware of swamps and leeches. Beware of wet saddles. Beware of men who wear spectacles." And she patted my wrist and whispered, "If you are sick and sad and alone, lying in a room full of vermin and with death in your heart, think of me, my lovely lad. Whistle in the night and I will come to you . . ."

1 February

To-day is Sunday. We set out for Anatolica at ten in the morning, just as the mist was beginning to settle over the water. We sailed for three hours through a reed-clotted bay. On our arrival we were greeted by exuberant salvos of musketry, and a cannon-ball came scuttling over the bay past our prow. Pietro wore his helmet and Loukas his spangled uniform, Mavrocordato his furry cap and I my gilded cloak. We walked through the streets on our way to the Primate's mansion, and women with yellow fans cried from their balconies: "Saviour! Deliverer!"

We sailed back at dusk. A squall came up suddenly and we were soaked by the howling torrents of rain. I saw that poor Loukas was beginning to shiver and I wrapped my thick, braided cloak about him.

There are times when I feel that there is a dream-like air about all this. Am I really in Greece? Am I really fighting for Grecian liberty? Is there such a boy as Loukas, and such a place as Anatolica?

*

My rooms were in the Great Court of Trinity, in what was known as Mutton-hall Corner. A stairway went winding up the tower to the little attic where I kept my tame bear, whom I called Ursus Major. Hobhouse and Matthews were my friends, and Ned Long and Scrope Davies: witty, middle-class friends, unlike my lordly friends at Harrow. Egg-faced Hobhouse and mop-headed Matthews, dumpy Long and cadaverous Davies: plain, sly, Platonic friends, not like my beautiful friends at Harrow. I still remember strolling at noon to the fencing-rooms in Portugal Place, or lolling on the banks with my Rousseau or Cervantes, or riding in the spring out to the orchards in Grantchester, or hurrying through the dusk to the lamplit coffee-house in Bene't Street and leafing, over my plum-tart, through some slim new volume of poetry.

I remember diving for shillings in the murky depths of the Cam and strolling by moonlight over the lawn by King's Chapel, which seemed transformed by the organ music of the Largo from *Xerxes* into a great harp-like instrument of brightly-shining stone.

At Cambridge, in my day, it was considered the sign of a gentleman to have a servant and a horse, to take a bath, to wear red kerchiefs, to belch with a casual resonance and fart with unconcern, and to talk of sodomy as though it were a perfectly humdrum occurrence. We were clever, terribly clever, but the cleverest of all was Scrope. He was a Fellow at King's, as well as a gambler and a dandy. He was gaunt, sly and caustic, with a slippery nose and owlish eyes. With all his

35

intellectual brilliance, with all his references to Kant and Aristotle, he had one little weakness: *id est,* kleptomania. On a hedonic level, I hasten to add; for zest, and never for profit. When we went to his rooms for tea we were sure to find a casket of marrons, nimbly filched from the grocery of Mr Muggins in King's Parade, or the latest French novel, bound in peppered brown calfskin, stolen from the stalls of the bookshop in Petty Cury.

"Well, Scrope, where did you steal this?" I said one day, pointing to a scarf.

"We are all thieves at heart," he said, and folded his arms tauntingly. "Some of us dare and some of us daren't, and that is the only difference."

"My dear Scrope," I said loftily, "this is utterly preposterous. You are far from impoverished. You could pay for fifty scarves if you wanted."

"You are quibbling, Byron, as usual. It isn't avarice which drives me but adventure. And perhaps a latent grievance against established British society. I would rather give rein to my instincts than conform to a prudish hypocrisy." And he squeezed his bony fingers with a leer of self-righteousness.

"Some day," I said darkly, "you will get into trouble, Scropie."

"Some day," replied Scrope, "we will all get into trouble."

The dearest to me was Hobhouse with his sad, sexless eyes, in which a glint of donnish merriment occasionally twinkled, rather wistfully. Dear Cam! Dumpy and slovenly, vicarious, viperish Cam! What was your secret tragedy, your worm of discontent? He never failed to twit me for my foibles. For taking a daily bath, he accused me of being a "sybarite". My preference for good food he called "blatant epicureanism". My taste in chemises he dismissed as "sartorial decadence", and my amorous by-plays he called "Bacchic", or even "Byzantine".

I said to him, "Hobhouse, I am obliged for your concern. I

36

shall take my daily bath, you may stink if you prefer. I'll have my lobster and claret and leave you to your haddock and tepid ale. I shall wear my Milanese scarves, you can wear your filthy flannels. As for sex, you are free to follow in the paths of virginity but I'll sleep with whomever I wish, though it end up with the clap."

Cambridge is beautiful, but the beauty is that of impenetrable seclusion. Clare bridge lies mirrored in the water like an ivory ring, or a ring of Saturn. The backs of King's and Trinity, all dotted with crocuses, have the air of abstract meadows never touched by a terrible reality. And the streets in the winter dusk, smelling of smoke and ancient masonry, have the black self-sufficiency of a hieratic universe, where pain cannot penetrate and where fear can never torture.

We rode out to Newmarket and bet on the races, and then we played hazard until three or four in the morning. We went shooting in the fens, and drinking in the taverns, but most of all we talked: we talked of anything and everything, but always with a gaudy and garrulous cleverness. Ursus Major, my bear, would listen carefully to these discussions, and then lick at the jam-pot and roll up on my bed.

We spoke of love from time to time, deep in the night over a jug of ale.

"Tell me this," said Scrope defiantly: "if true love exists, other than merely as a facet of the reproductive urge, then why is it always accompanied by such vulgar manifestations as penoid erections and seminal explosions?"

"Love derives," said Matthews primly, "from the reproductive urge, but people being what they are, affectionate by nature, idealistic by instinct, and much given to the habit of emblemization, they have built out of lust a superstructure of romantic love."

"Romantic love!" cried Ned Long. "Bless my soul, the forms that it takes! I happened to make use of a convenient wall on Jesus Green to-day, and a loving inscription was

37

written there in chalk. 'I was walking along Queen's Road,' it said, 'and was accosted by a young dragoon. He took me by the hand and led me into a dark deserted cellar. There he brutally stripped my clothes from me and chained me to the wall, whereupon he took a whip and lashed me fiercely across the belly. He had likewise removed his garments, except for his leather boots, and I was astounded by the size of his organ, which was ten inches long and as thick as my wrist. As he watched me squirming with pain it started to gush with sudden excitement, and the blood on my belly mingled with the torrents of boiling seed.' These are the words that I read. Is this a sample of romantic love?"

"Revolting," said Hobhouse. "These pathetic inscriptions, I would venture, are merely wishful imaginings rather than a record of actual occurrences."

"True, no doubt," agreed Matthews, "but all of love is a wishful image, and the actual occurrence never lives up to the paradisiacal vision."

I asked Hobhouse: "What do you see when you think of God?"

"I see a moon-faced monkey," said Hobhouse, "sitting on a mountain-top in India."

"And you, Matthews?"

"Something vaguely and improbably luminous, like an *Aurora borealis*."

"And what about you, Scrope?"

"I see a swamp with bubbles floating on top of it. Something imponderable, impenetrable, inextricable, and utterly useless."

"Well, then why," I insisted, "have men always believed in a God?"

"They say that God," said Scrope snappishly, "created man in his own image, but it strikes me as evident that the case is the contrary. The Hottentots too have gods, funny black ones with enormous *phalloi,* and the Chinese too have gods, with

38

pendulous bellies and sloping eyes. Why has humanity all these centuries indulged in such gross self-glorification?"

He strolled scornfully to the window and pissed into the court-yard. The rest of us, in the course of these ale-embroidered symposia, would reach politely under the table and make water into the chamber-pot; but Scrope, in the exuberant rebelliousness of his soul, would fling open the window and piss merrily at the stars.

"Scropie," I said, "why don't you piss into the pot like a gentleman?"

"I detest the sound of piss gurgling in a pot," said Scrope firmly. "And what is more, a stray drop always falls on the rug and the smell of urine in a room revolts me."

"Even your own?" inquired Matthews.

"All urine smells alike."

"You are wrong. A woman's urine," said Ned Long, "smells sharper than a man's."

"I have never smelled it, thank the Lord," said Hobhouse, wrinkling his nose a little.

"There you are. You cannot avoid talking about God," said Matthews indignantly. "As for me, I know nothing of religion. I see nothing good in religion. There are fools and impostors everywhere, in the church as well as the market-place. I disbelieve in immortality. When we die we die. *Ridens moriar.*"

Ridens moriar! Darling Matthews, how little you guessed what lay in store for you! Oh my bibulous, garrulous, querulous, unreal Cambridge! Oh mossy spires, oh foggy streets, oh piss-pots hurled into the night! How happy we all were, and how little we understood happiness! How wise we were too, and how little we knew of wisdom!

We spoke of the female pudendum. Scrope considered it purely utilitarian and of no artistic validity, compared to the *membrum virile,* which has a more definite character, being variable in shape, hue and behaviour.

39

"You are quibbling," said Matthews. "You are speaking from inexperience. Your opinion merely reflects your inflamed imagination."

"How can an orifice," said Scrope, "be as interesting, artistically, as an organ? One is an object, like a flute or a candlestick. The other is merely a hole. It is difficult to feel a connoisseur's enthusiasm about a hole."

"You are mistaken," put in Matthews, "and I speak from personal knowledge. Holes may vary quite surprisingly in grip and suction, as well as texture."

"Humbug, Matthews," said Long, wiping the ale-froth from his lips. "The vagina is merely a mechanism for giving pleasure to the male. Aesthetically it is a disaster. The evidence is clear. The great artists have always fought shy of the *labia majora*. Whereas the penis, since the time of Praxiteles, has been accepted as sculpturally adequate. I need not mention Donatello or Bernini or Michael Angelo. And think of architecture, please. Think of the minarets, the towers, the obelisks. Think of a damascened pistol, or even a gold-knobbed cane. Where do you find a similar glorification of the female cunt?"

"Long, my lad, you have lived too long in this rarefied atmosphere," said Matthews benignly. "Trinity College is not London, nor is Cambridge the universe, tempting though on occasions it may be to think so. The world is not merely an aesthetical laboratory. I might add that the glorification you so crudely deny might be found in Gothic naves, Byzantine vaults and Arabian archways. Not to mention a well-shaped urn, a Bohemian goblet or a Lowestoft gravy-boat. You must tear yourself away from this Cantabrigian academicism. The world is a bigger and rougher place than you imagine . . ."

Both Loukas and Pietro are down with a fever. I too feel unwell. Dyspeptic, dizzy, and distinctly *peculiar*.

*

I have always felt a compulsion to write journals, diaries and memoirs. Not, I fear, out of a yearning for self-elucidation but simply from a sort of inveterate garrulity. Hobhouse once accused me of "verbal diarrhoea". He may be right. Maybe it is time I stopped fiddling with the English vocabulary and tried to pin things down with strictness and exactitude.

What is style? Style is the cloak in which we clothe our spirits, said Montaigne. But what if this spirit is mercurial and evasive, perpetually changing? In my letters my style is chatty, rambling, fortuitous. In my conversation it is defiantly facetious or coquettishly digressive. In my verse it is mellow and playful: alliterative and allusive. I am none of these things by nature. At least not now. Not in essence. I have strutted about the world in numerous disguises, but here in Missolonghi I am reduced to only one. In these memoirs I shall strive for nothing but truth and lucidity. Can I force my meandering style into a submission to truth, to a crystal lucidity?

Hopeless, of course. The iron truth, the crystal lucidity—they don't exist. But at least, at this distance, staring at the violent stars of March, I can try to purge from my brain the false, the cloudy and sentimental and reach out, however ineptly, not like a compass on a mountain but like a claw in the ocean-bed, for that darting silver minnow which is the fabric of the past.

One spring day I was sitting in the Chapel, listening drowsily to the choir, when I noticed one of the choir-boys in

41

the second row to the left. A flake of sunlight fell on his face from the window overhead and I was reminded of the luminous cheeks of Lord Clare. When the service was over I lurked in the columns of the Court and when he passed I said demurely: "I beg your pardon, young fellow."

He looked startled and blushed. "Might I be of use to you, sir?"

"What is your name?"

"John Edleston, sir."

"You live in Cambridge?"

"I do indeed, sir."

"Well, Edleston, would you like to ride to Grantchester with me tomorrow?"

He lowered his eyes. "I should be happy to be of service to you, sir."

"Then meet me at the gate at half-past two in the afternoon . . ."

And that was how I met Edleston. We mounted our horses in the Peas Hill stables (his was a dappled mare which I hired for him and mine was a coal-black gelding) and we rode through the sunlight down the long road to Trumpington. The chestnuts were in flower, the air was noisy with birds, and we tethered our horses next to a low, drooping willow-tree.

We stood on the bridge and stared down at the mill-pool and the stream which went bubbling into the pool under the mill.

"Shall we swim?" I said casually.

"Let us swim," murmured Edleston.

Near the pool behind some aspens stood an empty "folly" in the Gothic manner (now no longer in existence, so Hobhouse informs me) and here in the darkness we stripped and hung our clothes. I can still smell the scent of the dusky wooden rafters, I can still hear the bees buzzing about in the cobwebbed stillness. We strolled through the grass to the edge

42

of the pool and sat in the shallow water and watched the gudgeons nibbling at our toes. Then we jumped into the pool and dived for the pebbles that lay at the bottom. Edleston cried out in panic as a tangle of weeds wound about him but I came to his rescue and tugged him back to the shore. We did cart-wheels on the grass and played leap-frog in the bushes, and Edleston stood on his head in the shade of the willow-tree. I still remember the shiny drops that rolled down his body, and the tight little scrotum upside down on his fuzzy groin. We stepped back into the summer-house and in the shade I whispered to Edleston, "Eddles, darling, tell me something. Have you ever been with a girl?"

"Never yet," said Edleston, blushing. (He blushed very easily.) "I have had no opportunity to do so. And what about you, sir?"

"Oh," I said with an air of nonchalance, "I have tried it occasionally, but sex is a distinctly over-rated commodity, to my way of thinking."

Edleston blushed a second time and glanced at me bashfully. I laughed and said gaily, "Eddles, my pet, you are beautiful. If you were a girl, I'd fall headlong in love with you."

"Hush," said Edleston, looking at the floor.

"It is true," I said quietly, and I folded my arms around him. I felt his body gradually yielding, and then growing rigid. I kissed him on the lips but he drew away shyly.

"What we are doing is wicked, terribly wicked," he purred.

"It is wicked indeed," I said. "All pleasure is wicked. I tell you, dear Eddles, I am ready to burst with sheer wickedness!"

We rode back through the twilight and had tea at a roadside inn, and finally we said farewell in the dusky stable at Peas Hill.

I was infatuated with John Edleston for three sunny months. We went riding to the Pike and Eel and sat fishing on the bank of the river, or out to the woods by Madingley where we shot at the archery targets, or up to the Isle of Ely where we strolled through the cathedral and ate a veal-pudding in the Red Grenadier.

Edleston much resembled Clare: the same blond hair, the same lean body. Only the eyes were quite unlike, Clare's being of a pensive violet, and Edleston's of a shallow forget-me-not blue. I shall never forget dear Eddles, though fate was afterwards cruel to him. Months later, in Constantinople, I had a letter from Frank Hodgson, and he told me that poor Edleston had got into trouble. He was caught one night by the watchman in the yard of the Purple Cow in a compromising posture with one of the grooms, a Toby O'Brien. True innocence is frail, alas, and youth is ever fleeting, and even the blue-eyed Edleston was flawed with the sin of the serpent.

Moral: Yes, there is a moral in this, and a most disturbing moral. I once presented a small carnelian heart to my Eddles, and I even wrote a poem in which I called him "Thyrza". But aside from the smirking poem and the heart of carnelian, we had nothing to remember the other one by, and my passion for Eddles rolled from my conscience like drops from a duck. But what of Eddles himself? That dismal night in the Purple Cow—the lusty young groom, the irascible watchman? Was it all my own fault? Am *I* the one to blame? Was it *I* who should have been hauled before the police? If we drop a sixpenny-piece from an upstairs window, and it falls into the hands of a half-witted sailor from Boscastle, who then gets drunk in the ale-house and kills a girl in a darkened alley, is it *we* who are the killers? Who are the innocent, who the guilty?

Was what happened bound to happen? Or was it all an unlucky accident? Or was it both, yet neither? A symphonic fusion of fate and accident, the melody being the black, secret flaw in our souls?

Postscript: Yes, there is a postscript, and a very sad postscript. Five years later, in October, I had a letter from Ann

44

Edleston. She wrote that her brother John had died "quite suddenly" the previous May. I felt a pang of sudden misery, but it was an oblivious, misty misery and I sat at my desk and wrote,

> The kiss, so guiltless and refined,
> That Love each warmer wish forbore;
> Those eyes proclaimed so pure a mind,
> Even Passion blushed to plead for more . . .

Charming, gay, sweet-singing Edleston! Even now I feel that I betrayed you. I betrayed you in the summer-house, I betrayed you in the woods by Madingley, and worst of all I betrayed you in that self-deceiving poem. Was it any comfort, when you died, to know that once I was in love with you? Was it any comfort in your humiliation to know that I remembered you as "pure" and even "seraphic"? Alas, in moments of anguish it helps us little to know we were loved. When we lie on our death-bed our absent lovers can do little to comfort us.

3 February

Excellent news. It appears that the *Anne* has eluded the Turks on its way from Ithaca, and has safely anchored at Dragomestre. They have begun to unload the supplies, which will be brought to Missolonghi by a fleet of fishing-boats.

A long visit today from wicked, equivocal Mavrocordato.

He sat down on a cushion and sipped at some *ouzo* and finally he said: "I am really, you know, a deplorable and bad little man."

"My good Mavro . . ."

"Please call me Alex."

"We are all of us deplorable, my good Alex."

45

"You see," said the Prince, "in my heart of hearts I am Asiatic. My speech is Greek and my manners are French, but my yearnings are Oriental. I should have been a pasha, I think, or a minor Maharajah."

The Prince's hair, which hangs in thin untidy strands, reeks of jasmine. He wears buttons of turquoise and a yellow handkerchief in his sleeve. He looks like a depraved but innocuous little scholar, and he speaks with a plangent, undulating lisp.

"Instead," he said, "of becoming an apostle, and such a puzzled apostle, of liberty, I should be lolling in idleness with sinuous ephebes scattered about me. But in every man's life comes a time when he gives up lewdness. I have decided to give up lewdness. I have turned to the bedlam of politics." He looked at me mousily. "Am I making a terrible blunder?" He fondled his glass for a moment and whispered with sorrow: "After all, I was never a beauty. For a beauty like you, to abandon the pleasures of love must be difficult. But for me, even at the best of times, reciprocated love was as rare as a dodo. Like you, I have turned to politics. For you it was a triumph, for me a surrender. Alas, dear Byron, I wish that my nature were better adapted to the spheres of the bellicose. I don't deny that there is a charm in the thought of a fine strapping soldier, but even as a child I recoiled from the thought of fighting other boys . . ."

*

One July morning in 1809 I sailed from Falmouth on the *Princess Elizabeth*. Sailing with me were my crony Hobhouse, my valet Fletcher, my page-boy Rushton, as well as a certain pimply and pot-bellied Herr Friese. Herr Friese was an obsequious Swabian who had been to Persepolis and Ispahan, not to mention the ruins of Antioch and the Sphinx

46

of Egypt. The captain was Captain Kidd, a gallant and stalwart spirit, and we arrived in the river Tagus four clear days after sailing from England.

Lisboa: what a filthy and exquisite, what an enchanted, execrable city! The rooms were seething with mosquitoes, the men with lice and the beds with bedbugs. I remember a dirty old friar sitting on the edge of a fountain, plucking fleas from his belly and cracking them briskly on the flagstones. Down by the banks, where the gulls came screaming from the sands of Capranica, the fishing-boys squatted (not to mention the stalwart young fishing-girls) and left a pestilential trail of excreta. The impoverished Portuguese wallowed in filth and degradation while in the background loomed the ubiquitous sidelong leer of the Papal establishment. Still, all can be forgiven Lisbon for its deep, caerulean beauty. The blue-tiled façades stretched to the moss-bearded quays and the gulls from Capranica flew through a deep prismatic light—a light that soaked the city in a cool evening shimmer, so that even the faeces and the fleas took on a mediaeval aptness.

We rode merrily out to Cintra on four tinkling donkeys. A tiny cloud, no bigger than a parasol, hung immovably over the hills. From the palaces of Cintra there is a view of the Atlantic and all around, in a sea of ferns, lie gurgling streams and hidden waterfalls. I have never in my life seen a place so beautiful as Cintra. But even here a kind of Lusitanian melancholy pervades the atmosphere, and the hush that hangs over Cintra is closer to hopelessness than to serenity.

I remember sitting in Cintra and sipping coffee under a trellis. Hobhouse was leafing through *Vathek,* trying to inhale the full "aura" of it, and Herr Friese was prowling through the bushes with his butterfly-net. He was an "Aurelian", as he put it. He wore a huntsman's cap and a plum-grey waistcoat, and squealed "Eureka!" when he caught a specimen and popped it into his bottle. Rushton and Fletcher were playing dominoes in the shade of a fig-tree. Bob Rush-

47

ton (a farmer's boy who worked for me in Newstead) had the rosy cheeks and coltish body of a typical Yorkshireman, while Fletcher, with his bulbous ecclesiastical nose, had the pallid angularity that is common in Cornwall.

I asked Hobhouse: "What made Beckford settle in a palace in Cintra? Was it the beauty of the place? Or were there other amenities?"

"There were *amenities*, no doubt," hinted Hobhouse with a sloping look, "but the thing that lured Beckford was the air of unreality. Think of Cambridge. It was the dream-like unreality that thrilled us at Trinity and gave us such a wine-like feeling of freedom. And look at Cintra. It is a myth. Totally unreal, totally free. Beckford did what he wished in Cintra. He cast off the chains of reality and played at being a sultan in the depths of Arabia."

We crossed the Tagus one morning and ate oranges in Sessimbra. Then we drove through the dark, rolling woods of Alentejo. We stopped in Aldea Gallega and started off again at sunrise. We rode through the dappled cork-woods to Los Prigones, where we sat under a pergola and drank the rosy wine and ate some fried mullet that were rolled up in bay-leaves. We rode on and came at nightfall to the inn of Montemenor, which lay tucked in the darkness of a forest of pines.

It was a hot, windless night. Hobhouse and I sat down in the tavern and talked until twelve about Dryden and Pope. Hobhouse idolised Dryden, while I much preferred Pope.

Hobhouse said that he found a greater "virile energy" in Dryden, and that Dryden was more capable of the "grand effect". I retorted that much of this energy was dissipated in "pseudo-heroism", and that it was exactly Pope's delicacy that gave him a truer intensity.

"Dryden," said Hobhouse, "portrays an epoch in its full robust flowering. Pope reveals it in a state of powdery decay."

"True," I said, "but an autumn copper is just as fine as a

summery gold, and it contains in its melancholy an even greater depth. I love the paintings of Watteau, which contain the poignance of foreboding. I much prefer him to Rubens with his buttocky vitality. A catastrophe came to Paris in 1789 and sent a tremor of panic through the whole of Europe. In Pope we already see the premonitions of the catastrophe, whereas old Dryden, with all his grandiloquence, was blind to the coming chaos."

"I quite agree," said Hobhouse mildly, "that Pope was a more intelligent man than Dryden. All the sadder, don't you think, that he chose to limit his poetry to what is nothing more than an exquisite *petit-point*?"

I said to Hobhouse, whose spaniel-brown eyes glowed in the candle-light: "Strange, isn't it, Cam? You are such a cool fastidious soul, and yet you admire the grandiosities of Dryden, and I am such a pompous grandeur-loving fellow, and yet I like the scrupulous needlework of Pope."

"We respond in art to our opposites, perhaps," ventured Hobhouse.

"Or perhaps we are all the products of a *coincidentia oppositorum*. Maybe, Cam, there is a hidden tempestuousness in your heart, and maybe there is a hidden scrupulosity in my own."

Hobhouse smiled. "Can you see me being tempestuous, Byron?"

I laughed. "Can you see me being scrupulous, dear Cam?"

Hobhouse picked up the candle and we threaded our way up the stairway. He opened the door of his bedroom and bade me good-night. I walked on, slightly tipsy, and turned the knob of the adjoining door and stepped into the pine-smelling darkness of my chamber.

There was a chair by the window. I sat down with a sigh. A lustreless moon hung over the black stretch of forest and shone into the stillness of the low, narrow bed-chamber. I reflected on the grandiose convolutions of *Alexander's Feast*,

49

compared to the fragile traceries of *The Rape of the Lock*. I heard a faint gurgle, and glanced at the bed. A naked shape was lying there with its head turned to the wall, arms spread over the pillow and the long legs outstretched. A thick Moorish bracelet shone on one of the wrists. It was a woman: the face was hidden but the body was slim and youthful and I caught a resinous whiff of the damp, sleeping flesh.

For a while I sat motionless, ten minutes maybe, with folded hands. I kept staring at the sleeping woman, whose face and name were quite unknown to me. I felt that I was being drawn into some deep animal intimacy; that I had known her since childhood, and that I knew her innermost thoughts. I rose from the chair and tiptoed softly to the bed. There I knelt, resting my hands on the edge of the bedstead, and watched the faint rising and falling of her breath. I noticed a small black spot on her hip. I thought at first that it might be a bedbug; then I realized that it was a mole. I leant over stealthily and touched a swollen nipple. Then I kissed, ever so lightly, the flat moonlit belly. The sleeper sighed lazily and murmured in Italian, without stirring: *"Miguel, mio carino . . . O Miguel, mio amore . . ."*

I knelt motionless a little longer, ten minutes maybe, maybe twenty. Then I rose and went tiptoeing to the black wooden door. I turned the knob and hesitated. The sleeper had lifted her head and was staring through the darkness with a look half-lustful and half-indignant.

I closed the door behind me and walked dreamily down the hall until at last I found my room, which was on the left, beside Bob Rushton's.

4 February

Numerous chests, sacks and boxes have finally arrived from Dragomestre. But today is a holiday and the Greeks (who are maddeningly superstitious) refused to carry them in from the rain. I ran down to the beach in a rage and started to tug at the ammunition boxes. A trio of sullen peasants finally came to my rescue and consented to drag the rain-soaked cases under a shed.

I have picked up my note-book and read through yesterday's entry. I cannot pretend, of course, that I recall all of these dialogues *verbatim*. Sometimes the words still ring in my ears. More often I am driven to conjecture. But the gist, no doubt, is there. And in any case, what people say is never quite what they mean. Conversation, even the simplest, such as "Pass me the salt, please", is really a series of psychological stratagems. The aim is not to communicate so much as to triumph; the purpose is not clarity but obliquity and circumvention. I never listened very attentively to what people said, nor tried to recall precisely the words that they uttered. What we said back in Cambridge was merely a *tu quoque* or a *jeu d'esprit,* or just a visceral grunt, or at best an approximation. When we say "I love you", the range of meanings is infinite and iridescent. Only when we say "yes" or "no" do we come close to verbal exactitude, and even these here in Greece (where the tongue is slippery as an eel) somehow manage to evade a definite commitment. "Yes" may mean "You are my superior; I intend to flatter you", or "I really have no idea but refuse to admit it." And "no" may mean "Yes, darling, but keep it a secret, please", or "Yes, but only provided that you give me more money."

*

We rode into Spain and came to the city of Badajoz. A woman in black stood waving her arms by the gate. She cried to us that the cholera had come to the city and that the streets were seething with rats and vermin. I peered through the arch and saw a procession crossing the plaza, each of the men carrying a large burlap sack which he placed on the pyre; the flames leapt upward and there was a chorus of lamentation.

We rode on. The land grew bony and abysmal, riddled with misery. We came to the village of Monasterio and spent the night in a courier's house. We ate shrimps and drank sherry (much drier than the one at Trinity) and for dinner we ate a chicken which was served with a fruit wine. The two waiters stood in the doorway, picking their teeth with little pins, and our guide Sanguinetti took his flute and played a fandango. Suddenly a huge-bosomed woman burst in from the kitchen and started to dance (quite gracefully, I thought, considering her immensity) to the high giddy chirping of Sanguinetti's flute. Some soldiers who were passing peeped in through the window and one of them shouted jovially *"Olé, Pepita!"* Pepita lifted a wine-glass and roared a deep *"Salud!"* at me, and then she slapped my back and kissed me lustily on the cheek.

Still, in spite of its outward gaiety, there was a bleakness about Spain. We went riding through the range of the Sierra Morena and watched the eagles circling over the cactus-filled valleys. Once, as I crouched under some rocks (I was plagued in Spain with diarrhoea), I saw a small adder crawl through the eye of a sheep-skull. An atmosphere of death pervaded the Sierra Morena and as I rode through the heather I was obsessed with the thought of death. I had always felt that death was an ugly and pitiful thing, but here in the Sierra Morena, I began to feel it was also majestic—a dark achievement, a metamorphosis, almost a sort of final triumph, whereby a man became a part of all that had ever happened in history; and that a man who was dying was no longer a single man but on the verge of becoming a hundred thousand men. He would smell in his death the leathery hordes of Attila, he would listen to the prayers on the shores of the Ganges, he would watch the Indian chiefs singing to the spirits of the Mississippi, he would drink the same hemlock which old Socrates had drunk.

We passed a row of muleteers and the road dipped into an

olive-grove, and then it crossed a bridge over a waterless ravine. It turned and in the distance we saw a hill with a tower on top of it, and the locusts started to scream in the motionless heat.

Suddenly Sanguinetti cried: "Quick! Take to the bushes, sir!"

"Why, what's wrong?" I called back to him.

"Robbers, Your Lordship!" cried the guide.

I glanced about but saw no robbers, and winked connivingly at Hobhouse. But at that moment three figures jumped out of a thicket and stood astride the road directly in front of us. One was a boy; he was brandishing a long shiny kitchen-knife. One was a one-eyed ruffian who was carrying a hatchet. The third was a white-haired patriarch in a threadbare tunic, and he was pointing (grinning cheerfully) a long black blunderbuss.

We halted by the roadside and I slid from my saddle.

"Careful, Byron," said Hobhouse.

"Don't be rash, sir!" cried Fletcher.

I strode up to the patriarch and patted him on the back while our guide stood behind me, quivering and gesticulating.

"What do they want?" I asked the guide.

"Money! Gold, jewels, haberdashery!"

"Well, I'll see to it that they won't think us stingy," I said briskly, and I walked to one of our donkeys and took a bottle from the hamper, uncorked it ceremoniously and passed it to the goat-faced patriarch. He sniffed it and drank. The ruffian did likewise. The boy sipped it suspiciously and broke into a grin. They passed the bottle about (it was an excellent brandy which I had bought in Lisbon) and their faces grew more and more mellow and conciliatory. I reached into my coat and took out a bag full of coins. These I handed to the patriarch with a courtly bow and a flourish, and instructed Sanguinetti to say to him, *verbatim*: "The English prince

53

presents his compliments to the noblest spirit of ancient Spain!"

The old bandit bowed with dignity, the boy and the ruffian did likewise, and we left them standing in the road with their bottle of brandy, waving good-bye mournfully to us with their dirty brown hands.

We entered Andalusia and came to the city of Seville. We stayed with two spinsters in a white-washed house surrounded by lime-trees, and at dusk we strolled in the small winding streets beyond the cathedral. There I watched the coal-black eyes which flashed behind the embroidered veils, and I thought that the Spanish women must be mysterious as well as beautiful. This, alas, was an illusion. We were invited, Cam and I, to a banquet held in the house of an old Marquesa. And here I found that these same dark beauties, with their palpitating lashes and equivocal glances, were obsessed with a single notion: that of shallow intrigue. Their eyes kept hinting at celestial joys and unquenchable sorrows, but the minute they opened their mouths it would be a meaningless giggle or a fatuous titter, or if they brought themselves to speak, it would be some devastating platitude. The more impenetrable the air of mystery, the more cretinous the giggle and lethal the platitude. The women of Andalusia were undulatingly beautiful but an instant's conversation with them filled me with panic.

The morning we left Seville, one of my fine moustachioed hostesses strode up to my stallion with tears in her eyes. She took a pair of scissors and cut a lock of her hair, which she folded trimly into a handkerchief and pressed into my hand.

"¡Adiós, hermoso! ¡Me gustas mucho!" she muttered quiveringly.

And we started down the white blazing road to Cadiz.

I have caught a chill in the rain, it seems, as well as a swollen tendon.

In the late afternoon Captain Parry came to the house, and we chatted together over a jug of cider. He is a bluff, barrel-shaped fellow with a thick ruddy beard. He smells faintly of ammonia. But I like Captain Parry.

*

I remember in Cadiz we were sitting in the sunlight by the sea, sipping peacefully at a glass of very dry manzanilla. The air in Cadiz is amazingly fresh and brilliant, and the sails on the horizon looked like a scattering of petals which had fallen from the clouds.

A man with a monkey passed and begged me for a coin. I gave him an Austrian *thaler* and he fell on his knees. The monkey jumped on my shoulder and stole an almond from the platter. Then it plucked at my ear-lobe and kissed it affectionately.

We spoke of Spain and the strange phenomenon which is called Spanish pride, and of the equally strange phenomenon which is Portuguese melancholy.

"No question about it," said Hobhouse. "People differ from land to land. A Cornishman is not like a Northumbrian, a Cantabrigian is not like an Oxonian, and the people of York differ considerably from those of Yarmouth."

"Partly the blood," I suggested, "partly the climate, and partly the atmosphere."

"What do you mean," said Cam, "by atmosphere?"

"A concatenation," I said, "of details. In York there is a cathedral. The presence of an Archbishop has infected the spirit. In Yarmouth there are haddocks. The people resemble fish. Have you ever noticed how a woman who is obsessed with things equestrian begins, after a while, to look like a horse?"

"There you go, making a caricature of the human spirit. Men's souls are moulded by subtler things than fish or archbishoprics. The Portuguese sadness derives from hopelessness in the face of poverty, combined with a spiritual stagnation, an insidious loss of national energy."

"And Spanish pride?"

"Due likewise to an obsolescence of the great traditions, combined with a silly emphasis on masculine bravado, a quality much admired here, where there is always a threat of death, by a stiletto or a bull's horn, or even by cholera."

"Now it is you, my good Cam, who are simplifying things. Things like sadness or pride are inherent in a person's character. They aren't caused by a pair of bull's horns or a bowl of watery soup . . ."

At this point we were startled by the sound of jeering and a rattling of chains. We turned and saw a straggling procession come down the street. A group of civil policemen, with black moustaches and tricorne hats, were leading a miserable creature who was chained by both hands, while a bevy of urchins were thumbing their noses and throwing pebbles at him.

I turned to Sanguinetti and said, "What has happened?"

"It would appear," he said (after a casual enquiry), "that this man, who is painted with rouge and is waggling his behind, has for long been disporting himself in an irregular manner. He has been seducing, in the shrubs of the park and behind the kegs of the wine-houses, and even in the transept of the local cathedral, innocent boys who knew no better and occasionally a sailor or even a priest. The governor of the city has decided to put an end to it. The poor devil is going to have his head chopped off in the plaza . . ."

The procession passed by and disappeared round a corner. But I noticed, not without poignance, that as the prisoner passed our table, even with the sentence of decapitation

56

hanging over his shaggy black head, he couldn't resist a furtive glance in my direction; and I saw in his eyes a quick and desperate flash of coquetry.

6 February

Nothing happened to-day. I wrote two letters. And I thought of England.

England, England! It is all so remote from the present reality that it looms beyond the night like a fog-bound paradise; like a haunted little park floating on the waves of the Atlantic. I remember the stink of smoke in Aberdeen and the whores pissing in Piccadilly, the wire-masked fencers in Portugal Place and the troll-faced mushrooms in Six-Mile Bottom. I remember the smell of cabbages and the stench of hypocrisy, the simpering dons and the leering duchesses.

And yet . . . England, England! I remember the moss on the Folly Castle and the salmon leaping in the crystal-clear Dee. I remember the violets in Harrow churchyard and the smell of clover in the meadows of Trumpington. What is the answer? Do we end by loathing the things that once we loved? Or do we end by loving the things that brought us misery and humiliation?

*

From Gibraltar we went sailing to the city of Cagliari, and from there we sailed to Sicily and the island of Malta. From Malta in September we crossed the Ionian Sea and dropped anchor in the Gulf of Patras. We stepped ashore. Hobhouse knelt and picked up a handful of dirt.

"The earth of the Peloponnesus!" he whispered reverently.

Far to the north across the gulf I saw (or thought I saw) a city. A heap of low black hovels rose from a flat brownish

57

swamp and beyond, ugly and ominous, loomed the hills of Chalkis.

Missolonghi! Even then (or was it only my fancy?) I saw something foetid in the contours of the place, as though it were a corpse left to rot in the muddy prairies.

Missolonghi . . . I look through my window. Stars are shining on the shore. The place is not a corpse, it is seethingly alive, and instead of despair I feel a thrill of expectancy.

Why? How? What? When? Something crucial is about to happen. I can smell it in the night, I see it hovering in the light of the flame.

I feel suddenly exhausted. I have worked too hard lately. I shall snuff out the flame and lie down on my couch.

7 *February*

Captain Parry has started to prepare the artillery corps. I have come to realize that I am expected to supply, for the siege of Lepanto, not only the money and the men but also the intelligence, the energy and the discipline.

The corridors of my house have grown noisy with polyglot tongues. I am pestered by obstreperous visitors, each one ready with his own advice—Swedish officers, German barons, Suliote chieftains, Baltic mercenaries, even an Austrian silversmith and a Hydriote philosopher. None of these creatures is of the slightest use to me. Each has his theory about the war; and each has his sly little eye on my purse.

I find myself surrounded by men whom I scorn and distrust. Aside from Fletcher and Tita, and my Newfoundland dog, I feel utterly isolated. I even quarrelled (quite pointlessly) with Pietro today. As for Alex, he is on the brink of total deliquescence. I detest the intriguing Moriotes, the farting Corinthians and the strutting Prussians. I am beginning to feel a nagging sense of self-pity.

But self-pity is certainly the most squalid of all emotions.

Whatever happens, I shall shrug my shoulders. I shall lift up my wine-glass. I shall laugh and keep listening to Mavrocordato's lecherous anecdotes.

*

We anchored off Preveza and hired a young dragoman. Then we started on our journey into the hills of the Epirus. We sailed to Salona in the dark Ambracian Gulf and headed for the mountains with ten horses and two guards. As we crossed the cool summits the hills suddenly opened. We saw a crystal lake reflecting the snow-white minarets which were shining through a grove of cypresses and orange-trees. This was Jannina. In Jannina I bought some magnifique Albanian costumes which were dappled with green and violet and gold.

I looked at the mirror and said to Cam, "I feel like a peacock."

"You look like a partridge," said Cam snappishly.

Two weeks later we rode into the mountains of Albania and finally caught sight of the towers of Tepelenë. It was late in the afternoon, the sun was ready to set, and the soldiers were strutting in front of the palace. Bull-faced Tartars in towering caps, Turks in turbans and pelisses, African slaves with snow-white horses, and grandest of all, the Albanians themselves in their gold-embroidered cloaks and waistcoats of red velvet, with silver-mounted pistols and daggers in their belts. I was reminded of my old *Arabian Nights,* and as I rode through Tepelenë I wanted to whisper, "Open, Sesame!"

And open it did, beyond a doubt. We were invited to the palace and I visited the Pasha in his cool marble chambers. Big red ottomans lined the walls and a fountain was playing in the middle. He rose from his couch and looked at me thoughtfully.

"You are young," he said gently. "Tell me, why have you left your country?"

"I like travelling," I said.

"Travelling!" he purred. "Travelling is dangerous! You are exposing yourself to unmentionable perils, my boy."

I sat down and he ordered some sherbets and a bowl of sweetmeats. This bloody tyrant, Ali Pasha, who had murdered thousands of men, was a person of exquisite manners and great mental subtlety. His face was dented and angular, his eyes were sharp yet gentle, his beard was soft and snowy, his lips were as small as a woman's. He wore a fez embroidered with gold and a black fur-collar, and his slippers were made of blue morocco tooled with gold.

He looked at me appraisingly. "I am told that you are a lord," he murmured. "I am not surprised. Only a lord could have such delicate hands and tiny ears. I much admire your magnificent sabre and your golden epaulettes. I am also charmed by your eyes and your sly, naughty smile. Please consider me your father while you are in Tepelenë. I shall expect you in my rooms at midnight. We will talk about poetry . . ."

We were accompanied to our quarters, which were in the western wing of the palace, and I said to Cam, "I can't help speculating about the Pasha's views on poetry."

Cam cocked his head and grinned. "He is an imaginative person, obviously."

"Doubtless," I said. "He has a wicked reputation, it seems."

"My good Byron," said Cam placidly, "you are quite capable of handling the matter. The Pasha's intentions are as clear as a crystal. You must prepare yourself for some Oriental blandishments."

"Should I go?" I said wistfully.

"You must go," said Cam coaxingly. "When in Cambridge you behaved like a Cambridge-man. When in Turkey you must act like a Turk."

I saw that Hobhouse, in his search for "marginalia" for his travel articles, was trying to goad me into my rendez-vous with the Pasha. I myself (aside from a certain sense of *noblesse oblige*) embarked on the tryst as a strictly scientific experiment, in order to learn what certain cronies of mine (Lord Ingoldsby, for instance) found so gratifying in what we called "the Ottoman posture".

I arrived in the Pasha's chambers precisely at midnight. An oil-lamp was burning, a smell of jasmine filled the room, and a pot of coffee and a bowl of almonds stood on the table. The Pasha was wearing a robe of scalloped satin, and he asked me to sit on the cushion beside him. A parrot sat in a copper cage which hung from the ceiling, and in the corner stood a Negro, tending the coals in a brazier.

We spoke of poetry for a while. The Pasha read me some verses which he had turned into Turkish from the French of Boileau. Not knowing Turkish, I was unable to judge their excellence. But I listened politely and nodded my head. Finally, the Pasha leaned over and said, "Enough of this poetry. Here, have some coffee and let me give you a kiss, my boy."

Now in retrospect, the occasion seems more ludicrous than sinister, but at the time I remember feeling distinctly uneasy. Only my wish to collect some data for Cam's "marginalia" persuaded me to submit to the Pasha's overtures. The lamp was snuffed out and we lay on a rug beside the brazier. Ali Pasha was clearly an expert and his manoeuvres were full of suavity, but when Hobhouse asked me later, "Well, Byron, did it hurt?" I was forced to reply, "Hurt? Of course it did. Damnably!"

I never was tempted to repeat my Albanian experiment. It was not, as they say, "my style". There is a streak of passivity in me, but it chooses a gentler and more hygienic outlet. And yet, as I think of the matter, and reflect on its subtleties, I realize that the occurrence was not without significance. All men are strange beasts. Their impulses are impenetrable. Later in London and Geneva, not to mention Venice and

Ravenna, I remembered my night with the Pasha with a mingling of merriment and revulsion. I told Caroline about this little episode one day, and her face grew quite solemn and she looked at me thoughtfully.

"Not your style?" she said softly. "Possibly not, my funny darling, but that night in Albania has certainly left its mark on you."

Has it indeed? Maybe it has. "Sex is a sphinx" (as Caroline put it) and there are moments when my mind roves back to that little "experiment" in Tepelenë. I still remember the young Somali peering out of his corner and the Pasha oiling his flesh with a pea-green ointment; I still remember the parrot chattering away in Turkish—not very flatteringly, I'm afraid, for the Pasha burst into a fury and threw a big black shawl over his cage.

8 February

I have had a meeting with the Suliote chieftains. I am sick of their chicanery. All the same, Suliotes or no, I am determined to march on Lepanto as soon as Parry can equip our artillery corps.

On my way back from the Seraglio I stepped for a moment into the church. I smelled the dusk of the smoking incense and listened to the slow liturgical cadences. I saw the silently burning wicks shining on the coal-black pulpit, the silver vessels and silver icons, the silver wings of the seraphim.

And it dawned on me that this place is no longer Hellas. It is and has been for centuries merely an outpost of Byzantium. The real Byzantium is no longer glorious or powerful or even Byzantine, and modern Greece is merely a sad shabby echo of a dead Byzantium.

Is this true? Or is there a deeper Greece still lurking, as

62

Alex insisted? With all of my boredom and disillusionment, the Grecian vision still has a grip on me—but a darker and more insidious grip than before. The old names, Agamemnon and Alcibiades, mean almost nothing now. Names like Petros, Jannaios and Aristoboulos are beginning to haunt me. I feel myself being sucked into a deeper and unknown Greece and being metamorphosed into a Greek, sad and sensual, tinged with the barbaric. A dreadful Greek duplicity is beginning to seep through me. The Greece of Pericles is dead but the Greece of Odysseus is still alive, with its smell of salted fish, resinous wine and dyed leather. I catch a whiff of a still older and pre-Athenian Greece in the smell of burning oil and freshly slaughtered goats, of the ships fresh from Ithaca and the sweating sailors as they drag their ships up the long red beach.

*

One day I shot an eagle on the slopes near Vostitza. I did not kill it, I only wounded it, and I took it back to my room and nursed it. But it slowly pined away and three days later it was dead. I shall never forget those fierce heart-broken eyes and the thick black tongue in the open beak; I shall never forget those bloody feathers and enormous, helpless wings. It crouched on my table and stared at me with a passionate intimacy, as though to say, "Yes, you love me, you are begging for my forgiveness, but there are things in this world that are unforgivable, Byron . . ."

I still remember riding through the rocky abysses with Hobhouse. The heat was intense and poor Cam was sensitive to the sun, and at times he was forced to open his little parasol. Poor Cam. Dowdy, scholarly, suspicious Cam. He was my faithful guardian-critic, more vulture-like than angelic, however, and always on the *qui vive* to detect my heel of

Achilles. He saw what was slack in my verses and slap-dash in my mind, and he never failed to inform me crisply about it. I felt grateful but resentful, cosy but touchy, superior yet humble. I sensed his admiration of me purely as an animal but sprinkled over it, like pepper, his dry appraisal of my moral failings. Poor Cam. Envious and dowdy in his thread-bare coat and mustard trousers, carrying a dusty blue parasol as he peered at the glories of Hellas! He climbed Parnassus with his map and compass, looking vainly for some ruined temple, and he chatted with the goat-herds of Epirus, trying to scrape up some legends of the region. But nothing came of it all. The temples turned out to be chicken-coops, and the legends were nothing but illiterate local gossip.

We rode quietly on our mules through the stone-littered valleys. I smelled the pines, I saw the falcons, I felt the breath of the mountain torrents. One day we rode out to the edge of Attica and climbed a mountain. On top of the mountain, so they said, was the secret grotto of one of the sibyls. We left the mules tethered to the fir-trees and entered with our guide, whose name was Vassily. We crept from tunnel to tunnel and deep inside the cave we came to a fountain which shone like mercury by the light of the torch. Vassily stripped and dived into the pool; I too stripped and dived in. But the water was like ice and I scrambled out as quickly as I could. The torch was growing faint and we started back through the grotto. We lost our way in the winding tunnels, the torch flickered and died; and we crawled after Vassily through the dripping darkness. Poor Fletcher grew terrified as we groped along the walls. "What," he said, plucking at my sleeve, "if we *never* get out again, sir?"

I too felt a little panic-stricken. (I have always suffered from a fear of enclosures.) I heard echoes all around us, delicate whisperings and titterings, and I knew we were being punished by the wicked old sibyl. "Absolutely shock-ing," said Cam. "Gross imcompetence on the part of the guide." But at last a flicker of light materialised in the distance and finally we came to the mouth of the cave. Hobhouse climbed on his mule with a splutter of indignation while I pondered on the words of Socrates: "All that we know is that nothing can be known."

We rode on through the dusty olive-groves and one evening we crossed the Cephisus and came to the low, grey walls of Athens. We entered the gateway just as the lamps were being lit. I still remember the hideous pang of disappointment as we rode through the city, which was nothing but a squalid and disorderly town like any other. A smell of burning oil leaked from the dirty little kitchens and the smell of stale fish infected the air. The place was alive with Turkish guards and Albanian soldiers, and we were bluntly informed that there were no inns or hotels in the city, or none which were even remotely inhabitable. So at last we were taken to the house of a Mrs Macri, who occasionally accepted "gentleman travellers from England."

The next morning I climbed the Acropolis with Hobhouse. The air was dusty, the sun was hot, and I was still suffering from diarrhoea. But I remember one moment, as I sat in the shade of the Erechtheum, when I was suddenly gripped by something that was like a trance. A feeling of supernatural envelopment came over me. The very air, the very light were invested with a sense of exactitude. And in that moment, sneezing and sweating, quivering with cramps in my bowels, my eyes were blinded with tears: I felt the miracle of Greece. It was an "accident", perhaps. I was struck by a headlong light. The squalor vanished away and I heard a voice like the sound of an organ, as though the rocks themselves were trying to say something to me. It lasted only a moment. Then the same old boredom swept over me again. I got up, feeling dizzy and captious and miserable. I said to Hobhouse: "This heat is disgusting. Let's go back to the villa and drink some wine."

65

Hobhouse cast a reproachful look at me. But then he understood. We got back on our *burros* and rode through the dust to Mrs Macri's.

No news. Mavrocordato is negotiating with the Suliotes, who want more money.

He came for a visit and we chatted over our *ouzo*.

"I have been reading some of your verses," said the Prince, with an ambiguous air.

"Indeed?" said I.

"There is much that is witty," he said, "and much that is musical. But only once, my good Byron, have you struck the chord of true grandeur."

"Ah," said I, rather testily. "And where might that be?"

"In your little song about going a-roving, I don't believe it has a title. I assure you it moved me to tears, which left a stain on the edge of the page. What struck you to write it? It is most un-Byronic, if I may coin the epithet."

I looked at the Prince with a jaded expression.

"Yes," he said, "it is exactly like a Mozart sonata. And an exceptionally beautiful one, I may add. It opens with an *allegro* in the first stanza, which sinks into a brief but majestic *adagio,* and in the third stanza you repeat the theme of the first, but with a magically tremorous deceleration. And the final line—oh, Byron, what a thumb-worn little phrase! *By the light of the moon!* Anywhere else it would seem outrageous. But here it is a miracle. You have transformed it into a sob. The effect, I must say, is utterly heart-rending."

I felt mildly disconcerted, but the Prince lifted his glass and embarked on one of his risqué anecdotes: how long ago, at the age of twelve, disguised as a goose-girl, he seduced a

66

young sailor on the isle of Corfu: an episode which left him bleeding but contented, and with a heightened insight into the nature of man.

*

Mrs Macri had three daughters whose names were Mariana, Katinka and Theresa. The loveliest was Theresa, who was barely twelve years old but already gifted with an instinct for coquetry. She had very long lashes and a nose that was slightly hooked, and her skin was the colour of the honey from Hymettus. I would sit in the garden scribbling away at *Childe Harold* while Theresa sat in the grass and played with the cat. She got up, peered over my shoulder and whispered, "What are you writing, sir?"

"A poem," I said, "Theresa."

"A poem! What about?"

"About a wicked poet who is in love with a little girl."

"Is it wicked for a poet to fall in love with a little girl?"

"It is," I said firmly. "Only the young should love the young. The old should love the old. And the Greeks should love the Greeks."

Theresa nodded sagaciously. But then she asked cunningly: "Then why do people fall in love with someone whom it is wicked to love?"

I glanced at her Syrian features and wondered vaguely about Mrs Macri. I caught the clovery fragrance of Theresa's young body, and I said, "My dear child, it is better never to fall in love. There is no point in falling in love. One should try to be happy, not to be sad."

I went bathing at Piraeus with my young friend Nicolò. Nicolò resembled Theresa: golden skin, long black lashes, and a nose that was oddly but amiably aquiline.

I remember sitting on a dock over the beach and saying to

Nicolò, as we watched the bathers gambolling in the water: "Why are some of them naked, and others not?"

"The Turks wear loin-cloths and the Greeks wear nothing at all."

I asked him why this was. "It is quite natural," answered Nicolò. "The Turkish men are circumcised and the Greek men are not. The Greeks with their foreskins never feel completely naked. The circumcised Turks feel very naked and a bit ashamed . . ."

One day, riding back from Piraeus with Nicolò, we saw a procession in the dusty distance. Some soldiers were carrying a burlap sack between two sticks and the sack kept wriggling about, as though it were filled with live chickens. I asked a shepherd about it, and he explained that the Vaivode of Athens had sentenced a Turkish girl, who was caught in an act of fornication, to be sewn into a sack and hurled into the sea. I rushed down the road and drew out my pistol and I ordered the startled soldiers to accompany me to the Vaivode. The Vaivode was a fat little man with twinkling eyes. I placed some coins on his table (artfully concealed under a handkerchief) and the Vaivode finally consented to free the poor hussy, provided she leave Athens before dawn on the following morning.

When the girl emerged from the sack I felt slightly disillusioned: instead of a sad-eyed little nymph, still dewy with offended innocence, I saw a fat young harlot with powerful calves and the voice of a baritone.

I said virtuously to Nicolò, "After all, love isn't a crime, is it?"

And Nicolò answered, "Not a crime, perhaps, your Lordship, but risky."

It was in February, in the shade of the Acropolis, that I explored my "Athenian profligacy". Not deterred by Theresa's virginity, which smelt like new-mown grass, or Nicolò's freshness, which smelt like the juice of an orange, I

68

embarked on a series of one-night liaisons which left my poor membrum seething with gonococci.

There was a brothel where the girls reclined in curtained alcoves, which were placed in a circle round a large pool, and I was escorted by a hunchback and allowed to take my choice. But I grew bored by the ease and blatancy of such a choice; I preferred another "brothel", a deserted stable at the edge of a park, where the whores lolled invisibly in the cattle-smelling corners and the lechery was spiced with all the abandon of anonymity. Even Fletcher was infected by this lewd Athenian atmosphere. He used to hide in the gardener's shed and coax the tittering Albanian washerwomen to stick little pins in his naked buttocks. Ah, England! Mysterious Albion! My hostess complained about this "chinoiserie" of Fletcher's, but I re-assured her and said it was merely an old Cornish custom.

I slept in Athens (I marked them in my ledger) with ninety-three women: some slender, some stout, some of them Greek and some Turkish, but the strange thing is that I cannot remember a single face, while I still remember the golden cheeks of both Theresa and Nicolò, sometimes the one and sometimes the other, and sometimes the two blended together.

O glorious Hellas, O verminous Athens! Yes, the two were blended together, and even now I can hardly distinguish them, they seem so interfused. I sat scribbling at noon in Mrs Macri's *giardinetto* and the lines of *Childe Harold* flowed from my pen with a giddy fluency, but all the while a strange ennui was gnawing away at my soul. My life seemed chaotic and rudderless and purposeless, and I was sustained only by a sense of my "inner" uniqueness: but what this uniqueness (if it was that) would eventually lead to, I had no idea, I could only dimly speculate. I kept hovering between fits of black melancholia and fits of equally causeless exultation and gusto.

I decided to leave the friendly little villa of Mrs Macri and moved to a Capuchin monastery which had a view of Mount Hymettus. It was a rambling and restless edifice, with chickens squawking in the court-yard, doves cooing on the roof-tiles, pigs guzzling in the outhouses and goats nibbling at the pergola. My life grew transformed from an Attic hedonism to a Spartan discipline. I was disgusted with my fat (Mrs Macri's dishes were soaked in olive-oil) and I forced myself into a diet of tea, toast and carrots. In the restaurants of Athens I rejected the woodcocks and mullet, not to mention the almond-puddings and the rich, dripping honey-tarts. Thrice a week I rode down to the *bains vapeurs* in the Turkish quarters, and at last I could look at my body in the mirror without nausea. In my lust for bodily slenderness I purchased a greyhound, as well as some skulls which had been dug from ancient sarcophagi. And when I sat in my room with Orestes curled at my feet and the four grinning skulls in a row on my desk, I felt that I had triumphed over the vices of superfluity, and my verses took on a cool, crisp "severity".

But this "discipline" and "severity" did not last very long. March came, the air grew mild and I longed once more to sail the seas. One breezy morning the *Pylades,* an English sloop-of-war, arrived at Piraeus and I booked a passage to Smyrna.

10 February

Favourable news from Lepanto. A Greek spy has just arrived. He tells me that the soldiers are so demoralised that the fortress will fall at the opening shot—"like a plum from a bough", as he put it.

I wonder: can one trust these people? It remains to be seen. The spy was a perfumed fellow with thick auburn curls. He wore a silver bracelet and a pair of coral ear-rings.

*

We sailed to Smyrna and saw the almond-trees blossoming by the harbour, and from Smyrna we sailed past Mytilene and the Troad. Of Troy, alas, I saw nothing at all: merely a mound-dotted plain, traversed by crevices and burrows. I crossed the Scamander and saw Mount Ida in the distance. I tried dutifully to think of Homer but the image of Homer remained nebulous. I saw some shepherds, but these filthy shepherds bore no resemblance to Ganymede. I tried to think of Achilles and Sarpedon. But their faces were as blank as the mounds on the plain.

So we came to the Dardanelles and I went bathing below the fortress, which juts into the sea below the inlet of Abydos. My valet Fletcher stood on a rock and tossed tortoises into the sea; and I dived and brought them up again and laid them on the sand.

Now it was May, the sun grew warmer, and my mind turned to Ovid. The vision of Leander grew more vivid than that of Achilles, and one day I said to Hobhouse: "To-morrow I'll swim across the Hellespont."

And so I did. The current was powerful and the sea was still cold, and once a large fish started to snap at my toes, but along with young Ekenhead (a lieutenant on board our ship) I swam for seventy minutes from Sestos to Abydos. When I crawled out of the sea and stood shivering on the gravel I felt that I had cleansed the Athenian lecheries out of my system.

What, I wonder, is the spell of the sea? The androgynous, snarling sea! The pre-historical, pre-rhetorical, all-forgiving sea! Why did I dive into the sea each day and glide through that coiling transparency? Was it my longing for adventure? Was it my lust for liberation? Was it my need for ablution? Was it animal delight? All of these, but more than anything it was my longing for oblivion, my longing to glide back into a cool and kindred element, those ever-eluding, ever-altering arms of the sea. There is something which the French call *"fornication avec l'onde"*. No doubt. But even the French cannot defile or degrade the sea. The sea is Love. It is also Timelessness. It is Unearthliness. It is Death. The filth and ruin of man are all about us on the land, but the sea is clean and empty, no trace of humanity is left on it, no trace of the blood and howling idiocy of human existence. My feeling for the sea lies deeper than fear or delight. And even now, as I look at the lagoon in the distance, the calm of self-forgetfulness steals through my spirit.

11 February

I have finally (after the usual bribes) obtained the use of the Seraglio, which is the biggest house in town, as a military laboratory and arsenal. The bull-buttocked Suliotes, who have used it as their barracks, and impregnated it with their vermin, finally agreed to get out. And my indefatigable Parry has already started to pave the court-yard and to train the soldiers in musket-exercise. He has ordered them to clean their uniforms, polish their boots, and repair their guns.

*

So we came to Byzantium. We sailed on the Sea of Marmora and caught sight of the domes and minarets shining through the mist, and at dusk we dropped our anchor near the cape of the Seraglio. We disembarked and threaded our way along the quay, and the first of several dark Byzantine visions met our eyes: two mangy dogs, as thin as skeletons, were gnawing savagely at a dead man's body.

We hurried on to a little wine-house where we drank some wine from Trebizond, and we strolled in the dusk into the court of a ruined mosque, where three dervishes were working themselves into a frenzy, screaming and jumping, spitting and bleeding and vomiting and ejaculating, and then falling

72

in a heap on the garbage-littered stones. And that night after dinner we strolled to the arsenal by moonlight, and witnessed the third of our sinister visions. In the shade of the arsenal, in a pit which was seething with rats, lay the body of a man who had just been decapitated.

The fourth of my visions was the following. One balmy afternoon, after lunching in Galata on a lobster in aspic, I decided to lose some weight in one of the local steam baths. I was led into a vaulted "aquarium" where some boys lolled by a pool, and thence into a "tepidarium", where some elderly gentlemen were reading their papers. From here I stepped into the steam-room, which was dimly lit by an oil-lamp. Naked figures moved slowly (as in one of Dante's circles) through the hypnotised stillness of the suffocating steam. There was a smell of cheap soap, human sweat, rotting masonry. I lay down on a marble slab and suddenly beheld, looming in the vapour, a decrepit old man gripping the edge of the slab. Behind him stood a barbarian, who looked like a gorilla, and he thrust his great obelisk into the buttocks of the moaning patriarch. I was about to jump up to rescue this maltreated person when I saw his grinning face: he was winking a wicked eye at me.

I fled back to the "aquarium" and reclined on the edge of the pool. Soon after, the white-haired patriarch emerged from the steam-room and sat down beside me on a leather cushion. *"Vous permettez?"* he said, and I nodded politely. We sipped some Turkish coffee, thick as syrup and black as pitch, and he explained in flawless English that he was a Marquis who lived in Gascony, but to escape from the rural monotony he sought diversion in foreign travel.

"You like Turkey?" I said.

"It has its own 'bouquet,' no doubt. I prefer it to Bulgaria, which is devoid of a cultural heritage, but I like it less than Egypt, which is filled with magnificent statuary."

"Did you like the pyramids?"

"I *adored* the pyramids but found them inhuman. To be quite frank with you, I find everything outside France a bit inhuman. The Egyptians have their Sphinx, the Greeks their Acropolis, the Germans their philosophers, and the Swiss their clocks. And the English of course have their clubs and cold mutton. I have travelled all my life and I still have a taste for *tourisme,* but the earlier *frisson* has begun to diminish. I shall go back to my château and spend the rest of my lonely days reading the plays of Racine and the sonnets of Ronsard."

"I admire Ronsard," I said, dipping my toe in the pool, "but I definitely prefer the poems of Villon. And as for *Phèdre,* I am struck by its icy perfection, but since you speak of humanity, I find much more of it in Molière's comedies."

The Marquis smiled. There was a hawk-like distinction about his face, which was wrinkled but finely-boned, with eyes as sharp as a falcon's. "It is all a question of what you mean by humanity. If you mean the clownish bustle and robustious gaiety of *Sganarelle,* very well, I agree that you'll find it in Molière. But if you mean the piercing gaze that goes to the core of human passion, then give me *Andromaque,* or *Athalie,* or *Esther.* And incidentally, in spite of my proclivities, I prefer heroines to heroes. A woman's grief is more dramatic than a man's. A woman's tears are more spontaneous than a man's, and the thought of a woman's death seems more poignant than a man's."

Two swarthy masseurs strutted past on their way to the steam-room and I said to the Marquis, "Tell me, do you find these proclivities satisfying?"

The Marquis regarded me wistfully. "Life is short, alas," he said, "and I try to make the best of my span in this vale of sorrows. I am no longer capable of an erection. Anal intercourse is all I am fit for."

"And do you really," I insisted, "find it all that amusing?"

"Well, I tell you," said the Marquis, folding his arms

philosophically, "the posture is gauche, the pleasure is debatable, and the after-effects are distinctly humiliating, but it leaves one with a feeling of inner serenity, and even a kind of secret emolument. It is certainly far from dignified but it has its little virtues. Back in my château in Gascony, while I am planting my tulips, I shall think of Byzantium with a misty nostalgia."

I too think of Byzantium with a misty nostalgia. Not in the way that the Marquis does (I can see him crouching in his flower-beds, muttering with Phèdre, *"Implacable Vénus, suis-je assez confondue!"*) but in the sense that here indeed was the city of exile, the city that was trapped between two blood-thirsty continents, whose grandeur was a mournful mismarriage between two cultures, and whose defeat left nobody weeping, since it was the defeat of an illusion.

12 February

The sunlight to-day looks grotesquely brilliant, like a flood of diamonds.

Sophocles said that his release from sexual desire in old age was like escaping from a mad, tyrannical master. My own release is like climbing from a leech-infested jungle into the dry, disconsolate desert-air.

All is parched and monotonous, and suddenly very lonely.

*

Back to England. Back to the fog, the leathery clubs, the cold mutton. I have half-forgotten my political ambitions (I took my seat in the House of Lords) ; the long ennuis of my financial entanglements (I was persistently in debt) ; and

75

even the anfractuosities of my literary career (my publishers were shocked by my "political iconoclasm"). I met the illustrious ladies—Lady Oxford and Lady Holland, Lady Mildmay and Lady Harley, not to mention Lady Melbourne and the Duchess of Devonshire. I met the famous poets—Sam Rogers and Tom Campbell, not to mention the "toast of the drawing-rooms", the snobbish Tom Moore (whose father it seems was a Dublin grocer).

All this I recall with a kind of vacant aimlessness. I remember the crystal candlesticks, the caviar and champagne, but the painted cheeks and the powdered faces I have all but forgotten. I remember the light of dawn creeping through the long French curtains, I remember the empty bottles, the dirty plates and the stink of tobacco. But the whispered flirtations, the "shafts of wit", the "stilettos of malice", all these are utterly gone and forgotten. The dancers in Devonshire House rattle in my mind like an army of skeletons, and when I think of their faces all I see is a row of skulls.

One day in late July I was packing my bag for a visit to Newstead when a servant arrived and told me that my mother had died. I drove immediately to Newstead and raced up the stairs. The curtains were drawn and a candle was burning, and I knelt in silence beside the bed. But why, oh why, was the grief so terribly slow in coming? My dreadful and devouring, my elephantine mother, whose very proximity I loathed but whom I needed so darkly and desperately! I sat by her bed all night and only when dawn stole through the curtains and dropped a greyish light on the bulging coverlet, only then did I finally confront the real loss, and the grief which had lurked in me burst suddenly into the open and I crouched on the carpet and shed bitter tears.

But even at this moment, hideous to relate, I looked at my prostrate body and I thought, "Yes, yes, he is capable of grief after all. There, behold, the brilliant poet, in all of his elegance and beauty, who lies distorted by an inarticulate sorrow!"

She was buried three days later in the family vault at Hucknall Torkard. But I refused to follow the funeral. I stood on the steps of Newstead Abbey and watched the *cortège* until it vanished behind the trees. Then I called to Bob Rushton. We walked into the refectory. I put on my boxing-gloves and started to spar with him. Suddenly he gave a small cry. One of my blows, unusually violent, had struck him in the eye and he started to bleed. I threw down my gloves and walked back to my room. I drew the curtains and lay on my bed and at last I fell asleep.

13 February

More chicanery amongst these infernal Suliotes. Pietro has discovered that their pay-lists were swollen with non-existent soldiers.

I keep wondering: is there anyone in this world that I can trust?

*

And now back to my memories. What a cool, ironical calm falls over me suddenly when I turn to my memories!

I lived for a while in Bennet Street. I hired a Mrs Mule, who was a hag as bald as a parson, with lips that resembled an anus, to come and be my fire-lighter and laundress. She would loom in my corridors at night like a ghost, muttering darkly to herself and frightening my late-departing "guests".

I asked Phillips, a fashionable painter, to let me sit for three portraits—in one of them, the most resplendent, I wore my red Albanian robe, with a striped satin turban coiled gracefully around my head. When they were finished, Hob-

77

house insisted that he saw no resemblance in any of them: the chin, the nose, the eyes were indefinably not my own.

"Your face," he said, "is uncapturable. Oh, yes, you have a face, no doubt, but it keeps continually changing and no painter will ever capture it."

And oddly enough, even the portraits themselves seemed to change. I placed one of them, the smallest, in a frame of red velvet and left it on the writing-table, planning to show it to Lady Holland. I noticed that the eyes, too vividly blue to be my own, were looking into space with an ironical expression.

On the following day, when I picked the portrait from the table on my way to dinner, I noticed that the eyes, now pearly grey, were gazing at my own and the smile on the lips seemed to have turned into a sneer. I took the picture and tucked it into the bookcase between *Don Quixote* and the *Decameron*.

After this I grew obsessed with the thought of another Byron—a deeper and purer Byron, a frailer yet stronger Byron, more intricate but more harmonious, less voluble but more discerning, and in November in the streets, when I saw a face loom through the fog, I was gripped by the appalling notion that the *real* Lord Byron was approaching me.

The leaves fell from the trees, the streets were coated with mud, and the chill of approaching winter crawled through the parks. Sometimes at night I watched the harlots wandering aimlessly in Piccadilly. Now and again one of them squatted behind a carriage to piss, and a friend would cry out to her "Yer petticoat's showin', Dolly!" or "Watch Out! Keep hold of yer purse, Babette!" Once I came upon one of these "sisters of the abyss" in a dark arcade, kneeling in front of a drunken sailor in the act of *fellatio,* and as I passed she glanced at me sidelong, her feathered hat still bobbing rhythmically, and she gurgled from the side of her mouth: "Wot's yer 'urry, duckie? Jus' wait, I'll take care of ye in a minnit, me lamb!"

One night in December I was sauntering through Hyde Park. The windows shone dimly through the mist in Park Lane and the boughs looked like snakes, black and shiny, shedding their drops. I was turning towards the Serpentine when a woman stepped out of the fog. She stood in the path in front of me with her eyes fixed on my face.

I halted and said politely, "I beg your pardon, madame . . ."

"Yes, yes!" cried the woman softly. "I have seen you before!"

"I rather doubt . . ." I began.

"No doubt at all," she said rapidly. "The same eyes, the same voice. I met you in Malta. You don't remember me?"

"I'm afraid I do not."

"Well, no matter," she said gently, more in sorrow than reproach. "On the quay at Valetta. You've forgotten, as is perfectly natural."

"Ah, indeed," I said thoughtfully. "It's quite conceivable . . . Yes, to be sure . . ."

"Come, sit down," she said quietly, and we sat on a bench. For several minutes we sat in silence, neither of us looking at the other. A carriage passed in the distance, the coach-lamps danced in the fog and the tapping of hooves died away in the wintry gloom.

I turned and looked at the woman. She was wearing a cap of fox-fur. Drops of mist clung to the fur and to her long black eye-lashes. She looked like a frightened animal that was trapped in the park.

"Tell me," I said, staring compassionately at her sickly face, "do you never . . ."

"Yes!" she cried, gripping my hand and holding it tightly. "The same reproaches! The same hypocrisy! The same meaningless philanthropy! I don't even know your name but I can read you like a book. I still remember your very words. 'Don't you ever,' you said kindly—oh, so kindly, I still remember! 'don't you ever grow weary of it all, my child?'

79

Well, I'll tell you the answer! Yes, I'm weary, heart-breakingly weary, but I keep right on with it and I'll never give it up! And why? Because I'm driven to it. It's my fate. It's my destiny. Oh my darling, if it were only a matter of lying on a bed and being mounted by a wearisome succession of strangers—if it were that and nothing more I'd have entered a nunnery long ago. But it is more than that, much more than that! I keep waiting for something to happen. All my long, lonely life I've been waiting for a miracle to happen."

"A miracle?"

"It would be a miracle, wouldn't it?" She stared at me feverishly. "To fall in love—yes, it's a miracle. It's as rare as the snow in August. Once it happened to me in Antwerp, in a little café near the port. My heart was broken in two. I was only twelve years old. And then it happened a second time—life is lunatic, isn't it? On the quay in Valetta. Just as simple as that, and just as terrible. But *you,* with your marvellous philanthropy, your hollow tolerance, your empty kindness (yes, I remember you gave me a gold-piece wrapped in a white satin handkerchief) —you'd rather not believe me! Just a sentimental lie! Just a prostitute's manoeuvre to get the best of a gullible customer! Yes, it's God's bitter truth and I'll spend the rest of my life waiting for it! Waiting for that simple and terrible miracle to happen a third time!" She turned and pressed her cold clammy lips to my cheek. Then she rose without a word and drifted into the night.

It was long after midnight when I came back to Bennet Street. Mrs Mule poked her head through the door in the hall. She raised her candle and grunted ominously, and then quietly shut the door again. I entered my chamber, lit the lamp, and stood silently by the window. I could see my face reflected in the fog-misted pane—lean and white and intense, not my own face at all: pale and bony and *souffrant,* and as chaste as a nun's.

Rain, rain, and still more rain. The lagoon has risen and is lapping at my door-step.

*

From Bennet Street I moved to fashionable rooms in Piccadilly. Mrs Mule insisted on accompanying me, but in deference to the elegant surroundings she bought a lace-edged bonnet and a poppy-coloured wig, and her mouth, when she spoke, took on a haemorrhoidal fastidiousness. Sometimes at night, after the departure of one of my female "guests", I would see Mrs Mule fluttering ghost-like down the corridor, wearing a long white night-robe and carrying a stubby little candle.

"Anything wrong, Mrs Mule?"

"*Everything* is wrong!" she growled balefully.

I bought a parrot and a macaw. I boxed and fenced daily. I was brilliant and celebrated, and I turned into a dandy. My two models at this point were my pugilist crony, Gentleman Jackson, and the suave and emaciated shape of Beau Brummell. I saw Kemble in *Coriolanus* and Kean as Iago. I went to fashionable teas in Mayfair and balls in Belgravia. I had turned into a lion; but a limping and rebellious lion, a surly and disreputable and fornicating lion.

I wrote *The Corsair* in ten days and *The Bride of Abydos* in four, but their easy success left me strangely disheartened. There were moments when I sensed that my verses were over-praised, and that I was squandering away my capability for great poetry. And there were other moments when I felt that I was hovering on the threshold and would turn, *dei volentes,* into an Ovid-cum-Catullus.

In my journal I made a "list", a kind of *gradus ad Parnassum.* I did not trouble with the ancients or with the French, or even the Augustans, all of whom I felt to be beyond the scope of personal rivalry. When Scrope Davies came to London I took him to dinner at the Cocoa-Tree, and there (over some cutlets cooked with mushrooms in a wine-sauce) we sat and made our list of poetical contemporaries. I put Scott at the top and Samuel Rogers in the second place. Moore and Campbell were together in the third, and in the fourth (rather indulgently, I thought) I bracketed Wordsworth, Coleridge and Southey. Below these hovered the "hacks", the "miscellaneous" and the "minor".

"I can't help wondering," said Scrope, "if your list is truly impartial. I can think of two young poets (I refrain from mentioning their names) who have more talent than Sam Rogers and Tom Campbell rolled into one. And where, by the by, do you place yourself on this poetical ladder?"

"I refuse to place myself on a poetical ladder", I said touchily, "and I hardly consider your hints in the best of taste, my good Scrope. Granted that Campbell and Rogers have a tinge of the 'academic', still they have earned a respectable place compared to your pair of young whipper-snappers. As for myself, please don't think that the *Bride of Abydos* is a serious effort. I am biding my time. My achievement lies in the future . . ."

Scrope grinned and winked at the waiter. I felt like slapping his pock-marked face. Still, I knew in my heart of hearts that for all his acid Cambridge "purism" he envied me desperately and also adored me, and hoped (even more than I did) that my achievement lay in the future.

What is strange is that I always wrote most easily in a state of confusion. Polishing my iambics every night seemed to soothe some deep malaise. When my liver was rebellious or my bowels refused to function the words came more nimbly than when I felt contentedly bovine. I planned an *"ars poetica"* called *The Knife and the Flower,* in which I compared a poet to a rare Brazilian flower which could only be prodded into bloom by the wound of a knife, *id est,* by the galvanising pain of deformity, which in turn could alone produce the intensity of poetry. But I abandoned this noble project, since the thoughts remained elusive, and *The Knife and the Flower* was doomed to remain unwritten.

15 February

Sunday again. Missolonghi is full of bleak and abysmal Sundays.

Something curious happened this evening.

At eight o'clock I went with Pietro down to the Colonel's rooms on the floor below. Good old Parry was waiting for us. The Colonel was working in the adjoining room. We drank coffee and talked of the rats, the lice, the mosquitoes, and the Suliotes. Pietro joked about the Suliotes, who have a reputation for "Bulgarianism", which in Greece is an euphemism for *coitus in anum,* and I suddenly found myself laughing hysterically. I was sitting on a cane settee. My sight grew blurred and filmy. The room seemed to turn into an enormous spider.

"Anything wrong," said Parry, "Your Lordship?"

"Give me some wine, please," I muttered.

"Would wine be quite the thing for you?"

"Give me some wine, damn it!" I screamed.

I drank a glassful. I remember slowly getting up from the settee, gripping the edge of the table, and then crashing to the floor.

A blackness followed, filled with the ceaseless whining of mosquitoes. Then I woke up again: everything looked strangely immobilised—the faces, the gestures, even the moths that hung in the lamp-light.

I felt obsessed with the terrifying thought that it was a Sunday.

"Is not this Sunday?" I demanded.

"It is Sunday," said Captain Parry.

"I should have thought it monstrous," I cried, "if this were not a Sunday!"

Colonel Stanhope, hearing the noise, emerged solicitously from his bed-chamber. "I shall fetch the doctor," he murmured, and not long after, Dr Millingen arrived with his tall black hat and his little black satchel.

I sniffed at some salts and finally grunted, "It was nothing. A bagatelle."

I felt dreadfully weak; but cool, collected, and totally aloof.

I woke up in the middle of the night. I could scarcely breathe; I felt I was suffocating. My capacity to think and my very identity were lost in a vacuum.

Then I noticed that the lamp was burning. The light was shining on Loukas's face. He lay sleeping half-naked on some cushions in the corner.

I said: "Luke!"

He raised his head and looked at me with a puzzled astonishment.

My jaw started to shake. I tried to speak but I could not speak. I leant back, closed my eyes, and my mind sank into nothingness.

*

One day the doorbell rang and Mrs Mule opened the door. "Miss Doossy Airs", she announced, and a dark young woman walked into my study. She moved in a hunched, crab-wise fashion and her face, slightly freckled, looked pinched and apprehensive and a little oily. She leant her umbrella against a chair and stood by the edge of the bookcase. She was wearing a checkered cloak and a big black hat covered with daffodils.

84

"Do forgive my intrusion, sir. I have come on a mission," she stammered.

"Your name, if I understood it . . ."

"Henrietta d'Ussières, Your Lordship. My mother was Scotch but my father came from Abbéville."

"And your mission . . ."

"I have come," she said, "to speak of your poetry." She crept sideways to my desk and rested her fingers on the ink-pot. "Forgive me, but you are frittering away your talent, Lord Byron. Instead of burning with passion your work is permeated with flippancy. You could be another Virgil, you could even be another Dante, but you are wasting your energies in a lascivious promiscuity."

I regarded her thoughtfully. "What is your profession, Miss d'Ussières?"

She hesitated. Then she murmured, "I am a student of the pianoforte."

I glanced instinctively at her hands and she started to blush. I saw that her hands were chapped and rather swollen, and not, I suspected, the hands of a pianist. She might be a governess, it occurred to me, or a nursemaid in Kensington.

"Dante too, for all we know," I said, "may have been guilty of lasciviousness. That scene with Paolo and Francesca has an autobiographical timbre. One can scarcely write about love, can one, without first having indulged in it?"

"Indulged!" cried Miss d'Ussières, wringing her hands in dismay. "What a false, degrading word! Love is not a luxury that one indulges in. It is a flame that sears, Your Lordship, it is a dagger that lacerates. No, sir, with all your talents, and with all your amorous entanglements, you keep scribbling about passion but you have yet to know the pangs of it."

"And what," I said dryly, "do you propose that I do about it?"

"You must learn," said the lady, lowering her lashes, "to *suffer.*"

As I watched the poor woman twisting her fingers with agitation I felt a demon of mischief rise up through my veins.

"I have no doubt," I said mournfully, "that you are absolutely right. I need instruction. Do you think you could help me in the matter, mademoiselle?"

A bashful smile twisted her lips and a glow of joy shone in her eyes. "In a sense," she began, "that is strictly Platonical . . ."

"But the flesh," I insisted, "is inextricably involved with the spirit. No spiritual vision is possible without a corresponding fleshly vision." I placed a thumb on my cheek and another on the tip of my knee. "Miss d'Ussières," I said gently, "would you be so kind as to move closer, please?"

Her lips started to tremble with glad apprehension. "Yes?" she said, stepping closer. "And what do you wish to confide to me?"

"Would you please, Miss d'Ussières, be so good as to lift up your petticoat? A vision of flesh, as I say, must accompany a vision of the soul." And I briskly grabbed her skirt and lifted it to her waist, revealing a patch of her emaciated thigh.

She recoiled as though struck by an adder. Her face grew terribly pale. She pressed down her skirt and covered her bosom with her arms. "Sir," she cried, "you are nothing but an animal. You are diabolically cruel! I can never forgive you for this wanton act of cruelty, Your Lordship!"

She burst into sobs and covered her face with both hands. Then she picked up her umbrella and with a last anguished look at me she slid through the door and went tripping down the corridor.

Poor Henrietta! Poor little fool! Poor little sly misguided hyprocrite! Yes, I was cruel, I was viciously cruel, but this, alas, did not end the matter. It did not deter Henrietta from subsequent efforts to save my soul. On these occasions, whenever the funereal Mrs Mule knocked on my door and an-

86

nounced that "Miss Doossy Airs" had come on a visit, I told her to explain that I was having a duchess in for tea, or was away on a trip to Brussels, or sick in bed with dysentery. Three long letters arrived by post and reproached me for my "Machiavellian lechery", and begged me to lift our relationship to a "more ethereal level". She spoke of "elective affinities" and of "mystical transcendentalism". She spoke of Leibnitz and Spinoza, and even of Santa Teresa. But in the last of these letters (all unanswered, I am sorry to say) she added in a postscript that she had pondered on my predicament, and that she was willing, if I insisted, to yield to my cruel postulate that "a fleshly vision, in its entirety, might be conducive to a spiritual *entente,* which in turn might lead to a flowering of the full poetic capacities."

16 February

I felt better this morning but strangely disarticulated, as though I were an insect fluttering in mid-air.

Parry called. I said, "Parry, what the devil happened to me yesterday?"

"I believe," said Parry thoughtfully, "that it was an epileptic fit. Your face was quite distorted. I detected no foam on your lips, however. You should eat more food, Your Lordship. And drink more brandy maybe. You are too thin. You are starving yourself in your obsession with bodily slenderness."

Bodily slenderness! I wonder what goes on in the mind of that burly sea-captain. Can it be that good old Parry has his own little suspicions?

Dr Bruno, that blood-thirsty idiot, has insisted on bleeding me. "There is always the danger," he hinted, "of a cerebral injury after such a seizure." He applied some leeches to my temples, and when he finally plucked them off again the blood still kept flowing. I fainted, Parry tells me.

87

When I finally came to, Dr Bruno was applying caustic. I remember crying out: "God help me, in this world there is nothing but pain!"

And pompous old Parry stroked my forehead very gently.

*

One day at Lady Jersey's I was introduced to Madame de Staël. She was being fêted and lionized on her visit to London. A formidable woman, cunning as a fox, hairy as a spider, fearful as a precipice. She looked at me fiercely, and turned away and whispered to my hostess: "*Qu'il est beau, ce jeune poète! Mon Dieu, qu'il est beau!*"

She drew me to a window and looked gloweringly at my face. "Strange man," she said finally. "You have the lips of a Laïs and the eyes of a Phryne, and you are leading the life of Aphrodite herself, so I hear!"

I was searching in my mind for a suitable riposte but she added calmly, "My dear boy, believe me, you will never be a *grand poète*. You are too beautiful. Women will batten and feed on your body. Women, remember, are much like harpies. When they are in love they cannot rest until they have ripped the heart out of their lovers, and sometimes even the testicles!" She glared menacingly at my midriff (I wore tight-fitting breeches) and I quickly crossed the room and started to chat with Lady Oxford.

When I think of Lady Oxford what I see is an autumnal radiance. I see a scene by Claude Lorrain of sloping light and ivied ruins. I catch a whiff of fallen leaves in a damp, shady wood. There were even moments when I felt a smouldering attraction to her elderly body, and for this she felt grateful and in the end she almost loved me. I remember sitting in the twilight under an elm-tree at Eywood, watching the children playing hopscotch beneath the honeysuckle.

"I am old," said Lady Oxford, "and no man wishes to sleep with me. But I am resigned. I should be horrified if a man were to make love to me. My dear Byron, be kind to women. Feel pity for women. Be compassionate. A woman's body begins to grow old at the age of thirty, and when she is forty she bursts into tears when she looks at her bosom."

"But after all," I said consolingly, "aren't there other things than bosoms?"

She smiled and cocked her head. "Be understanding, my dear Byron. A woman spends her life in unremitting anxiety. When she is young she is frightened, when she grows older she is apprehensive, and when she is old she is appalled. Nothing can change it. Wrinkles are wrinkles."

One night at Lady Westmorland's I met Caroline Lamb. I had heard of her often and I knew she was eager to meet me. She was the daughter of the Earl of Bessborough and the sister of the Duchess of Devonshire, and she was known as a "sprite", a "dryad", a "naughty Ariel", a "rebellious tom-boy", and her whims and eccentricities were the gossip of Belgravia. I was disappointed: she was far from beautiful. She was tall, thin and twitching, her face was boyish and her cheeks were flushed, and there was a disconcerting mockery in her hazel eyes. She glanced at me casually and was on the verge of saying something. Then she turned on her heel and walked to the other end of the room.

Some days later in Melbourne House at a *thé littéraire* (Tom Moore and Sam Rogers were invariably present at these teas) I entered the room and saw Caroline Lamb, still moist in her riding-habit, rise from the sofa and rush from the room.

Rogers said to me: "Lord Byron, you are a very lucky man. Lady Caroline, fresh from riding, has been sitting on the sofa in all her dirt. But the moment you were announced she flew from the room to take a bath!"

She returned to the room in a moss-coloured gown and

stood casually by the fire-place, fondling a long braided riding-whip. I walked up to her and said, "I am happy to see you, Lady Caroline. I was hoping for a chat the other day but you vanished into space."

"It is one of my gifts," she answered. "I adore to vanish into space."

"You preferred not to talk to me?"

"Not in a room full of rivals!"

"Very well, let us talk in solitude."

"What shall we talk of? Have you any suggestions?"

"Shall we start, perhaps, with literature?"

"I am not a literary woman. I am not like Madame de Staël, who has a fine red moustache."

"Madame de Staël," I said gently, "has her own special charm."

"You are omnivorous," said Lady Caroline. "You stop at nothing in your greed for flattery!"

Four days later I was invited to a ball at Lady Rancliffe's. It was spring, the lilies were blooming in the octagonal garden and the candles were burning on a table under a beech-tree. I was too shy to waltz with the rest of them because of my lameness, and during the waltzes I stood in the garden, chatting away with Christina Falkland, a young widow who kept gushing about my verses. A bell rang at midnight and the guests strolled into the drawing-room, where a buffet of lobsters and champagne stood on the table. I found myself next to Caroline Lamb, who had picked up a carving-knife and was pointing it at me playfully.

"Do you wish," I said, "to kill me?"

"I was toying with the thought," said Caroline.

"Be a Roman if you wish, Your Ladyship. But strike at your own heart, not at mine!"

"Byron!" she said. "You are a beast!" And suddenly tears welled into her eyes. She clutched the knife in her palm and started to run from the room. There was a scream from Lady

Rancliffe, who cried, "Caroline! What has happened?" Lady Caroline turned in the doorway and stared at me savagely; her left hand was bleeding and her costume was covered with blood. (She was wearing, I recall, the livery of a Neapolitan page, with sepia-brown breeches and a red velours-jacket.)

Out in the garden Lady Melbourne said: "What, my dear, did you do to Caroline?"

"Nothing of consequence," I said.

"She is fearfully sensitive," said Lady Melbourne.

"I called her, I think, a Roman."

"Strange, strange," said Lady Melbourne. "You have such a wicked reputation, but you are really touchingly innocent. My good Byron, it was your indifference which wounded my daughter-in-law. There are times when her fancy runs away with her, poor Caroline . . ."

Some days later at Lady Gosford's, when the last of the guests were leaving, I strolled into the empty ball-room, which was covered with mirrors. One last candle was burning and the floor was littered with petals, and the smell of stale food and rancid wine hung in the air. The dank light of dawn was already seeping through the curtains. I looked into a mirror and started to waltz, rather tipsily. I limped joyfully across the floor in my bright Albanian costume, watching myself reflected endlessly in the mirror-reflecting mirrors. Suddenly a figure stood behind me. I swung round: it was Lady Caroline. She was dressed like a Spanish courtier, in emerald hose and a ruffled collar. A trio of musicians was still playing in the garden, and through their "Good-Night" music I could hear the clatter of departing carriages. Caroline took me by the waist and we started to waltz together—she in brisk boyish movements, I in my clumsy gliding gait.

"You dance beautifully," she said. "But you are shy. You are painfully shy."

"Coming from you, Lady Caroline, that sounds like a compliment!"

91

The candles were dead and we came to a halt by the window. The musicians were packing their fiddles and the garden was suddenly empty. There was a swampy, crepuscular desolation about the place.

I glanced at Caroline. She looked vaporous, remote, like a "dryad".

"May I kiss you?" I whispered.

"Darling," she said, "don't be an idiot, please!"

17 February

I got up from my couch but felt too weak to go out.

A Turkish brig-of-war has gone aground some miles from the city. I can see it from my window, squatting like a sow in the mud-stained water.

The sun is setting. I shall write in my diary and then go to bed.

*

I feel, when I write of Caroline, that I am trespassing on the truth. With Caroline, and in Caroline's presence, there was no such thing as truth. When we sank to the littered floor and made love in the light of dawn, I saw thirty different Byrons embracing thirty different Carolines, whose figures receded, ever-multiplying and ever-diminishing, into the endless colonnades of Lady Gosford's mirrors. But what I saw was not Byron, it was a turbaned young pasha, and what I saw was not Caroline, it was a slim Venetian courtier. But then how, this being so, can I hope for exactitude? How can I hope to find my way through that maze of impersonations?

Was I really in love for a while, or were both of us playing a rôle? If it was love then it was certainly not a love that

92

could last. We were egoists and flirts, both of us. We were wayward and pampered and what we pretended, as like as not, was really the opposite of the truth. Even the act of coition took on a flavour of paradox. Her lust was exotic and exploratory, even transvestite, so that it seemed no longer sexual but almost maniacal. There lay food for uneasiness in the half-mad quixotism of her yearnings. It was as though, being sated with the customary practices, her only pleasure came from an ever-accelerating series of innovations. Some of these postures were humiliating, others eerie, others ridiculous. I remember lying on my bed with the naked Caroline crouching over me, her hair hanging in strands, her brow pearly with sweat, hacking away at my groin with a kind of vulturine fury. And her talent for the scabrous went even further on several occasions, when she embarked on what the Parisians call *"ouvrir la rose"*. (I am consoled, as I write these words, that no-one will read these Grecian memoirs!) Can one call such things "love-making"? No doubt one can and no doubt one must. All self-defilement, even the most ludicrous, can be forgiven in the "heat of passion". But was this passion? It struck me more as a desperate mimicry of passion, and poor Caroline, in her need to discover some new fillip for her jaded appetites, created a rarefied ambience in which love could not survive, any more than a rose can bloom on the slopes of the Matterhorn.

Sometimes her anecdotes could be amusing in a hot-house kind of way. She once told me of her adventures with the "Sapphic sorority" (or, as Lady Oxford called them, "the nymphs of Mytilene"). Having an appetite for the *outré*, she embarked on a Lesbian liaison with a certain Lady Breckenbridge, who raised wolf-hounds in Gloucestershire; and she promptly found herself enmeshed in an orchidaceous coterie (if such a phrase could apply to these strapping, pistol-shooting ladies). But she soon wearied of the scenes of perpetual jealousy and recrimination. Behind the air of bois-

93

terous ribaldry lurked tantrums and threats of suicide. Once she met a young woman in Regent's Park on a summer evening. She was taken to a near-by flat, which was decorated with whips and riding-boots. She sat down on a divan and leafed through an album of engravings until the lady (who had briefly absented herself) returned to the room. She was now dressed, to Caroline's amazement, in a splendid Guardsman's uniform. This in itself was not unpalatable, but then she strolled to the cupboard and took out a dildo (made of the best Algerian buffalo hide), which she strapped to her belt with a kind of butcher-like efficiency. Caroline burst into a fit of uncontrollable laughter, and as a result of this *contretemps* she thought it wiser to abandon the company of tweedy young ladies who lived in far-off country-cottages.

Yes, she could be charming, she could even be adorable with her Devonshire House drawl and the child-like lisp which decorated her witticisms. She could be as playful as a kitten and as gay as a butterfly, as delicate as a humming-bird and as lovable as a bear-cub. But underneath hovered a hint, or more than a hint, of sickness and aridity, and there were times when her face looked yellowish and parched, like an Egyptian mummy's. In the end I grew bored. I felt cloyed, shackled, suffocated. I even implored Mrs Mule, when Lady Caroline was announced, to explain that I had gone to the chiropodist's, or was riding in Hyde Park. There was something self-destructive in her crazy possessiveness. She knew that it could not last, which made her all the more clutching. I ignored the gathering scandal, but I hated the hysteria.

The most glittering ball of the season was held in honour of the Duke of Wellington at Burlington House on the 1st of July. There were 1700 guests (I remember the figure; I was deeply impressed by it) and it was announced as a *bal masqué,* so we all took pains over our costumes. Discarding my usual taste for a sultry exoticism, I came dressed as a monk of the order of Capuchins. It was not the most flatter-

94

ing of costumes but some of the ladies found it intriguing. The house was blazing with candles, which were carried by turbaned blackamoors, and Niagaras of satin and brocade flooded the stairways. I remember talking to a woman who was dressed as Catherine de Medici (she still wore her mask, but I suspected it was Lady Morgan).

"Tell me," I said. "What is your opinion? Turning from the realms of the purely spiritual," (we had been discussing the relative merits of Mohammedanism and Buddhism), "what arouses a woman's curiosity—a masculine virtue or a masculine wickedness?"

"My dear friend," said the lady, "I'm not quite certain of your identity, though I strongly suspect you of being a fashionable young versifier; can you doubt the true answer? Women are much addicted to jealousy, and they love to possess a man, but a virtuous man (quite aside from his sexual ineptitude) would certainly fail to provide an occasion for the requisite scenes of jealousy. If a woman were given a choice between a monk and a profligate, one out of ten would pick the monk; and her name would be Messalina!"

At this point (it was nearly day-light, and the blackamoors were asleep) a shape in sea-green pantaloons came prancing down the stairway. She was wearing a velvet mask but her costume gave her away: no-one but Caroline would have chosen that diaphanous attire of a Persian ephebe. Caroline was proud of her hips, which were as slender as an athlete's, and equally proud of her buttocks, which were trim as a boy's. (Once I said to her, "Caroline, your costumes are close to perfection and your figure is doubtless very much like a page's, but there is one little ingredient"—and I glanced at her groin—"which is blatantly missing!" After this she made a point of perfecting her disguises by tucking a rolled-up handkerchief in the left-hand side of the crotch.)

"Come," she whispered. "I want to speak to you." And she

drew me into a corner, where some cushions lay scattered in front of a balcony.

She looked at me feverishly and muttered: "I want the truth, Byron."

"What truth?"

"You know what I mean. You've been trying to keep it secret."

"I fear that I don't . . ."

"Liar! Pig and prevaricator! Who is she, you devil? Who is the latest victim?"

"I assure you, dear Caroline . . ."

"Don't try to enveigle me, please. I have long suspected it and now I am certain. You have embarked on a new affair. I can see it in your eyes. I can hear it in your voice. Oh, you lecher, you hyena, have you no instinct save that of seduction? Have you no wish but to defile? Have you no energy but towards destructiveness? Listen, Byron! You have caused enough misery to last you a life-time! The day will come when you'll pay for it. How I shall laugh! How I shall revel in it! That club-footed satyr with his vulgar snobbism and his stuffed-up poetry, weeping on the edge of a coverlet because his beauty has withered away—oh, I tell you, I'll laugh my heart out when the day finally comes and I see a drab old Byron, fat and bald and dribbling with syphilis, shuffling from Piccadilly to Mayfair, begging for a warm cup of tea!"

I reached out my hand and slapped her crisply across the cheek. Then I turned and walked back to resume my chat with Lady Morgan.

After that it was over. I still saw her occasionally but my boredom soon turned into a downright abhorrence. She grew thin and pitifully ugly, with deep pouches under her eyes. Once or twice I met her at a street-corner, looming in the twilight like a phantom and fixing her pearly accusatory eyes on me: they were no longer the eyes of an Ariel but of a thin, bristling Hecate. One night, after a ball, she stalked into my rooms unannounced, dressed in white embroidered breeches, like a Mesopotamian shepherd. I said quietly, "Forgive me, dear. I am tired. I am going to bed." And one night I came back to my study and found *Vathek* on the table, and on the fly-leaf, in Caroline's handwriting, were written (in red) the words: "Remember me!"

Oh, my chimerical, my hysterical, my costume-loving Caroline! Or am I being unjust to poor Bacchic Caroline? She represented, like Dionysus, a threat to orderly existence. Like Dionysus, she was innocence and abandonment, insight and madness, gaiety and cruelty. And yet, who knows, maybe it is the wild and elemental Dionysus who keeps our world from shrivelling, like Fragonard's, to a powdery lassitude.

THE
SECOND
NOTE-BOOK

This morning my men got ready to attack the stranded brig. The prospect of booty inspires them more than the thought of "liberty".

However, as usual, their sense of timing was sadly deficient. At two o'clock, during the siesta-hour, three Turkish boats approached the vessel, removed the stores and the ammunition, and set her on fire.

I can see the smoke still floating over the black horizon. It is illumined by the glowing ashes and looks like a vast and luminous bat.

I pick up my pen to write. But as I hold it between my fingers it seems to quiver and squirm, suddenly alive, like a little snake.

As I write in these note-books I grow aware of something strange. By turning these memories into prose (an alien element to me, unfortunately) I see that I am subtly transforming their texture, but in a manner exactly opposed to that inherent in poetry. Wordsworth called poetry a powerful emotion remembered in tranquillity. He was wrong, as I now see it. It is remembered in agitation, and it is the act of writing the poem which subdues it to tranquillity. But what of prose? Prose is indeed a recollection in tranquillity, but the act of writing these memoirs stirs my memories into agitation. What is happening? Why does my hand begin to tremble as I write? I summon lucidity, the essence of prose, and I reach for irony, the subduer of passions, and I look at the past with the beady eye of an indulgent cynic. But then why does my heart burst into flame all of a sudden? Why do these cool and caustic anecdotes (some of them tinged with the licentious) suddenly stir in my heart a secret joy which is close to terror?

*

I remember the snow was falling as we rode on the Great North Road. Towards noon it was so deep that we could hardly pass through the drifts. We went riding over a marshland which was sheeted with snow and the sun came from the clouds and hung over a flat horizon. The horse's breath steamed and the ruts squeaked under the wheels. The sun was ready to set when we drove through the gates at Six-Mile Bottom.

It was a dismal, ghostly place. A long avenue of alders, bristling with tufts of frozen grass, led up to the manor-house, which was a gaunt brooding edifice set in a copse of black yew-trees. I could see the diamond panes flash in the sunset and then die, as though the lights in the house had been suddenly snuffed. Some crows were still wheeling round the chimneys and when darkness descended they flew screaming into the stable.

Augusta was waiting for me in the library. She kissed me on the cheek. A butler brought us some tea and set it on the table in front of the hearth. I still remember the light of the flames which shone on the silver tea-pot and kept dancing in Augusta's happy brown eyes.

"And what," she said merrily, "are these terrible scandals I've been hearing about?"

"I see," I said sadly. "Your charming friends have been slandering me."

"Not in the least," cried Augusta. "It is rather flattering, I think, to be gossiped about. Gossip springs out of envy. You are envied. Be grateful for gossip. And besides, my dear brother, you are not a mimosa. You'll survive all this wicked wagging of tongues."

I was, of course, only a half-brother but Augusta called me her brother, and I called her my sister, which gave me a pleasant *frisson*.

We had dinner alone, face to face at the long black dining-table. I still remember the shutters which kept flapping in the wind. The walls were all mildewed and the ceiling was covered with stains. But Augusta's smiling face subjugated the demons of Six-Mile Bottom and we chatted about politics, about Piccadilly and Portugal. The two setters, Puck and Cleo, lay on the rug in front of the fire. Now and again they cocked their ears and started to whimper plaintively, as though worried by some queer little noise in the woods.

After dinner we strolled into the icy gallery in the east wing, where the portraits stared from the wall like a row of periwigged monkeys. The wind hissed through the panes as we hurried through the gloom. Even the elements were vengeful at Six-Mile Bottom, struggling, it seemed, to reduce the house to a physical decay which would equate the spiritual decay which had already overwhelmed it.

We threw on our cloaks and walked out in the snow, which now in the night looked quite lovely and almost comforting, with little white bonnets sitting on top of the bushes and the windows casting golden lozenges on the lawn. We looked at the stars, which were burning over the yew-trees, and Augusta said, "Stars! What are stars, can you tell me, darling?"

"I wish that I could," I said. "I have often speculated about the stars. Even as a boy I was baffled by those millions of stars."

Augusta gripped me by the arm. "I love to speculate about the stars! Are they hot or are they cold? Are they little or are they vast?"

"Since they burn they must be hot. And being hot they are

uninhabitable. Only a dragon could survive in the heat of the stars."

"Still," said Augusta, "it might be amusing to visit a star. They can't be so fearfully distant, when you really stop to think of it. Maybe the eagles fly occasionally as high as a star and then back to earth, disillusioned by all that emptiness."

"When I was a child," I said, "I wanted to be a bird and fly through the clouds. Now I want to be a fish and spend my life in the seas."

"Ah," said Augusta, tugging at her collar, "I would hate to live in the sea. Think of it, dear! The black sea-bottom! What goes on deep down in the sea? Horrible beasts with long white tentacles go prowling through the slime!"

Puck and Cleo were gambolling about merrily in the snow, but then abruptly, as we skirted the woods, they stopped dead in their tracks. Puck lifted his head and started to bay. Cleo cringed and with a strange little whine she ran back to the house.

Augusta turned and looked at me silently. I took her by the hand and we walked back hurriedly through the snow-filled meadow.

We entered the library and sat down in front of the fire. I glanced at Augusta from the corner of my eye. She was not beautiful, far from it. Her face was lean and bony, her brow was too high and her neck was too thin. Her eyes were like my own; they were set too close together. She was silly, she was scatter-brained, she knew nothing of Kant or Aristotle. She giggled at all my jokes, even the ones left over from Harrow. But then why did I fall in love with her? What was the joy that suddenly filled me? Why was she no longer a sister but a breath of consolation? Just sitting by her side brought peace and gentleness to my heart. Just hearing her laughter drove away some lingering ugliness. I saw in her loving eyes my own reflected image: an image drained of vanity, an image freed from anxiety, an image absolved by magic even from the threats of space and time: an image which was rescued by the very thrust into the forbidden from the guilts which clung to my hull, like a crust of old barnacles.

I sat on the floor beside her and listened to her chatter. The fire-light died and the wind grew still, and I raised her fingers to my lips.

19 February

Parry came for a glass of punch and we spoke of America.

Parry: "They are kind, they are generous, they are handsome, but they are crude."

Byron: "No matter the crudity. Crudity itself is of no consequence. They are children, but they are greedy and bigoted children. They have a rich new country to work on and a European heritage to work with. But alas, they have their vices. They are intolerant, it seems, especially in the north, where there is puritanism. And they love luxury, it seems, especially in the south, where there is slavery."

"And they boast," said Parry, nodding. "The Americans I have met were given to boasting."

"Yes," I said, "they appear to be egoists. And since their traditions are still fluid, their vanity is focussed entirely on themselves. An Englishman boasts of his country and he is called a patriot. If he boasted of himself he would be called an ass. An American boasts of himself and instead of being called an ass he is called (so I am told) a 'success', and a 'dynamic personage'."

"You have no wish to see America?"

"I have," I said, "and I haven't. Things seem to be going badly, but some fine day, when the Greeks are free again, I shall finally go and visit America."

"You look sad, a little, Your Lordship."

"My good Parry, I feel wretched. This place is growing intolerable. Foul weather, foul smells, and thousands of parasites, both human and insect. I must leave this filthy hole. I shall die if I do not leave it."

"But you will leave it," said Parry with a sidelong gleam in his little eyes, "not without a certain lingering regret, Your Lordship!"

I did not answer. I glanced at Parry, and he lowered his eyes discreetly.

*

Once we walked through the meadows (it was early in March, I think) and we entered the woods that lay to the south of Six-Mile Bottom. We had baskets and were looking for mushrooms—those white-turbaned mushrooms which Mrs Gutteridge, our cook, put in the pan with the gravy. We walked deeper into the woods, and suddenly the sky grew dark as a coffin. There was a rumbling of thunder and a zig-zag of lightning.

I looked around. Augusta had vanished. "Augusta!" I cried. "Augusta! Where are you?" I caught sight of her in the distance, running like a ghost through the vaulted trees. I ran up and caught her trembling little body in my arms.

"Augusta! What is wrong, my darling? Has anything happened?"

She looked at me and laughed, though her lips were still shaking. "Oh, nothing, nothing at all! I thought I saw a . . . *creature.*"

"A *creature?*"

"It looked like a calf with the face of a bull-dog!"

We ran back through the meadow and suddenly the storm burst in its fury. The drops lashed at our cheeks like a flood of angry tears, and the twigs slapped at our arms like little black whips. We walked into the library and sat by the hearth. Mrs Gutteridge brought us tea and a bowl of warm crumpets, and we crouched on the rug and played a game of Cat's Cradle.

"Aren't you sometimes," whispered Augusta, "just a little bit afraid, dear?"

"Afraid? Why on earth?"

"Nothing especial. Just the *world*. How I dread returning to London, with those wicked wagging tongues!"

Wagging tongues! I laughed at people who were worried by wagging tongues. What was the harm of a wagging tongue? Gossip was nothing but hissing air. Sticks and stones might break one's bones but the air of slander was merely disagreeable.

And yet, and yet . . . Here in the wet, storm-ridden loneliness of Six-Mile Bottom I began to feel the surreptitious terror of a pariah. That night, as we squatted cheerfully in front of the fire, I sensed something foul in the atmosphere of England. Or was it England? Was it the whole unwholesome world of humanity? No, it was England, it was surely England, and when I thought of the Mediterranean my heart jumped at the image of sunlit columns by a calm blue sea.

Oh, my scatter-brained darling, my berry-eyed Augusta, was I really in love or was it merely another mask? Did I love you? Or did I merely need your loyalty and laughter?

That night I sat by the fire after Augusta had gone to bed. I was leafing through the *Gulliver* which I found on the tea-table. All was still in the house, the storm had died, the animals were sleeping, and all I heard was the crackle of the burning juniper-twigs. I was reading the description of Gulliver's arrival in Lilliput:

I attempted to rise, but was not able to stir, for as I happen'd to lie on my back, I found my arms and legs were strongly fastened on each side to the ground, and my hair,

which was long and thick, tied down in the same manner . . .

I pictured myself as Gulliver, a ship-wrecked exile sleeping
in the grass and then awakening to find himself the prisoner
of a tribe of tiny philistines.

I dropped my hand lazily and felt the touch of a snout.
"Cleo," I murmured. "Good doggie!" But then I realized
that it wasn't Cleo. The thing that squirmed under my palm
was neither furry nor friendly, it was slimy and horribly
pimpled, like the head of a giant toad. I recoiled and sat
rigid, trying to gather my wits about me. Then I peered very
cautiously over the arm of the chair. There was nothing at
all. I heard a slithering behind the bookcase, as of soft scaly
paws, and I smelled something nasty, like a corpse found in
the woods.

I quietly closed my *Gulliver* and placed it on the tea-table.
Then I picked up the lamp, tiptoed slowly down the hall and
climbed the broad stairway that led to my bedroom. I locked
the door quickly and set the lamp on the chiffonier. Then I
walked to the window and stared into the night. Far in the
distance something white was loping swiftly through the
darkness and then vanished among the bushes which
bordered the swamp-land.

20 February

Colonel Stanhope left for Athens this morning. As he said
good-bye tears came to his eyes and his creased, protuberant
face looked more than ever like a crocodile's.

Oh, Lord, will I ever escape from this louse-ridden swamp?

*

One evening at Lady Melbourne's I was introduced to Miss Milbanke. She was a pale square-jawed woman with a country look about her, but the Viscountess warned me: "She is a formidable *bas bleu,* as well as a mathematical expert, my puss!"

Miss Milbanke looked at me coldly. I said, "Miss Milbanke, I am charmed to know you. I am told that you are a classical scholar, as well as a princess of parallelograms."

A bashful smile twisted her lips. She looked down at the floor severely. "I am neither a scholar nor a princess. I am nothing that would interest you, Lord Byron."

I drew her to the window and regarded her solemnly. I found her cold and irritating, yet I was teased by the air of abstraction, the philosophical chill which lurked in her eyes. We spoke of Swift and La Rochefoucauld, of Bolingbroke and Hume, and we spoke of Cowper's poetry, which she found especially congenial.

"You are a *femme savante,* Miss Milbanke, and an icy metaphysician. What draws you to the mild, half-witted melancholy of Cowper?"

"You are being unjust, Lord Byron; both to Cowper and myself. Cowper's poems are sad and autumnal but they are filled with spiritual insights. As for myself, I know about physics, but metaphysics: goodness, what are they?"

I laughed and asked her blandly: "What is poetry, then, Miss Milbanke?"

"Poetry," she said, looking at the garden, "is the lava of the imagination whose eruption prevents an even deadlier earthquake. Dear Cowper was mildly mad, but only his poetry saved him from lunacy."

I clapped my hands. "Bravo, Miss Milbanke! I have suddenly changed my mind. There is more warmth in you than I thought. Still, I am startled by what you say. You love poetry, it appears. But where does it rank in the scale of the intellect? Its essence is dreams. What use are idle dreams?"

"Exactly what I said, Lord Byron. Dreams are signals of warning, and talking about our dreams saves us from darker convulsions. Our demons lurk in our dreams, and in telling our dreams we banish the demons."

"Mm . . . I see. Poetry, in short, is merely a means to save the soul?"

"Poetry," she said, "in the purely decorative sense has no interest for me, Lord Byron."

She turned rather brusquely and started to talk to Sam Rogers, who as usual stood in attendance at these fashionable Whig gatherings. I regarded her from the back with a lingering distaste: her hips were too broad, her posture was hunched, her dress was dowdy. I glanced slyly at Miss Elphinstone, who was dressed in russet tweeds, and we started to chat about deer-stalking in the Grampians.

21 February

An insect bit me this morning and a spot like a raspberry has appeared on my wrist.

Mavrocordato came this evening. He was already a little tipsy, and our gossip grew somewhat blunter than usual.

"Tell me, Byron," he said amiably: "I feel you are hiding something from me. You have had, it appears, numerous liaisons with women?"

I nodded my head demurely.

"How many women, would you say?"

I made a rapid calculation. "It depends on what you mean by 'liaison'. If you merely mean the copulatory act, I should say three hundred or so. If you refer to a more prolonged relationship, involving the emotions, I should say seven."

"Seven. Not bad. Seven love-affairs. I wish I could say as much for myself. I was in love only twice, and neither was even remotely copulatory." He took off his spectacles and fixed a sphinx-like stare on me.

"Tell me another thing, Byron. I still feel you are not being frank with me. Have you ever had a liaison, copulatory or otherwise, with a man?"

I chuckled amiably; I knew that the Prince knew the answer to this ingenuous question. "To be honest with you, Alex, I must reply in the affirmative. Copulatory, four in number. Non-copulatory, only one."

"Honest answers to honest questions," said the Prince, leering smugly. "You are, I believe, what is called amphibious, or 'Janus-headed'. I have occasionally felt a doubt whether true amphibians really exist. One would suppose that they'd make their choice once and for all 'twixt air and water. However, let us assume that these amphibians *do* exist. The question is, are they equally partial to air and water, to an identical degree?"

"Nothing, I suppose, is ever identical in the sphere of carnality."

"True," said Alex. "And to generalise is also to obfuscate. All the same, since we are engaged in a highly-edifying symposium, may I ask you another question? Which of these branches of copulatory experience have you found the more pleasurable?"

"To that," I retorted, "the answer is simple. Women are constructed more adroitly than men."

Mavrocordato scratched his nose. "Well, I cannot help wondering. You may of course be perfectly right. One penultimate question, however. If you were crossing the hall in some little inn, shall we say in Seville, and had the choice between two doors, one leading into a room in which a naked female lay on the bed, and the other into a room with an equivalent male: which would you choose?"

"A darkened room or an undarkened?"

"Darkened. Naturally," said the Prince.

"I would choose the female," I said.

"And if undarkened?"

"The female likewise."

"And if instead of a room," persisted the Prince, "it were a sunlit forest, perhaps in Bavaria? Or some island grotto, shall we say in Sardinia?"

"You are indulging," I said, "in fantasies. Such things happen, but they happen rarely. What you are suggesting, my good Alex, is that the zest of a wood or a grotto is more linked with the forbidden than with the sanctioned and domesticated. But this has nothing to do with what you call amphibiousness. A beautiful man as well as a beautiful woman can make my heart skip a beat. And both women and men can be sadly tedious and disillusioning. One must, as you say, recoil from generalities."

Alex nodded. "Yes, yes. One must recoil. One must recoil. *Reculer,* perhaps, if only *pour mieux sauter . . .*"

*

In late July I drove to Hastings and rented a villa by the sea. My Augusta came to join me and we sat on the lawn reading *Waverley,* which had recently been published and which Augusta found "ravishing". We swam and ate turbot; we drank wine and walked on the cliffs, and at sunset we strolled on the downs.

"Darling," she said, "I think you should marry. Have you ever thought of marrying?"

"I have thought of it," I said, "but have rejected the notion. The thought of losing my liberty is more than I can bear."

"Liberty! What is liberty? How can any of us speak of liberty?"

"Freedom is happiness, my goose, and I refuse to abandon my happiness."

She took my hand; we came to a halt on the edge of a precipice. Below us shone the sea, clawing at the rocks with snowy breakers. A wisp of chestnut hair blew over Augusta's wind-flushed face and she murmured, "You are a child, dear. You have yet to learn how black the world is."

We walked home and sat in the garden, which was lined with the Muses. They stood in a row by the hedge, spotted with moss and sadly mutilated.

"Who on earth was Terpsichore?" said Augusta airily.

"Terpsichore," I replied "was the Muse of Dancing."

"And who, my pet, was Melpomene?"

"She was the Tragic Muse," I said.

"Look at the dear! Her nose is missing. And a pigeon has dirtied her brow. The Tragic Muse has lost her dignity, poor creature!" said Augusta merrily.

Then she looked at me carefully. "What did you think of that Miss Milbanke?"

"I have never cared for cultural females, as you know, my little goose."

Augusta looked glum and cast a worried look at Calliope. "I think you should marry. Have you thought of marrying Miss Milbanke?"

In September I drove to Newstead and saw that the leaves were turning to sepia. Augusta came in the evening and we strolled in the park. We sniffed the autumn air and felt the chill of seasonal change, the imminence of rot and the coming of upheaval. We walked to the Devil's Wood and carved our names on an ancient elm.

"Well," said Augusta. "What have you decided?"

"I have decided nothing," I said.

"Have you written to her?"

"Twice. But I wish that I hadn't."

"We must accept," said Augusta gloomily, "the edicts of society."

I turned on her fiercely. "Augusta, you are a coward! Why

should I give up my liberty? Why should I burden myself with society? Why do you insist on my marrying a mathematical equation?"

At dinner that evening, as we ate our gooseberries, Phipps the gardener came in and showed me a thing he had found in the flower-bed. It was my mother's wedding-ring which had been lost years ago. He had found it in the mould, amongst some withered chrysanthemums.

At that moment there was a thunder-clap and the rain began to fall. The door-bell rang shrilly and a gust of wind rushed through the dining-room. The door opened and Mullins the butler brought me a letter. I cut it open: it was written in a clear, symmetrical handwriting.

I have your second letter—and am almost too agitated to write. But you will understand. It would be absurd to suppress anything. I have pledged myself to make your happiness my first object in life. I will trust you for all I should look up to—and all I can love. This is a moment of joy which I have despaired of ever experiencing. There has in reality been scarcely any change in my sentiments. More of this I will defer. I wrote to you by the last post—but with what different feelings! Let me be grateful for those with which I now acknowledge myself

Most affectionately yours,
A.M.

I grew pale, my hand shook. I passed the letter to Augusta. Then I wiped my brow and muttered: "You see, it never rains but it pours."

Augusta stared at the ring and wiped it clean on the edge of the table-cloth.

"An omen," she whispered.

"God forbid," I said savagely.

Tears came to her eyes and she rolled up her napkin. I blew out the candles and we walked back to the library.

This evening, towards dusk, Loukas was sitting by my side and I was reading (translating into Romaic as I went along) the tale of Aladdin and the wonderful lamp.

There was a noise of distant rumblings, violent creakings and leonine howls. The house began to shake; the flame twitched spasmodically.

"An earthquake!" cried Loukas.

We ran down the stairs, which were dark as a tunnel. The Suliotes were rushing about in a hysterical scramble. I stood in the court-yard, watching them calmly, and I started to laugh at their clamorous cowardice. They reeled into the night, stumbling and swearing as though they were drunk. Even the house and the trees looked a little drunk, dancing in the darkness.

My heart suddenly tightened. "Luke!" I shouted. The boy had vanished.

I ran into the house and hurried breathlessly from room to room, crying "Loukas! Where are you?" No answer. The rooms were empty. The floors were shaking crazily and the walls squealed like rats. Then all grew suddenly still and the thunder died away, and I walked back to the court-yard, where a lonely donkey stood in the moonlight.

I called "Luke!" and there he was, strolling casually through the gateway. "Luke, my boy," I said softly and took him by the hand. I led him gently back into the gloom of the cold, empty house.

Love is something that we cannot control. It is frail as a moth and poisonous as a cobra. For Luke I am forgettable, and will soon be forgotten.

*

I started for Seaham the day after Christmas. I met Hobhouse in Cambridge and we drove through the snow-sheeted fens until nightfall. It was so cold that the servants moaned with misery on the box of the carriage. We spent a night in the town of Newark and another in Ferrybridge and a third in the village of Thirsk, which is slightly north of York. The next day, a Friday, was colder than ever. The harnesses shone with ice and the ruts glittered with crystals. At eight in the evening we drove through an iron gateway and followed the road through an elm-filled park. A butler stood by the entrance and led us into the hall, where Sir Ralph and Lady Milbanke were standing by the chimney-piece.

Lady Milbanke was dressed in grey, with yellow lace round the collar; her face was as dry as parchment, lightly tinged with disgust. Sir Ralph was a red-cheeked squire in dirty top-boots and leather-breeches and a long red waistcoat which reached below his hips. The other guests in the house were Mr Hoare and his pie-faced family (Mr Hoare was Sir Ralph's confidential counsel and agent) as well as a Reverend Noel, who was the Rector of Kirkby Mallory, a porous man with the teeth of a walrus and a nose like a spatula.

After dinner the rest of the company went to bed. I flung on my cloak and walked down to the edge of the sea. The wind was bitter cold and the stars shone on the beach, which crackled under my feet as though it were made of broken glass.

I caught sight of a figure hurrying towards me through the darkness. She came up and took my hand with a look of desperation.

"The sea!" she said softly. "Look—how black it is! And angry!"

"I have always loved the sea. But a bluer sea than this."

"You scarcely spoke to me at dinner!"

"Was there anything to say?"

"There are things that should be said, but to say them is difficult."

"Certain things," I said listlessly, "are too intricate for utterance."

She was shaking with the cold. "How is Augusta?" she said calmly.

"Augusta is well," I said, "and sends you her love."

We wandered down the beach and then back to the pine-copse. From here we could see the house, black and bull-like on its promontory, with one little light shining wickedly in an upper window.

"Certain things, dear Annabella, I would rather not talk about. I would rather, in the future, not discuss my sister Augusta."

She tightened her cloak about her and stared at the gloomy house. "Just as you wish," she said miserably. "Let us forget about Augusta . . ."

On Monday I woke up early and went for a stroll along the shore. The sea was ablaze under a bright winter sun. I walked through the pines and back to the snow-filled gardens, and then suddenly, with a pang of horror, I heard the tinkling of a bell.

The Reverend Noel, dressed in his canonicals, was standing in front of the fire, and beside him stood another cleric, a white-haired man named the Reverend Wallace. Sir Ralph stepped out of the library, wearing a black velvet waistcoat, and Lady Milbanke descended the stairs, dressed in a gown of brick-red satin. Hobhouse glanced at me guiltily from a corner by the window. He was wearing white gloves and an ill-fitting morning-coat. The clock struck eleven. The door of the dining-room swung open and my bride entered the room, accompanied by the governess, Mrs Clermont. She was wearing a loose-fitting dress of white muslin trimmed with wisps of ancestral lace, and a white muslin jacket.

We knelt on the cushions. The Reverend Wallace read the responses. Lady Milbanke pursed her lips; Sir Ralph wiped a tear. I remember stuttering a little when I came to the words: "I, George Gordon," and I glanced at Hobhouse slyly when I said "with my goods I thee endow". And all the while Annabella kept staring at me curiously, as though trying to detect some spark of emotion on my face. I placed the ring on her finger (my mother's wedding-ring, which was much too big for her) and I kissed her on the cheek and strode silently to the window. Annabella rose from the cushion with her eyes full of tears. She beckoned to Mrs Clermont and walked quickly out of the room.

The butler brought the punch-bowl and set it on the table. Then Mrs Clermont entered from the pantry with a pyramid-shaped wedding-cake. I spoke about her rose-garden to Lady Milbanke and about his horses to the shaggy Sir Ralph. "Don't be rough with the girl," whispered Sir Ralph with an amiable leer, and Lady Milbanke said, "She is brilliant but, oh, so innocent! Do be kind to her!"

Annabella returned to the room and sat down without a word. She was wearing a dress of slate-grey silk with a white fur-collar. The clock struck twelve o'clock when the carriage rolled into the drive and Hobhouse led my bride down the stairs ceremoniously. As we rode through the gate the church-bells rang in the village and the gardener's boy, Pippin, fired a musket from one of the gables.

23 February

My Loukas has just been here. He stood by the chair with his hands on my shoulder and gazed at my note-book, which I had opened to a new, blank page.

He kept smiling but said nothing. Why was he smiling? What was he thinking? Oh, what was my Loukas thinking while he stood there and smiled at me?

Missolonghi looms in the night like some menacing para-dox. All my life has been nothing but a snake's-nest of para-doxes. Oh, if only we could bring ourselves to look at the world impersonally! But no. Men are fools. They corrupt themselves with fear. They conjure up, like Hottentots, a whole hierarchy of devils. And in fearing and condemning evil, they contrive to create evil. Oh human hypocrisy, oh human intolerance, oh human malice and human lies, is it impossible for a man to love without defiling the thing he loves?

*

The boughs were blazing with icicles as we turned into the high-road. The clouds had gone away and the land looked white as Antarctica. My bride sat beside me without saying a word. When the sun touched her cheeks I saw that they were shining with tears. We rode past the fields and all of a sudden, as we passed a mill-pond, I burst into song: a song which Nicolò had taught me in Athens.

My bride looked rather startled. "What a curious song. What language is it?"

"Greek, my dear," I said gaily. "You and your learning—don't you recognize it?"

The cathedral-bells rang as we rode through the city of Durham.

"Ringing for our happiness," I muttered venomously.

"Or for our doom," said Annabella.

We entered a forest and I turned on her fiercely. "It won't work! It will never work! It must come to a separation!"

She stared at me desolately. "Then why did you ever propose to me?"

"Out of bravado, you little fool! Why else, may I enquire? If you had accepted me the first time it might have been salvaged. But you turned me down the first time. Out of a ludicrous female coyness. It was quite a relief, I assure you! But my sister kept insisting. I wrote you a second time, never dreaming that you'd accept. But of course you accepted. I shall never forgive you for it!"

We stopped at the inn in Rusheyford and had some ale and

an omelette. Annabella refused to speak. She nibbled at her toast and kept staring at the standing clock by the fire-place.

I was carried away by my daimon. I screamed, "Damn it, woman, you're as drab as a funeral! Can't you speak? Can't you smile? You are as cold as a lump of ice!" Then I added, half-aside, "How much longer can I stand it, I wonder!"

She said nothing. She kept twisting her napkin with an air of hopelessness.

"Very well! Keep on sulking! A miserable marriage, I must say. A brainless father, who stinks of the stables, and a detestable mother, who looks like a pickle, and a dowry so tiny it would scarcely feed a rookery. Well, I tell you, Annabella, it took courage to go through with it! I longed to break it off, but dear Augusta, the little idiot, kept in-sisting that I act like a 'man of honour', as she put it. Man of honour! As though honour had anything to do with this silly business! Yes, I've finally gone through with it, like a sol-dier and a gentleman. You're in my power, my little icicle, and I'll soon make you feel it!"

After this lunatic diatribe I lapsed into silence. Then I reached across the table and lifted her forefinger gently. "I am sorry," I growled. "Forget what I've said and please forgive me. Getting married, you know, is a desperate thing for a fellow . . ."

It was deep in the night when we finally came to Halnaby Hall. It was a chintz-cushioned country-house, well-suited to a pastoral honeymoon, with sizzling sounds that rose from the kitchen and a court-yard full of geese. I remember the cross-eyed butler opening the door of the carriage, and the look of nightmare misery that was frozen on Annabella. Her maid, a Mrs Minns, a waddling woman with a face like a cauliflower, took us up to our rooms, which looked north over the meadows. Fires were burning in both of the chambers. The beds were curtained with damask. We dined on roasted pork and a bottle of claret in Annabella's bedroom, and after the servants had gone to bed I said dryly to Annabella:

"Well, Annabella, what do you wish? I hate to sleep with a woman, but, of course, it's your honeymoon and if you insist . . ."

"I insist on nothing," said Annabella, setting her wine-glass on the table. The wine had lifted her spirits and she looked at me with serenity. "I should like to insist on manners but since it is clear that you haven't any, I suggest that you wipe the crumbs from your insolent cheek and go to your bedroom."

I glanced at her with amazement and burst into laughter. "Well said, my chick-a-biddy! You've spoken your mind, for once in your life!" I emptied my glass and rolled up my napkin and went limping into my bedroom without further ado.

I lay in my bed and heard the clock strike one in the morning. A feeling of remorse and self-disgust was creeping over me. I got up and threw on my robe, which was made of Lombardy silk, and tiptoed through the doorway into Annabella's bedroom. The fire was still smouldering and as I peered through the bed-curtains I could see the glow of the coals shining on Annabella's face. She looked transformed; she looked like a cherub. Her lips were smiling drowsily. She lay lost in some secret and half-remembered happiness. I leaned down and kissed her very gently on the lips. Then I threw off my robe and with a sigh of resignation I crawled into the ember-lit cave of her bed.

I woke up when the clock struck two. The embers were still crackling, and they threw a reddish glow through the cracks in the curtain. I looked down at the sleeping head, with its tousled hair and opened lips. She looked like poor Proserpine, snatched away from the world of light, and I knew that I was trapped in my self-created Hades.

The weather has cleared. The sky is blue, the sea glitters. I went riding again. But I felt lonely and dispirited. I came home and lay on my couch and read in the *Fables* of La Fontaine.

Something is clawing at my heart, but I know not what it is.

*

I woke up at noon. Annabella had gone downstairs and I found her in the drawing-room, sitting on a rose-embroidered sofa. *A Sentimental Journey* lay in her lap and she was holding an egg-cup between two fingers.

"Good-morning," I said briskly. "You are bright and early, I see."

"Not inordinately," she said. "The sun is shining. I walked in the meadows."

"There is nothing," I said, "like a taste for the bucolic." I sank into a chair. "You've recovered, I hope?"

She set her egg-cup on the table. "Was there something," she said, "to recover from?"

We played cards in the library, which had a view of the snow-filled valley. My spirits were rising and I peered at my bride with curiosity. Her face looked bland and equivocal, quite untouched by the act of matrimony, except for a foxy little smile that hung on her lips. She was calm and composed. She looked at me aloofly. And oddly enough this very aloofness began to intrigue me. I called her "Pip", I don't know why. We went for a stroll in the icy park.

"Why are you smiling?" I said, slapping a rose-bush with my cane.

"Was I smiling?" she said, gazing at the clouds. "I wasn't aware of it."

"As though you had a secret . . ."

"I have a secret. But I shan't reveal it!"

We played, we wrote letters, we read verses in Halnaby Hall. I remember sprawling in a chair while my bride read *Don Sebastian* and watching the snow-flakes drift slowly past the window. Scott's *Lord of the Isles* arrived one morning by the post and we sat in the library and Annabella read it aloud to me. That same evening I wrote a poem, *By the Rivers of Babylon,* and Annabella copied it carefully in her neat Italian calligraphy.

"What do you think of it?" I said.

"It has music," said Annabella.

"Is that all?"

"It is sufficient."

"But the feeling! The feeling!"

"What is feeling?" said Annabella. "Sometimes we feel that we ought to feel something, and so we induce ourselves to feel what we think we feel. But is this passion? I doubt it. True passion exists in secrecy."

"And you? Are you capable of passion?"

"Only in secrecy," said Annabella.

I glanced at her face, which seemed enclosed in parentheses, and the drab, expressionless features were suddenly brightened by a cat-like glitter. And at that moment, for only a moment, I fell in love with Annabella. It was only a moment: then it was over. But it was love. Yes, it was love.

25 February

I took my corps in full dress on a brisk little march along the beach. Their buckles gleamed and their buttons glittered in the fierce, unnatural sunlight.

*

A hideous thought occurs to me. The real reason that I loved Augusta was that in her gay convivial way she never really understood me. And the reason I loathed my wife, and never forgot her or forgave her, was that in her cool feline way she saw through me and understood me.

She spoke of her "secrecy", but it was I who huddled in secrecy. I longed to hide my feelings in impenetrable secrecy. Secrecy even from myself; secrecy above all from myself. I tried not quite to face, not quite to grasp my true character. Why was it? Was it guilt? Was it a preference for mystery? Or was it the fear that full self-knowledge would extinguish the heat in me, and would wither the lust and capacity for poetry? All three of these, no doubt. And add to these the lingering suspicion, which I experienced even as a child, that "self-knowledge" was merely an illusion, and an illusion in the end more dangerous and stultifying than the life of instinct.

We returned to Seaham for a month and in the middle of March we visited Augusta. Spring came late to Six-Mile Bottom. The wind was cold and the trees were leafless. I remember my dark Augusta descending the stairway and greeting Annabella with a crisp cordiality. (They had never met before: and from that moment they were deadly enemies.)

Those terrible days at Six-Mile Bottom I still recall with a *cauchemar* vividness. The two women kept watching each other with a tigerish intensity. When we sat at the table I saw Augusta's large brown eyes secretly appraising the pale, rectangular face of Annabella. When we sipped at our tea I saw Annabella's eyes rove furtively over the Gainsborough-like features of my Augusta. I made a diabolical point of totally ignoring Annabella. I went for walks with Augusta, leaving my bride alone in the library. I joked slyly with Augusta, employing our own private *argot*. I sat on the rug and played Cat's-cradle with Augusta after dinner while Annabella sat on the couch with her copy of Leibnitz. I kept hinting perversely at the unmentionable secret I shared with Augusta, and late at night, as we sipped our brandy, I would turn to my bride and say: "Go to bed, Annabella. Augusta and I would like to chat a while . . ." And when I finally came staggering into the bedroom at midnight, I glared at her and groaned, "Move over, for God's sake, woman! It's late. I wish to sleep. I am not in the mood for concubinage . . ."

What possessed me? What drove me to this lunatic brutality? I am moody, I am irritable, but I am not (I think) unkind. I was punishing Annabella for a crime she had never committed; indeed, I was punishing my wife for my own secret crime, as though her suffering might atone for all the sins that still lurked in me. Was this the reason? Was I turning Annabella into a scapegoat? Or was it that I loathed her for depriving me of my liberty? Was it some elemental instinct common to all captive males? Or was it deeper still? Was I punishing all of England, was I punishing the whole heartless world of my ancestors?

What is strange is that her suffering, while it maddened me at the time, did eventually produce in me an equivalence of suffering. Slowly and secretly and invisibly she created her own revenge. I cannot think of Annabella without a twist of pain in my heart, and it is strange that in this desert of pain and humiliation a tiny flower did finally grow, and that this flower is still alive in me.

26 February

To-day it is cloudy again. The sea keeps heaving and bubbling, as though some irritable sea-beast were prowling in the depths of it.

I keep waiting. For what? For the door to open? For

someone to enter? Is it as simple as that? As weak as that, and as sad and as silly?

The wind whistles, the curtains sway. And I keep on waiting.

*

We returned to London in April and lived in Piccadilly Terrace. I promptly installed Mrs Mule, who exchanged her red wig for a white one, and whose accent grew more farcically *raffiné* than ever. I slid merrily back into the grooves of London society, and I found some compensations in Annabella's society. I discovered a hidden warmth below her chilly exterior, and even a certain charm in her broad marble features.

We spoke of poetry. My Annabella, who after all had a "brilliant intellect", had read Tasso and Voltaire, not to mention Pindar and Lucretius. Our conversations began to mellow; I started to listen to what she said. The relationship grew tolerable and at times even playful. When she copied one of my poems in her fine Venetian script she sometimes called my attention to a limping cadence or a cloying epithet. She occasionally hinted at the need for "Attic purity" and "Gallic discipline". Once she even referred to a thing she called "cerebral incorruptibility". She warned me against my leaning towards the "merely mellifluous" and gently reproached me for my penchant for the "gaudily exotic".

I said, "Pip, my dear creature, you are turning into a prune. Poetry is not, as you suppose, a thing of purities and disciplines. It is a thing of force and fire. Thank you for your hints, which I deeply appreciate, but may I suggest that you have the mind of a governess?"

Sometimes we spoke of religious matters. (Annabella was deeply concerned with these.) I used to ridicule her religiosity, but there was an ambivalence in my agnosticism. I believed and disbelieved. God existed yet could not exist. Immortality was inconceivable, but death for ever was unimaginable. I posed as a sceptic and even an atheist. But I was in fact as superstitious as a Senegambian savage. I believed in omens: black cats, shooting-stars, broken mirrors. The fact that our house was numbered 13 never ceased to cause me anxiety. I believed (and still do) in gipsy fortune-tellers and Arab astrologers, in the portents of dreams and the meaningful bulges of phrenology.

I said to Annabella: "Pippin, my dear, we are utter opposites. You are rigid and cold as an icicle, I am capricious and hot as a flame."

"Ice eventually must melt," she said, "and fire must turn into ashes."

"To you the human soul, Pip, is a mathematical matter. You see it all in black and white, never in grey, speckled or mottled."

"I am not," she retorted, stirring the sugar in her tea, "either so stupid or intolerant or cold as you think."

"You are, my dear Pip, too methodical to be interesting. It would be a relief if you burst into a sudden rage and spilled your tea."

"And you," she said quietly, "are wholly unpredictable. Your savage moods frighten me and your jovial moods disturb me."

She pressed her hands together and looked at me intensely. "Something," she said, "seems to haunt you. What is the demon that keeps haunting you?"

Spring passed, summer passed, autumn came and the fogs descended. Our truce came to an end and I drank myself into a stupor. Annabella lay in labour and one day in mid-December I was taken to her room and saw a creature in the bed beside her. I leaned down and tickled its nose and then whispered exultantly, "Oh, what an implement of torture I have acquired in you, my darling!"

I adored my little Ada, but little Ada was not enough. My

abhorrence of Annabella grew obsessive to the point of paroxysm. There were times when I could hardly control myself in her presence. I was hot with an urge to wound, to defile and excoriate, and I spoke with a gathering blatancy of my sexual escapades—the mountains of Albania, the shades of the Acropolis, the forest by Trumpington and the harlots of Paddington.

"You never loved me," I muttered. "You are incapable of passion."

"I love you. I would kill my love if I could. But I cannot."

"You call it love. Is there love in a mathematical formula?"

"There is love even in that if you only trouble to look for it."

I got up and strode furiously to the window. Then I turned with a leer and said in slow, honeyed tones:

"You keep talking of your own undeviating rectitude, my dear. Oh, how I long for a bit of filth, a bit of slovenliness, a breath of humanity!"

I stared at her face, which was puffy with misery. And I detected in her eyes a new and horrible alertness. She understood a great deal. More than I, and more cruelly than I. She had suffered, she was willing to suffer, she had learnt to accept her suffering, but the worm had finally turned. As she turned the golden ring on her thin little finger I saw something new in those tear-reddened eyes: in her heart a slimy hatred, like a fat white larva, was beginning to feed on her rotting love for me.

"You are perpetually avenging yourself. Oh, what crimes have you committed?"

"Crimes," I said, "that have a name. Yours is a crime without a name."

I stared at her viciously. I knew that my guilt had turned into a weapon, and that it had dug a deep, festering wound in her character. And I also knew that henceforth, whatever might happen to either of us, she would always be a dark and destructive woman.

Was it "fated", was it inevitable that the whole thing should crumble? It was; yet it was not. It was "doomed", but never hopelessly. Even at the end I might have saved it. But my "agoraphilia" got the better of me. The clammy English weather began to asphyxiate me, the English hypocrisy was beginning to paralyse me. My longing for "sunlit arches" and "caerulean bays" grew irresistible. One evening I said to my wife with a baleful finality: "Do as you wish. For me it is over. It was a blunder from the beginning . . ."

I saw her for the last time on an evening in the middle of January. She came calmly into the room where Augusta and I were sitting, and she reached out her hand and said, "I have come to say good-bye, Byron."

I folded my arms and walked nonchalantly to the chimney-piece, I looked smilingly at Annabella and then indulgently at Augusta. "And when," I said grimly, "shall we three meet again?"

"In heaven, I trust," said Annabella, buttoning her gloves.

She slid out of the room and closed the door behind her. I heard her rustling down the hall, soft as a serpent, and that was the end of it.

27 February

A young American named Finlay came today, with a friend named Fowke. We spent the evening over a wine-jug and talked about Goethe. They are both *précieux* of the American variety, and alternate between an affected enthusiasm and a spinsterish fastidiousness. Finlay was dressed in a pale-green waistcoat which he had purchased in Paris; Fowke wore liver-coloured tweeds which he purchased in Edinburgh. Fat little Fowke worships Goethe and called him an "all-enveloping genius". Prim, prism-faced Finlay called him "conceited" and *"pomposo"*. True, no doubt. But in a genius one can forgive conceit and pomposity. And even worse, I hinted slyly. Fowke giggled, and Finlay wriggled.

"What does he look like?" I asked Finlay, who had visited him in Weimar.

"Oh, handsome, unmistakably handsome, with a face like a marble monument. But his eyes—well, there is something very curious in his eyes, something dark, something twisted, something positively diabolical . . ."

Annabella once told me that I lost my innocence the day I was born. And yet to myself I still seem so stupidly, incurably innocent.

I have never brooded enough. There is not enough evil in me for magnificence.

*

So we parted. Not in "silence and tears", as I might have wished it, but in a chaos of groans and recriminations. I prepared for my trip to the Continent with a feverish gusto. I was nearly penniless but my leaning for luxury was uncontrollable. I bought swords, guns, pistols, even a Florentine stiletto. I bought mahogany dressing-cases and a small folding writing-desk. I ordered gold-embroidered uniforms and a dozen nankeen breeches, as well as some coats of military scarlet with golden epaulettes. I also bought some gifts which I planned to present to "foreign potentates": golden snuff-boxes set with rubies, golden brooches set with sapphires, even a gold-enamelled music-box with figures set in pearls. I bought a trim little *calèche* for my servants and dogs and I ordered from Baxter's a preposterous carriage, which was modelled on Napoleon's great coach of Genappe. It was equipped with a chest of plates and a set of fine Bohemian wine-glasses, as well as a rose-wood "library" and a collapsible *lit de repos.*

One windy April morning I set out for Dover. I rose at dawn and hurriedly breakfasted (I was expecting the creditors at any moment) and then headed south in the direction of Canterbury. Hobhouse and Davies came along to see me off on the boat, and I was accompanied by Dr Polidori and my valet Fletcher and my "page" Bob Rushton. We walked down the quay and I boarded the packet. Then I stood on the deck and waved my cap to Cam and Scropie. I watched the snowy cliffs (shall I ever see them again?) until they finally vanished behind the waves of the English Channel.

We landed at Ostend and spent a night at the Impérial, and we rumbled along towards Ghent through the rain on the following morning. We paused in the town of Bruges, where Polidori bought me some walnuts, and long after midnight we drove into Ghent. My magnificent *carrosse,* followed by the humbler *calèche,* rode up to the door of the Hôtel des Pays-Bas and the grumbling old inn-keeper (still wearing his night-cap) cooked us a fine Flemish guinea-hen which was stuffed with mushrooms.

The next morning (which was sunny) I spent in looking at the cathedral, which was followed by a dutiful visit to the *École de Dessin.* Polidori was an eloquent partisan of the paintings of Flanders, but in spite of his enthusiasm I found Rubens repugnant. Polidori spoke of the subtle "Baroque intricacies" of Rubens but all I could see was a conglomeration of buttocks.

We lunched in the city of Antwerp and rode at nightfall into Brussels. Here at the Hôtel d'Angleterre occurred a typically Flemish calamity. My room was a charming chamber with a large oriel window, which was curtained with *cretonne* in a tasteful pattern of lilies and buttercups. On the table by my bed lay *Orlando Furioso.* I awoke at eight in the morning and rang for my breakfast. As luck would have it, I had taken some salts on the previous night for my constipation (which continued to plague me until my arrival in oily Italy). The maid knocked at the door and entered the room with her tray: and at that moment a hideous Niagara burst from my bowels without warning. I kept a dignified countenance and drew the sheets more tightly about me. The maid, whose name was Isabella, placed the tray on the dresser and then moved to the window to draw aside the curtains. The sun streamed into the room, the birds were twittering on the window-sill. The maid came up to the bed and set the coffee-pot on the night-table. As she leaned over the bed I could see her nipples beneath the muslin. I was hot with a humiliation which was tinged with lust and hilarity. The maid hovered about me in a state of expectant coquetry until I roared, "For the love of God, will you leave the room, please, my good woman?"

She left. I sprang from the bed and washed the filth from my body. I ripped off the sheets and rolled them quickly into a ball, and called Fletcher and asked him to make the best of a sorry business and transmit the linen (with a generous gratuity) to the hotel *blanchisseuse*. Then I dressed and paid my bill. Such are the hazards of foreign travel.

We rode on in Napoleonic splendour towards the Kingdom of Prussia and came to Cologne, where we slept in the Hôtel de Prague. The next morning we went for a visit to the Church of St Ursula, where we were shown a veritable mountain of ancient skulls and skeletons. These had therapeutic qualities, since they were virgins, as the guide explained to us.

"Why virgins?" I asked, delicately fondling a femur.

"Virginity," said the guide, "preserves the juices of propagation, and the bones of a virgin cure sterility as well as impotence."

My stay was too brief for a serious study of the German character, but as I strolled through the streets I was struck by something oppressive. Aside from their porcine faces and their pendulously bourgeois postures I detected a certain musk that exuded from their bodies: a smell not like the

English, which is compounded of mutton and cauliflower, but distinctly acidulous, suggesting herring and pickled pig's-feet. They love music, which appears to be their great redeeming feature. They fiddle away merrily in beer-gardens and wine-cellars but a heaviness hangs about them, an air of the theoretical. They keep farting incessantly and their urine has an especial pungency, and their leaning towards philosophy has a tinge of the philistine.

I went back to the hotel and lay down for a rest. I rang for the inn-keeper's wife and asked her to prepare a hot bath for me. She dragged in a tub, which was lined with polished zinc, and emptied three buckets of steaming hot water. Then I stripped and sat in the tub while she rubbed my limbs with soap, occasionally pausing to caress some sensitive area. I invited her cordially to step into the tub with me when Herr Stolz, the red-faced inn-keeper, came storming into the bed-chamber. He stared at me savagely (I was in a state of lathery erection) and shouted, *"Schmutziges Schwein! Heraus mit dem Englischen Lord!"* A bevy of maids lurked by the door and peered at my ignominy, and Herr Stolz dragged his wife out of the room by her braids.

This contretemps I likewise subdued by a tactful gratuity, but the pleasures of *tourisme* seemed more hazardous than ever.

28 February

Nothing happened to-day. It was exactly like yesterday. Except, of course, for the flood of thoughts that poured through my feverish brain.

Is this what is called the "life of the spirit"?

*

The gentians were blooming when we rode through the Jura and one day, clear as a looking-glass, I caught sight of Lake Geneva. We drove towards the city and spent the night at the Hôtel d'Angleterre, which was kept by a mincing mountebank named Monsieur De Jean. On Monday morning I crossed the lake with Polidori to look at a villa which was said to be available for the rest of the summer. On our return, as we stepped on the pier by the hotel, we were greeted by three figures, angular and wind-blown, blatantly British. The younger woman (in a big straw hat) was Claire Clairmont, whom I met in London, and the older was her step-sister Mary, who was William Godwin's daughter. The man (in a voluminous pea-green jacket) was Percy Shelley.

We walked to the hotel and had coffee in the sunlit pergola. My first reaction to Shelley was disparaging, almost hostile. His features were like a whippet's and his skin was flushed and freckled. His voice was high and strident, with little bursts of a warbling ecstasy, and his character was totally devoid of a sense of humour. As we sat in the pergola he seemed petrified with shyness and I said to him finally, "Well, Shelley, what do you think of it?"

"Think of what?" whimpered Shelley.

"Think of the world!" I answered resonantly.

"Ah," said Shelley, blushing slightly, "I have my opinions, as do all of us, but do I need to air them at every opportunity?"

I laughed. "Let's forget about the world," I said gently. "Let us talk about poetry. What do you think of William Wordsworth?"

Shelley glanced at me sideways with a wispy little smile. "Alas, it would take me an hour to say what I think of William Wordsworth. What is Nature, you might ask? And how should a poet respond to Nature?"

I put down my cup, which was decorated with moss-roses, and looked at young Shelley with an air of smirking tolerance. I could see that Mary was watching us with a glaze of apprehension and Claire Clairmont, her dark eyes flashing, radiated a school-girl eagerness. Polidori cast a furtive look of warning across the table and I folded my arms and murmured: "Very well. Let's talk about Nature. Clouds, mountain-tops and waterfalls. Do these things, taken in the abstract, provide a suitable theme for poetry?"

Suddenly Shelley lost his shyness and looked at me with a glow of enthusiasm. He spread out his fingers and said softly, "What are waterfalls? Are they merely a mass of water tumbling down a cliff, or are they an expression of a planetary plenitude? When I look at a waterfall I see a marvellous excrescence of energy, which manifests itself in a kind of ever-changing loveliness, and I am driven to ask myself, 'Is this loveliness merely an illusion? Is it merely a fancy of man's, or is it a symptom of a greater harmony?' And clouds. I must refrain from speaking of clouds, my good Byron, because clouds have a singular and inexplicable appeal to me. A waterfall reveals the pantheistic spirit in its effervescence while a cloud reveals it in a state of luminous metamorphosis. Which is the truer state of existence? An effervescent sparkle or a luminous changefulness? I often ask myself this question, which strikes to the core of modern poetry."

I looked quietly at Shelley, who lifted his cup to his lips and then stared at the jam-pot with sudden agitation. And at that moment, in the act of secretly laughing at his absurdity, I was struck by a sudden tenderness: I was touched by the presence of purity. A breeze passed through the pergola, and we sat in silence, listening to the waterfall.

1 March

The weather is vile again. I had an attack of dizziness this morning, and it seemed that my sabres were waltzing across the wall.

Dr Bruno has frightened me. What is this talk of a "cerebral injury"? He has been looking at me curiously, as though I were hovering on the brink of madness. All my life I have been haunted by two fears: fat and madness. My corpulence I have conquered. I live on carrots and soda-water. But madness? Was that too, like a leaning to fat, a gift of inheritance? (The difference being that it was my mother who was uncontrollably fat and my father who was an arrant and irresponsible lunatic.)

What is madness? Is it a sickness which separates the mad from the rest of the world? Or is it a law in nature which presents the mad as a terrible warning—a hint of the gnome of madness who is lurking in all of us, who is lurking in all of history and in every society, to be snubbed or ignored only at the risk of that convulsion which would grip the human race if all men were totally "sane"? Or is there a third possibility? That madness in fact is a part of wisdom, and that no vision is valid without a flicker of madness in it? Look at the thinkers and poets who were tinged with semi-lunacy. Look at Swift and Cowper and Blake. Behind their madness loomed the shadow of wisdom.

Am I too going mad? No, it is Bruno who is an idiot. It is Bruno who is mad, with his lust for blood and his passion for leeches.

*

Madame de Staël, who lived near by, asked me to visit her for tea. I recoiled from the stuffy Calvinistic air of Genevese society but the château at Coppet contained a more amusing ambiance, where political symposia blended with the music of a clavichord. Here I met a Monsieur de Bonstetten, an elderly person wearing a monocle, who had known Jean-Jacques Rousseau as well as Voltaire at Ferney. There was a whiff of the eighteenth century about this Monsieur de

Bonstetten, who had also been a close and admiring friend of Thomas Gray. He still thought of poor Rousseau as an "uncompromising innovator" and of lemon-faced Voltaire as a "formidable iconoclast", and the poetry of Gray still struck him as "audaciously *avant-garde*". It was touching to see this gentle white-haired patrician, whose manners and garments were antediluvian, still pride himself on his radical opinions, which had already receded into antiquity.

I asked him about Voltaire. He looked at me sadly. "Voltaire," he said musingly, "was a man of the utmost cruelty. He was viciously intolerant of any form of stupidity. His mind burned like a flame but his heart stank of sulphur. Once I spoke to him of the need to succour the savages of Africa and to bring them into the fold of more emancipated modes of thought, and he said, 'My good Bonstetten, you are talking like an ass. It is infinitely preferable to let these blackamoors pray to their demons and roast our crazy missionaries over the fire, than to coax them into wearing flannel breeches and tall black hats. Let them continue to be naked and grovel in their superstitions rather than turn into monkeys and ape our fraudulent modernism!' "

We spoke of Gray. It was his opinion that Thomas Gray, for all his talent, had sacrificed his poetry on the altar of "experimentalism". "Tom," he said, "had a brilliant intellect, but he was dry and a bit inhuman. His eyes were like a wasp's. His limbs were as brittle as a mantis's. The curious thing in Tom was that his poems, and especially the *Odes,* were intricate at times to the point of opacity, and yet were entrenched in a nostalgia for the past. He was torn between two epochs. He was tortured by this dilemma, but since his blood was ink-like it never attained the fullness of tragedy."

Madame de Staël loomed over her tea-table like Vulcan over his fire, with her aggressive hairy chin and her fierce virile eyes. Her teeth were sharp and greenish, her tongue was coated with mauve, and her hands had a velvety, almost paw-like look to them. Being dyspeptic, she was given to flatulence; but she let her farts with a fine precision, as though she were delivering some deep Delphic utterance. Still, with all of her oddities I began to like Madame de Staël. She was never a bore. She was loyal and tolerant. She was even kind.

We spoke of the Deity, a subject much in vogue on Lake Geneva. Once she asked me, did I accept, however hesitantly and reluctantly, the necessity of an All-Pervading Principle? I said nervously that I hadn't quite decided about it.

"My dear boy," said Madame de Staël, tapping me briskly with her fan, "you have been shilly-shallying long enough. Make up your mind. Do you believe in God?"

"With my mind I say no. But my instinct says yes. I hover between the two. One day it is this, one day it is that."

"Perpetually equivocating," said my hostess impatiently. "Yours is not, it is evident, the sphere of the intellect. You are a sensualist and a pagan, and what is worse, you are lazy." She glared at my foot. "You are a *diable boîteux.*"

We occasionally spoke of poetry, on which my hostess held definite views. "Should our poets," said a certain nit-witted Madame Eynard, who wore a wig, "be allowed to rule the world, as someone has suggested? They could hardly do worse than our monarchs and statesmen!"

"A poet," said Monsieur de Bonstetten, nodding his snowy old head, "feels certainly more concern for spiritual values than a politician."

Madame de Staël snorted vigorously. "Does he indeed? I dispute it. Poets love ruins and avalanches, they love darkness and bloodshed. Poets sing of death and destruction, not of chemical discoveries or of medical progress. A poet's approach to diplomacy would hardly be healthy."

"A poet would be sincere, at any rate," said Monsieur de Bonstetten.

"No poet is sincere," retorted Madame de Staël. "If he

138

said precisely what he really felt, his poetry would be worthless. All poetry is insincere. An exalted insincerity is the earmark of a poet. He must transcend and universalize, he must transpose into the chords of language all the foibles and fears of his miserable little self. Poetry, like music or painting, is a triumph over reality. It is a victory over the pettiness and mortality of the individual. But for the struggle to develop in the first place the poet *must* be petty, and his poetry is a soaring of the soul out of its prison of loneliness."

One day an unfortunate little accident occurred. Madame de Staël was wearing an oyster-grey gown embroidered with pansies, with a very low collar from which her breasts protruded like quinces. We were speaking (as I recall) of the transmigration of the soul. Madame de Staël rose from her chair to fetch the muffins from the mantelpiece. I noticed a small red stain on the tapestried arm-chair (which depicted the fable of the fox and the grapes). She walked back to her chair and looked down with a startled air. But far from drawing a veil over this disconcerting episode (I noticed at this point a stain of blood on the back of her dress), she gave vent to a series of ahems and alack-a-days, as though wishing to draw attention to her menstrual tenacity. Madame de Staël was a very brave woman, but she was also extremely vain.

One evening I came back from a stroll in the woods, where I happened to meet a milkmaid crossing a bridge with her pail. I dropped in at Madame de Staël's, where the talk revolved on the gods of antiquity, and specifically on the functions of Mercury as compared to the Grecian Hermes. I grew aware of a conjectural gaze from Madame de Staël directed at my person. I glanced down and saw some drops of half-dried semen clinging to my breeches. I flicked out my kerchief and drew it swiftly over the tell-tale mucilage, but Madame de Staël refused to be pacified. She turned to me and said, with a baleful look at the rest of the company, "You are incorrigible, Byron. I keep trying to improve your mind,

but there you sit, unabashed, fresh from a bout of philander-
ing . . ."

Madame de Staël was a clever woman, but she was also
very tactless.

I am sitting by the window, looking at the motionless calm
of the moonlight which falls over the marshes and the dark
Morean hills. The lamp burns on the table and my shadow
stirs on the wall. What am I writing? Is it the truth? Why am
I writing? For the sake of truth? No. I am not a philosopher.
Philosophy has always been alien to me. I write because I am
driven to write: to placate my furies and propitiate my demons.

Fowke and Finlay came for a visit, and we spoke about
music. Finlay admires Haydn for his "pastoral clarity" while
Fowke prefers the "crystalline complexities" of Mozart.

Madame de Staël (who speaks boldly) told me that Mozart, in speaking of his music, said that it came to him as
naturally as pissing to a sow. The magical thing about Mozart
is that his ceaseless awareness of death only succeeds in
making more beautiful (like a cloud passing over a wheat-
field) the casual and careless flowering of life. And what is
amazing is that Mozart, an earthy and bucolic soul, should
have produced, by an act as humdrum as that of a pissing
sow, a world of music so sublimely soaring, so piercingly
delicate, and so hauntingly subtle.

It is pleasing to think of an artist secreting his art like a
pissing sow. I prefer Mozart's theory to Aristotle's, or to that
of our Edinburgh pedants. But maybe the truth, though
equally earthy, is a little more mysterious. Coleridge (if I
remember it rightly) said that a poet's imagination reveals
itself in the balance of opposing or discordant qualities, that

is to say, in the fusion of emotional anarchy with an equally-powerful feeling of order. As in music (though differing in texture, since music is actual, a thing of the present, and poetry reflective, a thing of the past) a poem strives with its rhythm to impose a reconciling harmony on a Bacchanalian darkness and chaos. One might also put it as follows. An oyster, to shield its membranes, secretes a beautiful shell round an ugly and irritating granule. An artist secretes a shell round an ugly and alien deformity in order to protect his own quivering membranes. A man who is happy and natural has no need to be a poet. No man, perhaps, is happy and no man perhaps is natural; and every man, no doubt, is in secrecy a poet. Maybe the galvanizing deformity is not a Byronic foot or a Popeian dwarfishness, but something less tangible: an Aeschylean awe or a Sophoclean terror. The real deformity in the poet's heart is his life in an ugly world. Only in Goethe do I fail (like Fowke) to detect this *morbidezza*: unless his very Olympian perfection is itself a horrible deformity, and the granule in his soul is a disgust with his god-like image and a yearning for some saving and humanising weakness.

*

I rented the Villa Diodati, which was on the southern shore of the lake, with a splendid panorama of the Alps in the distance. Shelley and his wife, along with Claire, used to breakfast in my arbour, and we gossiped about the latest publications from London. The Shelleys had taken a house which lay on the other side of the vineyards, and at nights we went rowing over the moonlit water. At these moments my poor Claire (whose importunate intimacies I already regretted) would squeeze my hand and murmur, "Look, darling! Cassiopeia!" or "I wonder, shall we ever know what goes on in the Milky Way?"

I could not bring myself quite to break it off with poor Claire. I liked her vivid eyes, which kept fluctuating from a tender idolatry to a mournful reproachfulness. She did her best, poor little Claire. Her body was raw but her heart was fertile. She kept trying to improve her mind by reading the German philosophers, and she even tried her hand at some sonnets in the style of Petrarch. She begged me to allow her to copy out my poems and she made a careful transcript of some stanzas of *Childe Harold*.

One night it started to rain and we sat by the hearth at Diodati. We were pondering as usual on the deep conundrums of life and death. Mary was wearing a Grecian smock embroidered with fylfots, and her hair was wound in a voluminous braid round her head. In her very scorn of affectation there was a touch of affectation. She was a typical poet's wife, with an air of earthy common-sense to offset and mitigate the lunar delicacies of her husband. She had strong nordic features and a cleft in her chin; her eyes had a rich, almost Junoesque placidity.

As for Claire, she looked wayward and wind-tossed as usual. Her hair looked like a gipsy's, her gestures were rhapsodic. She too, I dare say, longed to become a poet's wife, but her character was too *schwärmerisch* and flighty for such an ordeal. She was wearing a muslin dress dappled with wands of asparagus and her shoes (purchased in Burgundy) had silver buttons shaped like snails.

Polidori sat on the rug, fondling the cobra-headed poker. My feelings towards the doctor (Polly-Dolly, as I called him) were dangerously volatile and increasingly intolerant. He was a handsome young bully with Tuscan features and Titian curls, but his touchiness and vanity sometimes bordered on the hysterical. Once he thought that Shelley had insulted him with some casual little gibe of his, and he challenged poor Percy to "a duel of honour". I curtly informed him that if this challenge were declined (which was only too likely, for

Shelley disapproved of duelling) I would feel myself obliged to accept the challenge in his stead. Polidori stammered nervously and agreed to drop the matter, and thereafter he and Shelley were on the friendliest terms imaginable.

The clock struck twelve. A gust of wind went whistling through the ivies. The flames writhed and darted, as though snatching at something invisible. The thunder kept booming and suddenly a window flew open and a fierce shaft of wind snuffed the flame in the oil-lamp. I jumped up and closed the shutters and turned back to the room, where my guests sat huddled in front of the fire-place.

"You will have to spend the night, I'm afraid," I informed them. "I'll ask Fletcher to get ready the guest-rooms up-stairs."

I opened the cupboard and brought out a bottle of *pflümli,* and we sat by the fire-light and started to tell ghost-stories.

Polidori told of a castle on the island of Crete, where a bull-headed spectre roamed through the halls at midnight. Some travellers were stranded in this castle during a storm and were found the next morning in a state of raving lunacy. Claire told of a night she had spent in an inn near Marl-borough. She awoke from her sleep and saw a man with the head of a dromedary who snatched at her coverlet and sud-denly vanished. Mary told of her visit to an abbey near Basel where she met in the cloisters an elderly nun with a face like a turtle's. I told about a night when I strolled by the Acrop-olis and saw a silhouette leap out of the bushes, half-trans-lucent and riddled with worms: but the face had the un-mistakable features of Socrates.

"Isn't it plausible," said Polidori, with an air of astuteness, "that some essence lingers on, and that a sensitive mind responds to this essence? I had a spaniel named Poof. When-ever he passed a certain door his hair stood on end and he started to whine. Later I learnt that a well-known chemist, a

Doktor von Waldhausen, had been murdered in this room by a Catalonian sailor."

A dog bayed in the distance; or it might have been a wolf. Shelley glanced at the window and Claire stared at me feverishly. The flames threw our elongated shadows on the wall, where they danced and gesticulated like witches over a cauldron.

"Has it ever occurred to you," said Mary Shelley, staring at the flames, "that if science progresses sufficiently the labours of child-birth will be unnecessary, and that men will be artificially fabricated, like an elaborate cuckoo-clock?"

"Such a man," said Polidori, "would certainly be a monster. A creature like that would be incapable of human emotions."

"And if he felt them," said Claire, "they would find some terrible outlet. Such a man would turn into a torturer or a madman, or even a murderer."

I lit a candle and set it on the table. Then I stood in front of the fire and recited some verses from Coleridge's *Christabel*. I lowered my voice to a low ghoulish tone when I read about the witch, "Hideous, deformed, and pale of hue . . ."

At this point poor young Shelley, who sat in the corner, uttered a shriek. He snatched at the candle and went racing out of the room. I ran after him and found him in the library, leaning limply against the mantelpiece. He seemed stricken with ague and on the verge of epilepsy. I threw water in his face and Polidori gave him ether. Then we led him back to the drawing-room, where he sank into a chair.

"It is dangerous," said Mary, glancing irritably at her husband, "to excite such an elfin-spirit with tales of monstrosity."

We climbed to our bedrooms and I lay on my bed, hoping to finish *Moll Flanders* before blowing out the candle.

The thunder had stopped and I nibbled at some grapes. There was a knock on the door and then another, very delicate.

"Who is it?" I snapped.

The door opened: it was Claire.

"Forgive me," she said, tightening her nightgown about her.

I said crossly, "It's three o'clock. Rather late for a visit, isn't it?"

"I couldn't sleep. I kept hearing strange noises below my window."

"Ghosts, presumably."

"Could it be burglars?"

"My dear Claire," I said acidly, "they are neither ghosts nor are they burglars. They are figments of your fancy. Go to bed."

She looked at me desperately and sat down on the edge of the couch. "My dearest Albé," she whispered (she had invented this silly nickname), "you probably think that I'm nothing but a harlot . . ."

"Not in the least," I said sarcastically. "You are as pure as the driven snow."

She leant over and fondled my shoulder-blade. "Cruel!" she purred. "You prancing centaur!"

"Claire," I said, "this is not the moment for verbal convolutions. Go to your bedroom and we'll save all this nonsense for the breakfast-table."

She lowered her head and laid it on the pillow and peered at me kittenishly. "Naughty Albé," she whimpered. "Have you no sympathy with a soul in torment?"

"You are merely a school-girl who is suffering from green sickness."

"A school-girl!" she cried. "Listen, Albé! Little you know! You would shudder if I told you some of the things that I did in London." She looked at me solemnly. "Yes, I'm a harlot, a Messalina, and if I told you some of my doings you would blush with disgust. Well, I shan't. You're too naïve. Oh, you think of yourself as a profligate, but it's clear to a practised eye that you're as innocent as a new-born baby. Poor little

145

Albé, if only you knew . . ." She turned over and gazed at the ceiling, and one of her breasts slid through the lace of her collar.

My poor Claire! What is wickedness? What is innocence, what is guilt? Who can tell? Maybe you were right, maybe it was you who were rotting inwardly, and maybe it was I who was still cradled in Edenesque simplicity. Maybe there is a wickedness that festers in chastity and a purity that flowers in profligacy. Maybe, maybe. I am never sure. One can never be sure. Love is a conundrum.

3 March

Young Loukas has just left me. I can hear his footsteps down the hall. I can feel the touch of his hand on my wrist, as light as thistledown.

Is there a pattern in all this? Is there a meaning in this sprawling destiny? Is it a destiny? Or just a series of charades *en route* to Nothingness? All the follies and cruelties, the lusts, the betrayals—were they sign-posts on the path to peace and salvation? Or were they merely the wild gesticulations of a madman?

I am afraid that I shall never know the answer to this question, which is the deepest and most formidable of all my questions.

*

How gently the morning came, how quietly the evening fell! How green were the trees, how white the mountains, how clear the water! The air of summer hung over the place like a glass bell, and even the birds were scarcely audible as they twittered in their branches.

One fine morning Shelley and I started on a trip from Diodati. We packed some sausages and cheese and set forth in our little boat. We followed the shores of the lake as far as Meillerie. It was a warm and windless day and we looked at the "land-marks" of Rousseau, whom both of us venerated, though Shelley more than I. We had tea with toast and honey, and I said to him casually, "It is rather a relief to be away from the women, isn't it, Shelley?"

"One is always," nodded Shelley, "rather on tenterhooks with women."

"I am not," I said, "a pederast, and I find women sexually delectable, but their psychological intimacy grows tiring after a point."

Shelley looked at me reproachfully. "You are putting it rather brutally. If you think of the female sex purely as copulatory receptacles, then their company grows cloying, I quite agree, like a puff of cream. But I regard them as human beings. They are generous and subtle-minded, and I find them much more patient and compassionate than men."

"True enough," I retorted, "so long as they are sexually satisfied. When their passions are unreciprocated they turn into witches. If I were stranded on a desert island, with nothing but coconuts and pineapples, I'd rather be trapped with a male than a female, I assure you."

"Strange," he said. "Your very virility makes you intolerant of women. And I suppose it's the female element in me (though I am far from being a pathic) which makes me sympathetic to a woman's mentality."

"Speaking," I said, "of desert islands: imagine yourself on a lonely isle. Which books would you choose, if you were restricted to only three?"

Shelley smiled like a child. He licked the honey from his spoon. "A tantalizing choice. Shakespeare, of course, with all his vulgarities, for Shakespeare alone has a way of perpetually renewing himself. I've read *Hamlet* seven times and each

147

time it seemed utterly new. And why? Because he never pronounces a fixed set of opinions, so that his lines perpetually shimmer with fresh and startling undertones."

"I too would pick Shakespeare," I remarked, "but for different reasons. Shakespeare alone, as you say, defies critical analysis. But while you are dazzled by his intellectual fluidity, I am beguiled by his human subtleties. His characters live in a world which is as legendary as Homer's, but unlike Homer's they keep revealing the ambiguities of human nature. Their behaviour is never stylized, it is never predictable or true to a pattern. They are never merely literary. They shiver and reverberate, like life itself."

Shelley glanced at a wasp which had fallen into the tea-cup. "Look! How beautiful it is—all black and yellow, like a little jewel!"

"And after Shakespeare?" I insisted.

"Oh, after Shakespeare . . . Nobody, nobody! I might pick Sophocles, but even Sophocles would hardly survive a diet of coconuts. No, leave me alone with my darling Shakespeare in the Pacific. Even Homer would wilt away in a climate of typhoons . . ."

The sky was blue as an iris when we sailed from Meillerie, but then it suddenly turned a menacing purple. The peaks, which had flashed in the sunlight, now shone with a liverish pallor. A violent wind came up and great waves slapped at our boat. We had an idiot of a boatman who refused to lower the sail, and it seemed that the craft was going to be driven under the water. My jacket was dripping and Shelley's face was covered with foam. I grabbed an oar and passed it to Shelley (who had never learnt to swim) and said firmly, "If the boat turns over, cling to the oar and I'll tug you ashore. But be careful not to struggle. All will be lost if you start to flounder!" And Shelley answered coolly, "My dear Byron, please don't fret about me. I'd rather drown quietly than drag you along to the bottom of the lake . . ."

The storm sank to a lull and we slid into shelter at St Gingolph, and walked to an inn which was hidden behind some elm-trees. We bathed and had our supper and then sat in the wine-cellar, where Shelley spent the evening reading Jean-Jacques Rousseau. The next day was calm and we sailed to Chillon, and from there we sailed to Clarens and Vevey and Ouchy. It was at the Hôtel de l'Ancre in Ouchy that the rain started to pour again, and I stayed in my room and wrote *The Prisoner of Chillon*.

We met for dinner in the dining-room, which was bleak and deserted, and we dined on boiled trout, followed by a bowl of wild strawberries.

Shelley said, "I have just finished reading the *Nouvelle Héloise*. Rousseau was a genius undoubtedly but there are moments when he seems like a fool."

"All geniuses perhaps have a touch of the asinine about them. Look at Shakespeare himself. Why on earth did he marry the Hathaway?"

"If Shakespeare were to walk into this dining-room," said Shelley, "do you think that we'd recognize him as an extraordinary personage?"

I reflected for a moment. "Far from likely. His face was amorphous. His head was shaped like an egg and his eyes looked like a rabbit's. If he came and sat at our table we'd think he was a draper from Nottingham."

Shelley looked at me sadly. "Yes, I knew that you were arrogant. Mary told me that you spoke of Keats as a 'potato-eating poetaster'. Tell me, Byron, how do you reconcile your anti-oligarchal theories with your scorn for those poor devils who are afflicted with a Cockney accent?"

"Theories are one thing," I said loftily, "and God knows that I'd like equality. But such being not the case, at least at the present point of history, I prefer my friends to smell like roses rather than stink like old billy-goats."

Shelley glared at me furiously and set his wine-glass in the middle of the table, where a bowl of half-wilted daisies was sitting. "You of all men," he squealed, "have least reason to be a hypocrite! You keep damning the English hypocrisy, and you're totally right in doing so, but I tell you, your pose of a so-called liberalism is a sham! You're a snob! You positively reek of a country squire's smugness, and permit me to say that your verses will suffer as a result of it!"

His face was pink with rage and I took his hand gently. "Forgive me. You are right. I'm a snob as well as a hypocrite. I only hope that the passage of time, with its attendant humiliations, will eventually purge my spirit of arrogance and fraudulence."

Shelley looked at me furtively, not quite sure whether I was teasing him, but then he smiled sweetly and we started to speak of other things, such as Mary's idea for a novel, which was to deal with a fabricated monster, and Polidori's poeticizings, which struck us both as ludicrous. The light was shining on Shelley's face, which changed continually, like a fluttering leaf. The irises of his eyes kept changing colour with his changing moods. I watched his face intently but I could not get at the secret of it. I felt that I was sitting beside a water-sprite or a merman.

The rain came to a stop and we strolled along the shore. A path led past a wall and through an alley of *arbor vitae*. At an end of the alley stood a bench beside a fountain. We sat and looked at the stars, which shone with a post-tempestuous brilliance.

"Assuming," said Shelley, "that the stars are an assortment of bodies, some of them vast, some of them small, some of them hot and some of them icy, it seems reasonable to suppose that some of them are inhabited."

"Reasonable enough," I agreed, "since there are millions and millions of them. Some no doubt are sheeted with fire, others with stalactites of ice, but of those millions of stars two or three are doubtless inhabited. But inhabited by what? Titanic monsters or tiny fleas?"

"Both, no doubt. If you go far enough, among those millions of planets, you'll surely find a star which has a species resembling our own. And keep on searching and you'll find (for that is the meaning of infinity) a planet which exactly resembles our own. It is even possible, indeed it is probable, that amongst all those millions there is one where a pair of poets, named Shyron and Belley, are sitting on a bench and looking at the galaxies, and wondering whether somewhere there are poets who resemble them."

I looked at Shelley teasingly. "It is conceivable, but fantastically improbable."

"It was already," he said, "fantastically improbable that we should ever be sitting here!"

Curious, I thought, and I still think so. Shelley's mind was the opposite of mine, yet an undercurrent of harmony existed between the two of us. We were both of us exiles and both of us rebels, but he was soaked in abstractions while I revelled in realities. He was far more intelligent than I: he was capable of deep concentration, and he moved from thought to thought with an effortless coherence. My mind compared to his was as wayward as a butterfly's. And still, in spite of his sincerity, I found him unfathomable. He was tinged with an inner ghostliness. Even his face had a silvery abstractedness. I never saw him naked but it was hard for me to visualize, under those loose-fitting clothes of his, two testicles and a penis. As for myself, women have told me they can read me like a book, and that my character to them is as "clear as a window-pane". And yet Shelley, with all his insight, utterly failed to grasp my nature. There we were in Ouchy, sitting on a bench beside the lake and gossiping away with the greatest spontaneity. And yet we were as impenetrable, each to the other, as the Sphinx. Shelley's heart was as fresh as a child's and his mind was as pure as a crystal: beside him I felt shaggy and brutish, like a satyr. But I never understood him. He remained a total mystery. Him alone I adored unselfishly, and him alone I loved without fleshliness.

But then why, after a while, did I come to resent the man?

4 March

I have read through yesterday's entry. I cannot help wondering. In this struggle for exactitude am I being led astray? Do I imagine certain tiny details which never existed? Was there really a wasp in the tea-cup and an aisle of *arbor vitae*? When things flow into the cave of the past they are gone for ever, whatever the clever philosophers may say about the matter. And what we recapture is only an emblematic fragment which is suited to our emotional demands at the moment. I remember the rain dripping from the ruins at Newstead Abbey, I remember King's Chapel by the light of the moon, but my memories, however vivid, are merely selections and distillations. And all those accompanying elements, the rattling leaves and the thundering organ-music, I merely remember as a hiatus, like a forgotten line in a sonnet. I know that they existed but their actual texture I conjure out of nothingness. And thus we are forced into falsity by our very search for the truth.

And still, I must go on. I must try to remember, even though falsely.

*

The chrysanthemums lost their petals and the air grew crisp and burnished. At night I could hear the crab-apples falling into the grass. Autumn came and the visitors moved away from their villas. Tufts of pine-smelling smoke rose from the cottages of the shepherds.

The Shelleys, along with Claire, had left Switzerland for England, and Hobhouse came to Coligny and we decided to drive to Venice. So we stepped one autumn morning into my Napoleonic coach and we followed Napoleon's road in the direction of the Simplon. The road grew steadily steeper, we passed chasms and cataracts, and the horses started to pant as they climbed up the slopes. The oaks gave way to evergreens and the evergreens to lichen. The cow-bells were tinkling on the grassy mountainside and once we saw a goat-herd playing his pipe on top of a cliff. Once we heard the sound of an avalanche falling in the distance, and once we saw a waterfall that looked like a braid of snow. It was a world of transparencies, wild and ancient and patriarchal, and as we climbed it seemed to recede into its pre-historical guiltlessness.

We crossed the great pass and rode down through the ravines and entered the darkening valley of Domodossola. We stopped at Lake Maggiore and rowed out to Isola Bella, where I looked with veneration at the bed of Napoleon Bonaparte. We rose before dawn and crossed the meadows of Lombardy, where the poplars were bright with the gold of autumn. It was dusk when we came to the walls of Milan and we stopped at the dirty old inn of San Marco.

I took a box at La Scala. We saw an opera by Paisiello—something silly about two princesses disguised as a pair of milkmaids. During the interval a Frenchman, a certain Monsieur Beyle, one of Napoleon's former secretaries, was brought to my box. We chatted about Italy and I said, "Do you like Milan? Aside from the cathedral I see nothing that appeals to me."

"Milan," said Monsieur Beyle, "is a special taste, like a trout in aspic. The Roman god is Eros, the Florentine god is Vulcan, the god of Venice is Mercury, and the Milanese god is Mars. The Milanese are bigger and braver than other Italians, and if their manners seem aggressive, well, just remember, it's the tradition."

"You prefer the Italians to the French?"

Monsieur Beyle regarded me shrewdly. He was a big-buttocked person with a face like a bread-pudding, but his eyes, though blurred with myopia, shone with a pitiless intelligence.

"The Italians are adorable but *au fond* they lack mystery. Life is exquisite in Italy but in the end atrociously boring. The French are occasionally nasty but at least they have depth. The Italians live on the surface. Their life is in the piazza. They feel passions, *bien sûr,* but they are the passions of the opera, full of gestures and grimaces, accompanied by a fine melodious resonance."

I liked this Monsieur Beyle and I called to an usher and asked him to bring us a bottle of champagne. The chandeliers were burning, having been lit by a bevy of pages, and the audience was walking about in the corridors. I looked at the pit, where a number of ladies were reclining, and I was struck by the cataract of silks and brocades. Milan is the city of silk as well as the city of Mars, and under its war-like surface lurks a wild, steamy opulence.

"And the English?" I said. "What do you think of the English?"

"Ah, the English!" Monsieur Beyle lowered his face and frowned a little. He looked like a bull-dog, blunt and formidable, yet beguiling. "I have always revered the English. They glide through the sea with a ravishing elegance but their eyes have a chilly, almost treacherous gleam in them. Even their bodies have a piscine musk that clings to them, though whether it's merely the effect of a diet of fish, I cannot say. I venerate the English and especially 'the happy few' but I'll never put my eggs in the basket of an English bosom!"

He raised his champagne-glass and patted my arm affectionately. "Always excepting your beautiful self, needless to say, Your Lordship! You are English but thoroughly un-English. You will never be buried in Westminster Abbey!"

I rode back to the hotel and climbed to my room, still reflecting on the words of the ambiguous Monsieur Beyle. I stepped into my night-shirt and was about to blow out the candle when I saw in the mirror that the door was opening behind me. I had forgotten to lock it; I reached quickly for my pistol, but then I saw that the silhouette was that of a woman.

I turned suavely and bowed.

"Might I be of use to you, madame?"

She was wearing a sea-blue dress which was studded with emeralds. In her hand she held a fan; a withered rose was pinned to her breast. She was tall, blonde and slender: not my sort, as it happened. Her dress had a mottled and undulous look to it. She might have come from a ball, disguised perhaps as a Swedish sea-goddess. She was wildly, unbelievably, and almost ludicrously beautiful.

The expectant smile on her lips died abruptly when she saw me. She blushed and recoiled. "I beg your pardon. I have made a blunder . . ."

I looked at her guiltily, as though it were I who had intruded on her. I stepped behind the table where the candle was burning, hoping to mitigate the look of my night-shirt.

"Not in the least," I said quickly. "Where have I met you? Was it at the opera-house?"

She shook her head mournfully and opened her fan a little.

Then she whispered, "Good-night, my dear . . ."

"Please!" I pleaded. "Won't you stay for a moment?"

She merely smiled with a desperate melancholy and then stepped into the hall again and closed the door silently but firmly behind her.

I stood paralysed for an instant. I ran to the door and

threw it open. I held up the candle and peered into the corridor. There was nothing to be seen except, for a brief illusory moment, a faint shred of light that resembled a floating handkerchief.

I quietly closed the door again. A breeze seeped through the window and I caught, ever so faintly, a whiff like a cadaver's.

5 March

A young Suliote is singing in the court-yard below my window. His voice has a melancholy whine to it, eerie, barbaric. Is he serenading me? I doubt it. But in Missolonghi nothing is impossible.

A magnificent moth, a Death's Head, has flown into my room. It settled confidingly on the arm of my chair. I put down my book and crushed its body between my fingers. I watched its pointed penis twisting and jutting as it died. Then I opened the window and threw the corpse into the night. My fingers are still covered with the scales of its abdomen.

The Suliote fell silent, but now he has started to sing again.

And a sickening surge of self-hatred has filled me.

*

And so finally we came to Venice. I left my coach at an inn in Mestre, and as we stepped into a gondola the rain started to pour again. We slid over the water towards the island in the distance, which was hidden by the rain and the thick black curtains of the gondola. Then the rain stopped abruptly. The lights of Venice shone in front of us. We entered a canal and watched the palaces glide past us. Our boatman cried "the Rialto!" We passed under a bridge and soon after we touched the pier of the Hotel Grande Bretagne, where a servant seized our bags and led us to a damask-lined drawing-room.

We dined on little prawns with a green garlic sauce. Then we sauntered down the alley towards the Piazza of San Marco. We walked through an archway and beheld a looming emptiness. I was fiercely disappointed. It looked desolate and gloomy, spreading darkly behind its monotonous colonnades. Then we stepped into the Piazza and through the gloom, like a sea of phantoms, the breath-taking splendour of the place suddenly revealed itself. At the end, half-invisible, crouched the ancient basilica with its gold shining dimly behind the lamps like an opening Sesame. Beside it rose the fierce phallic spire of the Campanile. We stood in an isolated world where time and space had coagulated, and the strangest feeling of all was that I had been here before, not in my present random identity but in some twin-like embodiment, which had experienced in the past some lurking intensity which still awaited me.

I paused in the archway, trying to absorb this adumbration. Then the lights in one of the coffee-houses started to twinkle. Hobhouse took me by the arm and we strolled through the columns and over our cups we chatted merrily about Goldoni.

We went prowling, sniffing and fondling and peering for several days. Once we visited the monastery on the isle of San Lazzaro, and once the isle of Murano where the glass-blowers live. I decided to abandon the costly Grande Bretagne and found some rooms in the Frezzeria, not far from the basilica, in the house of a chamois-eyed draper named Segati. I settled in my lodgings (which cost twenty francs a day) and decided to soak myself in the full Venetian atmosphere. I took lessons in Armenian at the flea-ridden monastery. I scrutinized the manuscripts in the Marciana library. I stared at the great deluge of Tintorettos in the Doge's Palace. I went to the plays at the Fenice and to the *balli* at the Ridotto. I bought some lace handkerchiefs and a dozen fluted goblets. I behaved quite naïvely and impeccably *en touriste*.

One day I was sitting in my room, scribbling busily at *Manfred* (which I now can't help thinking was a rather hectic concoction). The sun streamed through the window and the townsmen lay in their siesta. There was a rap on the door and Marianna, the draper's wife, poked her curly little head through the opening doorway.

"Are you busy, Your Excellency?"

"Not inordinately," I said, and I placed my pen in the dolphin pen-holder.

She walked towards the desk and lifted her hand with a woeful expression. "Forgive me," she said. "There's a splinter in my thumb . . ."

I nodded and held her hand. Then I took a pin from my waistcoat and very deftly, with an air of gravity, extracted the splinter. A drop oozed from the finger-nail and (stirred perhaps by some childhood memory), I leant down and licked the blood from the tip of her thumb.

"Oh, Your Excellency!" she cried.

"Hush," I said, "or someone will hear you."

She smiled. "He's sleeping soundly. There's no danger of his hearing us . . ."

Marianna, like Mary Chaworth, had enormous brown eyes. But Mary Chaworth smelled like a rose-bud and Marianna like a full-blown tiger-lily. We lay on the couch in the deep yellow sunlight and I whispered: "But your husband? He'll be furious if he ever discovers us!"

"Not in the least," said Marianna. "Like as not he'll be pleased as Punch. If you were a Venetian he would kill you. But being a Lord, he'll take it as a compliment."

I murmured, "I see. A Venetian custom, I presume."

158

"The Venetians," she said, "are pardonably proud of their hospitality."

I was delighted with Marianna, but Marianna was not Madame de Staël, and after a fortnight or two her line of chatter grew repetitious. Every day, on the stroke of two, she crept to my room with a furtive air (which, since secrecy was superfluous, had a purely aphrodisiac intention). We lay naked in the sunlight, nibbling at a bowl of candied cherries, and she told me how the butcher had cheated her out of a cutlet or how she had bought an apron in the Campo San Lucca. She told me how her cousin Angela was suffering from piles and her uncle Peppino was down with gonorrhea. Gradually our gossip grew fitful and we subsided into coition. Marianna's sexual repertory was more varied than her conversational one, and I remember how once, when one of the cherries had mysteriously vanished, she forced me to find it blindfold with the tip of my tongue.

"Naughty girl," I said reproachfully. "Did you invent this prankish game?"

"It's an old Venetian custom," said la Segata with a casual titter.

6 March

Something queer has just happened. I was leafing through an old book which I bought in Ravenna.

I was looking at a picture of Penelope with her suitors. She was wearing a large perruque in the style of Madame de Pompadour. Suddenly I noticed a brownish spot at the bottom of the page. I ignored it and continued to gaze at the engraving, especially the little spaniel who was nibbling at a bone under the banquet-table.

Then I saw that the spot had moved. It had crept from the edge of the picture and was lodged on the floor between

Penelope's slippers. I drew my thumb across it, trying to rub it away. It refused to be budged. It looked like a stain of wet tobacco.

I kept studying the picture, one of the suitors in particular, a young athlete in a helmet who reminded me of the Cid. Then I saw that the spot had moved again. It was crouching on Penelope's shoulder. I touched it: it felt warm and slightly hairy, like rabbit's fur. It resembled, it occurred to me, a very small orang-outang.

I picked up some sandpaper and tried to erase the spot. It refused to be erased and kept on staring at me balefully. Finally I ripped out the page and held it over the candle-flame, and as it burned I could hear a vicious little scream, like that of a rat.

*

More and more I am coming to realize that these "memoirs" are not really memories. I write down what I remember or think I remember: but immediately a three-fold screen arises between the words and the reality. First, my vision becomes selective: out of the jumble of the past it chooses not the ordinary (which, after all, is the flesh of life) but the strange, the enigmatic, the bizarre, even the repulsive. I choose to remember not a milkmaid carrying her bucket but a withered old duchess dying of cholera in Cadiz. And second: in the act of putting my vision into words, I am embellishing, distorting, I am stylizing and dramatizing. For it is language, perversely, which strives for exactitude, yet falls further than music from human truth or sensual exactitude. I start a paragraph: and I am raising the curtain on a stage. I choose an epithet: and I am placing a mask on the truth. And third. Try as I may to distil the essence from each memory, strive as I may to pierce the core and discern the fateful significance, I know that I fail. The hidden meaning remains elusive. I struggle to unveil the mystery only to confront a deeper mystery. As I weave this passionate web of bygone terrors and delights, there is born a new capacity for terror and delight. And so the poet, with his three-fold screen, is not only looking for immortality but is locked in a feverish struggle with his fear of approaching death.

Venice! Yes. Let me try to recapture the "human truth", the "sensual exactitude".

I never grew weary of exploring the labyrinths of Venice. I loved to follow the alleys towards the northern quays of the island and to peep through the doors into the candle-lit shops. I watched the cobbler hammering at his leather and the tailor stitching his uniforms. I watched the carver blowing the gold-leaf on his fluted candelabras and the puppet-maker gluing the wigs on his puppets. A whiff of warm loaves came filtering out of the baker's shop and in the butcher's a row of ducks hung from their hooks, upside down. Towards nightfall the air was filled with a furtive animation. The pimps peered from their doorways and the smugglers unfolded their wares. In a nook near the Campo San Angelo some rascals gathered at night and hovered behind a trellis. Some of these *ragazzi* were pale and effeminate, fluttering their arms and chirping like sparrows; others were stalwart and athletic, with blue-striped shirts and burlap breeches. *"Bello, bello! Carissimo!"* cried the sparrows, rattling their bracelets, while the bullies growled softly, *"Ciao, signor! Un piccolo pompino?"* Once I saw, as I stepped behind the trellis to relieve myself, a little white jelly-fish floating in a pool of stale urine.

(Every Italian metropolis had its sexual speciality, I discovered, as though the centuries of tradition had wrought their own little propensities. In Pisa it was one thing and in Genoa it was another. In Padua it was sodomy and in Venice fellation. Some great scholar may eventually make a study of

161

this phenomenon and produce a learned treatise on the influence of geography on lust. It is time that the realms of sex were removed from mystification. What old magician, with his wicked wand, has touched each precinct with its own dark longings? Why do the Turks go in for buggery and the French for *soixante-neuf?* Why do the Germans like to whip and why do the English like to be whipped? Why do the Hottentots love toes, why do the Eskimos love noses? Is it all to be ascribed to a thing of local ingredients, like a Frenchman's love of truffles or the Portuguese love for cod? Cunnilingus, I hear, is very prevalent in Persia, and a worship of boots in Mecklenburg-Schwerin. I am unfortunately not a scholar and my experiences are sadly limited, but the crannies of human lust cry for an explorer as much as the jungles of Borneo.)

Winter came and the season of Carnival. Gilded lanterns hung from the gondolas and the sound of violins echoed from the shades of the Rialto. The secrets of the city emerged through the fogs of mid-February. As I crossed the flooded Piazza I saw a raft of drunken revellers. As I stood under a window I saw a medley of lamp-lit dominoes. As I strolled down the *riva* in the mist before dawn I saw two little waifs making love in a watery portico.

Late one night I was returning from a *bal masqué* at the Countess Albrizzi's. The city was dark and the noise of revelry had ended. I was drunk from too much wine and went staggering past a bridge. Humming a tune from Pergolesi (*La Serva Padrona,* as I recall) I opened my flies and started to piss into the darkness. But alas (as sometimes happens) a casual fold diverted the stream and soaked my samite breeches in a cataract of urine. I growled with dismay and was in the act of adjusting my buttons when I noticed a young lady hurrying through the darkened colonnade. It was a girl in a white perruque, dressed in a voluminous silken dress. She had the air of a raffish, slightly elongated du Barry.

A little black beauty-spot was glued to her painted chin. Behind the mask I could see that her features, though angular, were young and beautiful. She paused and boldly approached me on the moonlit *fondamenta.*

"Alone, at this hour?"

"Quite alone, as it happens."

"Are you English?" said the lady.

"I am Patagonian," I said genially.

"Ah," she cooed, "you are trying to fox me! I know an Englishman when I see one. As for Patagonia, I rather doubt whether such a country really exists. My mother, who comes from Mantua, said that there are dragons in Patagonia. I don't suppose that you are willing to throw some light on the matter?"

"Your mother spoke the truth. There are dragons in Patagonia, but they are harmless and quite tame, and are used at night instead of warming-pans."

The lady flicked her wrist with a graceful coquettishness. "What a liar you are, signor. Warming-pans! I refuse to believe it. Once I heard that in Scotland they use snakes as a cure for sterility, and in Sicily they put spiders in the soup to cure lumbago."

"You are an expert," I said, "of medical lore, I am glad to see."

She looked at me thoughtfully and murmured, *"Molto bello!"*

She drew me under the bridge and kissed me on the cheek. Then she calmly, without preamble, opened the buttons of my breeches. She knelt and fondled me lightly (though with obvious expertness) and I lifted her skirt, which was of a Nattier-blue taffeta, and started to explore the hidden realms of her anatomy. She shrank back at the crucial moment, muttering something about a "lunar affliction", and begged me to do with a "second-to-best", which meant, as it developed, a *coitus in anum.* (This wasn't the first time that I had

163

to do with this slovenly substitute, for Lady Caroline, once or twice, offered a similar suggestion.) During the process, however, as I toyed with the lady's thighs, I was shocked to discover that it wasn't an orifice I was fondling but a blunt and rigid article, the approximate size of a cucumber. I finished my performance in a state of dejection (I had abandoned all such practices since my visit to the Greek peninsula) and murmured with regret, *"Buona notte, signor."*

"Arrivederci, amore," chirped the scoundrel unrepentingly. He patted his skirt into place with a wink and went waddling cheerfully off in the darkness.

I am offering this sultry episode to the pages of my notebook not in a spirit of vulgar ribaldry, nor even of moral didacticism, but merely as a comment on human ambivalence. Are we guilty of a sin though unaware that we are committing it?

But such was Venice. Like vice itself, she was a woman with many faces. She was grand but also stinking; she was wise but given to folly. Some great scholar one day may explore the delta of human frailties, but even he will hardly suspect its infinite rivulets and tributaries.

7 March

Fowke and Finlay came again, and we had some solemn conversation. I cannot help wondering, are they inspired by a zest for true enlightenment? Or is it merely a kind of *parvenu* curiosity, a desire to return to Boston with a feather in their cap?

"Herr Goethe," mentioned Fowke, "spoke of Your Lordship with enthusiasm. He stated that your talent is infinitely greater than you realize. But I suspect that he regards you as a symbol rather than purely as a *Dichter*. His admiration (as he put it) was that of Apollo for Bacchus. He envies the 'elemental fire' in you, compared to his own marble discipline."

"Herr Goethe," argued Finlay, "was fiddling with words, I can't help thinking. He himself is really a blending of Apollo and Bacchus. His Apollonian side is touched with a burning nostalgia and his Bacchic side is controlled by an iron sense of form. Where in England do you find such a blending of two opposites?"

"These two opposites," I hinted, "are only apparent. They are not real. Every poet contains a blending of Apollo and Bacchus. Apollonian, Bacchic—do these words have any meaning? The true Apollonian, as opposed to a dusty pedant, is merely an artist who moulds into shape the Bacchic urge in him, and the true Bacchic, as opposed to a common *débauché*, is merely an artist who sets fire to his sense of order. Indeed, the convergence of these two is the secret of poetry. I am convinced that there is a single essential ingredient in all great poetry. It is hard to find the word. Let us call it divination. Forget the passion, forget the intelligence, forget the music, forget the imagery. These together will blend into poetry, but the ultimate magic will still be lacking."

I could see that Fowke was listening with his owlish eyes a-glitter, and Finlay cocked his head, as though making a mental transcript.

"Think of Shakespeare," I went on, carried away by my bibulous fluency. "Shakespeare is the Satan of the Rationalists, the Great Enigma, the Prince of Paradoxes. There have been other poets as great, perhaps, but none quite so spectacular. How did he do it? Heaven knows. Homer is plausible, Dante is plausible, but Shakespeare alone defies rational explanation. We are forced to conclude that poor old Shakespeare was a monster. Only a monster could have produced that preposterous magnificence, which is held together by no discernible mental coherence, no moral postulate, no human philosophy, no stylistic redundancy or emotional consistency. No, there is nothing to suggest that a single man could have written the plays, except for that one ingredient: a miraculous power of divination."

Finlay said: "Don't you feel that a poet has a duty to society, Your Lordship? If a poet were to preach wickedness would he still be a poet?"

"Plato," I answered, "in his arrogance (or maybe it was treachery more than arrogance) excluded the poet from his perfect Republic. He regarded the poet as a disrupter, a force for anarchy and decadence. Blind old Plato! Couldn't he see that only the poet's challenging anarchy can save a society from being strangled by the dogmatists and the men of science?"

"You hate men of science, Your Lordship?" murmured Fowke, wincing slightly.

"I neither love them nor hate them. They have done some things, no doubt, that are good for us. But in the end, five hundred years from now, when *homo sapiens* has reaped the fruits of science and the individual spirit has been snuffed out by the dogmatists, the end will finally come. The *raison d'être* will have vanished. It has happened to other animals when the fire has gone out of them. It will happen to man when the zest for life has been crushed in him. The wish for death will prevail and the human race, having multiplied beyond endurance, will rush headlong into suicide."

"You said decadence, Your Lordship," put in Finlay. "What is decadence?"

"It is a natural phenomenon, like the plums that rot in an orchard. There are virtues in decadence, just as there is beauty in a tree in autumn. The poet, in his indifference to the scientists and the dogmatists, can see what they cannot see: the secret sources of life. And that is what I mean by the poet's power of divination. Our *zeitgebundene* moralities have no relevance to truth or poetry. A poet speaks into

Eternity; our social edicts last only a decade—and a dismal and soul-diminishing decade at that!"

"It is all," said Fowke sadly, "most confusing and contradictory."

I filled up my glass. "Forget what I've told you," I muttered. "You will be so good as never to repeat it in Boston, I hope. And now, my good Finlay, tell me more about Herr Goethe. Does he wear gloves? Does he take snuff? Do his breeches fit him? Does he carry an umbrella?"

It was long after midnight when the two Americans said good-night to me. I sat with my glass and meditated in the dark as the dawn crept closer.

I spoke of the poet as a sacrificial goat, as it were, slaughtered on the altar of society for the sake of its own survival. And yet, and yet . . . There had been nights when I suddenly woke up in a fit of terror and felt that poetry in the end is only a futile, dangerous dream.

And yet, and yet . . . To the poet himself it may be a futile dangerous dream. For the poet himself the "salvation" is only momentary. Maybe the poet in the end does have a duty to society—though a darker obligation than is commonly supposed. Every poet must go through suffering: without suffering no poem can materialise, any more than a pearl can be created out of water. But in his poetry he finds the secret of subduing his hidden crisis, and this "victory", which he presents to the world in the form of a poem, is also a miraculous medicine in which his listeners find the strength to look at the chaos of existence and pronounce it bearable, and even magnificent.

*

Fowke and Finlay have exhausted me. I shall write no more to-day.

167

Again my boy Loukas is laid low with a fever. He lay sweating among the cushions. His eyes were glazed and his face was flushed. I have carried him to my couch and rubbed his forehead with cologne. Then I lay on the floor beside him and tried to fall asleep.

But I could not fall asleep. I got up in the middle of the night and started to scribble in my dirty little note-book. Now I sit with my pen in hand and my eyes keep turning towards Loukas. He is sleeping uneasily. He has thrown aside the coverlet. His mouth is half-open and his eyelids are twitching. His body is more slender than the usual Greek body; his chest is still hairless and a curving crease, like a youthful smile, reaches down from his hips towards the hairs of his pubis. He is uncircumcised; even his phallus has a dark, feverish look to it. As I look at Luke sleeping I feel that I am old, irrevocably old; and ugly, dreadfully ugly, phantasmally ugly. I feel that the sleeping boy is a reincarnation of my youthful self, and that I have turned into his ancestor, a wicked and ape-like ancestor.

I have opened the window. The smell of spring has invaded the air.

> *O Primavera! gioventù dell' anno!*
> *O Gioventù! primavera della vita . . .*

*

We rode down to Rome through the gullies of the Apennines, but my mind grows strangely lethargical when I think about Rome. The Forum, the Pantheon, the Colosseum—nothing but dust. The Tiber—nothing but a sewer. St Peter's —nothing but a hodge-podge. Hobhouse took me to the studio of a certain Herr Thorwaldsen, who finally agreed to make an illustrious marble bust of me. But something in the bust struck me as posthumous and even corpse-like. Everything in Rome struck me as posthumous. The dust of death hung over everything.

When I strolled in the Protestant Cemetery I caught the smell that rose from the graves. When I walked on the Palatine I saw the rats burrowing in the tunnels. When I sat in the Forum, gazing at the Arch of Septimius Severus, a dove fell out of the sky and lay bleeding at my feet. And one night in the Piazza di Spagna, on my way to the Opera, a horse suddenly collapsed and lay dead beside the fountain.

Even the sunlight in Rome had a posthumous glint to it. Walking down past the Quirinal I saw a pair of enormous horsemen whose bodies seemed to stir in the heat like awakening Titans. At dusk the Spanish Steps flowed down from the Trinità in a golden waterfall and the city sank back into a mythical stillness. In the Villa Borghése the tufts of light under the pines looked like a flock of sheep in Virgil's *Bucolics,* and the aprons of light under the arches of the Colosseum were toga-clad ghosts waiting for the coming of the lions.

Rome is beautiful no doubt. But its beauty is tinged with the cadaverous. I remember one day going to a public execution. Three thieves were to be beheaded in the middle of a piazza. Hobhouse thought this outrageous but I was driven by my taste for the sinister. I wore a *tête-de-nègre* waistcoat and fawn-coloured breeches and a sky-blue kerchief round my neck. I carried a cane and a pair of ivory opera-glasses, and I took my seat in the shade of a balcony. The procession entered the square, led by a row of masked priests, who were followed by a pair of half-naked executioners. Then came the trio of manacled criminals, followed by the effigy of the Christ of Death. Some soldiers surrounded the scaffold and the thieves approached the block. The first of the victims refused to die. He kept howling and kicking in spite of the priest's admonitions. He was a big thick-necked fellow and the hole in the head-block was too small for him and they pounded and squeezed his miserable body until it fit. The axe flashed and fell. The body jumped like a Punchinello. The head rolled from the block with its mouth still open in a scream. The blood shot from the neck like a burst of black oil. I felt dizzy and feverish. I took a generous pinch of snuff and then lifted my glasses to witness the second beheading.

Strangely enough, I hardly remember the second and third beheadings. The ferocity of the first had blunted my sensibilities. Even the two remaining victims themselves looked rather listless, as though the howls of their predecessor had drained them of feeling. The first beheading I watched with horror and the second with distaste, and the third with an indifference which bordered on boredom. I rose from my chair and wiped the sweat from my forehead. Then I threaded my way through the crowd towards my carriage.

What else is there to say? The sight of death is a frightful thing. Then why did I grow so jaded by this horrible spectacle? Was it (like copulation, which it strangely resembled) a feeling so climactic that it left me drained and impotent? Or was it *au fond* touched with a heart-rending banality, each death being in essence so very similar to other deaths, so that my mind refused to dwell for very long on the sight of death? *Hélas,* familiarity breeds contempt even for Death, and the crowd waddled home to their wives and maccaroni.

I hated Rome. I breathed a sigh of relief when I stepped into my carriage and headed for the cool, clean air of the Apennines.

9 March

No news. I had a silly little squabble with Mavrocordato, who insisted that one of his captains be given epaulettes for his uniform.

I feel slightly unwell. My head is throbbing. Have I caught malaria?

*

I returned to Venice for the summer and took a villa on the Brenta, some six or seven miles from the shores of the lagoon. It was an old converted convent with Palladian columns attached to the front of it, and it looked upon the dusty yellow highway to Padua. I sat in my garden and worked on *Childe Harold*. I rode in my gondola and swam in the Adriatic. At sunset I took a horse, usually my gelding, Bambino, and rode along the reed-speckled shores of the river.

La Fornarina! O, my bull-throated, lion-hearted beauty! Your teeth flashed like lightning, your voice boomed like a sea-gong, your love was like the waves of the Adriatic in a storm. But then why is my memory of your character so nebulous? Why have I nearly forgotten you? Why is your soul (for you had a soul, surely) no more vivid in my mind than that of my gelding Bambino?

One day I tethered my horse to a tree and sat on the shore, watching some women from La Mira flogging their laundry on the pebbles. It was a sultry afternoon; the daisies nodded their heads and the dragon-flies flashed in the sun like chips of mica. A shiny green frog sat on a stone and cocked his eye at me. One of the women caught my eye: a wild-eyed beauty with coal-black hair. She turned and started to whisper to the woman beside her, who pointed with a grin to the little copse which rose behind them, where a tumbledown chapel was tucked in the shade of the oleanders. My beauty grew pensive. She cast a slow, conniving glance at me. Then she rose from the grass and (ignoring the titters of her colleagues) walked sedately down the path and disappeared into the chapel.

I meditated a moment. Then I rose from the grass and

(likewise ignoring the leers of the laundresses) strolled casually towards the chapel. I opened the little door, which creaked on its hinges. The place smelled of mould and withered begonias. It was startlingly dark, for the oval window was covered with cobwebs. A rake and hoe, broken and rusty, stood in the corner. Along the wall stood a row of flower-pots and a dusty old wheelbarrow. And at the end (where once, no doubt, an altar had stood) sat my fiery-eyed laundress, half-invisible in the dusk but clearly in a state of amorous expectancy.

O dusty chapel, O broken flower-pots, O leaf-littered wheelbarrow! No longer lifeless and rejected but suddenly symbols and conspirators, yielding their own earthy spice to all the ceremonies of love! No bed was ever softer than those weed-tufted tiles, no perfume more suggestive than those wilted begonias! We made love without a word and without the usual courtly skirmishes, and at the end, after kissing both of her nipples, I murmured:

"What is your name, my pretty raven?"

"Margarita," she growled.

"Margarita what?"

"Margarita Cogni."

"And are you married?"

"I certainly am! My husband is a baker and they call me La Fornarina."

"You are charming, Margarita. Will you meet me again?"

"When, for instance?"

"Tomorrow?"

"Very well. Let's make it tomorrow."

"Here in the chapel?"

"Good enough. At ten in the evening. I'll carry a lantern."

"You won't forget?"

She snorted cheerfully. "I am not one to forget, *carino*. I'll tell my husband that I'm visiting my cousin Simonetta."

"Is your husband a jealous man?"

"Fearfully jealous. But a little stupid."

"You are a lamb, my Fornarina."

"And you are a bad, blood-thirsty wolf!"

"Good-bye, my lovely lamb . . ."

"Good-bye, my wicked wolf . . ."

And those were the nicknames that we clung to. She was my lamb and I was her wolf. But truth to tell, our rôles were altered as the summer gradually deepened. We made love on the shores of the Brenta by the light of the stars, we made love under the acacias to the chirping of the crickets, we made love in the stables with my gelding looming over us, we made love under the bridge behind Dolo by the light of the lantern. I grew more and more lamb-like in my meekness and docility; she grew more and more wolfish in her sumptuous southern energy. La Fornarina was certainly, of the women I have known, the most Bacchantic in her postures and the most Gargantuan in her appetites.

Late at night, when I sat alone by my three-armed candelabra, I struggled half-heartedly to finish the fourth of my cantos. But something was wrong. The "creative fire" had gone from my spirit. Could it be that the continual fountain which kept gushing from my membrum had desiccated the deeper, darker fountain of the mind? I grew haunted by my imperfections. I saw nothing but flaws in my verses. There were times when I even felt that I had gone wrong from the very beginning. Instead of achieving a "marble perfection" I had merely dabbled in lyrical felicities. Instead of reaching out for splendour I had merely indulged in a pyrotechnical onanism. I even suspected, at gloomy intervals, that poetry was not my calling. I grew more and more disgusted with the aimlessness of my life. Late one night, as the clock struck two, I even toyed with the thought of suicide. I picked up the small Castilian knife which lay on my desk and ran it over my wrist in a speculative way. Then it dawned on me that even in this there was a whiff of histrionics. I looked at the mirror:

and those deep, burrowing eyes of mine positively glowed with a fashionable, self-admiring misery. I burst into laughter and tossed the knife on the table. La Fornarina had emptied her poison into my bloodstream, but it was a venom of the flesh, thank God, and not of the spirit. I winked at my bust, with its cadaverous solemnity, and I blew out the candles and slipped cheerfully into bed.

10 March

I have been glancing through some entries in this miserable little journal. If a stranger were to happen upon these parts (which Heaven forbid!) he might feel that I am obsessed with the lower anatomical intimacies.

This is true and yet not true. All mortal men are thus obsessed—both potentates and plough-boys, the saints as well as the sinners. There is no escaping these lower intimacies, which are inevitable as the setting sun.

Throughout the history of literature there has been a certain primness, one might almost say a conspiracy of primness about these matters. I think of the poet Archilochus as a noble exception to this rule. The fragments of Archilochus radiate an earthy virility, which (far from being vulgar) is touched with elegance and even with heroism.

Madame de Staël once informed me that the tales of the Cherokee Indians have a similar sturdy testicular truthfulness. I wish that Madame de Staël had learnt a lesson from these savages. She was a highly intelligent woman. Why, when she picked up her pen, did she lapse into idiocy? I could hardly read *Corinne* without blushing at its vulgarity—for vulgarity consists of hiding, as ostentatiously as possible, certain natural and inevitable attributes of man. A fig-leaf is more vulgar than the naked membrum of Priapus himself.

The poetry of life does not reside in ornamentation: in

visions of roses and moonlight and nightingales. It lies in darker things. There is a link between dreams and poetry. I have never in my life dreamed of a rose or a nightingale. I have dreamed of snakes and spiders, of werewolves and vultures. I have dreamed of doubt and shame, and of terror and enigma. Why do we waste our precious life in conjuring up a substitute for it, in disguising our true selves and in living in a world of masks? To achieve a sense of existence we must dig into the dirt. To discover our own reality we must confront the Great Gorilla. There is more poetry in the seam of a scrotum which Archilochus celebrates than in a swarm of Johnny Keats's mellifluous nightingales.

*

The rains began to fall; the leaves of autumn swam on the Brenta. I left my coach and horses in their stable in Mestre and rode back to Venice in a golden-prowed gondola. There I settled for the winter in the Palazzo Mocenigo. It was a sumptuous gloomy edifice, quite the grandest of my residences, but (as usual in Venice) the rot of the sea had invaded it. The stairs were discoloured by floods and the damask hangings were rippled with mildew. Whole dynasties of rats had made their nests down in the cellar, where long-empty barrels lay floating among the garbage. I chose for my study a large vaulted music-room, whose walls were lined with mandolins, piccolos and flutes. Down below, in the butler's pantry, I kept my private zoo which consisted of three dogs and a cat and a magpie, as well as two monkeys called Rosie and Hannibal.

I was thirty years old. I stared at myself in the mirror, appalled by even the faintest suggestion of a gorbelly, and haunted by those half-perceptible folds above my hips. I struggled still more fiercely to control my silhouette. I went back to my diet of magnesium and soda-water. Even in

October, when the Lido was windy and desolate, I took my daily bath in the chilling Adriatic. And in November, when it finally grew too cold for a swim, I took my horses on a ferry and went galloping on the sands, sniffing at the cool salty air and watching the gulls circling dismally. I still remember riding back in my gondola at sunset with the mists gradually enveloping the city: the walls of the Doge's Palace catching the glint of the setting sun, and the bell-tower rising grimly over the gold of the basilica.

Late one night, after a particularly lavish ball at the Rezzonico, I was standing on the quay, slightly drunk, waiting for my gondola. I grew restless as my boatman threaded his way through the maze of gondolas. I snatched a torch from the doorman and jumped briskly into the water. (I was dressed, as luck would have it, as a periwigged Poseidon.) I swam through the swarm of gondolas which were waiting for the guests, holding the torch high over my head and singing an aria from *Figaro,* until finally my faithful Tita (his eyes full of tears) dragged me out of the water and tucked me safely into the gondola.

They called him Il Barbone (or even Il Barbaccio) but his name was Giovanni Battista Falcieri. (I can hear him at this moment snoring on his couch out in the hall.) He had thick curly hair and a prodigious-looking beard. His Herculean chest was covered with hair as thick as a bear's. He carried a stiletto and two pistols in his pocket and he looked distinctly formidable from a distance, even terrifying. But I knew my gentle Tita. His heart was like a child's. One night he came back to the palace reeling drunk and I said, "Where have you been, Tita?"

"Down by the Rialto, with the *ragazze,*" he chortled.

"How can they stand you, those *ragazze?* You stink like a turkey-cock."

"They love me, those *ragazze.* Stink or no, they still adore me."

"Women's tastes," I said deploringly, "are a mystery. No doubt about it."

"Not in the least," he said with a hiccup. "They are as simple as a pussy-cat. You keep wondering why the women love me. Here is the answer, Your Excellency!" He opened his flies, with an air of bravado blended with apology, and drew out his *cazzo* (which was certainly the biggest I had ever seen). He regarded it with the air of a youthful artist who is studying his masterpiece and pointed to a wart which was placed strategically at the end of it. "There is no mystery about it, Your Excellency. Women are beasts like all the rest of us. I give them pleasure, turkey or no, and they end by loving your dirty Tita!"

I decided rather desperately that my cultural tastes were being neglected. I embarked on a series of visits to La Fenice, the Venetian opera-house, where I saw that frightening work by Amadeus Mozart, *Don Giovanni*. (I won't embark on the numerous reflections which the structure of this work inspired in me, nor on the emotional revelations which were provided by its music.) I attended, at San Benedetto, the oratorios by Handel and Haydn, and in the lamp-lit Piazzetta the *Stravaganza* of Vivaldi. I also studied conscientiously the works of the great Venetian painters. I was awed by the Veronese's elegance and piqued by the fancies of Carpaccio. I was touched by Titian's tenderness and stirred by Tintoretto's grandeur. I infinitely preferred the floating cherubs of Tiepolo to the pissing little brats of the Flemish Rubens. But most of all I loved Giorgione. What I loved in Giorgione was something subtly similar to what I loved in Amadeus Mozart. In both I sensed the yearning for a world of human perfection against the ominous background of a dark and impenetrable Nature, which gave to their vision of life both a sensual delight and a brooding sadness. But I was struck by a crucial difference between the darkening skies of *Don Giovanni* and those of Giorgione's musical picnic, for Giorgione had taken refuge in the world of his dreams while Mozart was still bound to the joys and miseries of humanity. When I asked myself which was the more akin to my own talent (putting aside, of course, their incomparable artistic superiority) I realized that in my youth I had clung to the paradise of my dreams and that I was now being sucked, slowly but surely, into the mire of humanity.

As for Venice, in spite of its filth I found it more and more congenial. Plato said that the secret of art was to render visible the things that are invisible. The secret of Venice is the revelation of a world of darkness in terms of light, and its magic is nearly identical with the magic of art itself.

11 March

I am obsessed with the thought of Lepanto. Everything seems to hinge on Lepanto. Will I ever get these bullies on the road to Lepanto?

I have been noticing something curious as I write down these memoirs. I am not a superstitious man. I don't believe in apparitions, and I have never in my poems (unlike Coleridge or Shelley) been preoccupied with what are called "phantasmal phenomena". But something has changed of late. Is it the air in Missolonghi? Or is it that these ugly little note-books have been bewitched? My memories, as I write them, seem to slip into a new dimension. I smell, I hear, I feel, I shiver and sweat with the past. I ride on my chestnut stallion, I go rumbling through the Alps, I glide in my gondola past the stink of the Giudecca. But is it really the past or just a conjuring up of fancies? I experience once again all the deliria of the past: but their very immediacy makes them suddenly suspect. Were they real, these bygone passions, or is there something *trompe l'œil* about them? Do they merely *seem* real while the real events were crucially different? I cannot quite be sure. One can never be quite sure. And this plethora of memories has finally succeeded in changing my character—colours have changed, appetites have changed, even the style of my prose has changed. I used to like apples. Now I much prefer oranges. I used to like blue, now I definitely prefer crimson. I used to laugh at ghosts. Now I am wheedled into believing in them.

Is it the air of Missolonghi? Or is there a demon lurking in these note-books?

*

Shelley came. We went galloping down the Lido on our mares, and in the evening we rode back towards the darkening canals. On sunny afternoons the Euganean hills shone in the distance and the clouds had a towering, almost Himalayan look to them. I recall that once I asked the gondolier to pause for a moment and I pointed to the madhouse with its cone-topped bell-tower, which was ringing just then to call the lunatics to prayer.

Shelley shook his head wistfully. "Must even a madman pray to God?"

"The madman most of all! But is it God," I said, "or the Devil?"

We talked until midnight in my mandolin-lined music-room, especially about the riddle of Free-Will and Destiny.

Shelley reproached me once or twice for squandering my energies in debauchery, and I said: "You say I am dissolute, but how can this be evil? If it is my destiny to be dissolute then it would be evil to live in chastity!"

"Well, in that case," murmured Shelley, pressing his hand into a triangle, "you might as well argue that nothing in the world is really evil, since all that we do is merely in obedience to our animal destiny."

"Precisely," I retorted. "Would you call a cobra evil

179

merely because Nature has endowed it with a poisonous pair of fangs?"

"Then there is no such thing as Evil?"

"Only hypocrisy," I said. "For hypocrisy is a lie and a denial and a falsification. It is a nasty little mask which hides the truth of our character."

Shelley shook his head sadly. "I refuse to accept your theorem. You are reducing human beings to the level of animals. Evil exists, good exists, and they are both of them controllable. My very soul rebels at a denial of this. My faith in human progress is the very basis of my being. Without it there is no meaning in such thoughts as perfectibility. Without it we are slaves, nothing but slaves, eternal slaves."

"You are a Utopian, my good Shelley, and I am an irredeemable pagan. But it strikes me as odd that you are emotional in your very rationalism, while in my very instinctiveness I am calm as an oyster. Your bent towards transcendentalism springs from a streak of hysteria in you. The roots of your so-called 'liberalism' lie in a flutter of feelings and not, I'm afraid, in the coolness of reason."

There was a twanging of guitars below the triple-arched window. We walked across the room and leant over the window-sill. Two large lamp-lit gondolas were passing below us. In the first six musicians (all in black) were playing their water-music, while in the second some masqueraders (still wearing their masks) were singing and drinking. One of the ladies, dressed like Juno, with a peacock on her shoulder, lifted her arm when she saw Shelley, and waved at him coquettishly. Poor Shelley blushed like a child and waved his delicate fingers back at her. Then the boats slid off in the night and I murmured to Shelley, "Ah, the coolness of reason, Shelley! What wouldn't I give for it!"

What is truth? What is poetry? I used to feel like Mephistopheles. Now I feel like poor old Empedocles squatting on Etna. What is our malady in this age of "feverish excitements" and "gnawing melancholy", sultry longings for opium and oblivion-bringing climes?

It is the severance of our minds from the sensuous and visible world, of our inner convictions from humdrum reality; of the arrogant and dogmatical separation of faith from that very human plight which the dogmatists pretend to ennoble. And that's why dogmatists are swine. Seeking ostensibly for truth, they wallow in the mire of their own self-falsification.

In short, what has happened to many of us, to Wordsworth, to Shelley and even to myself, is the severance of our inner from our outer existence, and the severance of the outer from the world of our imagination. It was never true of the Augustans. It was never true of Pope. It was never true of Shakespeare or Dante or Rembrandt. We have plunged, whilst making a gesture of plunging into reality, into a world of intellectual phantoms which we have chosen to call reality.

Poetry is truth, but it is the truth seen by a richer and wilder light. There are five or six creatures hidden in my self as a human being. As a poet there are only two. One is infatuated with heroic gestures, sonorities of phrase and lugubrious images. This is the poet of *Childe Harold*. The other loves the smells and sounds and sights of our earthly existence, digs for truth in the humdrum and loves to laugh at animal man.

It is the second, who wrote *Don Juan,* whom I recognize as the better one: or perhaps even the *only* real poet all in all. The first one, *hélas,* was always a bit of a gesticulator. I should have left the clouds to Shelley and the intimations to Wordsworth. I cannot read my *Maid of Athens* without a wriggle of embarrassment. The grandiose gesture comes easily enough, though it isn't easy to make good poetry of it. But to see splendour in a worn-out shoe or a jug of ale is not so easy. And I prefer a humble Murillo or a sketchy Rembrandt to a Michael Angelo.

*

In spite of Shelley's warnings I continued my life of profligacy and eventually I was punished by a dose of the clap. (This was the second time that I was afflicted with a tiresome gonorrhea, the only difference being that the first I obtained from a common prostitute whereas the second was given *gratis* by an elegant lady named Elena da Mosti.) I was forced to abandon my rides on the Lido and for a fortnight I led, under the doctor's orders, a life of strict celibacy. When I was well I sent a note by a special messenger to the Fornarina and begged her to pay me a visit. She arrived on the following day, wearing a bright yellow dress. And thus I slid back into a state of "monogamy".

One day she arrived at the palace in a frenzy of indignation. She had quarrelled with her husband, whom she called a tubercular cuckold (*un becco etico*), after he had squandered the money I gave her in a night of drunken gambling. She insisted on moving promptly into the Palazzo Mocenigo and had brought a wicker box, two canvas-bags and a bundle of underwear.

La Fornarina was a dark, tempestuous, gipsy-like woman who looked splendid and dignified in her peasant *fazziolo*. But after her arrival at the palazzo she decided to put on airs. One day she went and purchased a hat of green satin with an ostrich-feather perched grotesquely on top of it. I roared with laughter. I ripped off the hat and hurled it briskly into the fire. "Beast!" she howled. "Filthy octopus!" And she clawed my cheek until it bled.

She had her little whims and fooleries (aside from the hats, which she kept on buying in the conviction that a hat was the ear-mark of a lady). Out of sheer jealousy she learnt the alphabet, in order to intercept my letters and decipher in secret what various ladies had written to me. With all of her lechery she was also pious in a primitive way, and if it happened that we lay in bed when the bells rang for prayer, she called a halt to our operations in order to cross herself hurriedly.

The weather grew stormy. One day, *en route* from the Lido, a dark *temporale* burst suddenly out of the sky. A white stab of lightning shot down at the Giudecca and a moment later there was a violent outburst of thunder. Our hats blew away and went dancing over the white-caps and the gondola was suddenly filled with water. My good Tita, who had lost an oar, struggled bravely to steady the boat while young Tullio kept bailing out the water with a tea-kettle. We paddled laboriously, the wind subsided and darkness fell, and finally we landed safely at the Mocenigo, drenched to the skin.

My gipsy Fornarina was standing on the steps in the violent downpour, her hair streaming down over her cheeks and shoulders. She screamed with joy when she saw me and threw her arms round me passionately. Her eyes were flashing with joy, rage, triumph and indignation. "Ah!" she cried, shaking her fist. *"Can' della Madonna, xe esto il tempo per andar' al' Lido?"*

For the first time in my life I was quite sure that someone loved me. She dragged me up to my room, where a coal-fire was burning, and ripped off my clothes and rubbed me down with alcohol. Then she sprang into my bed with a loud triumphant purr, like a tigress who has just recovered her cubs. She leant down and kissed me on the cheeks again and again; then she stared at me with a kind of dazed incredulity. I remember how her eye-brows almost met over her nose, and the small beads of sweat that hung like tears from her lashes.

One day I informed her, after an unusually violent tantrum, that my gondola was waiting below to take her home. She burst into tears and went to her room and locked the door. That night as we sat at the table we heard a shattering of glass. The Fornarina had burst through the door that led into the pantry. She strode to the table, eyes aflame like a she-wolf's, and picked up a knife and stabbed me viciously in the thumb. I called Tita and ordered him to drag her down to the gondola. Then I filled up my wine-glass and calmly resumed my dinner.

But suddenly there was a turmoil of shouts and lamentations. I stepped into the hall and met Tita on the staircase. He was carrying the dripping body of the Fornarina up the stairs. She had hurled herself into the stinking canal in a fit of fury. They laid her out on the billiard-table and covered her with blankets.

After dinner I strolled into the billiard-room and looked at her solemnly. "It won't do," I said gently. "It's quite impossible. Now or ever."

She was strangely submissive. Tears shone in her eyes, and she peered at me with a look of animal hopelessness.

"As God wills it, Your Excellency," she whispered with trembling lips.

"Good-bye, then," I said. I pressed a bracelet into her hand.

She humbly took the bracelet, kissing my hand as she did so.

"God bless you, Your Excellency."

"Good-bye . . ."

"Good-bye, my darling!"

13 March

I drilled for an hour in the Seraglio with my artillery corps. I still keep hoping that I can capture Lepanto with my little army.

I have just read through last night's entry, and I am struck by a paradox. In my very effort to pin down the past in its exactitude, I am in danger of defeating the thing I strive for, namely, to conjure up the past in its full-blooded power. In this frenzied insistence on a microscopical clarity I destroy the emotional impact, whose essence is imprecision. But to this I add another paradox. The past is gone. It is irrevocable. But the ghost of the past can be recalled by a sleight-of-hand. The "full-blooded power", with all its tremors and arpeggios, for better or for worse, can never be recaptured. But a crafty and convincing similacrum can be created, even more vivid than the original, even more passionate and more luminous. And the simulacrum, by adorning itself with an array of bright irrelevancies, can become even more meaningful and truer than what happened. And thus memory, the power of longing, the transfiguring magic of the heart itself, ends by winning its victory over the merely historical.

*

There was a lady in Venice named the Countess Benzoni. She was a garrulous old coquette who had dyed her hair the colour of a pumpkin. She still had amorous pretensions in spite of her growing corpulence and she was still known indulgently as the "Toast of the Grand Canal". I remember a ball at the Grassi which was in homage to the French Revolution. She was dressed as *La Liberté* in a Greek-looking petticoat which was slit on both sides as high as the hips. Her breasts were quite naked and they bounced about gaily as she danced a fandango with the illustrious Ugo Foscolo.

One day I called at her house for her "five o'clock tea". (I had forgotten, unfortunately, that it was a Thursday instead of a Wednesday.) I arrived in the hope of some cultured conversation, but the butler looked puzzled and asked me to *"aspetti un momento"*. Some minutes later the door swung open and La Benzoni entered the room, totally nude except for a lengthy delphinium-tinted veil. She pretended to be startled by my unexpected presence but she rapidly recovered herself and sat on a velvet couch.

"*Entre nous,* there's no reason to insist on ceremony, is there, Byron?"

"Certainly not, my good Contessa. I forgot the day. I must apologise."

"Well, now that you're here we might as well have a bit of gossip." She tugged at the bell-cord and ordered some tea. Then she glanced at me coyly and draped the veil more gracefully about her. "You like Venice, it seems, Your Lordship?"

"I find Venice delightful."

"But," she said with some asperity, "you look down on the Venetians, don't you?"

"Quite the contrary. I admire their wit, I adore their complexion and I envy their morals."

She opened her fan and fanned herself musingly. "Our cultural heritage, to be sure, is incomparable. But there are moments when I doubt whether we exploit its full advantages. I like to pride myself on my weekly tea-parties but I can't help wondering whether they are up to Madame de Staël's."

I tried to reassure her. "They are on a comparable *niveau.* Here in Venice you speak of the opera, whilst in Coppet it was mainly philosophy."

The Countess smiled. "You have put it in a nut-shell. I prefer the theatre to philosophy, though which is the loftier is open to argument. I remember a Monsieur Beyle who came to my Wednesdays once or twice. He paid me some charming compliments. He thought me far from insipid. Once I asked him, 'Monsieur Beyle, you are an expert on *l'amour.* Will you answer me a question which has haunted me for years? When a woman tires of a man it is for a single concrete reason, I need not cross my t's, I am sure you know what I mean. But when a man grows tired of a woman the reasons are more elusive. Is it a psychological satiety? Is it a man's instinctive polygamy? Is it that a wrinkle more or less can make or break a man's fidelity?' "

"And what was his answer to this question?"

"He refused to answer," said the Countess cheerfully, "and the reason, just between us, was that he didn't know the answer. The fact of the thing is that there is no simple answer. When a woman leaves a man it's for a crystal-clear cause: when a man leaves a woman the reasons are slippery and manifold."

She lifted her cup and nibbled pensively at a raspberry-biscuit. Then she nimbly readjusted the folds of her veil, so that it flowed over her left breast and down under her right, settling cosily into a misty-blue swirl in her lap.

"What is your secret, Your Lordship? Why do the women all adore you?"

I blushed and said demurely, "You are too flattering, my dear Contessa. There are many who are indifferent to me and there are some who even detest me."

She lifted her veil and peered at me mousily over the edge of it. "I hear, from reliable sources, that you are *toujours prêt*. Only one man out of a hundred is *toujours prêt,* as the saying goes, and that one is usually a bore when it comes to other things. It is obvious that your secret springs from an unusual juxtaposition, namely of an amorous alacrity with a spiritual expertise, and this is as rare as an orchid in Spitzbergen."

The Countess had collected some pieces of Meissen porcelain, which stood on the mantelpiece under a painting by Canaletto. I remember a shepherdess with a lamb and an elegant little greyhound reclining on a cushion.

A breeze passed through the drawing-room. My hostess looked at me placidly and her face, in the gathering dusk, looked like the face of a Siamese cat, with its fine silky whiskers and ambiguous sea-blue eyes. I caught her musk in the air, which was like a freshly-peeled banana. She sighed and then smiled with a mute, forgiving melancholy.

She rose, deftly straightening her veil, and said, "Well, *à bientôt*. It has been a most instructive chat and let us resume it next Wednesday, if the Gods are willing."

I kissed her hand politely and walked back to my gondola. *Hell hath no fury like a woman scorned.* True, perhaps, as a general theorem. But it has its exceptions and there are times when a woman scorned grows mysteriously docile, and even angelic.

14 March

I slept badly and rose at noon. There was a letter from Augusta. She tells me that the yews at Six-Mile Bottom are starting to rot, and that the cook is sick with the dropsy, and the stable-roof needs mending.

Memory! What is it? Is it a betrayer, a consoler or a redeemer?

As I grope ever more deeply among the marsh-lands of the past, the further back I go, the more my memories are shrouded in fog. But then why do I remember a pimple on May Gray's ear-lobe more vividly than last night's supper with Captain Parry? Was there really a pimple? Did she really smell like a haddock? Did she really read aloud to me from the Book of Ecclesiastes? Oh, yes, these things were true but in my memory truths are nothing and emblems are gradually turning into everything. It is not the fact but the revelation that lingers, not the incident but the awful poignance of it, not the passage of days but the premonition of death.

Human life keeps flowing past us in a kind of incommuni-

cable secrecy, in a procession of *états de l'âme* that are closer
to hallucination than to history.

But I hate hallucinations. I hate what is fraudulent or
chimerical. Give me plainness, give me the strength to see the
world in a common light!

*

One evening I went to a late post-prandial party at La
Benzoni's. I arrived at twelve o'clock after crossing the storm-
tossed canal in my gondola. The guests were drifting in after
an early evening at the theatre. The candlelight shone on a
row of coloured aspics which were moulded in the shape of
chickens, porpoises and rabbits. I was sitting on a sofa opposite the door of the drawing-room. I remember that the clock
on the mantelpiece was just striking when a woman in a lace-
collared dress entered the room. La Benzoni greeted her
effusively with a kiss on both cheeks and then led her to the
sofa and tapped me with her fan. "Come, get up, you lazy
boy. Let me introduce you to the Countess Guiccioli."

I smiled amiably and the lady murmured, "I am happy to
see you again, Lord Bairon."

"Again?"

"We met last year, I think."

"Did we really? I'd quite forgotten."

"We went together to the Albrizzi's, and looked at a statue
by Canova."

"Yes. Niobe. I remember."

"Was it Niobe? I thought it was Helen."

"You've just arrived in Venice?"

"Last night. I came from Ravenna."

"You live in Ravenna?"

"My home is Ravenna."

"Ah. Ravenna. I must visit Ravenna."

"Ravenna is gloomy but it is civilised."

189

"Dante's tomb is in Ravenna, isn't it?"

"Have you read Dante?"

"Have *you* read Dante?"

"I was raised on Dante," said the Guiccioli, laughing. "I was taught by the nuns at the little convent of Santa Chiara in Faenza, and there we all read Dante, the whole of the *Paradiso* and some of the *Purgatorio*. We omitted the *Inferno*. It was unsuitable, we were told, for girls."

I looked carefully at the little lady, who had beautiful brown eyes and a quick spontaneous smile and a voice that rang like a bell. She was quite un-Venetian in her chestnut-haired plumpness and her face had a glowing, slightly moon-like rotundity. I stayed until one and when I left I said to the Guiccioli: "Forgive me, but would it be possible to see you tomorrow?"

She blushed and said hurriedly, "I shall be at the Albrizzi's for tea, of course."

I said: "I meant alone."

She caught her breath and glanced at the door.

"Well," I said, "what is the verdict?"

"Let me think for a moment . . ."

"Never *think*, my dear Contessa!"

"Well, at three o'clock, perhaps, when my husband takes his rest. We could go for a stroll in the public gardens . . ."

I waited for her in my gondola at three o'clock punctually, but instead of walking in the gardens we rode to the Lido, where we stopped at a *casina* and drank some Turkish coffee.

I pointed to a cloud. "Look," I said, "it is shaped like a donkey."

She smiled. "So it is. How very clever of you to notice it." She grew thoughtful. "It was most imprudent of me to come in your gondola."

"Imprudent? Is it imprudent to admire the clouds and the water?"

"We do not live, alas, in a society of cloudlets and wavelets." She looked at me anxiously. "You are frowning. Why are you frowning?"

"I often frown for no reason at all. I've been told that a frown becomes me."

"You look sad. Has your acquaintance with humanity made you sad?"

"Not sad so much as speculative."

"And what are you speculating about?"

"I was wondering how old you are."

"I am nineteen years old."

"Even younger than I imagined." I took hold of her forefinger. "Last night, when you walked through the door, it was like an apparition."

"But you didn't even recognize me!"

"You had changed . . ."

"It was *you* who have changed, Lord Bairon."

"In what manner, Contessa?"

"You are more serious. You have lost your frivolity."

"A funny thing to be happening in Venice."

"Venice is not the city of frivolity, as you seem to think," said the Contessa. "It is the city of masks and under the masks lurk apprehensions."

"You are a very perceptive woman."

"Not in the least. I am rather stupid. When people talk of philosophy I hardly know what they are talking about."

"There are other things than philosophy."

"Such as what? Love, I suppose."

"Yes, love for example. What are your notions on love, Contessa?"

She laughed. "It is growing late. The bells are ringing five o'clock. We'll meet tomorrow, if you wish, and continue our conversation."

So we met on the following day and we rode past the Rialto and stopped at a *casina* which was euphemistically known as the House of Roses. We drank some tea in a private room which was decorated with cupids in the style of Tiepolo. My darling had already accepted in her mind what was inevitable, and when I kissed her on the shoulder she offered no resistance. She slipped off her dress and we lay on the ebony couch, where the sun through the blinds had dropped a golden ladder. I remember her little breasts drooping sideways, with their pink *ocelli,* so that they looked like the wings of a large golden butterfly. She wore a golden chain with a crucifix at the end of it, as well as a snake (against sickness) , a horn (against the *mal' occhio*) and a medal of St Christopher (for safety on voyages) . As I laid my head on her breast my hair caught in the necklace, and she laughed as she untangled the little horn and the snake and the crucifix.

Once we lay in the House of Roses and Teresa fell asleep. I picked up a pencil and started to make a little drawing of her. But the drawing was so clumsy that I tore it in two. I drew the pencil very gently over her snowy white belly and made a *graffito* of a heart pierced by an arrow, which gradually developed into a bawdier configuration, so that the fur-tufted arrow became a symbol of virility and the chastely-scalloped heart a stalwart pair of labia. She woke up and smiled when she saw my lewd drawing, but then she grew angry and slapped me on the cheek.

"So this," she cried bitterly, "is your version of love! You transform an emotional poignancy into a crude sexual travesty. Oh, dear, what a beastly farce it all is! Why must love create its paradise in these filthy appendages?"

And still, all in all, there was no question about it. I was in love. Not painfully or piercingly but gaily, rhapsodically. As I rode in my gondola I leant back and closed my eyes. I turned into a feather and floated up towards the basilica and tickled its saints in their golden noses. I went floating past the bell-tower and over the ducal palace, touching the marble lianas and sea-shells as I passed. I went floating along the quay and out over the inlet, which shone like a fan sprinkled with coal-black sequins. I flew higher and higher. I flew up as high as the clouds, which even now in the gathering darkness were still touched by a hint of sunlight, and reminded me that happiness, though rare and ephemeral, was still possible.

15 March

I went riding with Pietro and suddenly lost my temper when he let his stallion spatter my breeches with mud.

I am living on the brink of my strength. My nerves are like needles.

*

I left Venice on June the 1st and rode through the dusty heat to Padua. I looked at the paintings of Mantegna, I visited the church of St Antony and I drank the frozen coffee for which Padua is famous. I rode to Ferrara and visited the cemetery of La Certosa. I still remember (perhaps with an added poignance nowadays) the music of the epitaphs which were scattered among the cypresses: *Lucrezia Picini—Implora et quiète,* and *Martini Luigi—Implora pace.*

I strolled back to my carriage and rode on to Bologna, where I slept in the suffocating heat of the Pellegrino. I ate some green *lasagne* cooked in the Bolognese fashion but I was sick during the night and had to vomit from my balcony. From Bologna I rode on over the plains until sunset, when I caught sight through the quivering heat-waves of the towers of Ravenna. It was dusk when I rode through the gates. The streets were swarming with people (it was the feast of *Corpus Cristi*) and a group of noisy urchins kept crowding about my carriage. The lights were being lit when I arrived at the hotel, which was a dingy little hut called (rather fancifully) the Imperiale.

I was desperately eager to see my darling Teresa but I decided to put this off till the morrow. I requested the *portiere* to deliver a note to her, as well as a letter of introduction to a Count Alborghetti, who immediately wrote back to invite me to his box at the theatre. The Count turned out to be a pudgy little man with three chins, who greeted me effusively and held out his snuff-box.

"Do you have," he inquired, "any acquaintances in the city?"

"I am a friend of the Count and Countess Guiccioli," I said blandly.

"Ah, poor Teresa!" said the Count despairingly. "She is lying at death's door!"

I caught my breath; then I cried desperately, "Good God, what is wrong with her?"

"Poor Teresa," said the Count, "had a miscarriage on the road to Pomposa and a fever has set in, aggravated by the moistness of the marshes."

I grew pale, my lips shook and I clutched at the iron balcony. The Count seemed startled by my emotion and said gently, "Be calm, Your Lordship. Perhaps the doctors have exaggerated a little . . ."

I hurried back to the Imperiale after the play was over and wrote a second note:

My sweetest Soul (I think these were the words) —Believe me, I live for you alone and do not doubt me. I shall stay here in town until I know what your wishes are. Even if you cannot contrive to see me I shall not go away. I beg you to command me as entirely and eternally yours. I would sacrifice all of my hopes for this world to see you happy, and I cannot think of your present state of health without tears. Alas, *mon trésor!* How much we endure and shall have to endure! And you so young, so good, so beautiful—you are suffering through my fault!

I kiss you a thousand, thousand times with all my soul.

B

I did not sleep that night. On the following morning I had a message from Guiccioli, and he called on me in the evening to accompany me to the palazzo, where Teresa, white and wide-eyed, lay in her poppy-curtained bedroom. I lifted her hand and regarded her thoughtfully. But I felt the Count watching me and I said calmly, "Is it the climate? I hear that Ravenna is dangerously humid."

Teresa smiled; and she seemed already on the way to recovery. Five days later she rose from her bed and we rode in her carriage through the pine-woods. The heat had gone from the air and the crickets were squealing noisily, and the nightingales were singing as we entered the twilight. We heard the ringing of bells in the purple distance, and Teresa was reminded of a scene in the *Inferno*.

"Those bells tolling so mournfully—they make me think of Dante! And those women in black by the gate—they remind me of Dante! Dante frightens me, darling, for nothing in Dante is trivial or casual. In reading Dante I feel that everything that I do is pre-ordained and that I walk through existence like a sort of somnambulist. I feel that life has turned into a menacing pantomime. Tell me, Bairon, is life itself merely a menacing pantomime?"

We made love under the pines, ignoring the goat-herds in the distance and quite indifferent even when a fisher-girl passed with her basket. After this we went riding every day in the *pineta* and Teresa shed her malady with startling rapidity. We spoke of fishes and flowers, or Tasso and Ariosto, of Tintoretto and Titian, of partridges and guinea-hens, and my life in Ravenna grew idyllically monotonous. Only the Count continued to lurk in the background disturbingly, and when I asked Teresa about him she said: "He is a Sphinx *senza misterio.*" So I tried not to worry about the Sphinx-like Guiccioli.

On rainy days instead of riding into the woods we met in the palazzo, when the stillness hung heavily in the halls during the siesta-hours. We soon enlisted the connivance of

195

Father Fabrizio, her priest, of little Poopoo, her blackamoor, and of her chambermaid Carlotta, and as the Count lay fast asleep in the *piano nobile* the rest of the household hovered about like conspirators. Once, indeed, when I heard a rustling out in the hall I opened the door, only to find that Pino, the pantry-boy, had been peeping through the keyhole and was masturbating merrily as he did so. I ordered him briskly to wipe off his breeches and go back to the kitchen where he belonged.

But even as I settled into the role of a *cavaliere servente,* in accord with the usual Italian traditions, I felt a certain anxiety which derived from the Count's own character. He was old, he was rich, he was elegant and he was wily. When he spoke to me he smiled and lifted his monocle, and our talks dealt with book-bindings, mushrooms and cheeses. He vanished from sight during the hours of the siesta and when he drifted into the drawing-room, where the coffee-tray was waiting for us, he regarded me with a crafty, faintly sinister benevolence.

16 March

I have seen it again.

I was reading my Montaigne. (It was the twenty-seventh essay of Book II, about the difficulty of persuading oneself that one will die.) He quotes Virgil:

Provehimur portu, terraeque urbesque recedunt . . .

At this point I noticed a hole torn in the yellowing paper. Through the hole I could see a curious dark stain on the following page. I turned the page and was startled to find no stain at all. Nor, on closer inspection, was there a hole in the previous page. I went on reading. And again, through some

196

maddening optical trick, the hole appeared in the page, obliterating the words *urbesque recedunt.* This time the stain was somewhat larger and was shaped like the head of a beast—a bull-dog, perhaps, or an otter.

I tore out the page, rolled it in a ball and hurled it through the window. But as I hurled it I felt a sudden pang in my thumb. And now, as I look at it, I can see the pin-pricks of two tiny fangs.

*

August came. The heat in Ravenna was growing intolerable and Count Guiccioli with his wife rode in their carriage to Bologna. I left on the following day, starting at three o'clock in the morning, and at nightfall I rode through the gates of Bologna. I took my former rooms in the Hotel Pellegrini, which were furnished in a fashionable Napoleonic blue. That night I went with the Guicciolis to see Alfieri's *Mirra,* in which the illustrious Madame Pelzet was playing the heroine. In this play the innocent Myrrha fell in love with her father and gave incestuous birth to the beautiful Adonis. I was so agitated by this theme that I burst into tears and was forced to borrow my Teresa's *sal volatile.*

I spent a month in Bologna. I filled my hotel-chambers with bowls full of flowers, two African parakeets and a cage of Swiss canaries. I worked feverishly on *Don Juan,* which came to obsess me more and more (its very playfulness, I found, began to exert a curious spell on me) and in the evenings I called on Teresa in the Savioli Palace and we chatted over our coffee in the many-arched loggia.

Teresa at this point was reading *Corinne* by Madame de Staël, and I made fun of her fondness for this silly female novel. (Her own copy I remember was bound in violet plush, with a withered fleur-de-lys which she used as a book-mark.) I explained that Madame de Staël was really an earthy old soul, and that her novels were totally out of keeping with her character, but Teresa refused to accept this and said that an artist reflects his soul, however equivocally, in that saintly secretion which is his art.

At this point I must digress for a moment. I have spoken little of my daughter Ada, though I begged my dear Augusta to keep me informed of Ada's progress (she was a clever little girl, it seemed, with a penchant for geometry). I have failed to mention, I think, that I had a second daughter, Allegra, whose mother was the mournful and calamity-prone Claire Clairmont. This little child was developing into a highly-intelligent creature, and I insisted that she be left under the care of an elderly nurse, a woman with a goitre whose name was Elise, who accompanied the girl to my villa on the Brenta. Now I decided that Allegra should visit me in Bologna. She arrived in late August and I used to play with her in the garden, where a twisted old ilex shaded a large pool of goldfish. My Allegra (her name was an irony) was very different from little Ada: her eyes were blue and her hair was dark, she kept scowling and frowning, and her leanings lay towards music and fairy-tales rather than geometry. She spoke French as well as Italian with a strong Venetian accent, and she would sit under the ilex with her doll and sing songs to it.

I confess that I felt only moderately paternal towards my daughters. One was the child of a frigid blue-stocking and the other of a lecherous blue-stocking. Oh why, I often wonder, am I always victimized by blue-stockings? What crime have I committed that I should be haunted thus by blue-stockings? I have always carnally preferred the baker's daughter to Madame de Staël. But there it is—I am inevitably entangled with these blue-stockings—their odours and odes, their otiosities, their offspring.

And in any case, what emotions should a father feel towards his daughter? I can't help wondering if it is a wholly wholesome relationship. I felt guilty about my lack of paternal solicitude, but both Ada and Allegra were, in a sense, freaks of accident, and the results of an unfortunate emotional *malentendu*.

In September I got ready to go back to Venice. I discreetly arranged with the Count that Teresa should accompany me, on the pretext that she needed to consult her physician, Aglietti. So I set out one morning in my Napoleonic carriage (which was showing signs of wear—the leather was cracked, the paint was peeling) and Teresa followed after me in the coach-and-six of the Guicciolis. We went climbing through the heat into the green Euganean hills. We stopped by a crucifix and turned into a side road, which was marked by a weather-beaten sign: *To Arque*. Teresa's favourite poet was not Dante but Petrarch, and Petrarch lay buried under the cypresses of Arque. The road grew more stony and eventually impassable. So we got out and walked, following a thistle-edged mule-path. I kept sneezing with the dust and perspiring with the heat, and I groaned periodically with the corns on my feet. But Teresa was in ecstasies. She gazed skyward and fluttered her fingers and recited some lines from one of the sonnets. We entered the house and wrote our names in the visitor's book. Then we stepped into the garden and drank from the fountain.

"Ah," said Teresa, glancing about her, "how delightful to be free again! Free from the shackles of society, of domesticity, of connubialism . . ."

"One can't," I said gently, "live in a vacuum, dear Teresa."

"Why not?" she cried gaily. "We could sail to Madagascar, or live on the palm-shaded shores of Ceylon!"

I wiped my brow miserably. "Nothing but heat and perpetual sunlight . . ."

"Very well. We could sail to the Norwegian fjords, which

are cool, or even the woods of Lapland, which are downright icy!"

We rode through the heat and slept in Padua the second night. On the next afternoon we arrived at La Mira. We had supper under the plane-trees of my pink Palladian villa. We ate a trout (which was served with an egg-sauce) and watched the boats on the Brenta. My memory wandered back to the sultry nights with the Fornarina, but I smiled resolutely and passed the grapes to my Teresa.

Dusk fell and we watched the urchins who were splashing about in the water. A far-away look crept into Teresa's brown eyes. I said gently, "You look thoughtful. Is anything worrying you, *carina?*"

"Dearest one," she said softly, "there is something I ought to tell you."

"Yes? What is it?" I said with a pang of apprehension.

"I blush to tell you."

"Don't be shy."

"I am suffering," she said, "from piles. They seem to run in the family. My mother endured agonies."

I sighed with relief. "It might be worse," I said sagaciously.

"And there's another thing," she hinted.

I lowered my cup and looked at her tensely.

"I suspect," she went on wistfully, "that I am afflicted with a *prolapsus uteri.*"

I picked up the cup again. "I shall send for Aglietti tomorrow."

"Isn't it dreadful," said Teresa, "to be a member of the female sex? Instead of those simple male contrivances, which seem to operate so painlessly, we are burdened with a multiplicity of little sacks and receptacles, any of which is apt to rebel at the slightest provocation. I can't help wondering if the threat of pregnancy is really conducive to the pinnacles of passion. Wouldn't it be lovely, *amore,* if both of us were boys and could carry on idyllically, like Damon and Pythias?"

Still, in spite of these sallies of unexpected wit, my life with Teresa was Saturnian rather than Mercurial, and the programmes at La Mira were tinged with an autumn gravity. A growing uneasiness was beginning to settle on me. I loved her, to be sure: but the love was fringed with restlessness. I grew jaded in my role of an Italian *cicisbèo*: a carrier of fans, a flatterer of bosoms, a singer of duets, a sniffer of rose-water. I grew weary of being a *cavaliere servente*. I grew bored with being a slave to the whims of the womb.

17 March

Spring has come. I saw a swallow and wrote a letter to Teresa. I went riding, fired my pistols and read Diodorus Siculus.

Mavrocordato came in the evening for a sip of *eau de vie*. This is rapidly becoming a habit of his. He says that he is able to *"se détendre"* with me. By this he means that I am willing to listen to his more salacious confidences.

He always begins by hanging his fur-cap on top of my trumpet, and then admiring the effect with a concupiscent leer. Then he wipes his gold-rimmed spectacles, unbuttons his waistcoat, and squats like a frog on the velvet cushions. He talks about politics for four or five minutes, about military matters for three more minutes, and then lapses into a recital of some new peccadillo.

To-day, he said, being balmy, with butterflies hopping about, he decided to go for a stroll to the Seraglio. He entered the court-yard and saw some Suliotes taking a bath. They were soaping themselves beside a big wooden trough. They were especially zestful in the washing of their pudenda, merrily pulling back the foreskin and rubbing the glans with a fistful of lather.

"I watched them," murmured the Prince, "with an air of scrupulous severity. I did not feel that it was appropriate for me to join them in their fun. And as I walked back through the meadow, watching the grasshoppers in the clover, I pondered on the fact that the Suliotes, with their massive noses and thick broad fingers, are also gifted with size in their other protuberances. For this reason I have always avoided men with aristocratic nostrils and tapering finger-tips. I always sensed that these ear-marks were distinctly inauspicious."

"So you judge," I said dryly, "desirability in terms of inches?"

"Not in the least," retorted the Prince with an air of offended delicacy. He added slyly, "Not exclusively at any rate. I disapprove of my Athenian cronies, who keep insisting (for reasons of their own, no doubt) that size is all that matters. I feel that this is much too gross an approach to the matter. After all, the *membrum virile* is like a human being. One must not judge it by size alone. It is the *tout ensemble* which counts. By that I mean (and I thank you for listening so patiently, dear Byron) not only the sculptural elegance, the silkiness of texture and the richness of content, but also the whole *chiaroscuro* of responsiveness, intensity, and general playfulness. I do not wish to sound prudish but I have always objected, as you know, to what I consider the single-track mentality . . ."

*

Tom Moore came for a visit and he said: "You have changed, Byron."

"Yes, I have changed. I have lost my looks."

"No," said Moore, "you are still magnificent, though slightly more adipose, if you will pardon my saying so. What I meant is that your face has lost its spirituality. Your hair hangs down to your neck. And look at your whiskers! You look positively waggish. Apollo is turning into Pan, it seems."

I filled his glass with *grappa* and said idly: "And what about London?"

"London is wet, just as always."

"What do they think of *Don Juan?*"

"They are shocked by *Don Juan.*"

"Well," I said, shrugging my shoulders, "nothing seems to have changed. In dear old London the power of cant has always been stronger than the power of cunt. I know both of them intimately, and I hold no brief for either of them. But of the two I must say that I distinctly prefer the latter."

Moore looked at me thoughtfully. "You are homesick for England."

"I hate England and English hypocrisy. But I still am obsessed by England."

"I suspected as much," said Moore. "You love what you hate." He leant back in his chair. "Your life in Italy is a charade. How much longer will you be able to keep it up, my dear friend?"

I have never quite decided how I felt about Moore. He was amiable, even charming, but there was something oily in his amiability. He was handsome but there was something rather sleek about his looks. He had talent but there was something gratuitous, even vulgar in his poetry. He was a dandy, but his clothes (all bought in Paris) had a *parvenu* look to them. His lips were full and luscious, his chin was dimpled, his complexion rosy. His face had the look of an over-ripe peach.

After dinner I took Moore through the canals in my gondola to look at *Venezia illuminata*. We were mellow with the effect of our dinner in the Piazza and I started to sing some of my old Albanian songs. We passed the Salute, which looked especially fine that night as it basked under the clouds in a demi-lunar quicksilver. We passed the great palazzi, the forbidding Gritti and the brooding Vendramin, the pigeon-spattered Labia and the matronly Rezzonico, and as we slid under the Rialto (it was two o'clock in the morning) Moore murmured:

"There is something rather ambiguous in your soul, I have noticed."

"Be explicit please, Moore."

"You won't be offended?"

"Certainly not."

Moore fondled the carnation which the *maître d'hôtel* had given him. "I couldn't help observing the looks which you cast at the waiter. You make love to the women but you love, *au fond,* the men. You sleep with the women but you yearn for the men. Your flesh lusts for women but your mind lusts for men. Am I exaggerating, Byron? Please tell me the truth, now."

"You are exaggerating, Moore. You deduce too much from a merry wink."

"Very well. I was mistaken."

"And in any case, Moore, even supposing that you are right, why should you call this ambiguous? It is perfectly natural. The men I distrust are the ones who pose as womanisers. We all of us admire both the male and the female principles and it is habit, or largely habit, which moulds our sexual vicissitudes. Haven't you noticed how a woman admires the breasts of another woman? Is this Sapphism? Certainly not. It is merely the sign of a healthy animalism."

"Aren't you quibbling a bit, my friend? Do you seriously suggest that there is no such thing as pederastical lewdness, as opposed to the garden variety?"

"Sexual habits bring in their wake a certain stylization. Men become the thing they do. They surrender to a pattern. But this isn't the root of the matter. What we love in another man is an idealization of ourselves, something heroic and unattainable and perhaps even mythical, and we are constantly reminded of our own littleness. But in loving a

woman we love our own opposite and we bask in our masculinity, we grow inflated and slightly bovine. Who can say
which is better, or more inducive to a spiritual flowering? I
have no idea whether Marlowe was a *better* man than Mas-
singer, or Virgil than Horace, or Leonardo than Titian. Only
one thing I can say. There's a twilight quality in pathic love,
and wallowing in twilight leads eventually to illusions. I like
daylight better than dusk. I don't say that it is *better*, I
merely prefer it."

"And yet," said Moore, tossing his flower into the foul-
smelling water, "there is a part of you, Byron, which longs for
dusk and gropes for the hallucinatory. And that is why I call
you ambiguous, if you will forgive me for my rudeness."

"Call me ambiguous, then," I muttered, and I burst into
laughter. The clock struck half past two and we rode back to
the Mocenigo.

18 March

Torrential rains.

Strange, strange. As the days slip past in Missolonghi, so
the years slip past too. I write of the passing days and the
vanished years loom behind them, and both seem to move
(like the hare and the tortoise) towards a hidden meeting-
place. More and more darkly the days go by; more and more
swiftly the years go following them. But the meeting-place?
What is it? What will happen when they finally converge?

I wait. I wait and wonder. What is the future? *Is* there a
future? What happens to a man when the past and the
present finally converge? Is there a chemical explosion, followed by a stench of sulphur, or merely a delicate unison,
like two voices blending in harmony?

*

I was helpless. I was sucked into my Italian rôle as into a whirlpool. Everything—the climate, the siesta-hour, the mentality of the domestics—conspired in favour of clandestine adultery. December came and I followed the Guicciolis back to Ravenna, where I settled into the topmost floor of their palazzo. I turned gradually from a *cavaliere servente* into a *cavaliere schiavo*, doing my sexual duties as *cicisbèo* during the Count's siesta-hour, while the blackamoor Poopoo kept watch at the top of the stairway. We had dinner and chatted about sorcery and astrology and heraldry, and after dinner we occasionally rode to the theatre, where the famous *improvisatore* Sgricci held forth.

Poor Sgricci! He was handsome in a twisted sort of way. His face was a perpetual grimace, his physique was a writhing question-mark. He wore powder and lip-salve and what little hair was left he wore in a series of lubricated curls. He was a celebrated sodomite, clever, vain, affected and vicious. In Italy they no longer burn the sodomites, they merely laugh at them, and certain ladies piously hoped that Signor Sgricci would be "saved", *id est,* converted to the usual fornications.

Once I wandered back-stage and had a chat with the fellow. He was fluttering about his dressing-room, trying now this wig and now that one, dipping his fingers into the salves, patting his cheeks with rouge. He had finished his act of a Neapolitan fortune-teller and was getting ready for his impersonation of Don Quixote. Finally he flung on his armour and looked at me with a crafty glitter.

I said amiably, "Do you like Ravenna?"

"Ravenna has its charms," he said, "but I prefer the headier bouquet of the Veneto or even Tuscany. Ravenna has nothing to offer, in the line of amorous novelty, which is equal to the nooks of the Lido or the Cascine on a summer's night."

I said, "Do you never grow weary of these so-called amourous novelties?"

"In my body," he said, "yes. But never in my mind. If you asked me what one triumph I long to achieve before my death-bed, I would say, not fame nor riches (though both of these appeal to me), neither an ermine-lined coat nor a carriage with six horses, neither a world-famous *Hamlet* nor a villa in Sorrento, but merely a single night of all-engulfing passion, an experience so exquisite that it would comfort me for ever, and even reconcile me to my inevitable voyage to the Inferno."

I was struck by Signor Sgricci's somewhat flowery Stoicism, and since we still had a moment before the rising of the curtain, I asked him to elaborate on his views of humanity.

"Is there really, Signor Sgricci, such a thing as good and evil?"

"Well," said Sgricci, with his big painted eyes flashing wickedly, "every life reflects *in pètto* the whole labyrinth of human existence. Some of us more than others, of course. Some men are odourless, others stink. Oh yes, there are saints and sinners, the saints all goodness, the sinners all badness, but the rest of us are merely a warmish bowl of *minestrone,* in which the chunks of good and bad lie floating about like beef and carrots, the flavour of the one gradually seeping into the other!"

The curtain-bell rang. Signor Sgricci fastened his armour and then threw a wilted rose at me as he waltzed into the wings.

19 March

Is this Purgatory? I lie alone in my darkened room and remember my follies. I remember how I snarled at Caroline, or snapped at Teresa, or sneered at Claire. Sweat drips from my temples. I writhe at the thought of my brutality. Just as the beauty of the past is enhanced by the magical properties of memory, so the dark spots grow darker, more grim and ineradicable.

And suddenly I fall asleep. My thoughts turn into dreams. But there's a very strange thing about these dark incessant dreams of mine. I dream of Lady Caroline: she has turned into a cow-eyed blonde. I dream of Annabella: she has turned into a *houri*. I dream of my mother. Her face is dark as an Indian's. I dream of Claire Clairmont. She has turned into Medusa. What is the answer to this riddle? That others play their rôle in our lives not as they are in actuality, but merely in the mask which our dreams have frozen on them? Our relations with other people are not an embrace between two realities, but a masked minuet between two self-created fancies. And even I, in the limbo of dreams, have turned into a stranger to myself, a hunted and fatuous fool who is trembling with panic on the Tower of Pisa, floating like a duck on the Lake of Geneva, soaring high over Piccadilly, pissing in the nave of San Marco, or cavorting stark naked in the drawing-room of Lady Blessington . . .

*

I was infected with a sense of impending calamity. The dampish sea-wind brought a twinge of sciatica; only an access of dysentery saved my waist-line from disaster; and the white-headed Count grew more sphinx-like than ever. The news from abroad filled me with deepening alarm. Beau Brummell had fled to Calais to escape from his creditors. Scrope Davies had fled to Bruges to escape from *his* creditors. Hobhouse was sent to jail (he was indiscreet politically) and Bonaparte was sent to the tropical isle of St Helena. I too was an illustrious exile, and in the gloom of the Palazzo Guiccioli I felt like Marius in Carthage or Themistocles in Magnesia. I felt rootless and alienated. My ties to England were withering away. Annabella was still obdurate in her refusal to write to me and my darling Augusta had caught a cold in Six-Mile Bottom.

And there was something disconcerting in Ravenna itself. Of all the cities I have known its streets are the narrowest, its walls the grimmest. The grip of Byzantium still holds it in thrall. The men walk about with enormous sad eyes, the only men in all of Italy who refuse even to smile. I wrote busily at night in my chilly upstairs chambers but I could hear, like the padding of a puma, the approaching tread of unpleasantness.

One evening the Count had gone for a stroll in the park. Teresa and I lay entangled on a red-plush sofa (on which, with the lapse of time, some smallish stains had appeared). We were studying a painting by Palma Vecchio on the wall, which showed Delilah in the act of cutting Samson's tresses.

The clock struck half past five and at that instant the door swung open and the Count stood in the doorway, holding his hat in his hand. It was precisely the situation I had often anticipated, but repeated imaginings had steeled me for the actuality. I rose casually from the sofa and said with a grin:

"The Countess has been so kind as to sew a tear in my trousers. She is as nimble with her thimble as she is brilliant at the harpsichord . . ."

"We will do," said the Count, "without the circumlocutions. Be so good, my dear Teresa, as to leave us for a moment."

Teresa threw her shawl about her shoulders and left the room. I walked sheepishly to the fire-place and folded my arms. The Count stroked his nostrils and looked at me glassily. In his eyes there was a blending of amusement, calculation and hatred.

"Well," he said, "what course of action do you think would be suitable?"

"I regret," I said hurriedly, "any misapprehension . . ."

"I could, of course," he said, "insist that you leave the

house immediately. I could challenge you to a duel. I could beg the Pope for a separation. I could even . . ." He grew thoughtful and took a pinch of snuff. "Never mind. I'm too old to fight a duel, alas. A separation would be awkward, as well as costly to me personally. However, even at my age, I have no wish to keep playing the rôle of a complacent cuckold indefinitely. It is up to you to decide, and handle the matter discreetly."

I nodded. "Let me ponder the matter till the morning."

Count Guiccioli smiled primly. "A good night's rest will surely do wonders for you."

It was always somewhat of a scandal. Now it turned into a gigantic scandal. Servants, relatives, priests, cardinals, all were mixed up in the quarrel. Count Gamba, Teresa's father, even appealed to the Pope. He begged His Holiness to allow the separation of his daughter from her sinister husband, including, of course, the payment of a "suitable" allowance. As always in Italy, an adulterous scandal developed a host of ramifications, tribal, political, religious, financial, with a tinge of blackmail and general hilarity.

Finally His Holiness the Pope gave his consent to the separation and one day, while the Count was napping, Teresa stepped into her carriage and drove to the country-house of the Gambas in Filetto. I myself insisted on keeping my rooms in the palazzo. (After all, I had redecorated them at my own expense, not to mention the private zoo which I kept in the ante-chambers.) Except for Teresa's absence life went on more or less as usual. When I met the Count in the hall, we both nodded coldly. We met in the garden occasionally and spoke about the weather. I grew convinced that what chiefly concerned him was the financial side of the matter, but Tita (who had followed from Venice) hinted darkly at other things. The Guicciolis, he said, were a proud and irascible race, and he expected to find me lying in a pool of blood one morning.

Summer faded. The apples fell and the Michaelmas daisies shed their petals. One day I rode to Filetto to visit the rambling Gamba manor-house, which was set in a spacious vine-encircled valley. The leaves on the plane-trees had turned to a speckled yellow, and a table with tea-cups had been set in the shade. The entire family was out on the lawn, awaiting the eclipse. They stood about with smoked glasses and a variety of optical instruments, the men with tall hats and the ladies with parasols. The Count rang a bell and they peered at the sky, where the moon was beginning to creep across the sun. No-one spoke; everyone was solemnly engaged in watching the phenomenon, which was drawing its shadow over the meadows and forests. Soon the sun emerged again and we all chattered merrily. The children played and the country cousins started to bowl, and I was challenged to a bout of archery by Teresa's brother, Pietro (who is sleeping at this moment in a room across the hall). Pietro was an intelligent and spirited youth, with excitable brown eyes and a faunish body. He too, like the rest of the family, was an ardent political idealist.

"What," he said, adjusting his bow, "do you think of the moon, Your Lordship?"

"I think highly of the moon, though with certain reservations."

"No, seriously, I mean!" He laughed and aimed at the target, where his arrow struck an inch or two south of the bull's eye.

Then he said: "Is it inhabited, for example? And if so, by whom?"

"I doubt it," I said. "The moon is covered with ice. There might be seals and even penguins, and perhaps a few Eskimos."

"But," said Pietro, "if there are Eskimos, how the devil did they get there? Did they fly there on wings or did they develop independently? It is hard to imagine a human race arising separately, with bodies like our own, with two arms and two legs."

"Not to mention," I said bluntly, "a pair of balls and a dangling dildo."

Pietro blushed. "Still," he said, "look at the Indians in America. They sprang up spontaneously on the shores of the Mississippi, and the only difference is that their skin is as red as a cock's comb."

"And on the moon," I retorted, "they may also be nearly identical, with phosphorescent skin and six testicles and a three-pronged penis."

"In which case," said Pietro, scratching his ear-lobe thoughtfully, "the lunar ladies would habitually give birth to triplets."

"And the pleasures of fucking," I said, "would be three-fold."

Pietro looked at me reproachfully. "Yes," he said, "they are perfectly right. They all told me that you are obsessed with the copulative process. Oh, Your Lordship, how is it possible that such sexual naughtiness can accompany a lofty poetical inspiration?"

"Life is a puzzle," I said.

"I quite agree," said Pietro gloomily. He took my arm and we wandered back to the leaf-sprinkled lawn, where the ladies were lolling in the shade with their tea-cups.

20 March

Dismal rain. Read some Grillparzer. A letter from Hobhouse, another from Moore. Stayed in bed until noon and then dressed to go riding, but returned in a rage when it started to rain again.

There are rumours (brought to me by a page from Mavrocordato) of a big Turkish force ready to march from Larissa.

My life for over a month has been the life of a monk. I have scarcely touched a woman, let alone lain in bed with one. In Genoa I already suspected that impotence was creeping over me, and more than once I was unable to come to an orgasm. It even seemed that my cock was diminishing in size, and my balls hung listless and limp in their scrotum.

Things have changed, it appears. The sexual note has returned to my dreams, tinged more strongly than ever with an adolescent poignancy. They are voluptuous yet tense with a half-blind yearning. I wake up with a powerful erection and a residue of images, which are bizarre in their lubricity but even stranger in their emotional fever. What does it mean? Just at the point when I was about to abandon sex, a new and fierce eroticism is rising within me. I have heard of such crises in connection with the menopause. Do men too have a menopause? I am not young; but I am young for a menopause.

Whatever the cause, I find that my "idylls" are more gripping in retrospect than they ever were in their actuality. Often the prospect of coition is more thrilling than the performance, and often in practice an anti-aphrodisiacal note intrudes on it—a fleeting odour, a hank of hair, an ill-turned phrase, an ill-timed gesture.

My life, as I look back on it, has been a series of copulations. This seems anything but glorious, and there were times when I felt ashamed of myself. Now I find that this series of fucks (a repulsive little word, and I use it only in the broadest possible connotation) takes on a fascination and even a splendour which hardly seem inherent in such a crude grotesquerie. I find that the memory of a fuck can outshine even the reality, and that the intensity of love can be posthumous as it were, finding its apogee long after the object itself has fled from the horizon.

I am not young; but a flickering of youth still hovers about me. I look at my face. It seems curiously alert. I gaze at my body. It is smooth as a statue's. It almost seems that I am being groomed by some dark little demi-god for a last and spectacular amorous climax.

Is it possible? Can it be, after those grandiose excursions, those beds of satin and chinchilla, those sloe-eyed harlots and perfumed countesses, those fields of clover and rustling laurel-woods, those desperate kisses and betrayals, those *billets-doux*, those curtained gondolas, those feathery fans and gilded dominoes, those half-hysterical acrobatics by the light of the setting sun: can it be that my last delirium, the most painful of all, should come with a shy caress, a furtive glance, a hidden tremor, an inarticulate sob beside a dirty old divan?

*

In the absence of Teresa my thoughts turned to politics. I grew absorbed in the "Revolution", that spasmodical Italian effort to throw off the yoke of the Austrian occupation. But the Revolution melted, as it were, before our eyes. The Neapolitans defected; the chiefs were betrayed; the plans slowly crumbled and the Austrians, the "blond barbarians", stood on the banks of the River Po with their tents and cannons.

I remember one night visiting some neighbours in Ravenna, where there was to be a *soirée* with a harp, a flute and a piccolo. A young lady came towards me with tears in her eyes. "And now," she cried bitterly, "we must abandon the hope of unity. *Quelle tragédie!* The poor Italians must go back to writing operas."

But in fact, it was a tragi-comedy more than a tragedy. Yes, the Italians would go back to making operas and macaroni. They are not suited for political matters: they keep squabbling among themselves and the ideal of "unity" plays second fiddle to personal emolument. There is no Italy in the strictest sense. There is only a dusty old boot that protrudes into the blueness of the Mediterranean. There is only a conglomeration of cities and provinces, and the patriotic postures soon descend to the operatic level. They are beautiful, they are clever, they are adorable, but they are hopeless.

And yet, shall I ever understand the Italians?

One day I rode back through the forest at dusk. Tufts of mist were beginning to float through the pines. I saw in the distance another horseman riding in the twilight. He guided his horse in my direction. We met and nodded politely. He was a handsome young officer with slate-blue eyes and a brown moustache, and he said:

"*Buona sera.* Commandant del Pinto, Your Excellency."

I said amiably: "There's a chill in the air. Winter is coming."

"Ah, the winter," said the Commandant, "is coming earlier every year. When I was a child it came in January. Now it comes in November."

There was a sad and strangely searching expression in his eyes. He blushed all of a sudden and gripped the buckle of his belt. A vein in his temple was throbbing nervously. He caught his breath and lifted the reins, as though in sudden anger. His skin was rather tawny, such as one finds in the Alto Adige, and the fog had drawn a fine pearly sheen over his forehead. His uniform was made of a coarse grey flannel. The braid on his coat was of a tarnished gold. He wore a thick golden ring on his left forefinger, and as he spoke he kept turning it round rather uneasily.

I said, "Have we met before?"

"We have, but you don't remember me."

"Here in Ravenna?"

"In Padua. I passed you in the street."

"Did we speak?"

"Not a word."

"Then how did you know my name?"

"I do not know your name."

"But you called me, I thought . . ."

"I merely called you Your Excellency."

"You live in Padua?"

"I live in Bolzano."

"Yes, there is an Alpine look about you. I might have guessed you came from the Dolomites. The eyes of the mountain-dwellers have a different look from those of the plain-dwellers. As a child I lived in the mountains. But I hated the mountains. I felt trapped among the mountains. I longed for the sea."

During this meaningless (and perhaps slightly feverish) monologue, Commandant del Pinto kept his eyes intently fixed on me. He said nothing; and when I finally in sheer embarrassment said *"Buona sera,"* he looked at me with a deep and almost dream-like intensity. *"Buona sera,"* he said very gently and almost inaudibly, and he slowly turned away and rode off under the umbrella-pines, like a wanderer drifting off into the night, alone, irrevocable.

On the evening of December the 9th (I remember the date: it was the date of Clare's birthday which I noted in my diary), I was sitting in my bedroom in the Guiccioli palace, bathing my feet in alcohol in order to soothe some bleeding blisters. The clock struck eight o'clock; I called Tita to fetch a shirt for me, and at that moment I heard a pistol-shot directly below the balcony. I ran to the window. It was drizzling imperceptibly, and I saw a group of men who were hurrying through the darkness. I flung on my dressing-gown and ran down the stairs and Tita, with my shirt still in his hands, came running after me. A crowd had gathered under a tree at the end of the garden. I walked up; the crowd parted; and I saw the body of a young Commandant who was lying face down on the rain-soaked grass. I ordered two guardsmen to pick up the body and carry it up the stairs into my bedroom.

The servants stripped him naked and the family surgeon arrived with his instruments. He examined the wounds in del Pinto's bleeding body. The poor fellow had been shot five times in the groin and the belly. (A rusty pistol was found in the grass near the body.) The physician was in the act of wiping the blood from his flesh when del Pinto opened his eyes and cried, "*O Jesù! O Dio!*" Then he closed his eyes again and breathed a powerful sigh, and a moment later he quivered and expired.

There was nothing more to do. I ordered that the corpse be left till the morning. Tita covered it with a sheet and placed two candles beside the bed. Then he got ready a bed for me in the adjoining study. I asked Diego to ride to the Cardinal's house to report the news, and a young lieutenant named Antonio (who was del Pinto's closest friend) sat down and lit his pipe and kept watch over the body.

Who killed him? And why? The truth was never established. The Commandant was disliked because of his Tyrolese origins; perhaps (who can tell?) he was an agent of the Austrians. I got up during the night and peered into my bedroom. One of the candles was still burning. The young lieutenant had fallen asleep and his pipe was lying on the floor beside him. He was a slender young fellow, some years younger than the Commandant, and he likewise (I was told) came from the city of Bolzano. He had taken the death of his friend very casually. He had merely shrugged his shoulder and loosened his belt-buckle. But he had taken (as a last act of friendship, I suppose) the dead man's hand from under the sheet and was holding it tightly in his own. I still remember his head lolling sideways over his shoulder, and his sharp white teeth shining through the half-open lips, and the buckle on his belt rising and falling with his breath, and the gleam of the dead man's ring on his forefinger.

The sun was out and I went riding. Beside the road not far from the town an old woman suddenly waved from the window of her cottage. Then she limped through the door with a bowl of curd-cheese and a cup of honey. She curtsied and said softly: "For the English prince who loves Greece." She refused to take money. I was deeply touched. I shall send her a present.

Mavrocordato, who came for dinner, said, "I have heard an amusing rumour. There are some elements in Athens which are planning to make you King."

"Preposterous," I muttered and looked at him tensely.

"Not in the least," said Mavrocordato, reaching calmly for the pepper-shaker.

My heart beat more rapidly. "A poet for a king," I said. "Extraordinary, isn't it?"

"My good Byron," said the Prince, "you would love to become a king. Don't deny it. Just think! King of Greece! Monarch of Hellas! The crowned ruler of the land of Plato!"

A gnome-like smile played on his lips. My heart sank as I cut my mutton-chop. Mavrocordato is an insidious, very cruel little man.

*

Winter came. The Palazzo Guiccioli was plunged in a torpid gloom. I decided to keep a journal (my first since my tour of the Alps) and as I listened to the wind whistling viciously though the corridors, I jotted down my thoughts, my daily boredoms and exasperations. I *was* bored. I *was* gloomy. Boredom and gloom were part of my nature. But why? Was it merely a matter of a constipated anatomy? Even wine and champagne left me sullen and brooding. A good dose of salts raised my spirits momentarily and a ride in the woods soothed my dark irascibility. A bout of coition usually stultified my nerves, so that for an hour or maybe two I felt relatively cheerful. Even in my youth I was given to moodiness and the fits of gaiety had a frenzied ring to them. There is a paradox in the fact that after embarking on *Don Juan,* my temper (as though in mysterious obeisance to the tone of the work) grew increasingly mellow and predominantly ironical. And here in Missolonghi, which is saturated in boredom, I find that after embarking on these memoirs of mine, I feel increasingly detached, even to the point of impersonality, as though in subtle obedience to the style of these note-books.

I kept searching for a "deeper purpose", a "spiritual call", a "dedication". I thought that I had found them in my zeal for the Revolutionaries: in my hope for Italian freedom, my hatred of Austria, my rage against tyranny. But I soon came to realize that I would never be a part of Italy. I would always be an exile and my political ardour had a hollow ring to it.

I read Mitford's *History of Greece* and Xenophon's *Retreat of the Ten Thousand,* not to mention Spence's *Anecdotes* and the *Lugano Gazette.* I played with my mastiff and fed my little monkeys. I listened to sonatas played on the cello and the clavichord. I played Lotto and Faro (at which I caught Il Conte cheating) . I bought a beautiful new carpet and a set of old etchings. I went riding in the woods and fired my pistols out in the meadows. I toyed with the notion of a play about Tiberius, and the anguish and despair which lead to those last vicious pleasures of his.

I finally embarked on *Cain.* I resolved to put into this opus the deepest reflections of which I was capable: the speculations on immortality, the meditations on fate, the conjectures on human identity which had engrossed me even in childhood. Why, I wondered, and still wonder, do we find a worm in the core of love? What venom is lurking in love, fame, pleasure, luxury, fulfillment? What shadowy anxiety keeps hovering over all this? Is it guilt? Is it the suspicion that these joys are unearned, or is it the fear that the greater the joy, the darker the plunge that will follow? Or is it an even gloomier conviction, namely that love, luxury and fame are merely momentary pauses, merely stepping-stones in the torrent, which if anything impede the natural flow of our destiny—that in short only a Spartan strength of heart and a Stoical fortitude can carry us through the darkness of grief and disillusionment? For grief and disillusionment are sure to come, like night after day. Power alone cannot bring happiness and even the Gods are not happy.

Two men died. One was Napoleon. His death left a void in the world, which now seemed delivered *in toto* to mediocrity. It is increasingly difficult for greatness to survive in our society. Men are reduced to a monotonous littleness. The heroes have departed.

The other was Keats. One day a pamphlet arrived by the post. It was a poem which Shelley had printed in Pisa. I read it reluctantly. I had never cared much for Keats, neither his verses nor his theories, which included an attack on my idol Pope. Yet on reading *Adonais* I felt curiously troubled. I sensed that there was something I had somehow failed to grasp. Poor little Keats had burst a blood-vessel in Rome, so I was told, in vexation at the hostile reception of his poetry. He died young; he died poor; he died neglected; he died miserable. I decided never to speak another word against Keats. I sat down and read *Hyperion*. I recoiled from the style, I disliked the vocabulary. But I was touched. There lay buried in its thickets a hint of magnificence. I put it back on the shelf and decided to cultivate "suspended judgements".

Shelley arrived at the palazzo at ten o'clock one night and we chatted in my library until five in the morning. We spoke of Pope. (Shelley disliked him, though to a lesser degree than Keats.) We spoke of Allegra. (Shelley told me she was spoiled and tempestuous.) We talked of Clare. (Shelley was puzzled by the purity of Clare's character.) And we talked of Keats. (There were tears of indignation in Shelley's eyes.)

Finally I read him a newly-written canto of *Don Juan,* and Shelley said:

"To be quite frank with you, I found *Childe Harold* a little ponderous. But what you have just read me is superlative, Byron. It is alive, it is fresh, it is witty. And oddly enough its gaiety has something curiously touching about it . . ."

I went with Shelley to visit the tomb of the illustrious Theodoric and the sinister old church of Sant' Apollinare. Shelley was stirred by the gold mosaics and the brooding black elegance, but it struck me that an atmosphere of the tomb hung over Ravenna. My terror of enclosures rose up in me again, and I finally decided to depart from Ravenna. In any case, a certain unpleasantness was developing there. Aside from Count Guiccioli's adroitly-veiled hostility I noticed something else: the police-spies were following me. I caught them lurking at the street-corners and peering through the hedges. (It even occurred to me that Commandant del Pinto had been spying on me.) I made no secret of my liberal politics and of my hatred of the Austrian oligarchy. The Ravennese authorities thought me a dangerous revolutionary.

But it was more than that, of course. I was stale and discontented. I was only thirty-two but I felt old, irredeemably old. I felt Time passing perilously; my life, my survival demanded a change.

One day I wrote to Shelley and told him I was planning to move to Pisa.

22 March

Rain again. Missolonghi lies half-drowned in the lagoon. The clouds are the colour of bat-wings. I feel an oppression in my chest.

Something dark is awaiting me beyond the horizon. But

then why do I soak in this steam-bath of reminiscences? What earthly sort of use is there in this wallowing in memory? No use whatever, I suppose, if no strength is to be gained from it. For the only use to be gained from anything is a greater strength, a greater fortitude. What is strength? What is courage? Simply this, I imagine: the will to keep on living amid darkness and destruction and the capacity to keep on loving amid loss and despair.

And so, in pursuing the past with an ever-increasing urgency (which amounts almost to a panic these last few days) I detect the need to see my past again in its full regalia before the curtain falls on the drama. I find a witch-like process changing the past before my eyes—like those dry Chinese flowers that Augusta brought one day, which spiralled into orchids as I dropped them in the water. New colours and new shapes are brought out from their years of hiding. Little things that I had forgotten suddenly blossom into a passionate vividness.

Memory! Yes, a redeemer as well as a liar and betrayer. Like a mediaeval alchemist it takes the cheap baser metals and triumphantly turns them into a pure-glowing gold; and the memory becomes more precious than the things that really happened.

Is this, after all, the final recompense of existence?

*

September passed, the leaves fell, the autumn rains started to fall. I roamed restlessly through my rooms, like a cheetah in his cage. I was followed about on these strolls by my little menagerie: my two cats, Lulu and Emerald; Moretto my bulldog and Rebecca my spaniel: Puck the terrier and Prattle the whippet; my sly little badger, Sardanapalus, my falcon Orestes, my eagle George, my crow Sally, and my two monkeys, Ahasuerus and Hortense. There was also a sleek little billy-goat whom I called Perkins and a splendid Egyptian crane whose name was Osiris. All of these heterogeneous beasts got on well together (aside from an occasional little quarrel about the food) and roved about freely in my rooms. They were reasonably clean (except for Sally, who was incorrigible, and dropped her little seals on my manuscripts with a crisp disdainfulness). When I worked at my desk they sat silent and attentive, no doubt realizing that I was engaged in a matter of importance. But the moment the door was opened and my maid appeared with the tea-tray, they gathered in a circle and begged noisily for crumbs of cake (the badger in particular had a passionate sweet-tooth and learnt to sit up and beg for sugared almonds). Sometimes, when she was good, I gave a fig to Hortense, and Osiris loved especially those little *délices de Parme* which came in gilded boxes and were shaped like violets. The monkey Ahasuerus struck up a friendship with Sally and they would sit on top of the bookcase, plucking the lice from one another, he with his fingers, she with her beak, and their mutual love was sweet to behold. I bought a silver necklace with a bell for Sally and a velvet coat with golden epaulettes for Ahasuerus, and after this they frequently posed in front of the mirror, side by side. They started to stay aloof from the rest of the menagerie, feeling vaguely aristocratic and glancing scornfully at the other animals.

After tea-time they all loved to cuddle on my bed, the cats along with the dogs and the eagle beside the badger. The coverlet grew dappled and frayed with their visitations, but this was their cosiest hour and I could not bring myself to discipline them. They were happy on the whole. They liked to play games. Lulu and Prattle used to play hide-and-seek behind the sofa. Little Hortense played *Button, button* every morning with Rebecca, but unfortunately their games often ended in a spat, with mutual accusations of unnecessary roughness, and even cheating. Sally the crow was a kleptomaniac, almost as bad as Scrope Davies, and hid my golden cuff-links behind the bust of Pallas Athene. Puck and Perkins loved to play with a large ball, and were watched with fascination by the eagle and the crane, who clucked and nodded wisely, appraising the finer points of the game.

Not that things were wholly idyllic. There were feuds and vendettas. Once the crane had a savage encounter with the billy-goat, and the crow was on icy, almost venomous terms with the terrier Puck. Blood-stained tufts of fur or feather were sometimes found on the tiles, and I was awakened from my siesta by squeals of rage or howls of anguish. My servants glumly tolerated these highly-strung creatures, with their repertoire of whims and noises and caprices. The falcon insisted on using the gravy-boat as a latrine; the crow kept absconding with the forks and the spoons. But I needed to have my own little menagerie, for even the wildest and wickedest beasts seemed loving and loyal compared to men. But it was more than that, no doubt. I needed the flurry of fur and feathers, I needed the medley of croaks and cackles, I needed this miscellany of life around me in my gathering alarm at the thought of death.

Finally I prepared to leave for Pisa, where both Shelley and Teresa were awaiting me. Shelley arranged to have eight waggons sent from Pisa to Ravenna in order to carry the furniture and beasts back to Pisa. I watched them loading my books and my sofas on the waggons, and a curious reluctance to leave Ravenna suddenly came over me. Was this merely a spasm of homesickness asserting itself? Or was it an instinctive apprehension about Pisa? Soon my rooms in the palace were empty and desolate. Only a table and a bed remained. Even the rugs had been removed. I roamed at night through the hollow chambers, wrapped in a black, aimless melancholy. My animals were infected by my own forebodings. They looked worried and dejected. They followed me about in my candle-lit wanderings, whimpering and mewing uneasily, trailing their shadows along the wall. The rooms echoed sadly to the restless padding of paws, the pattering of hooves and the scraping of little claws. A jungle-like anarchy seeped through the zoo. The monkeys swung silently from the glass chandeliers, vaguely frightened by this new and disconcerting loneliness. The rooms began to stink of cat-shit and monkey-piss, not to mention the subtler effluences of the goat and the badger. The place began to seethe with thousands of fleas, lice and ticks. Little paw-prints and claw-prints covered the dusty old floors, which were littered with fossilized turds and fallen feathers.

My heart still burns painfully when I think of my departure. Most of the beasts had been led to the waggons, two by two, as though to the Ark, but five I left behind under the care of old Ghigi. I waved good-bye to the two old monkeys who crouched mournfully on the sills. I patted the little badger who lay curled on my bed, and I stroked the ancient crane who sat immovably on his perch. And finally I said good-bye to poor old Perkins, the billy-goat, who had broken his leg and lay dying in the library. He looked at me gently with his enigmatic eyes, and then feebly butted his horns at some invisible adversary.

23 March

I kept waiting for the soft double-knock on my door. Finally at midnight I heard it. I said hoarsely, "Come in, Luke."

He is flattered when I call him Luke. He feels that it makes him half-English.

He stood shyly by the door. I beckoned. "Come. Have some brandy, Luke."

And as he sat there in the lamp-light I said, "Take off your clothes, my boy. I'll try to make a drawing of you. In Venice I took up drawing . . ."

I picked up my note-book and started to draw. The pencil shook in my hand, but I started with the profile and then proceeded to sketch the shoulders and the arms and the belly. And then suddenly as I looked up at him I saw that he was blushing and that my excitement, silently communicating itself, had touched his rising phallus.

*

I stepped into my coach on a cold October morning and went rattling through the dark dripping streets of Ravenna. The land rose gently towards Imola. The sun came out and the vineyards glistened. The road twisted around a half-ruined monastery and joined the stony highway which led to Bologna. I rode at the head of the column in my fine heraldic coach and the long trail of waggons came lumbering after me. Once we passed by a fountain to fetch water for the animals, who lowered their heads and lapped thirstily at the bucket. Then we climbed up a hill. On the peak stood a crucifix, and in the distance rose a ghostly old castle on a mountain-top.

I was gazing at the view when I saw another coach in the distance. It was climbing the steep mountain-road in my direction. I glanced through the window and caught sight of a familiar face.

I leaned out and cried "Clare!"

Lord Clare leaned out and called "Byron!"

The two coaches came to a halt and I ran across the road. He reached out and grasped my hand. And for a moment the familiar face, which I had recognized instantly, grew alien and blurred: it was the face of a stranger. But then the veil fell away again. It was Clare after all, and the delicate tranquil face had scarcely changed at all, except for a hint of dryness around the mouth and a touch of hopelessness in the eyes.

"You have changed," he said, "Byron. Yet you have hardly changed at all."

"You too have scarcely changed, Clare. And still you too have changed!"

Clare smiled. "We all keep changing and yet we never change."

"A part of us keeps changing. And a part never changes."

"Do you remember," he said, "how we sat in Harrow churchyard?"

"Yes, I remember," I said quietly. "We talked of Death and Eternity."

"And you wondered how you turned into Byron."

"And I wondered how you turned into Clare."

I stepped into his carriage and we sat without speaking. I thought of the mossy gravestones and the clouds overhead; I thought of the mysteries of coincidence and the deeper mysteries of identity. I took his thin-boned hand and held it gently in my own. Then I stepped from the carriage and said, "Fare thee well, Clare!"

And Clare called softly back to me, "Fare thee well, Byron!"

And so we parted again, saying little and knowing less, and we went on our separate ways, he to Rome, I to Pisa. I was still shaking with excitement when the road entered the valley; but whether it was grief, or love, or amazement, or an invisible terror, I do not know.

24 March

The olive-trees in the meadow are writhing like souls in torment. But of course they are merely olive-trees and the world is merely the world, and love is nothing but a silent perambulating phantom.

Something is wrong. I feel horribly weak. I tried to walk to the close-stool and suddenly I fell down and started to vomit uncontrollably.

I shall pour a glass of brandy and try to gather my wits about me.

*

I met Rogers in Bologna. We rode together over the Apennines, which were soaked in a smouldering glow which made them look like volcanoes. We crossed a stony pass where the eagles were circling and we paused by a farm-house and watered the horses at a trough. The water came gushing from a mossy old lion's head and I dipped my face in the icy coolness. I still remember the laundered petticoats which hung from a pear-tree and the smell of hot loaves which flowed from the kitchen. I bought a loaf of bread and some cheese and a jug of wine. Then we sat under a pine-tree and chatted away peacefully.

Rogers munched at his crust and peered at me quizzically. I never trusted Sam Rogers. He was calculating and cunning. His face was as white as a parsnip and his eyes were black as raisins. His verses (I once admired them) were sleek but dull and desiccated. And his character (for all its suavity) was caustic and malevolent. But he was a stimulating conversationalist. I loved to gossip with Sam Rogers.

"What," I said, "do you consider the secret, Sam, of poetical craftsmanship?"

Sam replied: "The whole secret lies in a mastery of prosody. The choice of words is subsidiary. Even the play of the mind is subsidiary."

"And whom," I said amiably, "do you consider a master of craftsmanship?"

"Certainly not Shakespeare," said Sam loftily. "Shakespeare was brilliant but erratic. And scarcely Dryden.

Dryden's music is monotonous in its very sonority. Spenser definitely. But Spenser moved within too narrow an orbit. Which leaves us with Pope. Pope's metrics were as bright as a diamond."

"Poetry," I hinted, "is surely more than a matter of impeccable prosody."

"To be sure," said Sam Rogers, tossing a crumb to a sparrow. "But show me a masterpiece where the prosody is not impeccable."

I said: "I idolize Pope. But didn't he deliberately restrict himself in clinging so slavishly to the Heroic Couplet?"

Rogers grinned and pinched an imaginary gnat in mid-air. "Ah," he said, "the Heroic Couplet! What a blessing it is! The grave becomes graceful, the tragic becomes ironical, the witty becomes incisive, the wise becomes supple. All passion grows civilised in the cool embrace of the Heroic Couplet. The Spenserian stanza is treacherous, and the *terza rima* is outlandish; iambic tetrameter is gauchely primitive, the dactyl and anapæst are antiquarianisms. Even the sonnet (though I love the sonnet) suffers from coyness and rigidity. Nothing will ever take the place, for spice and variety, of the Heroic Couplet!"

"And what," I snapped, "of Scott?"

"Scott wrote songs," said Rogers airily.

"What," I growled, "of *The Ancient Mariner?*"

"A lugubrious *tour de force.*"

"And *Intimations of Immortality?*"

"A vaporous excrescence," cackled Rogers.

"You cling to the traditions, don't you, Sam?"

"I cling to discipline," said Rogers smugly.

The animals were becoming a little restless in their waggons. Moretto kept barking and Lulu mewed plaintively, and Orestes the falcon started to hack at his cage.

I said icily: "I should like you to explain what you mean by the 'treachery of the Spenserian stanza'."

Rogers leered at me maliciously. *"Touché!"* he snapped. "Your little Achilles heel! *Mon cher* Byron, I know you are sensitive regarding the merits of *Childe Harold,* and the vulgar success of the work has failed to endear it to me. But your use of the Spenserian is quite embarrassingly self-conscious. At the end of every stanza comes a grandiose flourish, with a glance at the audience. No, no. It won't do. I prefer *The Castle of Indolence.* Even Keats did it better in *The Eve of St. Agnes.* And Shelley did it with infinitely greater flair in *Adonais."*

I was blushing with rage. "So Keats and Shelley have become your models?"

Rogers patted me on the wrist. "Forgive me, Byron. Another Achilles heel. No-one admires you more than I. I have always defended you against the critical purists. But every poet must learn to move within his own limitations. Stick to *Don Juan,* my friend. *Don Juan* is a minor triumph. Your penchant for the self-congratulatory finds its perfect outlet in the bawdily cynical . . ."

Rogers glanced about absently. Then he rose and said, "Excuse me, please." He dipped through a fence and crouched clandestinely behind a bush. He was still wearing his London hat and gripping his gold-headed walking-stick, but even these could not give elegance to the excretory posture. When he returned, wiping his brow with his *crêpe-de-chine* handkerchief, I said to him cheerfully:

"My dear Rogers, it is always edifying to listen to your critical diatribes. It is equally instructive to watch you following the call of nature. When I saw you squatting in the bushes it occurred to me that even Dante had to pause from his glory and lower his breeches to take a shit. Henceforth, in moments of gloom, I shall always draw sustenance from the recollection of your bare white bottom and your tapering grey hat. I now realize that there is nothing incompatible between a spiritual refinement and the intestinal processes."

Rogers looked at me with acerbity. "It is a lesson I thought you had learnt. How often, my dear Byron, while reading your finer emotional outbursts, I was driven to picture you in the act of *coitus interruptus!* And I consoled myself by murmuring that there is nothing incompatible between magniloquent verbiage and the thrust of a well-oiled penis . . ."

After this acidulous tit-for-tat we got into the carriage and proceeded on the road that wound into Tuscany. The sun sank and the lights of the farm-houses twinkled in the distance. Our coachman stopped and lit the lamps of the carriage. It was night when we entered Florence. We dined in an inn near Giotto's tower and at midnight we rode to our hotel by the Ponte Vecchio.

The next morning Sam Rogers came and woke me out of my sleep. We had breakfast in the Piazza and then went wandering to Santa Croce, where we dutifully inspected the marble tombs of the dead. One by one he intoned the names of the illustrious Florentines: Lorenzo and Dante, Galileo and Giotto, Machiavelli and Michael Angelo, Botticelli and Boccaccio . . .

But the old irritability swept over me again. I took a violent dislike to the city of Florence. Whereas the circle and the curve reigned supreme in Rome and Venice, Florence was a maze of squares and triangles, of cubes and pyramids and parallelograms. I have never cared for squares, nor for cubes or parallelograms. What was more, I suddenly found myself in a quagmire of onlookers, and once again I was reminded that I was an infamous celebrity. English spinsters craned their necks when I drank my tea beside the Duomo. A girl approached me in the Piazza and asked me to sign her *Childe Harold.* And when I left on the following morning and stepped into my coach there was a face at every window to watch my elaborate *embarquement.*

I rode gloomily through the cypress-laden sceneries of the Arno and at dusk I entered the city of Pisa.

The Turkish forces in Larissa seem not to have materialised.

We keep waiting for something heroic, something spectacular to happen. But nothing at all happens; nothing visible to the naked eye.

Mavrocordato came and said, "This war is a whimsical business. We wait for the Turks to pounce on us. But the Turks refuse to pounce on us."

"You look cheerful," I said, "Alex."

"I *feel* cheerful," said the Prince. "I was wandering through the woods to-day and what did I see? A young shepherd lay snoring under a large bushy evergreen. I knelt down beside him and meditated on his rustic loveliness. Then I gently caressed him. He still kept sleeping but his flesh responded. It was most gratifying, my good Byron, it was deeply reassuring. If we cannot capture people's hearts by the cruel light of day, we can sneak into their spirits by the dusk of their dreams."

"You speak most poetically, Alex."

"It is an astonishing thing," he said. "When I have done something virtuous, such as posting a letter to London, I feel mentally stultified. I feel drab and prosaic. But when I have done something deplorable, such as fondling a shepherd's testicles, I feel the veil of poetry descend on me like a blessing."

"Poetry springs, perhaps," I said, "from a violation of the usual proprieties."

Alex grinned. "I shall go home and write a poem about my shepherd. Rather in the style of Virgil's Eclogues, with a whiff of Gongora."

"I can't help wondering," I remarked, "if your shepherd deserves a poem."

Alex regarded me with horror. "I am shocked, Byron,

shocked. That you of all creatures should utter such a heresy! Everything is worthy of a poem, even an egg in a frying-pan. My shepherd will emerge from my poem bigger and more beautiful than he really was, just as Troy emerged from the *Iliad* grander and nobler than it ever was!"

*

Ravenna was damp and menacing. Pisa basked in the Tuscan sunlight. Ravenna was dark and lonely, and I never spoke English in Ravenna. Pisa was cheerful and sociable; I spoke nothing but English in Pisa. I rented the Casa Lanfranchi on the banks of the Arno and the Shelleys lived in the Tre Palazzi di Chiesa across the river. Mary Godwin was by now appropriately legalized as "Mrs Shelley". She had published her *Frankenstein* and was already posing as a literary celebrity. Aside from the Shelleys there were Tom Medwin and his crony John Taaffe and the amiable and erudite Ned Williams and his wife, as well as a certain Signor and Signora Mason. The "Masons" were actually a wealthy expatriate named Tighe and his mistress, Lady Mountcashell, who lived together in the Casa Silva. The Lanfranchi very shortly became an open house for the lot of them. They were welcome at all hours, for luncheon, tea or dinner. We'd go riding after luncheon to Cisanello, not far from Pisa, where we practised pistol-shooting in the court of an empty farmhouse. We came back in time for tea and my Teresa presided at the tea-table, which was spread with bowls of jam, heated muffins and sliced *prosciutto*. We played billiards after tea or sat in the garden and spoke of poetry. We drank claret after dinner and kept on chatting till three in the morning.

George Tighe was a bulging person in a brightly-checkered waiscoat, and his mistress was a fragile, feathery lady with the eyes of a marmoset. Medwin was lean and parsimonious, with

233

an interest in "druidism", while Taaffe was chubbily garrulous, with a fondness for macaroni. Ned Williams was a
gentle though pedantic young man with a defect in one eye
and a mole on his lip. He kept listening attentively during
our claret-spiced evenings, peering sidelong at Shelley, whom
he worshipped and idolized. Jane, his wife, was an inarticulate woman in a rose-dotted dress, who kept nodding her
head rapidly and grinning with horse-like teeth. They were a
dim and rather untidy couple, earnest and pallid and opin-
ionated, utterly charmless but utterly kind.

But it was Shelley of course who mattered. When he
greeted me on my arrival he exclaimed, "How thin you are,
Byron! You have changed, you have changed incredibly.
Your appearance, like your character, is strangely Protean."

"We are all Protean," I said. "You too have changed,
amico."

"But *you*," insisted Shelley, "are truly and essentially Protean, and the core of your being is a perpetual changefulness.
You keep darting about endlessly, like a brook in the Highlands, while the rest of us lie pickled in the same little bodies
and the same little souls."

"I too lie trapped," I murmured, "in the same club-footed
body."

"Fiddlesticks, Byron. Your body is beautiful. You are very
proud of your beautiful body."

"I too lie trapped," I whimpered, "in the same old profligate soul."

"Nonsense, Byron. You are profligate but you are also in
your way ascetic. I have pondered upon your character. You
are everything and the opposite of everything. No generalities apply to you. You are like quicksilver. There is no
capturing you. Even your thoughts, your very instincts dart
about like drops of mercury. You have, like Shakespeare, no
philosophy: you merely have whims, insights, attitudes."

I was flattered by Shelley's effort to decipher my character, but at the same time I felt that he had somehow missed the "crux" of it.

"I am not," I said mournfully, "nearly as intricate as you think. I am really very simple. I am an animal. I am merely an animal."

He too had changed, I thought. He seemed frailer, more flamingo-like. He stooped forward rather awkwardly so as to seem less tall than he was. His hips were broad like a woman's. His legs were a little knock-kneed. His clothes were drab and slovenly; his shoes were worn and his breeches were stained. He wore a brown school-boy jacket, much too tight and frayed at the elbows. Yet there was something about Shelley that made him graceful and almost elegant. His head was strangely small; it was poised on a thin white neck. The hair on his head had a dishevelled, fuzzy look to it. His face had a frail and almost china-like texture, with lips like a doll's and cheeks so pink that they looked painted. He moved in a sinuous, undulating way. I called him "the Snake": referring to the nephew of Eve's serpent, who walked on the tip of his tail, precariously balanced, like Goethe's Mephistopheles. I might equally well have called him "the Bird" (referring to the Phoenix who springs from his ashes) : his voice was thin and bird-like and he fluttered his arms like wings.

There were moments when I felt a bit uneasy in Shelley's presence. He once said, quite unaffectedly: "You are the sun to my glow-worm, Byron. I can never hope to rival you. You will always overshadow me." But I knew better. Though they occasionally seemed too nebulous and rarefied, I knew (and more than ever after reading *Adonais*) that there was something in his poetry which I hopelessly lacked. Rapture and Delirium are the essence. Wordsworth has Rapture, Coleridge Delirium. But there is more to it than that. An "intellectual ardour" for one thing. Shelley had it and I did not. And a "spiritual dedication". Shelley had it and I did not.

And a capacity for "the sublime". The sublime, I fear, was never my *forte*.

"Why," said Shelley, "do you keep on flitting from subject to subject, like a butterfly? Why do you refuse to argue coherently? Why not be serious, just for once? Why do you joke about everything, even about God and even yourself? It is charming, it is beguiling, but it is wasteful. It is frivolous, Byron."

"I am a frivolous man," I said.

"You are," said Shelley, "a tragi-comedian."

After the rest had gone to bed we used to talk by the flickering candlelight: about painting and about politics, about Beauty and about Divinity. I do not wish to create the impression that we were a pair of bloodless aesthetes, given to vaporisations about pale artistic principles. We also spoke of horses or wine or tobacco. But certain talks we remember more vividly than others, and certain talks cast more light on human character than others.

One night we went strolling along the Lungarno. A stairway led to the water and there we sat down, watching a boy who was fishing in his boat by the light of a lantern.

"What is beauty?" murmured Shelley. "Is it merely a human concept? A woman looks beautiful because we appraise her in human terms. Would she seem equally lovely to a whale, or a man from Mars? The unimaginable shapes of the ocean-bed, or the miracles of Saturn—can these also be called beautiful, though never to be seen by human eyes? Does beauty exist as a Law? Did it exist before Adam and Eve? Will the *Odyssey* still be a glory when Man has finally perished? Will the *Primavera* still be a masterpiece when only the insects are left to admire it?"

"The *Primavera* will still exist as an object in space. But will *Figaro* still be beautiful when nobody is left in the world to sing it?"

"There are questions," muttered Shelley, scratching his

temples, "that have no answer. Some men say that all art is merely the reflection of an age and a locality. Is *The Rape of the Lock* merely the squeal of a dwarf in Twickenham? Only a brute or a vulgarian would think such a thing. Great art is not just an echo of a place or a time. Great art creates its own world. It lives in timelessness and placelessness. It soars across history like a falcon over a valley."

"Beauty," I said, nodding wisely, "is a human concept, as you say, but it also transcends the values of mere humanity. A peacock will still be beautiful even when Man has ceased to exist, for Nature has obviously intended that a peacock should be beautiful. But the rest of the birds, while suspecting his beauty, will fail to appreciate it. The triumph of *homo sapiens,* and his only claim to glory, is that he alone of the animals sees the magnificence of the natural universe."

Shelley smiled and took my hand. "There are moments," he said, "when I love you, Byron. I myself struggle laboriously to produce an *aperçu.* To you it comes spontaneously, like chirping to a cricket."

"Which, alas, does not make it any more precious," I said.

"Nor any less precious, thank God," retorted Shelley.

Suddenly the boy lifted his pole with a cry of delight. A small silver fish was wriggling at the end of the line. He plucked it from the hook and clapped it briskly into his basket and then he reached for the oars and rowed slowly down the Arno.

"There is something," I said softly, "that we have omitted to mention, Shelley."

"Yes? Namely?"

"Poetry," I said, "has something akin to terror in it. All my life I have felt that I was skating on a sea of chaos. Has this anything to do with those Natural Laws which you describe?"

"Terror exists in the world," said Shelley. "And maybe terror is an aspect of beauty. Pope closes *The Dunciad* with an invocation to terror:

Nor public flame, nor private, dares to shine;
No human spark is left, nor glimpse divine!
Lo! thy dread empire, Chaos, is restored;
Light dies before thy uncreating word;
Thy hand, great Anarch! lets the curtain fall,
And universal darkness buries all.

"Our terror nowadays," I said, "is a different terror from Pope's. The world has become a vaster and more unpredictable place."

"Yes," said Shelley, "but a glimpse of terror in a world of order and security is more frightening than its presence in a world of disorder. A flash of lightning striking a tea-pot which stands under an arbour is more disturbing than the howling of a storm in the jungle."

"A matter of opinion, at best," I ventured.

"Or of idle fancy, at worst," said Shelley.

We rose and walked back to the Casa Lanfranchi.

26 March

Luke has just left my room. I can hear him tiptoeing down the corridor. I can feel the touch of his lips on my cheek like a burning coal.

A ghost. Only a ghost. The whole of humanity is nothing but ghosts.

*

One night I discovered that my *casa* was haunted.

It was a cold December evening, just a week before Christmas, and a white winter moon shone through the windows over the Arno. My friends had said good-night—Tighe and Taaffe, Jane and Edward. The glasses stood on the table amid a litter of almond-shells. We had talked of transmigration, the movement of souls from beasts to men, and in certain rare instances from men back to beasts. An arrow of wind shot through a crack in the pane and the candle-flame twisted and lunged, as though inebriated.

I was reaching for my atlas (I wanted to glance at the map of India) when I heard a little cry which was like the hooting of an owl. I picked up the candle and tiptoed into the hall which led from the library towards the store-rooms at the rear of the *casa*. The hallway was unlit but I noticed a patch of moonlight, which then vanished as a door seemed to close upon it noiselessly. I was determined not to be fooled by any hallucinatory nonsense, so I boldly crossed the hall and knocked at the door which had just been closed.

"Anyone there?" I said briskly.

There was no answer; I had expected none. I detected, however, a furtive rustling within the room, or rather a kind of brittle feathery vibration. I turned the door-knob (it was strangely warm, as though a hand had been gripping it) and opened the door, which creaked reluctantly, almost irascibly. The room was filled with trunks, wicker chests and *armoires*. The moonlight was hovering over a dusty disorder, with which it appeared to be mutely conspiring. Some old cloaks and faded ball-gowns hung on the wall to the right, along with the masks and rumpled dominoes of a bygone Carnival.

I was about to retreat (my hand still rested on the iron door-knob) when it seemed that one of the cloaks, by some half-perceptible movement, was deftly removing itself from the hook on the wall and assuming an independent, almost puppet-like rigidity. And by some similar sidelong movement one of the masks moved slightly leftward, so that it lodged, or seemed to lodge, on top of the russet-coloured cloak. I cannot swear to what extent this juxtaposition was a real one, or merely a *jeu optique* created by the dust-filtered moonlight. It crossed my mind that one of the maids (probably Giulietta, the laundry-girl) was hiding in the dark, waiting for an amorous *appuntamento*. This suspicion was dispelled, however, when the cloak slid languorously towards me and then turned about abruptly, revealing the face of a beautiful woman—no longer young, perhaps in her thirties, with a silvery tinge at the temples. But these putative thirties instantly turned into fifties, and I watched her in horror as the face dissolved into a mummy's, and a moment later into a maggot-riddled patch-work of skin, which then melted into ashes in front of my eyes as the cloak slowly crumpled into a heap on the floor.

I swiftly closed the door and hurried back to the library, but decided to leave my study of the Indian map till the following day.

When I awoke the next morning I ordered Tita to lock the cloak-room and make sure that it stayed locked during the rest of my residence.

He did so. But he mentioned as he delivered the key to me that he had noticed, when he entered the room, the corpse of an owl beside the window, and that he had wrapped it in a newspaper and buried it promptly in the vegetable-garden.

I may add that it seems strange that so many of my houses have been haunted. But "haunted" is a relative, even an arbitrary term, and quite possibly these same dwellings presented to their subsequent tenants a totally humdrum and commonplace appearance.

I am like a magnet, a reluctant magnet. I attract to my person not only women but also animals, phantoms, mosquitoes and leeches.

THE
THIRD
NOTE-BOOK

To-day we were planning to go to Salona to meet the generals. But the rain has turned the land into a slate-blue swamp and the slumbering streams into vomiting cataracts.

I happened to glance at my portrait: the little engraving which Kinnaird sent me. There comes a day, as a man grows older, when he suddenly sees himself from a distance. He sees his youthful self as an irrevocably-vanished creature. I looked at my portrait and I knew that it no longer was myself. I am only thirty-six but I am old, old, old. I see my younger self as a shadowy stranger: the late Lord Byron. The flesh has changed and the blood has changed, the heart is weaker and the spirit sharper, and all that is still the same (or nearly the same) is the skeleton. Polidori once said to me that in a man's entire body only the semen remains unaltered, and stays perpetually young.

Well, perhaps, some tiny essence in me still remains the same. Montaigne thought that *au fond* a human character never changes, and that all the apparent changes are only illusory. Youth hides a multitude of sins which the pouches of age expose into banality. I was no better when I was young, I was merely stronger and more beautiful, and beauty gave me pride and prodigality as well as cruelty.

Hester Stanhope once told me in her brusque, importunate way: "Your eyes are too close together. But they are the key to your fascination." Edleston told me: "Your eyes are frightening. They are almost like a hypnotist's." Hobhouse told me: "The top of your face is very strong and very masculine, but your mouth and your chin are strangely soft and almost feminine." And Constance told me: "You are the most beautiful human being I have ever seen but there is something perverted and destructive about your beauty."

Alas, the beautiful Byron no longer exists. But the perverse and destructive and tortured Byron still exists. Only now the destructiveness is directed against myself. Some men say that my character is baffling—chaotic, pagan and mercurial. Very well. But is this baffling? Sometimes, I admit, I too feel baffled. But is there anything baffling in being an *infans naturae*? Childishly happy and childishly gloomy, childishly affectionate and childishly venomous, easily tittivated, easily satiated—an animal in short, and wayward like an animal. I am really as transparent as an Alpine spring. I am sick of those prudes who despise a man who follows his instincts, who is indifferent to the smirks of the fashionable or the leers of the hypocritical.

I am sick of trying to analyse my own impulses and oddities. They are what they are, desperate and throbbing and equivocal, and to give them a name is to cloud their essence.

*

One wintry afternoon I was sitting at my window. A cold brassy sun was shining brightly on the Arno. Three men were crossing the narrow white bridge in my direction. The man on the left was Shelley; the man on the right was Williams. Between them walked a powerfully-built man in a long black cloak. Shelley was wearing his threadbare jacket and was gesturing with both hands. Williams wore a thick red coat and was plodding along sedulously. The man in the middle was walking in a careless muscular stride, listening calmly to the animated chatter of Shelley.

Five minutes later there was a knock on my door. Moretto barked; the visitors entered. Shelley introduced his friend, whose name was Edward John Trelawny. I felt a shock of excitement when I first laid eyes on the man. It was as though I had seen him long ago under rather "suspicious circumstances". I had never actually met him but his impact was so powerful that memories of my youth seemed to spring into life. He was handsome in a virile, piratical way. His beard was black and curly and clung to a finely-cleft chin. His lips were sullen and fleshy, with a contemptuous turn to them. His teeth were unnaturally white and very sharp, almost wolfish. His brow was high and bulging and his nose was sharp and arrogant. His eyebrows were bushy and met over his nose. His ears were finely shaped, like little pink seashells, and his eyes had a tense and somewhat predatory glitter.

I felt immediately, when I laid eyes on him, that something new had entered my life: not hostile precisely but somehow ominous and oppressive, in spite of his charm and animal vitality. I also felt (and continued to feel) that under his faintly obsequious manner lurked something else, a dark intention, a rather sinister intimacy.

I led them into the gaming-room and we played a game of billiards. Then we stepped into my study and sat down for a cup of tea. Teresa had returned from a trip to the florist's and joined us for tea, having placed some chrysanthemums in a copper vase. She seemed faintly disturbed by the dark flamboyant stranger and kept glancing at him covertly as she sipped at her tea.

Trelawny kept his eyes fixed intently on my face as I started to chat with a giddy vivacity. I turned to him and said:

"And now tell me about London, please."

"What do you wish to hear about London?"

"What about the theatre? Are there any new actresses?"

"I know nothing about the theatre, I fear, nor about the new actresses."

"What about boxing? Do you follow boxing?"

"I know nothing about boxing."

"What about gambling? Any scandals?"

Trelawny laughed scornfully. "You are a trifle out-of-date, sir. The gentlemen of London no longer gamble."

I blushed and put down my cup. I felt like an ass; I had vulgarized myself. And Trelawny had succeeded in establishing a relationship with me. And from that moment I both hated and loved Trelawny.

As time went on he came to remind me more and more of my own frailties—my self-display and my *passé* dandyism, my moodiness, my braggadocio. But there was also, with all his slyness, a masculine openness about Trelawny; he had a maritime flavour, a sailor-like elegance.

As we sat by the fire he unbuttoned his shirt and revealed a large tattoo between the nipples on his chest: a cobra which lay coiled round the stem of a lotus-blossom. Thereupon he embarked on a leisurely recital of his early adventures. After a miserable childhood in Cornwall (a drunken father who beat his mother) he ran away at fifteen and entered the Navy and sailed to the Indies. He was humiliated and tortured by the officers on board the vessel, and he was even, he hinted, sexually assaulted on several occasions. He deserted the ship in India and joined up with a Netherlands pirate, whose vessel used to pounce on the ships of the East India Company and carry off the booty to the shores of Mauritius. He took up Mohammedism and dressed as an Arab. (He still had a Barbary look about him.) He rescued (so he told us; Shelley later cast doubt on the episode) a beautiful Arabian girl whose name was Zuleika (or maybe Zela) whom he promptly fell in love with and proceeded to make his wife. When she died of an intestinal fever he burned her body on the desert sands and returned in despair to the stale corruptions of the European continent.

How much of this was true? I was never sure. Not much of it, probably. Trelawny had a way of extravagantly embroidering his anecdotes and at the same time tightening their tone with a few pedestrian truths. He did not lie in order to deceive nor even in order to impress. He lied out of self-love, and because of a loathing for authority.

But he was more than merely crafty. He was highly intelligent. There is no question that Trelawny was very clever. His talents were not dedicated to Truth or Benevolence, nor was I sure on the other hand that they were at the call of the Prince of Darkness. He never said what he really thought but beneath all he said lurked the flickering of a ruthless and adventurous energy.

I said: "And what have these adventures taught you about life, Mr Trelawny?"

"Nothing at all. Merely that men are a filthy and ravenous kind of beast."

"And what have they taught you about God?"

"Very little," growled Trelawny. "Except that God, to care about a horde of contemptible swine such as men, must be either outrageously stupid or deliriously perverse."

Williams said gently: "I think you are trying to shock us, Trelawny."

Trelawny smiled: a surprisingly child-like and beguiling little smile. "Perhaps you are right. Maybe it is I who am mad and perverted!"

The sun was setting when they said good-bye. I stepped to the window and watched them leave. I saw the trio walking briskly down the street towards the bridge. As they stepped on the bridge Trelawny turned in my direction. He glanced at my window, and for an instant I felt his eyes fixed on my own with a piercing, conspiratorial intensity. He turned away brusquely and the trio crossed the bridge and gradually vanished in the wintry twilight.

Teresa crossed the room and touched me lightly on the shoulder.

"Who was that wicked-looking man?"

"His name is Trelawny."

"He looks like an assassin!"

"My child, he is quite innocuous."

"He has the *mal' occhio*. I can tell by his eyebrows."

I laughed nervously. "How utterly delightful. I have always longed to meet a *mal' occhio*."

"It is dangerous to joke, my darling."

"Perhaps it is dangerous *not* to joke . . ."

I took her in my arms and kissed her thoughtfully on the ear-lobe.

28 March

For two decades I have indulged in pontifications about love. But I still don't understand it. I have never understood it. It is a longing for repetition—a nostalgia for the same low voice, the same responsive flesh, the same secret ceremonies. But it is also a longing for novelty, a perpetual need for change—the half-familiar voice is never saying the identical words, or if the words are identical their meaning is subtly different. The flesh is never the same; or if indeed it is the same, it seems to have changed mysteriously into the flesh of a stranger. The kisses are the same but the time and place have altered their flavour. The ceremonies are ritually regulated, but some detail is incessantly different. Thus love is simultaneously both faithful and promiscuous. In its very fidelity lurks an appetite for the stimulus of novelty. (With Teresa I closed my eyes and thought of my beauty in the inn in Portugal.) And in promiscuity there lurks a need to recapture an early love. (In Luke I find embodied the flesh and features of Lord Clare.) In my fidelity to Teresa I was being secretly unfaithful to her, and in my faithlessness to Clare I am bound to an unquenchable fidelity.

O England, my England! *O quando te aspiciam?*

*

One evening in March a thing occurred (or seemed to occur) which was at the same time both idiotic and fateful.

We were riding back from our pistol-shooting in Cisanello: Shelley, Trelawny, Pietro Gamba, a Captain Hay and myself. Some distance ahead of us Teresa was riding in the carriage with Mary Shelley. (These two ladies, and occasionally Lady Mountcashell, used to accompany us on our sporting trips.) My groom Papi was driving the carriage and Teresa's manservant was riding behind it. The sun was very low and shone directly into our eyes. The hills looked calm and still. The walls of Pisa gleamed in the distance.

I caught sight of our bibulous crony John Taaffe beside the road. He had been out for a ride with his Turkish *amico* and was walking beside his horse in an absent-minded way. The rest of us slowed down to keep pace with the pedestrian and we lazily rode abreast down the dusty white road. We chatted pleasantly about the play we had seen the night before—some nonsense or other about the Emperor Heliogabulus.

I remember saying, "One can hardly expect histrionic subtleties in a place like Pisa."

Trelawny said, "Was Heliogabulus a very subtle sort of man?"

Shelley said, "All wickedness is subtle. And that is why wickedness is more interesting than goodness."

"Ah, I wish that I could agree," said Captain Hay didactically. "I consider that virtue is even more intricate than vice."

Suddenly a horseman came galloping down the road behind us. The dust welled up from the hooves in ghostly little clouds. He went racing past Taaffe, whose horse reared in panic, and Taaffe cried indignantly, "My dear, have you ever seen the like of it?"

I put the spurs to my stallion and went galloping after the rider, who was dressed in the golden braid and golden epaulettes of a dragoon. Shelley came galloping after me on his piebald gelding, and just as we reached the walls he swerved in front of the dragoon and barred his entrance into the narrow stone gate.

Shelley flung up his arms and squealed in his shrill Italian: "Please explain what you mean by your conduct, you scoundrel!"

The dragoon looked at Shelley with a frozen expression. Then he bared his teeth and said: "My conduct is that of a soldier who follows his orders. Yours, signor, if you'll pardon my saying so, is that of a hysteric."

Trelawny rode up and came to a halt at my side. I said to him, "This man is insolent. What shall we do about it?" I reached into my saddle-bag and drew out a card and gave it to the officer, who said with a sneer: "I have no card, but my name is Sergeant Masi, if it pleases you. And I am ready to fight the whole lot of you, one by one!"

"Very well. Tomorrow," I said, "at twelve o'clock. We'll meet at the gate."

Then Trelawny approached the man and fixed his powerful black eyes on him. He said softly, "I add my challenge to that of the other two gentlemen."

The young officer (who was blond and very handsome) nodded silently. His lips were trembling, I noticed. He sat motionless in his saddle. At this moment Pietro Gamba, flushed with rage, rode up to the group. He cried out: *"Ignorante!"* and struck the Sergeant with his riding-whip.

Sergeant Masi's whole body started to quiver with fury. He roared: "You are all hysterical! You are all of you madmen!" He wheeled about his horse and rode on through the gate, shouting to the guards beside the gate, "Arrest these idiots! Arrest these lunatics!"

I laughed and shrugged my shoulders, suddenly recovering my composure. Gamba and I rode through the gate and Shelley and Trelawny were about to follow. But at this moment the wild young Sergeant swung about unexpectedly and started to slash indiscriminately with his sabre. Trelawny parried the blows but Shelley was knocked from his horse. He lay unconscious in the dust at the foot of the gate. Captain Hay (an elderly person who was wearing a monocle) now rode up with a puzzled air and was cut on the nose by the Sergeant's sabre.

I went galloping in a rage down the street towards my *casa*, which was only a hundred yards beyond the gate. There I ordered my butler to run to the *questura* and report the whole matter as promptly as possible. The carriage now drew up at the entrance to the *casa* and Teresa got out, screaming *"Dio! O Dio . . ."* Mary took her by the arm and led her calmly into the hall, and I stood on the steps and wiped the sweat from my forehead.

Suddenly I beheld Sergeant Masi riding up to the stairway. He leant from his saddle and stared at me with his wild blue eyes. Then he said softly: "Well, signor, do you admit that I have defeated you?"

My heart felt strangely heavy. I felt hypnotized almost. I looked intently at the young dragoon and cried out in a daze, "I don't admit it! You are a rascal! I demand satisfaction!"

Sergeant Masi leant closer and gripped my hand firmly. I caught the smell of his boots and the whiff of wine on his breath. There was hatred in his eyes. But it was more than merely hatred. It was like the culmination of a dark and unutterable relationship, in which hate was blended with pride and desire with a fiery jealousy. A crowd was already gathering in front of the house. The sun had set. It was growing dusky and the bells began to toll.

Masi and I stared at each other in silent rage, unable to speak. His hand around my own felt strangely hot; it was trembling feverishly. Then he dropped my hand suddenly and picked up his reins and briskly turned his horse and started back towards the Lungarno.

I heard a voice cry out *"Prego!"* and then another crying

"*Aspetta!*" A silhouette at the head of the steps was pointing a pistol at Masi. Then a second shape in black came gliding swiftly out of the door and lunged at Sergeant Masi with a long iron lance. This second shape, whose face was hidden by a cloak over his head, cried out hoarsely, "I hit him! By God, I hit the bastard!" And he darted into the crowd and vanished from sight.

Sergeant Masi started to lean over sideways in his saddle. He gripped at the reins and dug sharply with his spurs, but his helmet slid sideways and the *birretta* fell from his head. His arms jerked abruptly like those of a puppet. He cried, "They have killed me! Jesus and Mary, they have killed me!" He slid from his horse and fell heavily on the pavement in front of a little café at the corner. He lifted his head and looked back in my direction. Then he crawled on all fours through the door of the café.

I raced up the stairs into the Casa Lanfranchi. Teresa lay on the music-room sofa in convulsions. Shelley was crouching by the fire-place, vomiting into a copper bowl. Captain Hay was wiping the blood from his nose with a towel. Pietro Gamba was foaming with rage and Trelawny stood silently with folded arms. And Mary Shelley, as calm as a turtle, was giving smelling salts to Teresa and regarding the rest of us with sibylline disdain.

The candles were lit. Two bottles of Chianti were brought from the cupboard. A bowl of noodles was set on the table along with some Parmesan cheese. We ate and drank listlessly, waiting for something more to happen. But nothing happened. We talked of politics, we talked of noodles, we talked of theology. We talked of everything in short except of the blue-eyed Sergeant Masi. Teresa excused herself when the clock struck ten-thirty. And at half-past eleven the rest of my guests said good-night to me.

The next morning I called Tita to my room and said: "What news, Tita?"

"No news, Your Excellency."

"Is he dead?" I said softly.

"No, Your Excellency. He is still alive."

Sergeant Masi did not die, as I later ascertained. But the police arrested Tita, who had been seen pointing a pistol at Sergeant Masi. I asked Tita before his departure about the identity of the man with the lance. But Tita had not seen any man with a lance. I asked the rest of the servants. None of them had seen a man with a lance. I decided that the man with the lance must have been my coachman, Paolo Papi.

But I was never sure. I was sure of nothing in this hectic episode. After a while I even thought that it was a figment of my fancy, and that all of us, including Shelley, had been drinking too much wine.

But Teresa said darkly: "I have my opinions on the matter. Be careful, darling. It is an omen. It has all the aspects of an omen."

29 March

And so love (to continue with last night's digression) is in fact a kind of malady, an insidiously recurrent fever. (That is to say, if it is a passion and not just a bovine set of habits.) It moves constantly toward corruption, it is in fact a gesture toward death, and at the same time it is the supreme and unaltering symptom of life—perpetual change amid the unchanging, secret patterns amid the chaotic, a continual reaching out into the chasm of the future; a blending of delight, desperation and decay.

No doubt. But can it be that some loves are beneficent and others destructive? That certain loves contrive to strengthen us in our struggle with existence, while others gnaw at our strength and our very identity?

Homer said that Achilles "within his hairy chest hesitated

253

between two choices". I too hesitate. But my chest is hairless and my hesitation is not heroic. Nor, like Hamlet's, is it intellectual. It is merely tormented. Still, it has its own vehemence. It has its own poison. Achilles said to Lycaon (if I remember the words correctly) : "Even upon me will fall hard destiny and death." So it is. Even upon me will fall hard destiny and death.

*

I noticed again that I was growing a gorbelly. After my bath every evening I glanced at the mirror with disgust. Teresa forgave me (and even, I suspect, relished my obesity) but one morning I decided to put an end to it. I embarked on a diet of biscuits and soda-water, and when hunger grew too violent I prowled into the kitchen and stirred some rice with a bit of fish, spiced with vinegar. I wolfed down this pudding with a wince of disgust, and after a fortnight I saw that my belly had vanished. I stopped sweating. I stopped belching. My armpits smelled like figs. My piss grew clear as spring-water and my ribs grew once more visible. Even my scrotum seemed to shrink. I grew constipated for lack of oil. My sperm dwindled in texture as well as in quantity and my cock displayed a leaning towards *ejaculatio præcox,* an event which left Teresa even more disgruntled than myself. I continued however with this Spartan self-discipline, in expectation perhaps of some coming emergency, spiritual or pecuniary, as the case might be.

A second obsession now crept over me: that my childhood was returning. The *idée fixe* took hold of my mind that we were all still children, and that the appearance of maturity was only an illusion. The misty memories of my parents took on a new and harrowing vividness. My memories of Mary Chaworth and Lord Clare grew strangely luminous, and my thoughts of Harrow and Newstead took on a *trompe l'œil* effect, as though they had happened only yesterday, with a magical shifting of perspective. Dear Augusta suddenly turned into a spellbound little dryad and Annabella into a rosy-cheeked water-baby.

I now suspected that as we age we slowly slide into a world of fantasy, and that (unlike the usual assumption) reality lurks in childhood, where we still see the world in all its Easter-like freshness, free of slogans and clichés, free of dogmas and taboos. And our grief lies in the awareness of a heart-breaking loss: we thirst for the fountains of childhood in the deserts of our maturity, and we are driven to re-enact the enchanted patterns of our childhood. Not that childhood is pure or innocent. Childhood is vicious and unforgiving. I remember a dream in which I wandered across a sunlit meadow. A group of children with auburn locks and white lace-collars were playing at archery, and their feathery little arrows struck the bull's eye without piercing it. Suddenly these lovely young creatures turned into a band of howling pygmies and shot their arrows at each other's hearts, and the lawn lay covered with bleeding corpses.

I thought of Ada occasionally, but Ada had turned into a dream. I sometimes thought about Allegra, but always with guilt and apprehension. One morning Shelley said: "There is something that I wish to discuss with you."

"Yes? What?"

"About Allegra."

"Yes? And what about Allegra?"

"I hear that the convent in the Romagna where you have sent her is far from salubrious. The food is foul, the nuns are shrewish, the beds are damp, the air is malarial. Don't you think that Allegra might be brought up to Pisa, where she could live with a respectable family and take lessons in the pianoforte?"

I shrugged my shoulders impatiently. "Has Claire been talking nonsense again?"

Shelley's eyes grew blurred with fury. Tears of sweat shone on his brow. "Byron," he screamed, shaking his fist, "you deserve to be horse-whipped!"

April came. Showers fell. Violets were sold on the banks of the river. One day a letter arrived from my banker Ghigi in Ravenna, saying that poor little Allegra was sick with a fever. I grew pale with apprehension. I sent a courier back to Ravenna, asking that the nuns call in a doctor from Bologna if necessary. Ghigi wrote every day. At last he wrote that Allegra was better. She had begged the day before for some "Turkish paste", which she adored.

But two days later came another letter. Allegra had taken a turn for the worse. She was stricken with "catarrhal convulsions" the night before and lay in a trance. She died the following day. The nuns asked Ghigi about the corpse. He ordered it to be embalmed and put in a lead-lined coffin.

Teresa came into my study to break the sad news to me. But even before she spoke I said, "I know. Say nothing more about it, please."

I went to my room and lay down on my bed. I felt listless, almost indifferent. But then the thought of Allegra's death came welling over me like a wave. It was worse than sad: it was utterly unbearable. I felt cold and stiff as a stone. I kept staring at the ceiling, searching for a pattern among the cracks. The clock struck half past three. And I finally fell asleep.

Was it grief that I felt? Or was it guilt? Or was it horror? I had always preferred my Ada to my bright-eyed little Allegra. Even while Allegra sat on my knee my thoughts kept drifting back to Ada. The love which I owed to Allegra had already been fixed on the absent Ada. And now that Allegra was dead I felt I had killed her with my indifference.

Two days later a letter arrived from Shelley: "The object of this letter is to convey Claire Clairmont's requests to you, which, though melancholy as one of them is, I am sure you will readily grant. She wishes to see the coffin before it is sent to England; and she also hopes you will give her a portrait of Allegra and (if you have it) a lock of her hair, however small it might be."

I sent the lock, as well as the portrait, back to Shelley by a special messenger.

30 March

The primate of Missolonghi, amid much bowing and scraping, has presented me with a parchment decorated with golden flourishes. They have made me an honorary citizen. But I smell a rat. They want money.

I feel vaguely unwell again. What is wrong? Have I caught a fever?

*

Summer came. I yearned for the sea and looked for a villa beside the water. I finally discovered a country mansion near the village of Montenero, which lay on the shore some miles south of the city of Leghorn. The Villa Dupuy stood on a knoll surrounded by cypresses and looked over the blue, sunny sweep of the Mediterranean.

Life was peaceful in Montenero, and less gregarious than my life in Pisa. I spent the morning in my bed and usually rose at two o'clock. I lunched and read the *Gazzetta* and then bathed in the sea, and at six I went riding over the fields or through the pine-woods. The Shelleys were living in Lerici nearby but I saw them rarely. Shelley was piqued at me, it seems. And what is more Claire was visiting them. I refused to see Claire. It was heartless, but it was necessary. The thought of Claire Clairmont was very disconcerting to me.

One day I was told that the Mediterranean squadron of the American navy was anchored in the harbour, and I sent a letter to the Commodore. That same evening I received a note inviting me to visit the *Constitution*.

I arrived at noon punctually and climbed up the gangplank. I felt shy and rather uneasy when I saw the crowd of young sailors, rosily clean and radiantly handsome, speaking a curious kind of English and peering at me with their innocent, sun-drenched smiles. But I soon felt totally at ease, as though I had known them all my life. Captain Chauncey kindly accompanied me to a smaller frigate, the *Ontario*, where an even greater degree of informality reigned. The young officers (similarly rosy and radiant and snowy-toothed) kept watching me with an undisguised excitement and fascination. They edged closer, trying to touch me and hear what I was saying, and I caught the smell of soap and fresh starch that clung to their bodies. They invited me to sit and have a glass of wine with them. One of them asked me what I thought of the famous American poets, including a Miss Bradford (or Bradmoor or Braddleton). I explained apologetically that I was ignorant of American poetry, but that I would try to obtain a copy of Miss Bradford's effusions. He then, to my surprise, produced a copy of *Manfred* and asked me to inscribe it to him, which I did with delight. I felt touched that my reputation (which in England was dwindling rapidly) was beginning to blossom in the trans-Atlantic territories.

One day I was sitting in my library. I had finished reading the newspaper and was starting on a letter to Douglas Kinnaird. A servant entered the room: "A young American has come, Your Excellency."

I said rather musingly, "A sailor, could it be?"

He showed me the card: a Mr Bancroft, from Massachusetts.

Mr Bancroft was a tall and somewhat knock-kneed young

man of twenty-two, who had gone to Harvard and was now returning from his studies in the city of Heidelberg. He was grave and austere, yet somehow delicate and over-civilised, with a finely-carved nose and deep-set eyes and twitching jaw-muscles. We sat in the west drawing-room which looked over the sea, and we spoke of Washington Irving, whose *Knicker-bocker History* I had thoroughly enjoyed. Bancroft thought less highly of it than I did. He was a bit of a pedant, but at the same time he was refreshingly eager and open-eyed.

I said, "Am I what you anticipated?"

"Not quite, I confess."

"Do I look like what you imagined?"

"Older, a little."

"And less handsome?"

"Oh no, equally handsome, sir, but a little less myste-rious."

"What did you expect?"

"A more impenetrable, more tempestuous sort of man."

"More in harmony with my verses?"

"More morose and monosyllabic."

"My good Bancroft," I muttered, "whatever our nature may happen to be, we cannot spend our whole lives boiling away like a volcano. We must learn to relax. We must try to cool down. I look forward to growing old, when I can contemplate things peacefully."

Bancroft stared at me with bewilderment. "You will never grow old, Your Lordship!" He blushed and started to stam-mer. "I mean emotionally, of course, Your Lordship. I can-not picture you as an elderly bard. Your hair will never be white. You will never, I am sure, turn into another William Wordsworth."

"Mm. I see. Has William Wordsworth turned into a white-headed bard?"

"He is fifty, or even older. The flush of youth has gone from his poetry."

259

I grew thoughtful. "And how about Goethe, whom you visited in Weimar?"

"Goethe too is an elderly bard. The gleam of youth has gone from his face."

I felt faintly depressed after Bancroft's departure. Teresa entered the room and sat down at the clavichord. She started to play a little rondo by Mozart, and I walked to the window and looked towards the sea. Mr Bancroft was wandering down the path towards the highway, and his tall bony body dressed in black looked like an undertaker's.

In the middle of May three English sailors arrived in Lerici. They had brought Shelley's boat down from the shipyard in Genoa, and I was invited to Lerici to inspect the little vessel. Mary Shelley mentioned casually that it had been baptized the *Don Juan*, but that later they decided to call it the *Ariel*. I was piqued. I took a violent dislike to the *Ariel*. I urged Trelawny to hurry on with the plans for my own schooner, which arrived some weeks later in the harbour of Lerici. I called it the *Bolivar*. For a week I was pleased with it. But this pleasure changed rapidly into boredom and even bitterness. I strolled about on the *Bolivar*, fondling the cannons and sniffing at the cables, but something about the ship disappointed and even disgusted me. Trelawny had instigated it. Trelawny had planned it. I both hated and loved Trelawny but I merely hated the *Bolivar*. It had cost me a fortune but I promptly lost interest in it. I left the unfortunate *Bolivar* in charge of Trelawny.

"Well, you see," whispered Teresa, "everything he touches turns into ashes!"

31 March

The Turkish fleet is bearing down to blockade Missolonghi. An impressive sight, I must say. But at night our boats still manage to evade them.

260

Wrote a letter to Clare today to introduce Signor Zaimie. Clare has been in my mind of late. Why? Who knows? He is like a corpse to me.

There it is. This new passion, which I dare not mention to anyone, seems to hover over the chaos of my life like a mythical bird. A basilisk perhaps, which destroys with its stare.

I have grown very thin. My breeches are much too wide for me. I am haunted by crazy fears, weird alarums, sudden suspicions. I feel I am under a spell. I suspect that someone has cast the Evil Eye on me. Yes, there is something very strange in those owlish eyes of Mavrocordato. He is jealous, corrosively jealous. But why on earth should he be jealous?

Alas, the reason I dare not admit this new passion even to myself is not that it is wicked or forbidden, but that it is ridiculously painful. It is silly, it is hopeless, it is humiliating: but above all painful. I have kissed the lips, I have touched the body, but I will never touch the heart. I am in love, but for once my love will not be reciprocated.

Is this why men recoil from what Moore calls *Knaben-liebe*? Not because of an intrinsic evil, since there is no intrinsic evil, but because this search for beauty brings its own inevitable self-defeat, and paedophilia, like Narcissus, is left to contemplate its own pale countenance?

*

June arrived, the sun grew hot and a wave of indolence crept over me. One evening a dusty coach drove up to the door of the villa. I glanced through my window into the coach and I recognized the fine, frozen features of Lord Clare. I ran to the door and gripped his hand eagerly. Then I led him into the drawing-room and ordered some tea.

We spoke of Harrow. We spoke of Wingfield and Tattersall and the rest of them. We spoke of London. We spoke of Moore, we spoke of Melbourne, we spoke of Webster. And all

261

the while I stared at Clare, trying to penetrate the surface, trying to pierce through this effigy into the image of my memories. It grew dark, the lamps were lit, and it was time to say good-bye. We stepped into the garden, where a warmish breeze was stirring the leaves. Clare's face in the starlight looked suddenly young and alive again, and we stood in the pergola for several minutes without speaking. Thirteen years had passed by. They had shrivelled into nothing. The Clare who stood beside me was again the Clare I had known at Harrow. I flung my arms around him and kissed him on the mouth. He whispered: "My Byron. My friend. My beloved friend . . ."

And thus, by a delicate miracle, I succeeded in altering the past. The kiss which I denied him at Harrow I finally bestowed on him at Montenero. But it was a posthumous sort of kiss. It was almost like kissing a corpse, and only the power of my yearning, which had gathered impetus over the years, turned the corpse into a throbbing and loving reality. It was so strong that it swept us both back into the past again. We were nineteen years younger and the Villa Dupuy turned into a high-gabled school on a dark, windy hill.

He said quietly, "Fare thee well, Byron," and stepped into his coach.

I walked back into the drawing-room, where Teresa sat at the clavichord. She raised her hands from the keyboard and looked at me intently. The lamp shone on her face and on the black and white rectangles, which still seemed to stir under the touch of her fingers.

She said: "Why does Clare mean so much to you, Bairon?"

"How did you know it was Clare?"

"Oh, I knew it. I felt it."

"I loved him," I said.

She grew pale. "Did you love him physically?"

"I loved him physically," I said calmly.

"You should never tell me these things—they make me

sad," she said quietly. She looked at the music (it was a sonata by Couperin) and her lips shook a little as she turned over the page.

I smiled and took her hand. "You don't quite understand me. I was in love with Clare at Harrow, but I never touched his body. I have slept with men occasionally but I never slept with *him*. It was a different sort of thing. And now he is dead. He has gone forever."

Teresa lifted her eyes and stared at me with bewilderment. "You puzzle me, Bairon. You are a mystery . . . Do you really love me?"

I sank to my knees and buried my head in her lap. I took both her hands and pressed her palms against my face. And in the dark, protective warmth of her palms on my eyelids I loved Teresa at that moment more than I had ever loved her before.

1 April

I have seen it a third time.

I was standing in front of the mirror, studying the muscles in my chest (very fine muscles, even now) and assuming (as usual) a posture designed to hide my foot. I meditated on the incredible fact that this same naked body, even with its hideous deformity, had been loved in its day, both by women and men, both by countesses and milkmaids. Tiny nipples, stiff as shirt-studs, an invisible belly-button, and a streak of brown hair which points like an arrow to a slumbering penis—a penis which has been kissed, fondled, venerated and even celebrated. Yes, strange and incredible, and perhaps a little bit melancholy.

A breeze passed through the room, flattening the flame and swaying the curtains, and in the mirror I saw the door slowly opening behind me. A black hairy arm seemed to reach

263

through the doorway, but it quickly recoiled before I could be quite sure of it. I turned and ran to the door. Then I peered into the corridor.

"Anyone there?"

No answer, naturally.

I thought for a moment that it might be a burglar. Naked as I was, I stepped into the corridor. I tiptoed cautiously past Fletcher's door and slowly moved in the direction of the stairway. At the head of the stairs I noticed a dark shapeless mass—it might have been a cushion, or a heap of dirty laundry. As I stepped closer it disentangled itself abruptly and went flopping down the stairs, like a huge hairy toad.

I am not cowardly by nature but I scurried back to my room. After a minute's reflection I slipped on my dressing-gown, seized the lamp and the musket, and stepped back into the corridor.

The creature had vanished. There was nothing left but a smell of slime, and in the spot where it had lain something that resembled a piece of liver.

Is this an omen? Is it a punishment? Or is it merely what it seems to be—some filthy little monster who has crept out of the marshes?

*

We returned to Pisa and I went back to my old routine in the Casa Lanfranchi. I got up at twelve and lounged about in my dressing-robe. My valet Fletcher (who had returned) laid my clothes on the bed for me, and my faithful Tita (freed by the authorities) brought me my breakfast and the newspapers. I had my breakfast and read the papers, humming a tune from *Il Seraglio*. Then I took my hot bath and dressed tidily in my riding-clothes and joined Teresa in the *giardinetto*, where we gossiped till tea-time. When the heat of the day was gone I went riding in the forest, either in an open-aired barouche or on my gelding Otello. Sometimes Tre-lawny rode along with me, smoking a big black cigar. We wore riding-coats of a finely-spun mazarin blue and small velvet caps with black-satin visors. Sometimes we rode to Cisanello, where we used to shoot pistols, but the gaiety and cosiness had gone from our excursions.

I had dinner with Teresa and after the rest had gone to bed I sat in my study and worked feverishly on *Don Juan*. I sipped at my gin-and-water till the early-morning hours, and scribbled away briskly on dirty menus and old play-bills, and the world of Don Juan, built out of ink and paper and prosody, engulfed the Casa Lanfranchi and even invaded my own character: so that I turned, as it were, into the prevalent atmosphere of the latest canto.

Leigh Hunt and his family arrived from London one morning and in a moment of insanity I asked them to stay in my *casa*.

Hunt himself was an amiable though rather mischievous sort of man, with faunish brown eyes and a sly Puckish smile. His hair hung loose and oily, and his voice was bright and chirping. Shelley called him "the wren". A rancid odour hung about him. Once I begged him to wash more fre-quently. It wasn't necessary to stink, I said, in order to write good poetry. His nails were black with dirt and his tongue was coated with purple. Still, we all liked Leigh Hunt. He was so helpless, so utterly incompetent. The only thing that I couldn't tolerate was his way of picking his nose (in the midst of a discussion of the *Paradiso,* for example) and then devouring, quite shamelessly, the little tidbits which he ex-tracted.

Still, there were times when it was a pleasure to have Hunt in the house. I would sit on my *chaise longue* in the shady *giardinetto,* sniffing lazily at the orange-trees while I played a game of patience. I would call through the window: "Leon-tius! Come and join me!" Leigh strolled into the garden and

265

sat down in the grass beside me. He liked to talk about his contemporaries in a deft, disparaging way: of Southey's stupidity, of Coleridge's ugliness, of Wordsworth's crudity, and of Moore's obsequiousness. He spoke lovingly of Shelley and with idolatry of Keats, but even with these he couldn't resist inserting an occasional dart. He regarded all poets as his rivals and enemies. His favourite phrase was "He is finished". "Wordsworth is a corpse," he said. "He is finished." Even the poets of the past were not immune from his terrible obituaries. "Dryden is finished," he said. "His plays are exposed as mere balderdash." Or, "Spenser is finished. The *Faery Queen* will soon be tossed into the dust-bin." He was obsessed with reputations, which were invariably "inflated", and he whittled away at them till they were reduced to a heap of splinters.

He said: "You have scolded me for the infrequency of my baths. Are your callousness and promiscuity to be excused on the grounds of poetry?"

"My promiscuity has harmed nobody and has given pleasure, I trust, to many. And my callousness is merely the result of being pestered by parasites. I could alter these traits by some moral resurrection, perhaps, but all you need to do is step into the bath-tub."

Hunt's slovenliness I could bear. His wife's pretensions I could not. A stoutish person of Cockney origins, she cultivated a "refained" manner of speech and lost no time in loftily proclaiming her disdain for all titles. The aristocracy, she hinted, was merely a pack of degenerate sybarites. She wore poppy-patterned dresses which were stained under the armpits, and she had a way of farting at the tea-table, especially when there were muffins and Gorgonzola, each little fart being accompanied by a glance of startled innocence. The farts of Madame de Staël had at least a resonant self-confidence. The farts of Mrs Hunt had a cringing, hypocritical air to them.

Once Hunt asked her facetiously: "And what do you think of Byron's morals?"

Mrs Hunt pursed her lips and squealed, "Why, I didn't know that he had any!"

I had heard this sally before and went on calmly buttering my bread. But the Hunts clearly felt that a crushing witticism had been administered, and they sat and sipped their tea in a perfect miasma of self-complacency.

Leigh Hunt had six children. I called them the "Yahoos", the "Vandals", the "Hottentots". Like Hunt, they were black with filth but instead of smelling like billy-goats they smelled like a concoction of milk, leeks and cat-shit. They pulled each other's hair and threw their spoons at the cook, Elvira. They scrawled on the walls and ripped open the upholstery. They pissed in their beds and shat in the halls. They spilled their soup on the table-cloth and screamed like a flock of cockatoos. But their parents regarded them as talented little darlings.

I said, "My good Hunt, you must discipline these little beasts of yours."

Hunt said pompously, "I prefer them to grow up in spontaneity."

"My set of Ariosto is in shreds," I said grumpily.

"I despise Ariosto," said Hunt with a sneer.

"I found a turd," I persisted, "in the pantry this morning."

"One of your cats, or that bull-dog, I suppose," said Hunt acidly.

A sense of misrule and anarchy was gradually descending. Fame, money, love, allegiance, even my body seemed to be rotting. The Tuscan police were already keeping an eye on me (in Pisa as in Ravenna I was considered a dangerous revolutionary) and the atmosphere of the city began to grow poisonous. A small brownish spot appeared on my hand and I watched it growing daily, as though it were a symptom of leprosy. The fat on my body was no longer smooth and baby-like: it had a puckered, faintly corrugated look which dis-

267

gusted me. Flakes of eczema appeared on my legs and my velvet collar was sprinkled with dandruff. I was thirty-five years old but I was growing older with a sickening rapidity.

I was inclined to blame these ennuis on Hunt and his horrible family but Teresa said, "What did I tell you? All that he touches turns into dust."

2 April

It is long after midnight. The lamp has guttered and I have lit the candle. And by the light of the candle I have written a poem—the first I have written since my thirty-sixth birthday.

> I watched thee when the foe was at our side,
> Ready to strike at him—or thee and me,
> Were safely hopeless—rather than divide
> Aught with one loved save love and liberty.
>
> I watched thee on the breakers, when the rock
> Received our prow and all was storm and fear,
> And bade thee cling to me through every shock;
> This arm would be thy bark, or breast thy bier.
>
> I watched thee when the fever glazed thine eyes,
> Yielding my couch and stretched me on the ground,
> When overworn with watching, ne'er to rise
> From thence if thou an early grave hadst found.
>
> The earthquake came and rocked the quivering wall,
> And men and nature reeled as if with wine.
> Whom did I seek around the tottering hall?
> For thee. Whose safety first provide for? Thine.
>
> And when convulsive throes denied my breath
> The faintest utterance to my fading thoughts,

To thee—to thee—e'en in the gasp of death
My spirit turned, oh! oftener than it ought.

Thus much and more; and yet thou lovs't me not,
And never wilt! Love dwells not in our will.
Nor can I blame thee, though it be my lot
To strongly, wrongly, vainly love thee still.

I have read the poem again. I feel shocked and humiliated.
Dear Hobhouse would never approve. One stilted phrase
after another, as well as a split infinitive. "Were safely hopeless", "breast thy bier", and "reeled as if with wine." No, no.
Even at Harrow I would have been more fastidious. A clumsy
poem, hideously clumsy, like a turtle trying to fly.

But it was written in pain. Yes, it was written in anguish.
Good God, what is a poem if it is not a half-articulate cry of
anguish?

*

One day in July I looked through my library window and
saw Trelawny galloping up on a coal-black mare. Two minutes later, sweating heavily, he came rushing into the room.

He told me the following story. Three days before, after a
morning thunder-storm, Shelley and Williams (along with a
sailor-boy whose name was Charles Vivian) weighed anchor
at noon and turned the *Ariel* in the direction of Lerici.
Trelawny was on the *Bolivar* and intended to follow them,
but he was forced by the port authorities to remain in the
harbour of Leghorn.

Some time later Captain Roberts (who was a crony of
Trelawny's) was standing on the mole and saw a storm rise
up in the gulf. The sky turned to mauve, streaks of lightning
shone in the distance. He climbed the tower at the end of the
mole and looked through the telescope. He caught sight of

the *Ariel* some ten miles away, and it seemed that its passengers were taking in their topsails. Then the air grew swiftly darker and the mists hid them from view. He remained in the tower until the storm finally cleared. Then he peered into the telescope but the *Ariel* had vanished.

Captain Roberts and Trelawny waited in Leghorn for two days. They questioned the local fishermen but learnt nothing about the *Ariel*. So finally on the third day (the 11th of July) he came galloping to Pisa and informed me of the episode.

Hunt entered the room. I turned to him and said, "Please, Leontius, write a note to Mary Shelley in Lerici and tell her what has happened. Then we'll see what can be done."

The next day at midnight I was sitting at my desk with my pen in one hand and my gin-glass in the other. It was raining, I remember, with a dreary persistence. I heard the wheels of a carriage come to a halt below my window. Then the doorbell started to ring. I heard footsteps in the hall and Teresa's voice as she greeted Mary.

Mary cried, "Teresa, where is he? *Sapete alcuna cosa di Shelley?*"

The door flew open and Mary Shelley came striding into the room. She was followed by Jane Williams, who was wearing a slate-blue cloak. I rose and took Mary by the hand and said quietly:

"No news. I know nothing. We will do all that is possible."

Mary flung out her arms and stared at me desperately. I detected some passionate accusation in her eyes, though what she was accusing me of was a total mystery to me. I led Jane to the sofa and took off her cloak. Then I called Fletcher. I asked him to bring us some brandy.

"What shall I do?" cried Mary hoarsely.

"Spend the night here," I urged her.

"Utterly impossible," groaned Mary.

"You need sleep," I said gently.

But poor Mary, who was shaking feverishly and whose face

270

was wet with rain, refused to spend the night. She drained her glass and took Jane by the arm and said grimly: "Come on, Jane." I accompanied the two ladies down to the street, and they stepped into the coach and went riding off to Leghorn. Mary leaned through the window and stared at me balefully: there was hatred in her eyes, but it was more than merely hatred. I still remember the carriage as it rattled down the street and its lamps shining through the rain-drops as it vanished into the night.

Trelawny told me the rest. The two women arrived in Leghorn at two o'clock in the morning, and he met them at dawn and took charge of the search for the *Ariel*. He sent couriers down the coast with instructions to pause at the watch-towers and scan the horizon for any sign of the boat. He and the ladies left Leghorn and rode through Pisa towards Lerici, pausing for a while in Viareggio, where he asked a young lieutenant whether the *Ariel* had been sighted. It appeared that some fishermen had found a life-boat with a water-cask: it sounded suspiciously like the life-boat of the *Ariel*. They rode on in despair and arrived in Lerici at nightfall, and Trelawny stayed with Mary and Jane Williams at the Casa Magni.

On the 16th of July I had a note from Captain Roberts: "A boat came off this morning and informed me that two bodies had been thrown ashore some three or four miles above Viareggio. By their description I think that it must be poor Shelley and the sailor-boy. The third of the bodies has not yet been found . . ."

On the following morning Hunt and I rode in my coach to Viareggio, and we asked permission to see the bodies which were washed ashore the day before. We were shown two little mounds in the sand between the bushes. The health authorities had already ordered the bodies to be buried. We returned that same evening. I asked Hunt to write to Mary and invite her to stay in Pisa at the Casa Lanfranchi. The next day (the 18th) we had some further news: a third cadaver had been found washed up on the beach not far from Massa. Trelawny insisted on riding to the spot immediately, and he said on his return: "It was horrible, Byron, horrible. The corpse was hideously swollen. The face looked like an octopus and the skin was ripped into long green tentacles. In the pocket I saw a copy of *Lamia and Isabella,* and I knew that it was Shelley. There is no question—it was Shelley. They covered him with lime and buried him quickly in the sand."

I wrote piously to Moore: "There is thus another man gone, about whom the world was ignorantly and brutally mistaken. It will do justice to him *now,* perhaps, when he can be no better for it."

This, however, was not my true and secret feeling about the matter. I felt guilt and remorse and a kind of wan, inarticulate sorrow. I had grown to resent the man. I resented his "purity" and "integrity". But I also felt a playful and capricious veneration which was tinged with a childish kind of jealousy. But above all I felt terror. An invisible beast was crouching in the darkness, and the stench of chaos was hovering in the air.

3 April

I have read my little poem again. Wrong, wrong from the beginning. Poetry is not and it never can be a "half-articulate cry of anguish". If it is poetry then the anguish must be purged from its veins. Clumsy Wordsworth may be right. Passion must ripen into tranquillity. And if Wordsworth fails as a poet it is because of his blunted eye and execrable ear, and not because of any emotional distortion.

And my hideous poem fails as a poem just because it *is* such a bleeding cry: the emotion in its very immediacy grows distorted when put into words. And this distortion is reflected in the limping cadences and the trite vocabulary.

Well, so much for poetry. Now to more important matters. I received a letter from Mavrocordato. It seems that there is a kind of conspiracy. A man named Karaiskakis, who is the chieftain of Anatolica, is conniving with Kolokotrones against his rival, Mavrocordato. Should one believe this silly nonsense? If it is true, it is disgusting. If untrue, it is even sillier and equally disgusting.

*

Trelawny walked into my study and lookled at me triumphantly. "Well," he said, "I have finally succeeded. The health authorities have relented. They will allow me to disinter Shelley's body and take it to Rome. I have a *permesso* to cremate both Shelley and Williams on the beach. I have ordered from the ironmonger's a box for the cremation, as well as two coffins for the bones and the ashes."

On the 13th of August two coffins arrived at the *casa*. They were sprinkled with rose-water and placed in my carriage. On the morning of the 15th Hunt and I had breakfast together and then rode through the dust and the heat towards Viareggio. I caught sight of the *Bolivar* anchored off in the distance and we headed for the beach five miles south of Viareggio.

The carriage crossed a field and came to a halt among the dunes. The horses were sweating and wheezing with exhaustion and a fierce yellow light rose from the flat waste of sand. I stepped from the carriage but immediately got back in again, and watched from a distance Trelawny's morbid antics. He had gathered some fire-wood which he built into a pyramid. He was stripped to the waist and was watching the disinterment. The first of the graves was opened. Iron boat-hooks were lowered and a mutilated body was dragged from the pit. Trelawny waved his arms at me. I stepped from the carriage and strolled somewhat squeamishly to the edge of

273

the pit. It was a nauseating sight: the flesh was utterly shapeless—random chunks of a sand-caked purple, more like a shark's than a human being. But I cried with absolute certainty: "It is Williams! Yes, it is Williams!" The pieces were thrown in the box, which was then carried to the wooden pyramid. Trelawny lit a stick and tossed it casually into the pyre. The fire caught hold instantly. The iron box was hidden by flames, and we tossed some wine and incense into the flames to keep them burning. The intensity of the heat set the air all aquiver, and I watched the burning flesh gradually shrink into ashes. I noticed how the flames changed their colour during the burning: as the body turned into ash the flames themselves turned into silver.

I was seized with a kind of hideous, half-feverish exultation, and I threw off my clothes and went racing into the sea. I kept swimming (as I thought) in the direction of the sunken *Ariel* but I suddenly grew sick and started to vomit into the sea. Little flecks of black bile were floating about on the waves. I turned around grimly and swam back to the shore. The funeral-pyre was already reduced to a heap of ashes, amongst which were visible some broken bits of bone. Trelawny was scuffling about in the sand like a man possessed. His eyes were glittering wildly and the sweat flowed from his armpits. He gathered the ashes in a large canvas sack and threw them into the coffin, which was placed in my carriage. We headed back for Pisa. So much for poor Williams.

Charles Vivian, the little sailor-boy, was left in his sandy grave.

The next morning, the 16th of August, Hunt and I got into the carriage and we headed towards Massa, where Shelley's body had been buried. We came to a halt in the shade of a stunted pine-tree and walked towards Trelawny, who was standing on the beach. Two men were prowling about, looking for the unidentified burial-mound, probing the sand with iron spades and hacking about among the bushes. Finally one of them cried *"Ecco!"* His spade had struck the skull. Hunt and I hurried up. We watched as the men dug into the sand. They kept digging until finally the corpse was exposed. It was unutterable: it was even more hideous and putrefied than Williams's. The clothes had all turned to a black dough-like texture, and the body had fallen into iridescent ribbons. The smell was devastating. Hunt recoiled and ran back to the carriage. But Trelawny crouched grimly over the mass of green flesh and groped in the pocket for the copy of *Lamia and Isabella*. He pulled it from the slime with a snort of satisfaction. But for some mysterious reason only the binding was left. The pages themselves had disintegrated into jelly.

I felt dizzy with disgust, but something in the ceremony had mesmerised me. A passionate loathing for Trelawny welled up in my soul. I said fiercely, "Give me the skull. Do what you wish with the rest of the body but I insist on having the skull. Give me the skull, please, Trelawny."

Trelawny glanced at me furtively. A smile crossed his lips, and he started to twist the delicate skull from its spine. But then suddenly, as he tugged at it, it broke into pieces, which lay scattered on the sand like bits of yellow porcelain. I knelt and started to pick up the fragments of the skull. But the stench was too vile and I quickly turned away again.

Now Trelawny put a match to his pyramid of fire-wood. Hunt came scampering from the carriage with a bottle of olive-oil, which he poured on the flames with a badger-eyed solemnity. I had brought along some caskets of cinnamon and incense, and these I tossed on the corpse, turning the flames from red to blue. Trelawny opened a wine-bottle and poured it on the fire. The sweat poured down his face, mingling with the tears on his cheeks. His whole body was trembling. He lowered his head and growled feverishly: "I restore by fire to Nature the elements of which this man was composed: namely, earth, air and water. Everything is changed but nothing is annihilated. He is now once more a part of that which he worshipped."

I looked at him with rage. Then I said very gently, "I knew, Trelawny, that you were a pagan, but not that you were a pagan priest. You have conducted this whole ritual most convincingly, I must say."

I walked towards the water. The need for ablution swept over me. I looked back at the pine-grove, which was shuddering in the heat-waves, and I stripped myself naked and jumped into the sea. "This," I growled to myself, "will be *my* pagan ritual." The *Bolivar* lay anchored over a mile from the shore and I swam in easy strokes all the way to the ship. As I swam I looked back and saw the flames of the pyre. They sprang with a ghostly grandeur from the flat yellow sands. The pine-woods beyond looked like a pack of waiting wolves and the mountains in the distance shook in the heat like wind-blown tents. I climbed on board the *Bolivar* and lay on the deck. I asked the steward Giacomo to bring me some wine. I gulped down the wine, then dived into the sea and swam back again. It was late afternoon when I stepped on the beach. The body had burned for over three hours and was finally reduced to a heap of ashes. Except, uncannily enough, for a single small part of it: namely the heart, which lay nestling in the flames but refused to disintegrate.

Trelawny pierced the heart with a stick and plucked it out. He held it in his hand and sniffed at it inquisitively. Then he held it to his ear, shaking it gently as he listened. It was black and very wrinkled: it looked like a very large prune.

I poured wine on the heart and then oil and a bit of cinnamon. But the shrivelled little heart still refused to burn. I threw some more incense on it and Hunt brought out his brandy-bottle and sprinkled it with brandy, but it still refused to burn. It lay bubbling in the flames, exuding a syrupy fluid, and it gradually turned from black into a mummy-like violet. Finally Trelawny had the furnace carried down to the water. They dipped it into the sea, and a cloud of steam arose. Then Trelawny waded in and plucked the heart from the iron box. He stared at it with horror: drops of blood were still oozing from it. He dropped it in the wine-jug and gave it to Hunt, who carried it triumphantly back to the barouche. Then Trelawny gathered the ashes and dropped them in the coffin. He screwed on the lid and the coffin was placed in the barouche.

We washed our hands and faces and stepped into the coach. We crossed the sandy beach and headed back to Viareggio, where we arrived just as the sun was sinking below the Mediterranean. We went to a sea-side inn and dined on fish and roasted lamb, and we drank six jugs of wine in a state of dark exhilaration. We kept chatting as we sat on the terrace: about the Celts and the Druids, about Boadicea and Vercinge-torix, about Stilton and Parmegiano. We even talked about the Russians and the morbid strangeness of the Russian temperament. We talked about the Prussians, and the ghost-like cruelty of the Prussian temperament.

It was midnight when we stepped into the carriage again and the horses went galloping through the forest of Pisa, which seemed to my drunken eyes to be dancing like waves as the lamps tossed their billows of light among the tree-trunks.

I felt violently dizzy. My cheeks were aflame with sunburn and my body was seething with a frenzied exhaustion. The coach came to a halt at a bend in the road. We got out and pissed solemnly into the lamp-lit forest. Then we buttoned our breeches and rode silently into Pisa, where Tita was waiting beside the door in his night-cap.

4 April

The rumours turn out to be true. Karaiskakis's rebel soldiers have taken possession of the fortress of Vasiladi at the mouth of the harbour.

I went for a stroll in the afternoon, past the fields towards

277

the olive-groves. I sat down in the shade and something strange suddenly happened to me. A small blue flower, shaped like a buttercup but slightly frailer in texture, was growing in the moss among the roots of the olive-tree. I picked it from the stem and held it up between my fingers. It was odourless but the colour had a strangely-familiar look to it. It took me back to the forest beside the Brig o' Balgonie. There was a purity in the colour blue. It was the purity of self-forgetfulness. And for the first time since my childhood I was lost in self-forgetfulness. I kept staring at the flower with its marvellous child-like blue, and wave upon wave of self-forgetfulness swept over me. These waves were like the waves of the Tyrrhenian or the Hellespont; but they were even more calming and cleansing and redeeming. I sat for over an hour with the flower in my hand, and I sensed that something glorious, after all the years of waste, had finally and triumphantly entered my life again.

Was it all merely an illusion; was it all just a "poet's fancy"? No. I am old. I am old and weary. It was not an illusion. It was Truth.

*

I remember it now. It was Hunt who kept the heart. He kept it in a wine-jug in the corner of his bedroom. After a while he took the heart and transferred it to a spirit-jar, which he placed on his desk beside a set of *The Lives of the Poets*.

"You should give it," I said, "to Mary."

"I have offered it to Mary, but Mary recoiled at the thought of it," said Hunt.

Some days later (or maybe weeks) Mary Shelley came up to me and begged me to coax him to give her back the heart. But Hunt loved Shelley's heart. He kept it on his desk, where it gradually turned yellow as it floated in the spirit-jar. Once I

278

walked into his study and he picked up *Adonaïs* and read, somewhat drunkenly, the closing lines of the poem:

> The breath whose might I have invoked in song
> Descends on me; my spirit's bark is driven
> Far from the shore, far from the trembling throng
> Whose sails were never to the tempest given . . .

Tears shone in his eyes as he delicately fondled the spirit-jar. Then he lowered his eyes and read piously to the end of it:

> The massy earth and spherèd skies are riven!
> I am borne darkly, fearfully afar;
> Whilst, burning through the inmost veil of Heaven,
> The soul of Adonaïs, like a star,
> Beacons from the abode where the Eternal are.

He lowered his head and started to sob, and I walked from the room and slammed the door in disgust.

I was wrong, I suppose. Hunt loved Shelley, and he grieved for Shelley. But I was sick of the horrible forms that this love could assume.

(Later on, incidentally, after urgent persuasions, he gloomily consented to give the heart back to Mary.)

5 April

I ordered some gun-boats to be sent against the Vasiladi fortress. When they saw the boats the miserable rebels were filled with terror and fled instantly.

O Greece! O noble Hellas! Where is it gone, that rocky splendour?

There are times, in this maddening frustration, when I suddenly see a light. It is like a lonely little lantern shining in the middle of a forest. And I whisper to myself, "Enough of all this 'glory'. Enough of all this 'art', 'happiness', 'love', 'beauty', *et cetera*." I have searched long enough for beauty and happiness on earth. The search for beauty brought out all that was false in me and the search for happiness brought out all that was contemptible. A half-mad father and an ogress-mother brought me to feel even in babyhood that I would always be an orphan and a pilgrim on this earth. One looks for happiness in the life of the herd. I was not meant for the life of the herd. Those who look for a herd-like joy end by turning into worms. Their existence is meaningless. They grow slimy, gelatinous. Life is meant to be inexplicable, unpredictable and unutterable. Life is terrible and sublime for a man, not placid and slavish. And it is those (the priests, the preachers, the scientists and the dogmatists) who would like to reduce us all to a placid uniformity but who will finally destroy us on the pyre of a horrible boredom. Let us learn to be alone and to suffer and be singular, and to find our exultation in solitude and secrecy.

Is this what life has finally taught me? A curious lesson. But it will serve.

*

And now the old "fear of enclosure" swept over me again, as it had in Geneva and Venice and Ravenna. Only this time it was different. There were sinister undertones. I felt old, appallingly old. I felt parched, pitted, pendulous. The delight had gone from my heart and the vitality had gone from my body, and a chilling uneasiness hung in the air. There was disheartening news from London. The critics were chilly if not vituperative and the sales of my books were dwindling disastrously. There were no more rapturous letters from governesses in Somerset, and the letters from my bankers grew more and more ominous. The letters from Murray grew strangely impersonal and the letters from Augusta grew painfully aloof. The Gambas had been banished from Ravenna for their "Revolutionary sentiments", and the rumours had spread to Pisa, where they likewise became *non grata*.

One day Teresa murmured: *"Caro* Bairon, something is wrong. The Pisan climate disagrees with me. What would you think if we moved to Genoa?"

And so the inevitable finally happened. I was forced to move from Pisa. All my belongings, the books and beasts, the mangy dogs and screaming monkeys, the urine-patterned rugs and the heaps of dusty rubbish, all were piled in a large *felucca* which I rented in Leghorn; and I myself with Teresa (and three geese in a bamboo-cage) got into the old, creaking carriage and headed gloomily for Lerici.

In Lerici I met Trelawny. We went strolling along the beach. Then we stripped under a pine-tree and dived into the sea. It was a hot and glittering day. The waves were lapping lazily. The *Bolivar* lay anchored three miles off, beyond Lerici, and two fishermen were sleeping in their boat in a near-by cove. We sprawled on the golden sand and Trelawny looked at me wonderingly.

"Why do you look at me so strangely?"

"I am trying to read your thoughts."

"My thoughts! I wish I had some."

"Well, your feelings, then," he muttered.

He fondled his testicles with a sly, musing air and then looked at me calmly with his black piratical eyes. I felt drawn to Trelawny even while I secretly despised him. There was a tension between us, a kind of dark animal rivalry. I envied his boxer's body, with its tiny buttocks and massive calves. He sensed this envy, and his air of comradeship was tinged with coquettishness. I even suspect that he kept hoping for a sexual overture, which would provide him with the double pleasure of a moral triumph and an animal ascendancy.

He lay on his back with his legs spread apart. The salt of the sea left white streaks across his belly. I kept glancing at him furtively: at the huge hairy chest, at the thickly-veined penis and the sea-tightened scrotum. There was, I confess, a sexual curiosity in these sidelong glances, but there was also a wincing, almost morbid repugnance. I could see that he was watching me through half-closed eye-lashes. And he sensed, I am sure, the ambiguous nature of my attitude: a male detestation mixed with a female fascination.

We started to talk of Greece. He glanced across the bay. "You keep talking about Greece," he said. "Does Grecian liberty mean so much to you?"

"One must care," I said, "about *something*. I worship Greece and I long for her liberty."

"It is a personal thing, I'm sure, and not a political one, Byron. You long for your own liberty and the freedom of Greece is a symbol of it."

"Do you suggest, my dear Trelawny, that it is merely a form of vanity?"

"I do not call it vanity. I call it an inner rather than an outer urgency."

"Then all our political passions are merely the vapour of an inner turmoil?"

"Call it that if you wish. But what I mean is this, Byron. In your longing to fight for Greece there is a genuine hatred of tyranny. But you are also seeking another, more personal salvation. And you seek it by exalting yourself into the role of a liberator."

"You are being unjust, Trelawny."

"Of course I am being unjust."

"You keep looking for my Achilles heel."

"Because I once revered you . . ."

I rose lazily to my feet. "Come, Trelawny. I have a suggestion. You fancy yourself as a swimmer. Well, I challenge you to a race."

Trelawny smiled indulgently. "You are sure that you're in the mood for it?"

"I'll race you to the *Bolivar,* if you think you can manage it."

"Yes? And then?"

"We'll dine on the *Bolivar* and then we'll swim back again."

Trelawny shrugged his shoulders. "Well," he said, "if you insist on it. But," he added with a delicate twinkle, "I can't help wondering whether you're up to it . . ."

We dived into the water and headed across the bay. I immediately struck out and quickly forged my way ahead of him. I thought, Gain the lead, my man, and you'll manage to keep it comfortably. I was fifty yards ahead of him; I widened the lead to a hundred. The sea was warm and smooth, with a casual scattering of ripples which were blazing in the sunlight, almost blinding me as I swam. We were half a mile out when I realized that I was panting. The first little spurt was already beginning to tell on me. I looked back and saw Trelawny only a dozen yards behind me. I decided to speed up and keep my lead at all costs. Now I realized that I was paying the price of my Pisan indolence; the roasted ducks, the *foie gras,* the bottles of wine and *spumante.* My arms grew horribly leaden; my legs felt thick and sluggish. Gradually the *Bolivar* grew nearer. We were over half-way there. My heart began to pound at my ribs in an ugly way and my bowels squirmed uneasily, like a curled-up python. I kept my burning eyes fixed on the gleam of the *Bolivar,* and I changed to a restful though humiliating side-stroke. I started to count my strokes: fifteen, twenty, twenty-five, thirty . . . . . . I glanced around again. Trelawny had vanished from sight. The thought that he had drowned, half-hope, half-terror, shot through my mind. I paused for a moment and looked about appraisingly, and to my horror I saw Trelawny swimming far out ahead of me. He was steadily widening the gap, which was already a hundred yards or so. I kept swimming on desperately, filled with rage at my growing feebleness. I swallowed a jutting wavelet which left me spluttering for air. I was still three hundred yards from the stern of the hateful *Bolivar* when I looked and saw Trelawny climbing the ladder that hung from the side of it.

Ten minutes later I gripped the ladder and dragged my body out of the water. Trelawny came strutting across the deck with a grin. He had wrapped a white towel round his head like a turban. He gripped me by the arm with a loathsome leer of mock-solicitude.

"You are well, I trust," he purred.

"Oh, egregiously so," I growled.

"I have ordered," he announced, "our dinner. Roasted veal with a bit of ale. Some plums, if you happen to care for them. Plums are not a favourite fruit of mine . . ."

He lit a black cigar and started to smoke it complacently. He fondled it gently, as though it were a sign of his own virility.

"Excellent," I said, smiling breezily. "Just the thing for a summer's day. Tell the cook we'll have dinner down in the sea, please, Trelawny."

We climbed down the ladder and slid back into the sea. A wooden grating lay floating beside us, and the cook climbed down and placed our dinner on it. We kept afloat as we gnawed at the roast and drank our ale. My venomous humour gradually left me; I drained my glass and filled it up again. I happened to speak of palmistry and Trelawny held out his palm to me. "Do you see?" he said triumphantly, pointing to a line: "Victory by water!"

Finally I said, "Well, are you ready?"

"More than ready, my boy," he grunted, and we emptied our glasses and started to swim back again. The race was already lost but I was determined to keep my *sang-froid,* and I headed for the beach three miles off with an air of indolence.

I swam easily for several minutes. Then a fit of nausea seized me. I vomited out my dinner. Tufts of veal lay floating about me. My eyes were watering with pain and I paddled about miserably. Trelawny turned back when he saw what had happened. He swam up to me and said: "Please be sensible, my good Byron. Put your hand on my shoulder and I'll tow you back to the *Bolivar*."

I screamed: "Keep off, you villain! I'd rather drown than give in to you!"

Trelawny started to laugh. His hair hung black and streaming. He looked like a puffed-up malevolent water-god. He quoted Iago: "A fig for drowning! Drown cats and blind puppies!"

I shouted back at him: "Come on! Don't be a coward! We're swimming back!"

Trelawny reached out and put his hand on my forehead. "You are feverish," he said. "You need some grog to calm your stomach."

I followed him furiously back to the *Bolivar*. We climbed out on the accommodation ladder and called to Giacomo to bring us some brandy. We drank silently as we sat on the ladder, I with my feet dangling in the water and he two rungs above me, with his thigh against my cheek. I caught the musk of his dripping loins, faintly bestial, like a rain-soaked mastiff. I felt suddenly very fragile and submissive, almost humble. I gave Trelawny my goblet and he drained the last few drops in it. Then we slid into the sea again and headed towards Lerici. I kept swimming along listlessly, switching from a side-stroke to a back-stroke, and I finally crawled out on the sweet-smelling sand. I lay motionless, face down, sniffing at the sweetness of the sand, which had a caressing, almost womb-like aroma.

Well, I paid for my bravado. I lost the race both physically and morally, not to mention some auxiliary aspects, sexual and gastric as well as literary. I dressed and wearily dragged myself to the inn on the edge of Lerici, where I lay on a bed while Trelawny rubbed me with steaming towels. I lay caught in the clutches of a feverish rheumatism, compounded by a bout of biliousness, which turned into diarrhoea. I kept vomiting green bile and my teeth shook with ague while my stomach writhed murderously and my bowels grew stiff with pain. Good old Fletcher (who himself had just recovered from a "spirituous" ailment) hurried off to the apothecary's and brought me some ether and laudanum. Teresa sat by my bed and read aloud from the *Decameron,* and finally, after a hot glass of rum, I fell asleep.

On the fifth day I got up again. The Hunts had arrived in Lerici. We decided to head for Genoa on the following morning and I arranged to go by boat, to avoid the tortuous roads of the Apennines. The carriage was put into the *felucca* along with the horses. The Hunts sailed in one boat and Teresa and I in another while Trelawny was gaily cutting along on the *Bolivar.* My appetite returned. I dined on fish, wine and apricots. We landed at Sestri, where the road ran straight to Genoa, and we got into my carriage, where the geese still cackled indignantly. It was long after midnight when we saw the lights of Genoa and drove into the court-yard of the Casa Saluzzo.

6 April

I got up at sunrise to go to the close-stool (I had taken one of Millingen's vile-tasting purgatives) and I happened to see my face reflected in the mirror. A strange and foggy mask, still half-lost in the watery dimness. And it struck me that this creature wasn't Byron at all. But then I realized that this indeed was the real and essential Byron, haggard and bearded and desolate, caught for once without a pose.

And I asked myself: after all the metamorphoses which I

have gone through, am I now at long last turning into the real, the authentic Byron?

I lay on my bed and meditated (rather zestfully, I admit) on my character. I listed mentally my flaws and virtues. The flaws, no doubt, outweigh the virtues. Virtues: affection (when properly flattered), loyalty (when reciprocated), generosity (when appreciated), a love of liberty (for such as deserve it) and of course a certain talent (facile, I fear, and self-congratulatory). Vices: an all-devouring vanity; a superficiality of mind, concealed by dexterity; sentimentality and fits of passion rather than profundity of feeling; self-indulgence, alternating with spells of a lunatic self-discipline; self-love mixed with self-hatred; and a basic sloth, or acidia.

A frightening ledger, I suppose. But do vice and virtue really exist, when regarded in the light of fifty thousand jungle years? I am what Shelley called me: a shame-faced Manichean. Every virtue contains its vice and every vice its own virtue, neatly tucked in its folds like a walnut in its shell.

We are what we are, and the only ultimate virtue is a faithful acceptance and fulfillment of our animal selves. An animal integrity, in short. I have not always possessed this quality, but now, alone in my bed, I feel it falling on me like a breath from heaven.

*

The Casa Saluzzo in Albaro was the fourth of my Italian homes. It was a large cube-shaped dwelling surrounded by palms and acacias, with a court-yard in the back which was lined with bougainvillaea. Here my geese strutted about, pecking and cackling incessantly. They hissed at the maids and insulted the cats. I had bought these miserable geese with the thought of eating them for Michaelmas. But I decided to let them live. They turned into symbols of longevity.

287

The three Gambas—the venerable Count, the fiery Pietro and the doe-eyed Teresa—all had rooms which looked to the pine-studded hills in the north. My own rooms looked on the bay and the slopes of Genoa beyond the bay. The salty air of the sea mixed with the stink down in the gully. The local *contadini* had chosen the place as a public convenience, and as I sat by my windows, delicately reaching for a metaphor, I would see the young peasants squatting below me in the dust.

Sometimes in the evening I grew listless. I put down my pen and sat by the window. The boats in the distance sailed into a deeper, darker blueness. They kept sailing into a huge unimaginable freedom, and their sails in the setting sun shone like lamps in the wilderness.

O vieillesse! O senectus! I was oppressed by the gloom of exile. I had a disagreeable sense of being considered beyond the pale. I grew captious, even prim. I grew jaded with intrigue. I felt a Pharisaical yearning for peace and respectability. I resented the lady-travellers who raised their brows when they caught sight of me and gripped the pasty hands of their virgin daughters. I was no longer a *diavolo,* a phallic philanderer. I was turning into a crapulous, sphincter-mouthed miser.

I manoeuvered to keep the Hunts from moving into my *casa.* I paid for their lease on the Casa Negroto, which lay in the pines below my villa. They invited Mary Shelley to come and share the house with them, and on Sunday afternoons they came for tea in my shady pergola. Poor Hunt! He was never at ease with me. He was always on the defensive. Either he tried to be over-familiar, with some elephantine repartee, or he grew fawning and oily, in terror of losing his bread and butter. Or even worse, he tried to assert himself by sneers and petty impertinences. Once I called him "my dear Leigh" and he was touched to the point of tears. His bird-like eyes were aquiver with pleasure and gratitude.

The omens were far from encouraging. Two days after my

arrival a mirror fell from the wall, crushing my beautiful kitten Lulu. A rat was found one morning trapped in the strings of the pianoforte, and Teresa developed an agonising boil on her anus. One day there was a storm. Shafts of lightning struck at the hills. The sea was totally hidden by the colonnades of rain. A torrent came thundering down the slopes into the gully, carrying with it a mournful miscellany of goats, pigs and spinning-wheels. Two bridges were swept down. The neighbouring shops were scoured by the flood, and the streets were transformed into slimy canals in which lay floating the shoes from the shoemaker, the wigs from the wigmaker, as well as the duck-shaped gingerbreads from the gingerbread-maker.

One day the door-bell rang and Mary Shelley, wearing a shawl, came striding into my study with an air of the utmost urgency. She dropped her shawl in the arm-chair and walked solemnly to the window, where the light of the setting sun shone on her fine archaic profile. Her hair was drawn back into a large silky bun. Her chin was strong and stubborn and her lips were like a man's, very broad and aggressive, with a hint of a moustache. She was panting from the climb and her face was flushed and damp. She folded her arms and fixed her dark, philosophical eyes on me.

"I had a letter from Claire this morning."

"Oh, indeed? I trust she is well."

"She is living, as you know, in Vienna. She is desperately in need of money."

"My good Mary, I am not interested in the destiny of Claire or the state of her finances."

"Don't you feel," she intoned, "well, shall we call it a *moral* duty?"

"I emphatically do not," I said, staring beadily at my *pantoufles*.

"You are too irritable about poor Claire."

"I am bored to tears at the mere mention of her."

289

"You do, after all, have an obligation," said Mary pityingly.

"Do I? Why?"

She looked shocked. "Have you forgotten poor little Allegra?"

"Allegra," I said, "is dead."

"I find you appalling, utterly appalling!"

"Really, Mary, with all of your modern emancipated views, there is an amazing primness about you. You are an intellectualized governess. You see men as artificially constructed simulacra, which distress you the moment they behave unexpectedly."

Mary's eyes grew strangely limpid. A pensive smile appeared on her lips. I had always felt with Mary a certain *arrière-pensée* in the atmosphere, and she looked at me with a drooping, faintly basset-like expression.

"Are you happy?" she whispered.

I peered at her nervously.

"A poet must be more," she went on slyly, "than just an automaton. His verses must draw energy from a self-renewing vision. Oh, mind you," she said hurriedly, "I am not suggesting a deterioration. It is not for me to say that your verses have grown stale. I am no critic. Far from it. I quite ignore what the reviewers say. I am merely concerned with your spiritual welfare—your *sophrosyne,* as one might put it."

"You are being didactic, Mary. You are tiresome when you grow didactic."

"You need help," she insisted, tugging at her gloves. "I am trying to help you."

I leant back in my chair. "Yes," I said, "you are perfectly right. I feel stale. I feel cloyed. I am turning into a mushroom."

"Ahem. Do you think Teresa . . ."

"Do not mention Teresa, please."

"A change. That's what you need."

"And what do you suggest, *ma chère?*"

Her eyes grew bright with expectancy. "What you need is an intellectual equal. Not necessarily on an exclusively literary level, perhaps, though a meeting of minds is always refreshing. You looked for it in Leigh. But Leigh is whimsical and sponge-like. You looked for it in Trelawny. Trelawny is an adventurer. You looked for it in Shelley. Poor Shelley, alas, is dead. You are a fragile tropical flower that is wilting away in an alien clime."

I sighed. "Thank you, Mary. A most perceptive analysis."

"You need," she cooed, "a *change*."

"No question about it," I said gloomily.

I rose from my chair and calmly accompanied her to the door, through which she walked with a startled though dignified air. She climbed down the stairs and looked back at me waveringly, and I waved to her gaily as I leant over the bannister.

7 April

I had a dream last night. I usually forget my dreams, but this one I remember.

I was wandering along a path that led into a forest. At the edge of the forest stood a house with pointed gables. I paused in front of the house, which looked lifeless and empty. Suddenly a curtain was drawn aside in an upstairs window and a boy leaned out. He was wearing a tall black hat in which a fern had been stuck, like a feather. He called out to me, "Holla, Byron! What's wrong? Don't you recognize me?"

I mumbled: "Wait a moment. Yes, to be sure. Why, your name is . . ."

"You are wrong," she cried out (for I now saw that it was a woman). "I am Caroline! You didn't recognize me! You never recognized me! You always lied to me! You said that you loved me but you never loved me at all. You loved strangeness, novelty, darkness—in short, you loved yourself. Yes, I detected your guilty secret and I turned to disguises. I was a Mantuan page, an Arabian horseman, I was Adonis, I was Ganymede. But you saw through the fraud. You were slyer than I. And you ended by loathing me!"

I hurried into the forest. The trees grew vast and primaeval. It might have been a jungle in the depths of Brazil. A pool shone in the distance, reflecting the leaves in its coal-black mirror. Beside the pool stood a naked woman. She raised her arms, as though ready to dive.

Then she turned her head and saw me. Her face grew twisted with fury. Her eyes shone like obsidian, her voice was hoarse and passionate. "Ah," she said. "There you are! I have been waiting. Where have you been?"

"I have been visiting," I muttered somewhat shiftily, "my bygone school-days."

"Hypocrite! Liar!" cried Trelawny in a rage (for I now saw that it was a man, since a large dark obelisk had emerged from the vagina). "School-days indeed! You never even learnt how to multiply, you bastard. You cheated. Your translations from the *Georgics* were done by Tattersall. Oh Byron, I thought that I loved you but in reality I hated you. You broke my heart, Byron! I shall never forgive you!"

I ran back into the jungle and suddenly found myself by a sea. Decaying palaces lined the shore, rather in the style of Claude Lorrain. In front of me stood a row of weather-beaten statues. I recognized them all: Bacchus, Mercury, Minerva. One of the statues (it might have been Diana) raised her arm and beckoned me gently.

"Darling," she whispered, "did you really love me? Or did you merely love the forbidden?"

"Augusta," I cried, "forgive me!"

"There is much to forgive," said Augusta.

I walked on in dejection, haunted by an indefinable loneliness, and came to a manor-house covered with ivy. Dusk fell. I could see the flames from the hearth shining in the window. I peered through the curtain and saw a woman crouching on a lion's skin. She was fondling her nipples with a frozen look of misery. Suddenly she caught sight of me. She sprang to her feet and covered her pudendum with her hand. "At first I loved you," she said icily, "but you tried to grind me into the dust. You defiled me and humiliated me. Some secret vengeance, I suppose. But vengeance for what? I never knew. And I ended by hating you . . ."

Now it was night and I found myself in a cold black city. I was standing under a balcony. A door opened; a shape emerged. It was a beautiful young woman. I was transfixed with a sudden joy. I thought of Romeo and Juliet, and then of Dante and Beatrice. The woman leaned over the balustrade and leered at me voluptuously. Her cheeks were heavily painted and great rubies hung from her ear-lobes. Silently, with insidiously erotic gestures, she started to disrobe. Her breasts emerged and then her belly and her great hairy thighs.

"Is this what you wanted?" she said, and she pointed lecherously to her *mons Veneris.* "Are you sure? Well, you had your fill. I never stinted you, did I, Bairon? And what, may I ask, did you ever give in return?"

"Oh Teresa," I murmured, "I tried to be faithful. I really did."

"Faute de mieux. That's all it was. You filthy rogue! Swine! Crocodile!"

And as I watched her in horror great wrinkles appeared in her face, her belly grew pendulous and her pubic hair grew white as snow. Tears rolled down her cheeks and turned into icicles that hung from her chin.

And I kept on wandering into the endless, clattering darkness.

*

Yes—Teresa. It is time that I wrote about Teresa.

Why does my memory grow blurred when I think about Teresa? No creature was ever closer to me physically than Teresa. She was loyal and she was generous. She was amorously inventive, she was gaily domestical. She was never a bore. She laughed at my jokes. Her eyes were radiant and her voice was melodious. But then why, when I try to visualize her, does she fade into anonymity? I remember exactly the face of a cow-girl in Andalusia, or the face of a white-bearded priest in Previza. But when I try to visualize Teresa I see nothing, or nearly nothing. I knew her too well. I had seen her in too many moods. And this intimacy, instead of making her more vivid and comprehensible, in the end made her as nebulous and faceless as a phantom. I sometimes even wonder whether she had a definite character, or whether she entered my life as a kind of uterine force, whose *raison d'être* finally deteriorated into that of a sponge-like appendage.

I was deeply and dotingly and inexhaustibly fond of Teresa. But alas, I was no longer in love with her. I was flattered by her loyalty and touched by her idolatry. Claire was likewise idolatrous, even to the point of absurdity, but unlike Claire (whose very aroma, whose very touch I found exasperating) the nearness of Teresa had a sedative quality. I suppose that there is something chemical, even cutaneous, in our preferences. Teresa's hips were too wide, her legs too short and her breasts too drooping, but the sound of her voice and the touch of her skin were marvellously soothing. I loved the smell of her body. Even after her bath every morning her flesh exhaled its special fragrance, which was spicily pastoral, like hay after a shower.

She was only twenty-three but by a process of propinquity she grew infected by my own accelerating senility. She was by nature turbulent and stubborn. She grew pliable, phlegmatic. She grew fatter. Her eyes grew dim. Some greying hairs appeared on her temples. She took to eating creampuffs. She played dominoes instead of Mozart. Instead of Dante she read the gossip in *Galignani's Messenger*.

I embarked once again on an anchorite's diet. Maybe as a result of this stringency (or perhaps of earlier excesses) I found pimples on my back and tiny boils on my buttocks. The suspicion occurred to me that these were symptoms of syphilis, and I confided my fears one day to Teresa. She scoffed at the notion but immediately called a physician. Dr Alexander called at the house and prescribed a diet of salads and oranges. I grew thin as a skeleton. I swam occasionally but not far. I was soon out of breath and the memory of Lerici was a repugnant one. (I was still suffering from bouts of rheumatism as a result of that hideous episode.) I went riding in the cool of the evening but I abandoned my promenades. I had never liked to walk but now I liked it less than ever. Once Teresa and I walked down the path to the sea-shore. It was a coppery, windless day. I felt feverish and dizzy. We paused in the shade of a sycamore and I muttered: "I am growing old. I have lost my zest. I have lost my gusto. I am sick of living."

"Don't talk like that, my turtle-dove!"

I said: "I am sick of Italy."

"*O carino*, you mustn't say such things!"

It dawned on me that Teresa had transformed herself into an opiate. When I entered her room at dusk, with the shades discreetly drawn, I would find her on the couch, naked and fragrant, feigning sleep. But instead of lying beside her face to face, as in the earlier days, I proceeded on a never-ending series of innovations. I dropped my silken robe and pressed my lips against her belly. Then I straddled her shoulders, murmuring hoarsely, *tu quoque*, and pressed my frozen phallus against her cheeks. At first we scarcely moved but gradually our postures grew more fanciful until we finally subsided into the conventionalised gymnastics of a heterosexual orgasm.

I dwell on these devices, not in a spirit of prankishness, nor in a mood of onanistical fantasy, but because these animal truths, so long considered *contra naturam,* are in fact as natural and guiltless as eating a strawberry. I could go into a richer and more clinical analysis (e.g. the rôle of the clitoris, which with Teresa was a crucial organism) but at the moment I am more concerned with the philosophical nuances. Ah, *tristis post coitum!* After the pleasure, the philosophy. When I beheld, after the orgasm, the pearls of semen draped on her belly, melting like snow, growing translucent, flowing into the jungle of her pubis, I reflected: How much seed have I hurled into the female cavities, between their labia or their lips or across the whiteness of their bellies! Enough to fill ten buckets. Enough to beget a nation. Seed so precious and prolific that in a drop of this pale liquid lie a thousand possible lives, potential Dantes and Galileos. Yet we hurl it away, we toss it thoughtlessly into the chamber-pot, where these unbeggoten souls, these desperately-wriggling sper-matozoa, finally fade and expire like a vanquished army on the battle-field. And we commit this multiple murder just as casually as we swat a fly or kill a little worm that we find in our salad.

Our physical intimacy had grown complete and un-ashamed. Tom Moore once informed me that he could not bear to be near a menstruating woman. There was an odour, he protested, of disintegrating clams. There are aspects of the feminine processes not congenial to most males. Yet to me there is something comforting and almost maternal about it all. Annabella's lunar ailments seemed in discord with her character, but during Teresa's menstrual periods I felt a solicitude that was close to tenderness. God knows she was frank enough. She was refreshingly Italian. Not for her the perfumed euphemisms and circumlocutions of the English boudoir. To her a chamber-pot was a piss-bowl, a cock was a cock and a cunt was a cunt. She fondled my *cazzo* as though it

296

were a favourite lap-dog, and discussed its eccentricities as though it were a poem by Voltaire.

To Annabella coition was a blushful but inevitable ritual, wrapped up in a penumbra of unmentionable incidentals. She refused even to touch my *membrum erectum* and I abandoned all hope of a delicate Ovidian experimentation. Even Augusta, with all of her gaiety, chose her phrases discreetly and would say, "Really, darling! Not *again?* Goodness me!" Lady Caroline, in her penchant for the *argot* of Bermondsey, would say, "How about it? Shall we tear off a piece, Bibbsy?" But Teresa, at equivalent moments, would merely chirp "Shall we have a fook, *caro?*" When I farted she smiled indulgently, as though amused by the English accent of it. Speaking of farts, I have often noticed an air of hypocrisy in the matter. Human vanity reaches its highest, most idiotic pinnacle in the field of flatulence. Our own farts we accept with composure and sometimes even relish (I have even lifted the sheet for a furtive sniff of their bouquet) but the farts of another person, however lustrous or melodious, we tend to find ludicrous or downright distasteful. Annabella never farted, of course. Her control of the sphincter was phenomenal. Caroline's farts were a fine falsetto, and smelled of asparagus. Teresa's farts were of a warbling, almost effervescent quality, and their fragrance was that of a duck-pond on a midsummer evening.

Once she said, "Forgive me, darling. Those *fagiolini* were really too much for me."

I replied, *"Nihil humanum mihi alienum est.* I love you, darling, and nothing about you ever disgusts me, not even the musk of your genitals, which reminds me of truffles."

Shelley told me that the sight of of a woman pissing seemed absurd to him. (When I visualized Mary this *idée fixe* seemed comprehensible.) Teresa paid me a compliment. She said I was the first man she had met who struck her as dignified in the act of micturation. When I pissed into the pot, instead of shyly averting her head she watched me with a gentle, almost ruminating gaze. I felt flattered but reflected that the female pose is of necessity (as it is amongst dogs) less adroit than the male (though I am told that in Tunisia these positions are reversed). I remember in Rapallo once, on a mild November evening, a fat old woman walking by with a basket full of combs. She paused under a palm-tree with a far-away air, and a yellowish pool spread on the flag-stones by her feet. She regarded me with a glint of mournful complicity, shrugged her shoulders and strolled off in the direction of the harbour.

Ah, such memories are dreams made of! Why does there linger a mellow magic in this glimpse of a fat old woman pissing furtively on the esplanade? Because it was true, because it was human, because it was sad, because it was forgivable. Dear old woman with many combs, in my dreams I have come to love you!

I gave Teresa a little present: a golden brooch with an oval frame which was encircled by brilliants, delicately set in a cluster of grape-leaves. She gave it back with a lock of hair which was tied with a ribbon under the glass.

"A souvenir," she murmured.

"It's your own hair, is it, darling?"

"It is," she said demurely.

"It seems unusually coarse, and curly."

"It's an Italian custom, dearest. It's my hair, as it happens, though not from my head."

Alas, there are times when a man should refrain from telling the truth. I could not tell my poor Teresa that she had committed a *gaucherie*. Much as I loved her, the pubic hairs were not the most ethereal part of her, except by some extraordinary leap of the imagination. A man may love a woman but certain thoughts he must keep to himself. Teresa was intelligent but she was also naïve, one might almost say that she was incurably innocent.

Once or twice, when I failed to produce the customary

298

erection for her, she looked at me with a troubled, almost agitated air. I explained that fondness and loyalty were finer than lust and deeper than passion. But she knew that I was lying. How can one possibly explain these things? I was fond, I was devoted, I was even happy—yes, I was happy. Yet the need to escape from Teresa became so violent, so almost hysterical, that there were moments at midnight, as I lay in the bed beside her, when the sweat burst from my belly and I started to tremble, and I came very close to strangling the poor woman.

One evening the sunlight fell through the half-open shutters and the smell of dying fox-gloves hung unpleasantly in the air. Teresa sat by the window with lack-lustre eyes, lazily stroking the monkey which lay sleeping in her lap.

"What is it?" she whispered. "What has happened, *carissimo*?"

"What do you mean, *piccinina*?"

"Something has happened. You have changed."

"How, precisely?"

"The way you look at me. The way you touch me. I can feel it in your finger-tips."

"I am growing older, my cuckoo."

"I too am growing older."

"I still love you, *carina*."

"But you no longer are really in love with me."

"Fiddlesticks, child."

"Shall we say you are still fond of me. But the passion has wilted."

"Passion, my puss, is for the young. I am a middle-aged Englishman and the English, as you know, age even faster than the Italians."

"I too am growing old. Yes, *hélas*. So it is. A woman's body is not pretty when the youth has fled away from it . . ."

She looked suddenly ten years older. Deep furrows appeared in her face. She looked as though some illness had abruptly come over her. The realization that her flesh was no longer desired had aged her terribly in a single hour, like those Seminole Indians who have drunk from the Well of Youth and are suddenly deprived of the magical liquid.

8 April

All who loved me I eventually deserted. All, all of them. None remain. Sometimes at night I see their faces looking down at me from infinite distances. They hang in the darkness, sad and wizened but at last invulnerable. They hang suspended like pears in autumn, slightly silvered by an early frost, while I lie in a dirty bed in a filthy town by a muddy sea.

How can I ever describe it, this all-engulfing loneliness? This hideous knowledge that I once was loved, painfully loved and tenaciously loved, and that these loves now lie frozen in grey distances while I lie in my bed alone, alone and unloved at last? Unloved as all my life I maneouvered to be, in my suffocating need for a new *frisson*. I have scorched the land behind me. I have burnt all my bridges. I have wasted it all—the blood, the tears, the torrents of semen. All have shrivelled away in the cold sands. Alone. All alone to face the final Black Adversary. So it is. I swam the Hellespont. Now I must swim a darker and deeper sea, with nothing to sustain me but a blind and meaningless courage.

Wrong, wrong from the beginning. In everything I thought, in everything I felt. Wrong in those masturbative verses which I cast off at Harrow, wrong in the *dicta* which I sprinkled about at Cambridge like urine, wrong in my sickening conceit, wrong in my histrionic love-affairs, wrong in my clothes, wrong in my wit, wrong in my friends, wrong in my *snobisme,* even wrong in my ideals, those sad little scarecrows that dot my long pilgrimage towards obliteration.

I look through the window. It is nearly dawn. The sea is

brightening. A mangy yellow dog is prowling along the empty beach. Something frightens him and he scampers off with his tail between his legs.

A fishing-boat moves on the misty horizon. The tips of its sail have caught the light of the rising sun.

*

One night a luxurious caravan of coaches and *calèches* drew up in front of the Albergo della Villa in Genoa. (I did not witness the occasion personally but Pietro Gamba gave a vivid description of it.) This *cortège* of six carriages (which were filled with servants, including a blackamoor, and various pets, including a cheetah, as well as some dog-baskets with satin cushions and several picnic-baskets with golden cutlery) belonged to the Earl of Blessington, who had toured the Continent from Paris to Vienna and back by way of the lakes to the Mediterranean. The next morning the whole town was already buzzing about the "Blessington Circus", and I sent Fletcher to convey my greetings to the illustrious newcomers. I was sipping my coffee when I heard a tinkling of coach-bells and a barking of spaniels as a magnificent carriage entered my driveway. I peeped through the window and then hurriedly combed my hair and sprinkled my face with *eau de Cologne*. When I entered the drawing-room I saw the visitors already awaiting me. The room was transformed by an air of perfumed elegance, of rustling taffeta and *doubles entendres*, of flicking wrists and swirling handkerchiefs. They were four in number: the Earl himself, who was a wealthy dilettante with languorous gestures and a look of satiety; Lady Blessington, a gleaming beauty with rosy cheeks and ironical glances; her sister, Mary Power, a defiantly Amazonian type; and the Count d'Orsay, an undulous Apollo with a moiré waistcoat. (*Le Cûpidon déchaîné* we called him later, somewhat enviously.)

As I confronted these luminous guests I grew shy, even

agitated. My heart sank as I saw the twinkle in the eyes of Lady Blessington. She glanced at my coat, which was frayed and no longer fitted me, as well as my pointed shoes, which were sadly *démodé*. I tried to hide my lameness by gliding casually from chair to chair, but she detected my little stratagem, as indeed she detected everything, including the *passé* bits of slang which I still indulged in, and the greying strands of hair amid my thin receding locks. I knew I was being gauche and rather bumptiously ceremonious, so I immediately changed my tone and grew flippant and sarcastic. But even this did not deceive the undeceivable Lady Blessington, and the look in her eyes grew indulgent and even pitying.

I said: "Did you like Vienna?"

"Operettas and whipped cream, my dear!"

I said: "Did you like the Alps?"

"I liked the snow, but detested the cheeses."

I said softly: "I can see that you are disappointed in me, aren't you?"

"Disconcerted, a little. Disappointed, not in the least."

"I am not what you expected."

"Thinner a bit. And somewhat balder."

"Not romantic, to put it bluntly."

"Not the brooding, melancholy poet."

"Must a poet be always melancholy?"

She grew thoughtful. "Yes, I think so. A poet must be haunted by the *lacrimae rerum*. And in your heart of course you are sad. It is only outwardly that you are frivolous."

"So are we all," I said with a smirk.

"Am *I* frivolous?" said the Countess suspiciously.

I glanced sidelong at the beautiful d'Orsay. "You are still a stranger to me, Lady Blessington. But we all have our own little ways of being frivolous."

She was dressed in green silk, a tint unflattering to most women but on her as naturally appropriate as are the leaves to the lily-of-the-valley. She was the loveliest, in a spring-like way, of all the women I had ever seen, and the freshness of her beauty was enhanced (deliberately, I suspected) by the jaded *chiaroscuro* of her companions. Her eyes were very dark but extremely gentle and luminous, and at the same time as remorseless and impenetrable as a Polar bear's. Her skin was smooth as a water-lily and her hair was sleek as a seal's. But beneath this vernal lustre, this Botticellian limpidity, lurked a steely resilience and a positively Arctic impersonality. I immediately sensed that, putting aside her inestimable advantages of wealth and beauty and my own sad deficiencies of health and anachronism, I had met, as they say, my match. The combat was joined. After all, I had my own little armoury: the profligate poet, the notorious *débauché*. And it was a combat made all the more tittivating by the fact that no "triumph" would ever derive from it, and that it would remain on a purely symbolical and pantomimic level.

And so it turned out. I fell in love with Lady Blessington, but it was like falling in love with a porcelain statue. I never dreamed of tarnishing the image by stepping into bed with her. She was a sorceress. In her presence the world grew shimmering and oblique. She turned life into a succession of Guardiesque whimsies, a manoeuvering of masks and a sly staccato of clicking fans. And in this opalescent ambience I myself grew transformed. I grew strangely coquettish, ebullient, indiscreet. It is hard to define the equivocal essence of her charm. All I can say is that the moment I stepped into her periphery I was ridiculously happy, my soul grew young and I turned into a child again.

Teresa, of course, detected this, and felt a loathing for Lady Blessington; and while her jealousy was justified on a purely ornamental level, she failed to see that the perils of a sexual involvement were microscopical.

At first I toyed with the notion that this glittering quartet was engaged in a highly-sophisticated sexual quadrille; that is to say, each of the four with each of the others. But then I saw that the opposite was true: that in fact they were as frigid, and as ill-equipped for copulation, as a group of Nymphenburg shepherdesses.

I used to chat for hours on end with the garrulous Countess of Blessington. The Blessington Circus decided to settle in Genoa for the spring and I used to see her at tea-time, either in my own littered villa or in her cushioned rooms in the Albergo della Villa. Little by little she managed to badger me into a mood of "intimate confidences", and I told her things that might more prudently have been left untold. (It may even be as a result of these salty *tête-à-têtes* that I have slipped so spontaneously into the style of these "private" note-books.)

Once she said: "You have been too tolerant, and indeed indiscriminate, in your choice of *amici* and *innamorate*. You put up with mediocrities, and in fact you seem to prefer them, and the reason for this is either laziness or vanity."

"You are perfectly right," I said. "I *am* vain. I *am* lazy. And as you seem to insinuate, I love to feel lordly. I have never felt at ease in the presence of my equals, though frankly, I have found these equals to be as rare as the snows of Sicily."

"But what a hideous waste of time! You could be the lion of Belgravia, but here you are just a frog in a little pool in a suburb of Genoa."

"Well," I said, "I have always suffered from a *besoin d'aimer,* and this has finally dwindled into a *besoin d'être aimé.* And this *besoin* is more insistent than a merely mental discrimination. I see the faults of my various ladies. I keep loving them out of habit. Clever ladies are often thin, and I happen to like well-rounded ones. Thin women, when they are young, remind me of dead butterflies, and when they are old they remind me of spiders."

"I will tell you," she said, "what women find so irresistible in you. Not your burning eyes or melodious voice, not your illustrious profile or lugubrious verses, but simply this. The evident fact that you intensely desire them."

"Intensely? I wonder."

"What I mean is really this. We desire those very things we were not intended to possess, and the more elusive they are the more intensely we keep reaching for them."

"Women have never," I said recklessly, "been exactly elusive."

Lady Blessington smiled: a malevolent, mocking smile. "Precisely," she said. "They fell before you like a row of dominoes. And this led you into an endless and unassuagable search. You kept looking for that aureole-bodied *princesse lointaine*, that all-possessing paragon who would bring your search to its calm conclusion."

"This seems like a highly-generous interpretation of promiscuity. You might as easily explain it by merely saying that I found it enjoyable."

She regarded me stonily. "Is it *always* so enjoyable?"

"It is always fun to explore a beautiful new body, Lady Blessington."

"Men," she said, "are no better than mongrels, when you really come to think of it."

"No better and no worse."

"Adam fell because the serpent tempted him."

"It was Adam who tempted the serpent. The serpent loved Adam, and he discovered the only way in which he could finally possess him."

"You keep rambling along," said the Countess, "with an air of incorrigible flippancy, and you don't really mean more than a tenth of the things you say. Conversation for you is a diversion, like Cat's-cradle, rather than a meeting of intellects or a search for the truth. Don't you occasionally, Lord Byron, feel a need for the truth?"

"With you," I said gallantly, "I shall henceforth be truthful. No words but the true ones shall glide from my lips."

"The point," said Lady Blessington, "is that you create a false impression. People listen to you carefully, and they think that you mean the things you say."

"*N'importe!* Let them think what they wish to. One opinion is as good as another. The actual truth, Lady Blessington, as perhaps you suspect, is that I have no definite or identifiable character. I am so changeable, so fluid and ephemeral, such a mad *mélange* of the good and deplorable, that I doubt whether even a genius could describe my true character."

"But there *are* certain ingredients . . ."

"Only two," I put in hastily. "My worship of liberty and my loathing for fraudulence. And neither, I might add, has ever made a single friend for me."

We spoke of Greece.

"And so," she said, "you have finally decided?"

"There is no point in putting it off. I have decided to go to Greece."

"Are you sure," said Lady Blessington, "that your decision is a practical one, and not just a Quixote-like tilting at windmills?"

"The Turks are not windmills."

"But Grecian liberty—is it more than a chimaera?"

"Chimaera or no, I have decided to go to Greece and risk my life for it." And for once in my life I felt an impulse to tell the truth. I stared at Lady Blessington with a sudden intensity, and I put my shaking forefinger on her pearl-crusted wrist. "Life is nothing but a heart-breaking process of decay. My motives in going to Greece are private as well as public ones. It will be a journey of exploration. I wish to discover the *other* creature, if there really is another, who is hiding within me."

My chief pleasure all that spring was my daily ride with the Blessington party. I still remember the Earl himself in dark-red velvet on his mare Zenobia, and the Countess in green on her Arabian steed Mameluke, and d'Orsay in scarlet on the gelding Coriolanus: and how gracefully they went riding through the freshly-budding woods, where the leaves hung like tassels and the forsythia waved its plumes!

I tried to coax them into buying a magnificent villa near Albaro, a vine-encircled palace with Moorish turrets, called Il Paradiso. Their youthful elegance and beauty had become a kind of necessity to me, a veil which hid the loss of my own proud beauty and youthful elegance, and which seduced me into the illusion of a life still glowing and unalterably golden. I couldn't bear the thought of their departure. But depart they finally did. The Earl kindly offered to buy my ill-fated *Bolivar,* and I pleaded with the Countess to sell me her Mameluke. But as their departure grew more imminent my veil of illusion fell into shreds. I dropped my shell of elegance and became a miserable little huckster. I had spent a thousand pounds on the *Bolivar* and was planning to take it to Greece with me. But my avarice for gold induced me to accept the Earl's offer, which was finally stabilized at four hundred guineas. The Countess recoiled from the thought of parting with Mameluke, whose silky black mane and flashing eyes were a constant joy to her, but I hypnotised her into selling the horse for eighty pounds, and the glorious Mameluke is now in the stable below my window.

They departed in June for Naples. On the evening before they left the Countess took my hand and said, "And you are still a total mystery to me!"

"And you to me," I murmured.

"Women," she said, "are never a mystery. They merely hide their nakedness under a veil of ostensible mystery. But men are always a mystery since they are outwardly naked and the enigma in their hearts is impossible to fathom."

We politely exchanged some sentimental *gages d'amitié,* from her a golden snuff-box with a painting of Danaë, from me a golden brooch with a cameo of Napoleon. When I turned in the doorway for a last farewell look at her, her eyes were flooded with tears but her teeth were clenched in fury.

Two letters from England, one from Augusta and one from Hobhouse. I keep running my fingers over the pages to make sure they are real; that these words and these people really exist, and that England exists.

The sun came out and I went for a ride in the fields with Pietro. But of course it started to pour and we hurried back, soaked and sweating.

I am still shivering. I am stiff with rheumatism. I am going to be ill, I think.

Why do I scribble like a maniac in these ugly little note-books? (Sometimes I can hardly even recognize my own shaky handwriting.) Alas, is it only just to stay alive a little longer? It is all I can do to refresh this old heart of mine. Queerly enough, after despising all these years the "profession" of writing, and yearning all these years for a life of "heroical action", I am now being exterminated by the life of action and cling feebly for survival by the act of writing.

Why did I do these wicked things? (I assume that faithlessness is wicked.) Was it in order, by committing this hierarchy of sins like an elaborate ritual, to emerge from my own past like an insect from its chrysalis? God knows. Perhaps it was that. I am too weary to think clearly. All I can do is to keep on scribbling in the hope that these memories, finally recaptured in the Gulf of Patras, are my struggle for redemption.

*

I said gently: "Teresa, I have something to tell you."

She peered at the canary. "You need not tell me. I have guessed already."

"What have you guessed," I said, *"carina?"*

"You are in love with that horrible creature."

"What creature?" I said innocently.

"That conceited, sneaking vampire!"

"You are wrong, my dear child. I admire the lady but I find her icy. She is handsome but she is certainly not my sort."

"Well, what is it then, *caro?*"

"I have made a decision. I am going to Greece with your brother Pietro."

"Greece! Pietro!"

"*Pazienza,* Teresa. It is only a brief excursion. Your father has been invited back to Ravenna, as you know. Your exile is ended. You should go back, I think, to Ravenna."

"Never!" she cried. "I will never go back to that doddering old cuckold!"

"Not to *him,*" I said silkily. "Merely to Ravenna, which is your home."

She burst into tears. "Ah, it is true that your love is dead, then?"

I kissed her on both cheeks. "My love, *carissima,* is as strong as ever." I walked thoughtfully to the bookshelves, where there was a heap of dusty manuscripts. I gave them to Teresa with a ceremonious bow. They included *Cain* and *Sardanapalus,* as well as some cantos of *Don Juan.*

"They are yours," I said grandly. "You may do with them as you wish. Burn them if you like. Or sell them if you like. Some day, who knows, they may bring you a fortune."

"Do not leave me, *carino!*"

"I'll be back," I said guiltily.

Her face grew very calm. "You will never be back. I will never see you again."

"Do not say that, my parakeet."

"I have always known it. You will leave me for ever!"

And so it was done. The die was cast. I was leaving for Greece. Since the *Bolivar* was no longer available, I looked about in the port of Genoa and found a vessel, the *Hercules,* a sturdy ship of 120 tons. I engaged it for two months for the sum of £230. I wrote to Trelawny (who had gone on a hunting trip) and begged him to return to Genoa along with his two Hungarian horses. I embarked on a correspondence with the "London Committee for Greek Liberation", and assured them of my moral and pecuniary assistance. I engaged a ship's physician, a certain hook-nosed Dr Bruno, and I purchased a whole mountain of medical supplies, enough to last a year for an army of a thousand. I also ordered, as a sop to my vanity, some gold and scarlet uniforms and some ornamental helmets for Trelawny and Pietro and myself. These were inscribed, as an ultimate gesture of self-glorification, with my motto and coat-of-arms. *Crede Byron. Crede,* indeed!

On the morning of my departure I went for a stroll with Teresa. The sun was just rising. Flakes of mist hung over the sea and the leaves of the lime-trees were varnished with dew. An old woman was climbing the path to the village. She was carrying a little red rooster, upside down. The creature kept squawking and flapping his wings indignantly. She grinned when she saw us and waved the beautiful cock at us. Then she darted round a corner into the darkness of the eucalyptus-grove.

Now the sun crawled out of the water. A magnificent frigate in full sail moved slowly across the horizon, heading westward towards Spain, or perhaps even further, towards the savage Americas.

Teresa turned and stared at me with a shrivelled despondency. She uttered a squeal and flapped her arms helplessly. "I cannot bear it! I cannot bear it! I cannot bear it, I tell you, Bairon!"

I kissed her on the cheek and we entered the house for our morning tea.

I spent a feverish night. The pain pierced through my bones. All the same I insisted on riding again to-day. The sun shot spasmodically through the dark, bulbous clouds. I felt better but was troubled by the rain-soaked saddle which the groom had carelessly put on my horse.

I lay down when I came home again. But I could not sleep. I was in torment. I asked Fletcher to prepare a bath and then I went to bed again. I took a large dose of castor-oil and had three "evacuations". Bruno came with his leeches, but I refused to be bled.

I took some antimony powder but still I could not sleep. I have lit the Turkish lamp and picked up my pen again. My whole skeleton is aching. Will I ever be able to sleep again?

Yes, something amazing, something spectacular is about to happen. I can see it in the clouds. I can smell it in the wind. This morning I looked up and saw an eagle fall from the air. I heard the screaming of a million locusts and the galloping of far-off hooves. Tita tells me that he found a pregnant sow lying on the beach. She was dying, and her face was seething with flies.

*

And so I set sail in the *Hercules*. I left behind me my three Pisan geese, who had survived my Michaelmas dinner and who seemed destined for immortality. They had developed very definite and beguiling personalities. Clotho was a hoyden, Atropos a flirt, and dear Lachesis was a virago. They were fat but they were tough. They looked contented to see me leave.

I took along my valet Fletcher and my shaggy black-eyed Tita, as well as Moretto, my bull-dog, and my Newfoundland, Lyon. I took four horses and two cannons which had been removed from the *Bolivar*. And finally there were the chests, a regular Chinese Wall of chests: arms, ammunition, food and medicine, books and bottles, helmets and uniforms. I had planned to head directly for the island of Zante, which the good-hearted Colonel Blaquiere had recommended to me. But I decided to sail instead for the isle of Cephalonia, which was in command of a Colonel Napier, who was known as a partisan of Grecian liberty.

We weighed anchor at sunrise on the 15th of July. Several American ships in the bay, as a gesture of cordiality, sent their boats to tow us out of the windless harbour. We lay in the offing all day long under a bleak scorching sun. The deck-hands lay about on the deck, singing merrily. Finally the breeze set in at midnight. The wind grew more violent. The thunder began to roll, the sea got up and the spray went flying. The horses started to kick down their thin wooden stalls and Trelawny and his groom went below to nail them back again. Then he came to me and said, "We must bear up for port. If we don't we shall certainly lose all our cattle." I replied, "Do as you wish, please," and so we bore up, and after a wild clamourous night we anchored again in the port of Genoa. The wind died away and the sun crept out of the clouds, and the bleary-eyed deck-hands crawled on deck, scratching their belly-buttons.

And so we set sail again and headed for Leghorn. We sailed along the coast with its foaming rocks and snowy villages. I sat on a chair on deck and leafed through La Rochefoucauld while we sailed past Grosseto towards the rolling hills of Latium. We passed Ostia and Gaeta and sailed on past the Bay of Naples. We saw Vesuvius smoking in the distance and the cliffs of Sorrento. I read through the *Essais* of Montaigne as we sailed past the many-coloured grottos of Capri. Past Stromboli we sailed and past the red volcanic isles, and we skirted the capes of Sicily and sailed into the blue Ionian Sea.

312

And I slowly recovered my happiness. With each day the sea grew bluer, the air more golden, the Ionian horizon more majestical. I felt happy in this virile salty world of the *Hercules*. I joked with Tita, I fenced with Pietro, I boxed with Trelawny. We practised pistol-shooting at wine-bottles, cider-jugs and poultry. Each morning we dived from our dinghy into the sea for a swim, and a feeling of hope and exultation swept over me.

On we sailed, and late one evening we sighted the island of Cephalonia. We sheltered during the night and at dawn we anchored near Argostoli.

11 April

I feel feverish and rather horrible. Parry called in the afternoon and urged me to go to Zante, where there is an excellent English doctor.

But why bother to go to Zante? Why on earth go to Zante?

Lucretius said that the flesh grows old from an accumulation of sorrows while the soul perpetually renews itself, even on a diet of sorrows. My body has grown old with a witch-like rapidity. My soul? Is it young, still? Has it freshened itself on suffering?

This morning I crept to the window. The air was uncannily clear. I saw the hills in the distance rising higher and higher, soaring exultantly as I watched them into a row of icy minarets. Then I realized that these peaks were merely an imaginary landscape. Pain can become an outer thing, one can cast it off and regard it impersonally, as though it were a stone or a strange sort of bird. But my pain is a special pain, more elaborate than a stone or a bird, more majestic, less innocent, more remote, and alas more inexorable. It has risen, it has soared from a muddy plateau.

Out of pain can come an icy Alaskan magnificence. And out of pleasure? A wisp of wisdom, like a worm in a peach.

*

Yes, I was happy in Cephalonia. We lived gaily on board the *Hercules*. The waves shone in the sunlight and the sea was as clear as glass. Delicate ferns, fronds of sea-weed, swayed in the sea below our prow. Schools of circular little fish, as bright as silver coins, came and nuzzled at the anchor which lay caught among the rocks. I crossed the harbour each morning with Trelawny in a boat and we landed in an estuary and lay basking in the sun. Sometimes we took along our lunch and drank our wine under the pine-trees, and we lay in the shade, as naked as Adam and nearly as happy.

"You look young again, Byron!"

"An illusion. I feel like Methuselah."

"Look! You are laughing," said Trelawny. "You never laughed when you were in Genoa."

"Is laughter," I said, "necessarily a sign of happiness?"

"It is a sign of well-being, at any rate," said Trelawny.

I looked at Trelawny's body and grew mournful with envy. "Look at this foot of mine, Trelawny. I am sick of my ugly foot. I hope some Turk will chop it off. I wish I were rid of this ugly foot of mine."

"You are being unfair to your foot. You should not hate your foot. If it weren't for that foot you might never have been a poet."

Trelawny looked at me intently with his satyr-eyes. He ran his powerful fingers through his salt-entangled beard. At that moment, even as I sensed that Trelawny was plotting my destruction—in darkest secrecy, and driven by forces which even to him were incomprehensible—I also felt that he suddenly loved me, as men love what they kill, or as men kill the thing that they love but love guiltily.

314

I said, "Trelawny, you look like Odysseus!"

"And you like Achilles, with his heel."

"The chest of Achilles was a hairy one."

"Then like Nausicaä, or Penelope."

"Or like Circe," I said slyly.

I glanced at my chest, where the pectoral muscles (which my passion for swimming had magnified) once drove Caroline to remark, "Darling, I wish I had breasts like yours!"

"Circe. I see," said Trelawny with relish. "Who turns men into swine."

"Or women into sows, if you wish," I said grimly.

"Oh self-tormentor! Self-torturer! Superstitious yet sceptical, God-haunted yet atheistic, noble yet petty, beautiful yet twisted, both idolater and iconoclast, both Gerontion and Ganymede!"

I laughed. "You exaggerate."

"It is *you* who have always exaggerated!"

One day we sailed to Ithaca. It was a glittering day in August. We rose at dawn and rode on mules to the opposite shore of the island, and then we crossed the sea in a narrow four-oared boat. Towards sunset we set foot on the scalding rocks of two-hilled Ithaca. We passed the night in a hut which belonged to a Triestine merchant, and at dawn we started off on the dusty mule-path to Vathy.

Captain Knox, the English resident, invited us to a picnic on the following day. We were to visit the "all-remembering" Fountain of Arethusa. We left the village at nine and rode through the rocks for five miles, and we came to a mossy little spring beside a grotto. Two goat-herds, hairy as centaurs, were squatting in the cave. We sat in the shade and listened while the old one played on his flute and the young one did an ecstatic Pan-like dance in front of the fountain.

I felt dizzy with the heat and called to Tita: "Bring us the bottles!" We drank some grog in the tall green glasses which Pietro took from the picnic-basket.

"Drink deep," I said sepulchrally, "or taste not the Pierian spring."

"You have steeped yourself in the atmosphere, I see," said Trelawny.

"I am listening to the song of the Sirens," I said, rather irritably.

"You alone are allowed to hear it. You," said Trelawny, "are the lucky one."

When we sailed away at sunrise I glanced back at rocky Ithaca. It looked like a phantom. It was fading into nothingness. I stared until it was only a small blue bird afloat on the sea, and I felt that I had never really seen the island of Ithaca. I had visited an island that still called itself Ithaca but I had missed, in my fatal blindness, the real meaning of Ithaca.

12 April

Dr Bruno paid a call and ordered another hot bath, as well as a dose of castor-oil and more antimony powder. I refused to allow the leeches. I felt a pain in my rectum. I took some hot broth with the yolk of an egg beaten up in it.

Finally Bruno gave me some henbane before he left to dull the pain.

And now the night has come again, and my nightly struggle with fear. The sky is tightening its noose, its eyes are burning with frenzy, and now it is turning into a snake-headed Medusa. With a feeling of lassitude, I hear the waves sobbing below. I wait. But for what? What is the message? What is the verdict?

Someone wrote:

> Cut is the branch that might have grown full straight,
> And burnèd is Apollo's laurel bough . . .

316

And someone else:

> The soul of Adonaïs, like a star,
> Beacons from the abode where the Eternal are.

Comforting words, noble words. But my fate is neither noble nor comforting. No-one will remember me as a burning laurel bough. No-one will think of me as a beckoning star.

I remember in Malta a woman sitting under a fig-tree. She was holding a baby in her bony little arms. But as I rode closer I saw that the child was seething with ants and its face was eaten away by maggots. Oh God, what are we destined for? Are we destined to suffer always? I look through the window: a grey-haired woman is hurrying by—but no, it is only a cloud, it is not a woman, nor is it a ghost. Is this Hell? Is this the Inferno? Has this village been turned into Hell, all for my own very special edification?

*

After eight weeks of living on board the sturdy *Hercules* I decided to move to a villa on the island, at Metaxata. On the morning of my removal Trelawny came and said good-bye to me. There were tears in his eyes, and he kissed me on both cheeks. But even then, even at that moment when his mask fell for an instant, I felt the cool, steely touch of a hidden dagger. I said quietly "Fare thee well" and he said gently *"Arrivederci, caro."*

He sailed for Pyrgos on the mainland. I have not seen him since.

Metaxata: my twentieth home, and my smallest and humblest. It was a tiny pink house set among the vines at the edge of the village. Below the village lay the shining blue stupor of the Ionian and above the village, perched on a rock, rose the

317

castle of San Giorgio. The bottom floor of the house was a vaulted white-washed cellar filled with vegetables and fruits, barrels of wine and jugs of olive-oil. Pietro and I and Dr Bruno lived on the top floor of the villa and the servants spread their mattresses and blankets in the kitchen.

I sat on the terrace with my eager-eyed Pietro and we talked about Greece and the black-eyed Greeks. Sometimes Bruno would join us, and occasionally Colonel Napier.

We were waiting impatiently for our departure for the mainland, but Colonel Napier tactfully explained that the appropriate moment had not come yet. We must wait, he explained, for the final "signal" from Missolonghi.

Rumours came from the mainland of confusion, jealousy and ineptitude. One of their leaders, Mavrocordato, had quarrelled with another, Kolokotrones; the eastern chiefs had quarrelled with the western; the civil chiefs were squabbling with the military; and all the while the Grecian fleet was hovering feebly near the shores of Hydra while the Turks blockaded the coast all the way from Chiarenza to Missolonghi. The tyranny of the Turks had thoroughly depraved these charming people. They scrounged for dollars and they lied for favours. They fawned, they flattered, they cheated, they pimped. Was this what slavery had done to them? There were times when I gave up hope. For every honest courageous Greek there were a thousand thieves and cowards. They looked on me as a gold-mine and they slandered each other poisonously. How can one help these pitiful people who don't know the difference between truth and falsehood, who mix heroism with treachery and whose palms are soaked in grease? How long will it take to cleanse them of the vices of slavery?

"You are disillusioned with the Greeks," said Pietro.

"I am dismayed but not disheartened."

"You despise the Greeks, I think."

"I am appalled by what history has done to them."

Pietro stroked his moustache and regarded me wisely.

318

There was still a glint of bravado in his long-lashed eyes but his voice, like his father's, had a deep melodious melancholy.

Colonel Napier, who was a camel-faced man with a lisp, said sadly, "Ah, Your Lordship, one must try to be patient. Slavery begins by depraving the slave, but it ends by depraving the master even more than the slave. You are disgusted, you say, with the cowardly greed of the Greeks. You would also be disgusted with the brutal avarice of the Turks. Slavery corrupts and war brutalises and the whole peninsula is beginning to stink."

Napier rose and said good-bye and Pietro looked at me ruefully.

"Are there times," he said softly, "when you feel you are making a blunder?"

"I have been making egregious blunders all my life, my good Pietro."

"Greece has fallen into ruins."

"I will bury myself in the ruins."

"And you'll never go back to Italy?"

"I'll go to Attica and I'll live as a shepherd."

"Do you really believe this, Byron?"

"No, I don't believe it, Pietro. Life moves quietly and sluggishly and our spirit begins to rot until all of a sudden, as now with me, some hidden force takes hold of it. And where this force will finally lead me God knows, and God only."

We went to the beach by Santa Euphemia and had our picnic under the trees—a roasted chicken and a resinous wine and a bowl of black grapes. I told Pietro about my youthful adventures in English politics. I told him of my magnificent maiden speech in the House of Lords. It was an ardent attack on the Frame Makers' Bill. I felt passionately on the side of the poor, the hungry and oppressed. I was passionately on the side of a juster society. But I was, as luck would have it, not a born politician. I was too singular and too tempestuous. I was also too tactless. And now, in retrospect, I saw that my sense of justice was absurdly patronizing. I was merely an aristocrat who thought of justice as a gift to be given rather than a human necessity, like water, food, or sleep, to which all have a right, even the idiots and the murderers. Justice is really just a shallower synonym for human liberty. And liberty! It isn't a gift or an indulgence or a luxury, it is the air we must all breathe, like the lions in the wilderness, if we ever hope to taste the true flavour of our brief existence.

At twilight we set out for the monastery above Samos. When we finally, at sunset, climbed the last stony path, we saw a row of old sarcophagi standing in the dust outside the monastery. Night fell, the stars came out as we peered at the stony coffins. I laughed, and as a jest I lay down in the nearest one, and I shouted to Pietro,

> Alas, poor Yorick! I knew him, Horatio: a fellow of infinite jest, of most excellent fancy: he hath borne me on his back a thousand times; and now how abhorred in my imagination it is! My gorge rises at it! Here hung those lips that I have kissed I know not how oft. Where be your gibes now, your gambols, your songs, your flashes of merriment . . .

I caught sight of a column of monks who were emerging from the monastery. They all wore long beards and they were carrying pine-torches. When they saw us they gathered into a welcoming circle. There was bowing and scraping and a fluttering of dirty hands, the old abbot embarked on a flowery address, and a violent rush of nausea swept over me. I felt feverish; I was beside myself with fury and misery. I roared savagely at the innocent abbot, who smelled of garlic and urine, and I ran into the monastery, followed by the panicky Dr Bruno.

I lay down on a narrow bed in a tiny grey cell and Bruno gave me some liver-pills (*benedette pillule,* he called them).

I was sweating like a sow. My heart pounded crazily. I blew out the candle and sank into a procession of horrible nightmares.

13 April

I have just had another stinking and bloody evacuation. The heroic fate for which I was intended seems not to have materialised.

At dusk I took some broth and a spoonful of arrow-root, and since I was suffering from a violent flatulence, I also took a spoonful of Epsom salts. Good old Fletcher prepared a very hot foot-bath.

The lines above were written at midnight. Now I see the sun rising. I shall pick up my pen. I feel calm. The pain has gone. I feel refreshed, almost happy. A little bird with green feathers and a crimson beak is sitting on my window-sill. I feel a kinship with this bird. It is speaking to me; the voice is familiar. The merry little chirp is gradually swelling into a mighty symphony. I hear waves on the shore below me. Yes, all is in harmony.

A crazy hope has suddenly welled up in me. I will not die. I will never die. I will fight with death like a maniac. I will live on for ever. I will finally conquer death, and be unique in human history in my frenzied and lunatic victory.

*

There was a man in Cephalonia whose name was Dr Kennedy. He was an evangelical-minded medical officer, a red-haired man with fleshy lips, tormented eyes and a tremulous voice.

He came and spoke of God. "You don't believe in immortality, it seems, Your Lordship. I have noticed that in *Cain* you appear to cast serious doubts upon it."

I said: "I don't deny immortality, my good Kennedy. I merely say that I have yet to see convincing testimony of it."

"Aren't you frightened, ever, Your Lordship?"

"Oh, yes, I am frightened occasionally."

"You must look," said Dr Kennedy, lowering his voice, "for a cure for terror."

"When one is frightened one must be brave, not superstitious, Dr Kennedy. Superstition is a form of cowardice. It takes courage to confront one's terror."

We spoke of predestination. *"Why,"* said Kennedy, "do things happen? Why did you come to Cephalonia? Ah yes, outwardly it is perfectly plausible. But *inwardly,* Your Lordship? There are reasons which defy mere reason."

"I admit, my good Kennedy, that I have done certain things for reasons which elude me, or which are totally incomprehensible. Things happen which I never intended. But I accept this. I do not speculate. Things happen in our life in a dark mysterious way, and there are times when I feel that I am nothing but a puppet."

Dr Kennedy sighed profoundly. He gazed thoughtfully at his forefinger. "If that is so, then it would be foolish to punish men for their wickedness, wouldn't it?"

"It would indeed," I agreed. "Assuming that there *is* such a thing as wickedness, rather than men behaving merely in obedience to an animal destiny."

Dr Kennedy looked at me wistfully. "You *are* wicked, a little, Your Lordship."

I laughed and drained my glass. "And so are you, my dear Kennedy!"

Colonel Stanhope arrived in Cephalonia in the middle of November. He was a solemn and didactical person with glassy eyes and a malodorous breath.

"I am an agent," he announced, "of the London Committee for Greek Liberation."

"I am happy to hear it," I said somewhat wanly.

"There is much to be done," said the Colonel with an optimistic glitter. "Our task is many-faceted. The military aspect is merely a preliminary. We must instil in these pitiable Greeks a sense of true democracy. First of all, a free press. We must set up some printing-presses. There is nothing so conducive to the democratic spirit as a printing-press."

I felt dejected. I looked at Stanhope and asked him listlessly, "Have you brought some books for me?"

His eyes sparkled joyfully. "I have brought you Bentham's *The Springs of Action.*"

I lost my temper. "A brilliant choice, I must say, Colonel Stanhope! What in hell does that doddering fool know about the springs of human action? My cock has more spring in it than all his damned theories!"

Time passed in Cephalonia with a Limbo-like lethargy, as though in preparation for the darkness which loomed to the east of us. The days were sunny but a sheath of clouds hung over the Gulf of Patras, where the oyster-hued sails of the Moslem ships could be seen in the evenings. One day I stood on the cliff which jutted into the sea below my villa and sniffed at the evening air, trying to catch a whiff of Hellas. My shadow on the stone grew longer as the sun behind me approached the horizon. Something curious then happened. There was a stirring behind me, like a fluttering of wings, or the rustling of the wind in the thistles. And I saw another shadow, parallel to my own but slightly larger, fall on the gravel a foot or two to the right of me. I saw an arm being raised, the shadowy arm of a dark pursuer, and something pointed, like a knife, being lifted above my head. But at that instant the sunlight died and the shadows dissolved and when I turned and looked behind me I saw nothing, nothing at all.

One morning, on the road to Argostoli, I met Loukas. He

was sitting on a rock, whittling away at a piece of wood, which he was trying to carve into the head of a horse.

I said, "Good-morning, my lad."

He said, "Good-morning, Your Highness."

I looked startled. "But why . . ."

"Ah, everyone knows that you are a King. They say you will soon become the King of the Hellenes!"

He told me about himself. His name was Loukas Chalandritsanos. His family had once been rich land-owners in Patras, and Luke himself had been fighting in the Morea under Kolokotrones. He had fled to the isle of Ithaca with his widowed mother, whom he adored, and now he was yearning to go back to the mainland and start fighting again. He was fifteen years old. His face was like Apollo's. His eyes were extremely blue, which is a rarity among the Greeks, and his hair was touched with copper; also a rarity among the Greeks. His body was like a lamp, it exuded a gentle glow, as though a flame were burning under his lion-tawny skin. Even such dry and respectable gentlemen as Dr Kennedy and Colonel Stanhope opened their eyes a little wider when they looked at the beautiful Luke.

I said to him one day, "I will make you my page-boy, Loukas, and you will come along with me when I sail for the mainland."

We were wandering along the beach. The wind blew out of Hellas, and it carried the honeyed tang of the Grecian hills and the Grecian heather. The sun had set, the air was hushed. A single star peeped through the darkness, and the moon rose out of the sea, sly and suspicious, slippery as quicksilver.

I said, "You must promise never to lie to me, Loukas."

He laughed and looked at me mockingly. "What is a lie, tell me, Your Highness?"

Well, yes, I thought sadly, if truth does not exist, or at least can never be clearly identified as truth, then lies do not exist,

324

or at least can never be clearly identified. I turned my back to the moon and stared at the stars, which looked at that moment friendly and alive, almost human. What were their names? Capella, Betelgeuse, Cassiopeia and so on? Oh white Capella, oh ice-eyed Betelgeuse, oh singing Cassiopeia! No longer stars, no longer fire, no longer lost in the roaring infinitudes, but reaching towards the Earth with calm and pitying gestures, Cassiopeia turning her spinning-wheel, Capella hanging the laundry, and Betelgeuse, the blue-armed Betelgeuse, peeling potatoes in her kitchen.

A fishing-boat crawled slowly out from a cliff to the left of us. Its lantern shone in the water, beckoning to the lantern-loving fish, and somewhere in the night an invisible fish jumped out of the water.

14 April

I got up at noon but felt so weak that I went to bed again. Tita brought me my note-books and left them on the night-table. Loukas came with a bowl of those curious black hyacinths, whose odour struggles heroically with the foetid stench that seeps from the close-stool.

Towards dusk I had a fit of delirium, which lasted an hour. I felt hideously feeble, and refused to be bled.

"The lancet," I said stubbornly (and not very wittily) "has killed far more people than the lance, my good Bruno."

Yes, something momentous is about to happen. But one thing I'm not sure of: will it happen to me alone, or will it also happen to the rest of the world?

What is intolerable in the thought of death is that it will happen only to *us,* the rest of the world will go on just as before, the dandelions will bloom, the crickets will chirp, our friends will sit at the table and eat their pancakes. If *they* would die as well, if the flowers would shrivel and the birds

325

be still, the thought of death would be bearable. At least to me. At least today.

We cling to the hope of living for ever, the great and the small, the wicked and the good. Socrates said, "Whether life or death is better only the Gods can know." I do not know, not being a God, and being much less wise than Socrates. My own life has been full of ugly things and full of beautiful ones. (Oh yes, I have been lucky, fantastically lucky!) Someone else said that the immortality of the soul is *un grand peut-être*. A *peut-être* at best, maybe a big one and maybe a little one.

*

On Christmas morning the "appropriate signal" (as Napier called it) finally came. A brig appeared at daybreak in the windy waters by Metaxata. It had been sent from Missolonghi by Prince Mavrocordato, with the request that I should sail for Missolonghi immediately.

I got ready. But a strange reluctance, almost a terror, kept me from leaving. I cannot even say now whether it was a physical or a mental fear; the premonition of a vague disaster or merely my own inveterate acidia. I sat at night and stared at the clumsy little brig in the moonlit harbour. I knew that I would go, but the thought of going was strangely oppressive.

I waited for five days. Finally, on the 30th of December, I left. I hired two island boats, one being a swift and shallow *"mistico"* and the other (for the horses and the chests) a clumsy bombard. On the *mistico* I took along my valet Fletcher, my doctor Bruno and my page-boy Loukas, as well as my faithful old Newfoundland, Lyon. I also took some fire-arms and some sacks of silver dollars. Pietro sailed on the bombard, which was planning to follow the *mistico*. As we sailed through the night, with the stars overhead and the beast-like configuration of the waiting hills in the eastern distances, a wave of exultation did finally sweep over me. I felt war-like almost; the disaster-loving sea seemed to transfigure me into the warrior-like rôle I had chosen. The Suliotes kept crying to me, *"Derrah! Derrah!"* and I gaily shouted back to them, *"Courage! En avant!"*

We reached Zante in the morning, where we obtained some ship's papers, and at dusk we set sail for the lurking mysteries of Missolonghi.

The two vessels kept sailing side by side for three hours. The breeze was still favourable and the Cephalonian sailors started to sing. I sat on deck with a bottle of wine and soon I joined them in their singing. The breeze freshened and the little *mistico* started to gain on the heaving bombard. The billowing sails under the starlight, the snowy foam of the black Aegean, the Cephalonian singers and the smell of tar, the smell of honey, the smell of heroism—oh yes, a wave of dusky exhilaration did sweep over me and I sensed the enigmatical splendour which lay waiting in front of me. Pietro and I still kept calling, I from the *mistico*, he from the bombard, until our voices grew faint and finally inaudible. The night was quite moonless. We fired our carbines periodically, but the night grew intense and Pietro's bombard was no longer visible.

All was still. No-one spoke. I lay on the deck beside Loukas, with Lyon sleeping peacefully between us. I dozed off and suddenly woke up again (it was two o'clock in the morning) to see a large vessel looming directly in front of the *mistico*.

I muttered to the Captain: "Is it Greek?"

He growled softly: "No. It is Turkish."

But by now we were already trapped under the stern of the Turkish frigate. They had caught sight of us and there was a slow, inquisitive stirring of silhouettes. Not a sound rose from the *mistico*. The Captain turned the rudder violently

327

and we veered away from the Mohammedan vessel. We waited for something to happen, for the sound of a voice or a musket. But nothing happened. For some strange reason they allowed us to sail on. After an hour the Turkish ship was finally lost in the moonless darkness, and we hovered off the coast of the craggy mainland until sunrise.

In the light of early dawn we caught sight of a town in the distance. A large ship (Turkish, said the Captain) guarded the entrance to the port. Luke cried "Look!" and in the west we saw our bombard on the horizon, and a larger vessel (the Mohammedan frigate, so it seemed) pursuing it. We saw a Zantiot boat signalling to us vigorously from the shore, and the Captain said, "They are warning us. They are saying *Go away!*" So we went before the wind and headed for the cape which rose to the north of us, and there we dropped our anchor in an inlet behind the rocks.

It was New Year's morning, and I said to Luke: "Come, my lad, I will give you a letter and you and Stavros will cross over the hills on foot. You will reach Missolonghi and give my letter to the Prince."

So Luke picked up his shoes and went ashore with the sailor Stavros and I watched them as they waded through the creek along the estuary.

I called to him, "Don't let those brutes get hold of you, Loukas!"

He called back, "Never fear! I will kill them if they try!"

And he climbed over the hills and followed the path towards Anatolica.

We waited in the inlet but shortly after noon we saw a Turkish vessel approaching the estuary. We knew that it would be unable to enter the shallow inlet, but the Captain was afraid of being trapped by the Moslem boat and he shot out of the inlet and headed due north, following the zig-zag of the coast, sailing past Petola with its ruined watch-tower, and gliding uneasily past bay after bay, until at dusk we finally slipped into the harbour at Dragomestre. Here it was safe, and here we waited. I slept on board with my faithful Lyon, guarding my sacks of silver dollars and my precious box of fire-arms, and we waited two more days, hoping for news from Mavrocordato. Finally, on January the 3rd, three little gun-boats sent by the Prince arrived in the bay of Dragomestre, and on one of them was Loukas. He flung his arms round me and kissed me on the cheek, and we sailed out of the bay and headed straight for Missolonghi.

But the clouds grew black and menacing and a powerful wind swept down on us. Night fell and the poor little *mistico* fluttered through the dark like a wounded bird. We passed some towering cliffs and a stab of wind took the *mistico* and drove it on a foam-covered crescent of rocks. The waves swept over the deck as Fletcher dragged my sacks to safety while Bruno kept shrieking hysterically at the Captain. I gripped Loukas by the shoulder and held him tightly against my body while the breakers went crashing over the half-hidden rocks.

But the wind suddenly died, though the waves still kept pounding, and the clouds hurried westward and the moon shone over the water. We cast anchor between two rocks, and the air grew strangely balmy. I threw off my clothes, which were soaked with the sea, and dived into the water, which was sprinkled with silver, as though my sacks had split open and scattered their dollars over the sea.

And so at last, on the 4th of January, we sailed into the port of Missolonghi. The sun was shining brilliantly as I stepped into my braided uniform. The *mistico* approached the black-walled fortress which guarded the harbour and a small Speziot boat came out to carry me ashore. I could see the welcoming crowds, all white and yellow, along the shore, and the batteries of Vasiladi let go with a salvo of twenty-one guns. As the dinghy approached the mole the little children waved their flags, and the girls lifted their garlands and cried: "Saviour! Hero! Liberator!"

Dr Bruno and Dr Millingen came and begged me for my blood. They stood by my bed like a pair of vultures. "You are suffering," said Millingen, "from a bad rheumatic fever." "And bleeding," said Bruno, "will be the only possible remedy."

I growled, "Call for a witch, please, Millingen. I need a witch, I tell you."

"You are joking, My Lord," said Millingen.

"Never mind," I said angrily. "I beg you to bring me a witch, the ugliest witch in town, and she'll tell you if my sickness has come from the Evil Eye!"

Parry came to my room and sat in the dusk by my bed. I sat up and leant my head against the pillow. I felt quite calm.

"You look better," said Parry gently.

"It is curious," I said, "about fevers. When I am feverish I fancy myself a Moslem, or a Buddhist, or even a Jew. Eternity and space keep dangling before me like a pendulum. On one particular subject, however, I feel quite at ease. The thought of reviving and of living eternally is a debatable pleasure, Parry."

I looked at Parry ironically. His lips were shaking; tears came to his eyes. He picked up his cap and left. It was nearly ten o'clock.

I was seized by a fit of coughing and vomited in the bowl beside my bed. The door opened and Fletcher came creeping on tiptoe into the room.

"Fletcher," I whispered, "if I die what will they do with my body?"

"My Lord," said Fletcher softly, "what should we do but take you home again?"

"Is it worth taking this miserable body back to England? Well, perhaps, all in all, it might be best if they did . . ."

He left; Loukas entered.

330

"Luke," I said, holding his forefinger, "there in the corner, in the Captain's chest, is a bag full of dollars. Two thousand of them in all. That bag is for you, my boy."

Luke sat by my bed and started to talk about his mother. She was a paralytic widow who had fled with her children to Ithaca.

"Did you love your mother?" I asked him.

"My mother," he said, "was a saint. I loved no-one in the world except my mother, who was a saint."

And now I am alone. There is no-one I can confide in. Fletcher is stupefied with drink, poor young Pietro is weak with panic, Bruno is quivering with anxiety, and only Tita is calm and sensible.

Am I dying? There are moments when I feel that it would be folly to keep on living. It would be a betrayal of that fine "Byronic" legend to keep on living. The sirocco is blowing and the waves keep chattering, and down below I hear the Suliotes shuffling about, belching and bellowing . . .

*

"Saviour!" they cried. "Hero! Liberator!" I looked round glumly. I saw a village squatting like a *cauchemar* on the marshy peninsula, with its alleys squirming like eels along the edge of the lagoon. Far from heroic, far from Hellenic, merely dirty and desultory, as though rejected by the rest of Hellas and even by humanity itself. Scum-striped fishing-boats lay stranded in the ooze below the harbour and the fishermen's huts, suspended on stakes, crouched like spiders. Long red fishing-nets hung from the stakes or lay drying among the pebbles.

My good Pietro (whose bombard had entered the harbour two days earlier) stood on the edge of the mole, wearing his sword and his helmet. He took my arm and led me to the

square where my coal-black Mameluke was nervously awaiting me.

A young lieutenant, dressed in turquoise, stepped through
the crowd and bowed ornately. "I bring you greetings from
His Excellency, Prince Mavrocordato. He is awaiting you in
the house which we have chosen as your residence."

We rode along the promontory and came to a halt beside a
gate. A rain-streaked banner flapped listlessly over the entrance. In the doorway stood a sad, squat, mincing little man
with eyes which peered benevolently though rather shiftily
through a pair of spectacles. He wore a small furry cap and a
velvet coat with golden buttons. His cheeks were delicately
powdered, with a furtive flush of rouge. He had exquisite
hands and spoke beautiful English.

Tears shone in his eyes. "I am unutterably moved, Lord
Byron."

"I feel profoundly honoured," I said.

"And I similarly," he murmured. "It is a beautiful occasion—your illustrious poetry, your vast prestige . . ."

"Let us forget," I said curtly, "about the poetry, if it is
agreeable to you."

The Prince looked plaintive. "A pot of tea," he stated, "is
waiting in the loggia."

"I would prefer," I said briskly, "to have some wine, if
wine is available."

"As you wish," said the Prince. He rolled his eyes and
beckoned to me coyly.

We sat down in the loggia and proceeded to speak of
practical matters. The Prince sketched out his plans in a
somewhat absent-minded way, with much ogling and digression and a palpitation of jewelled fingers. He suggested that I
take command of a band of Suliote guardsmen, a clamorous
group of refugees who had settled in the Seraglio. These poor
Suliotes, he explained, had not been paid for nearly a year
and were sadly in need of nourishment, gun-powder and
soap. I agreed to maintain the Suliotes for a period of a year

at my personal expense. (I could see a bevy of bearded faces, gesturing greedily and whispering excitedly, peering in through the window in the course of the conversation.)

The Prince continued: "My plan is the following. Your army of Suliotes will capture Lepanto, which lies on the northern shore of the Gulf of Corinth. Once we capture Lepanto we can deploy our Speziot vessels and we will conquer Patras and the castle of Morea, and soon after we will control the entire length of the Gulf of Corinth, and Aetolia and Acarnania will be joined to the Morea. We will gradually gather strength for further attacks on the Turkish strongholds, which will soon find their position dangerously exposed and untenable. The advantages of this plan are that it is ingenious as well as infallible. It is superior to the nebulous fantasies of Kolokotrones and the other up-starts . . ."

I peeped through the window. The bearded Suliotes were waving a flag. Drums were beating, women were singing, and a patriotic ardour filled the air.

Mavrocordato looked at me wistfully. "Alas," he sighed, "they are nothing but children. They have forgotten their glorious past, the ringing cries of Thermopylae. They have never heard of Alcibiades. They are not inspired by mem-ories of Achilles. Plato is nothing but ashes. Who was Phidias, who was Euripides? The last time I visited the Parthenon it was littered with garbage. Even the language of the Greeks has sunk into a gross, inelegant demotic."

He lifted his wine-glass and his eyes grew cow-like. "Still, you must try not to lose your faith in us. Missolonghi! *Quel horreur!* The absolute dung-hill of the world, if you will par-don the expression. Nuzzling swine, swarming mosquitoes and nothing but drizzle, drizzle, drizzle. Ah, you should see the purple glow falling on the crystals of Mount Hymettus! Greece is a cliff and not a quagmire. Let us pray for the sun to shine on it!"

After this flowery salutation the little Prince sank back in his cushions. He took off his spectacles and wiped them carefully with a handkerchief. Then he peered at me playfully. "And now," he clucked, "to more congenial matters. Such as poetry, for example. What is your opinion of *Kubla Khan*? . . ."

This morning Dr Millingen slipped into my room on cat-like feet with Bruno behind him carrying a knife, a bowl and a bottle.

"I beg you, Your Lordship . . ."

"I refuse to be bled!" I shrieked.

"Allow me to suggest," said Millingen, "that if you persist in your resolution, the disease may well end by disorganising your cerebral system, and thus bringing on a state which might almost be called . . ."

"Yes. Madness," I muttered. "You are beguiling me with the thought of madness. Come on, then. Damn you, you are a pair of filthy butchers! Take all the blood that you wish but have done with it, please."

They opened the vein. I saw the blood spurt into the glass.

"Close the vein!" I cried wildly. "Enough of this! Enough, by God!"

But the blood kept on gushing until they finally filled the glass. Then they crept out of the room again on delicate cat-like feet.

I felt suddenly cold as ice but abnormally serene. I kept staring at the clock; but I could not fall asleep.

Three hours later they came back again. My heart was pounding savagely as though it were guarding what little blood was left in me.

"We must propose," said Bruno suavely, "another bleeding, Your Excellency."

"Damn you!" I screamed. "Stop tormenting me! You will have no more of my blood!"

Dr Millingen felt my pulse and gave me a dose of nitrates to ease my bladder. He brought out the chamber-pot but the urine came reluctantly, and when I looked down I saw it was the colour of coffee.

*

It was the house of a certain illustrious Apostoli Capsali, a peppery man with a thick blue beard who was one of the Ephores of Missolonghi, and it stood at the end of the spit which divided the gulf from the lagoon. In the distance rose the cloud-clapped peak of Varassova and far away, when the sun was out, I could see the mountains of the Morea. On rainy days, or at high water, the promontory turned into a swamp and the horses stood floundering in the mud in the outhouses. My Suliotes lived on the ground floor and Colonel Stanhope on the first. I myself lived on the second with Fletcher and Tita and Loukas and the blackamoor (acquired from Trelawny; a splendid groom and an ingenious cook). I covered my rooms with Turkish swords and Albanian bayonets, ancient helmets from the Epirus and silver trumpets from the Peloponnesus . . .

I am too weary to keep remembering. The past is a phantom. Or rather, it is a river whose infinite tributaries have finally entered the sea . . .

17 April

For several moments I shall be alone. Fletcher and Tita have left the room. After another spell of delirium I feel calm and lucid again. I shall try to remember what happened today.

335

After a bout of pills and purgatives (Dr Millingen's love of purgatives is almost as fanatical as his penchant for leeches) I lay down and tried to sleep. But of course I could not sleep. Millingen came again at noon and said: "You will sleep if you let us bleed you."

And I said: "Without sleep I will die or go mad. Of the two, to be frank with you, I prefer death to madness. Listen, Millingen, I would rather shoot myself in the brain than go mad!" Then I added more gently: "I am not afraid of dying, Millingen. I am fitter to die than some of you suppose. Go home, Millingen. You need a rest. You and Tita will both be ill if you keep on sitting by my bed all day long."

He left, and now it is night. I can see the moon through my open window and the light of the moon on the windless lagoon. I can see three drunken Suliotes staggering through the mud in their silvery splendour. One is carrying a lantern and the glow keeps dancing on their faces. One of them has stopped to piss into the dark, and the spray shines brightly in the glow of the lantern.

One of my fine Turkish swords has fallen from its hook. It is lying on the floor. But the moon still shines on the bayonets and trumpets.

*

The past! There is no past. All things converge into the present.

18 April

[Transcriber's note: This entry is written in a very uneven and child-like handwriting.]

I can hardly write. My hand keeps shaking, partly from fever, partly from exhaustion. Still I feel a compulsion to write what happened to-day. Things seem calmer and less sinister if they are written down on paper.

It is Easter Sunday. The doctors have left me and I am alone in my room, except for Lyon, who lies twitching on the left of my bed, and Tita, who lies snoring noisily on the right of it.

I felt cold as ice all day. Dr Millingen came at noon and applied a hot embrocation to my thighs. Some of the fluid leaked onto my testicles, but the sting of the ointment was almost a relief to me.

I dozed off. When I opened my eyes again I saw Bruno leaning over me. I tried to speak but I could not speak. With great suavity and cunning he applied twelve leeches to my temples (I counted them) and as I felt them sucking at my blood I felt, surprisingly enough, that I was gradually growing stronger. I felt that perhaps I might survive after all.

Pietro came and sat by my bed for a while, but said nothing.

In the early afternoon I heard the door opening softly and my blackamoor poked his head through the doorway. He looked at me solemnly and burst into tears. At that moment I knew the truth. I knew that I was dying.

The two doctors arrived at twilight and I said to them as they entered, "I must die, I suppose. But let me die in peace, I beg you!"

I gripped Tita's enormous hand and stared in terror at the doctors, who were gripping their umbrellas as though they were weapons. I screamed, "Tita, help me! These lunatic doctors are trying to kill me!"

I saw the tears welling into my Tita's enormous black eyes. I laughed and said: *"O, Tita mio, questa è una bella scena!"*

I closed my eyes. Tita's loving dark face faded away and another face appeared, pale, unloving and hauntingly beautiful. I whispered: *"Io lascio qualche cosa di caro nel mondo."* Then I grunted, "As for the rest of it, never mind, I am content to die."

It is nearly dawn. Tita is lying by my bed, fast asleep.
Yes, yes, I understand. I must go on. I must try to rem . . .

*[Transcriber's note: Here the handwriting trails away into
an undecipherable scrawl. There is a small brownish stain at
the bottom of the page.]*